D1564426

BEYOND THE RIVER OF THE SUN

Fredric M. Hitt

Illustrations by
Linda Silsby Hitt

This book is a work of fiction. Any resemblance to actual events or persons, living or dead, is entirely coincidental.

"Beyond the River of the Sun," by Fredric M. Hitt. ISBN 978-1-60264-075-7 (softcover); 978-1-60264-076-4 (hardcover).

Library of Congress Control Number on file with Publisher.

Published 2007 by Virtualbookworm.com Publishing Inc., P.O. Box 9949, College Station, TX 77842, US.

Manufactured in the United States of America.

To Christie,

Mother, poet, shining spirit
who loved words,
and the images they invoked.

Lexicon of Timucua Words and Phrases

Atichicolo-Iri -Spirit warrior

Chulufi-Yuchi -Crying Bird

Cimarrone -Outlaw, run-away

Holata -Chief

Holata Aco -Chief of Chiefs

Inija -Chief's next in command

Isucu -Herbalist, medicine man

Itori -Alligator

Jarva -Shaman, sorcerer

Nariba -Term of respect, old man

Niaholata -Woman chief

Paracousi -War chief

Paqe-paqe -Forgive, forget

Tacachale -Fire that cleanses and purifies

Yaba -Wizard, witch

Wekiva -Waters of the spring (Seminole-Creek)

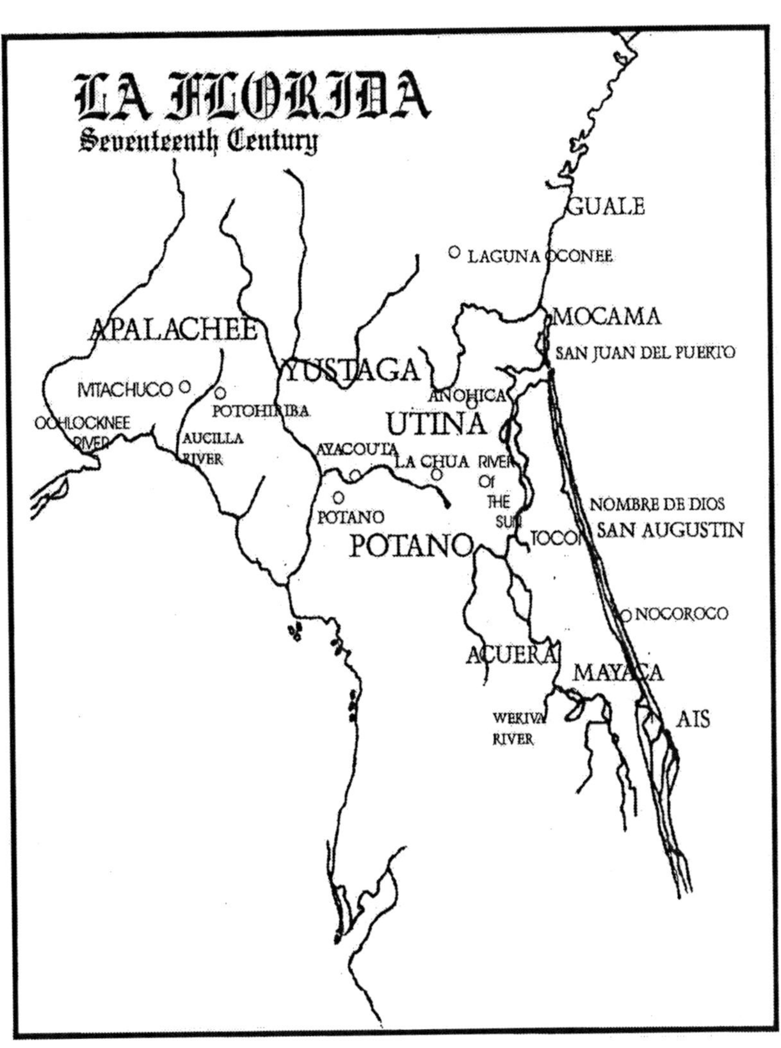
LA FLORIDA
Seventeenth Century
GUALE
LAGUNA OCONEE
MOCAMA
SAN JUAN DEL PUERTO
APALACHEE
YUSTAGA
IVITACHUCO
POTOHIRIBA
ANOHICA
UTINA
OCHLOCKNEE RIVER
AUCILLA RIVER
AYACOUTA
LA CHUA
RIVER OF THE SUN
NOMBRE DE DIOS
POTANO
TOCOI
SAN AUGUSTIN
POTANO
NOCOROCO
ACUERA
MAYACA
AIS
WERIVA RIVER

Prologue

San Augustín, La Florida
1602

When word of the deaths at Misión San Juan del Puerto reached the ear of Mendez de Canzo, Governor and Captain General of the Spanish province of La Florida, he reacted without hesitation, dispatching a brigantine under the command of Sergeant Major Vicente Gonsalves with a platoon of well-armed soldiers and two heavy cannon.

For good measure, the governor sent two squads of arquebus and musket-bearing men overland toward the mission twenty leagues to the north.

Four years earlier, Canzo had been called before the Council of the Indies to answer for his slow response to the revolt among the Guale Indians, and he was determined to deal with any uprising among the Timucua-speaking Indians firmly and expeditiously.

Still, Canzo had his doubts about the magnitude of the problem. To the governor, the most frustrating aspect of service in this God-forsaken outpost was the unreliability of reports from the frontier. The Indian runner told an improbable tale of revolt among the Mocama Indians, an explosion and fire that destroyed the mission, and many deaths among the soldiers quartered there.

Canzo's cynicism was confirmed seven days later when Gonsalves returned to San Augustín and reported that there had, in fact, been a fire that had destroyed the military barracks and blown up a powder magazine. The mission church and convento, however, were untouched. More importantly, the mission friar, Francisco Pareja, informed Gonsalves that there had been no uprising by the Indians and that the fire may have occurred when Sergeant Suarez, acting on his own authority, attempted to burn a rebellious Indian at the stake.

Four of the eleven men stationed at Misión San Juan del Puerto died, and their squad leader, Sergeant José Suarez, was badly burned and disfigured by the explosion. He had been delivered by Gonsalves to Our Lady of Solitude, the only hospital in San Augustín, where he would be cared for by the Franciscans.

Questions remained, and Gonsalves recommended to the governor that an *audencia* be empaneled to investigate further. The sergeant's culpability in exceeding his authority with regard to the burning, and his negligence in lighting a fire so near the powder magazine, could be looked into if he survived his injuries, though that appeared unlikely.

Other unresolved questions bothered Canzo. While the sergeant and three of the dead men had suffered concussion injuries and severe burns about their bodies from the accidental explosion of the munitions depot, another of the soldiers appeared to have died from a knife wound to his throat. The Indian who was to be burned had somehow escaped in the confusion, and was nowhere to be found on the island.

The sergeant major concluded his report to the governor by saying that the Timucua-speaking Mocama were not upset, but were happily going about their business of raising corn for the governor's needs in San Augustín and attending Mass regularly. Father Pareja had enlisted the help of the Indians in cleaning up after the fire, and they had done as he asked, removing every vestige of the military barracks from the mission grounds.

The surviving soldiers were brought to the presidio for questioning and reassignment. Perhaps there was no further need for a military presence at San Juan del Puerto, as Father Pareja had repeatedly suggested.

The friar had been summoned to San Augustín by his superior, Father Marron, and was expected within a day or two. Perhaps he could provide answers to the lingering questions.

Escape To Wekiva

Chapter 1

Lower San Juan River
(River of the Sun)

The river by night was a new experience, one for which life at the Spanish mission had not prepared the twelve-year-old Indian boy. Shadows hovered overhead as the dugout canoe glided along near the shoreline. Trees that were ordinary elm, hickory or bay in the light of day were now frightful beasts and evil spirits in the darkness, their limbs armed with sharpened claws reaching down to rip at his face.

The boy sat in front, staring ahead as he had been instructed, searching the blackness of the water for snags that might strike the bow, and the shadows above for limbs that might sweep them all into the murky river. He could sense the four Indian men behind him watching, judging him harshly, alert to his every move, to any sign of weakness, or to the fear that clutched his chest.

"Beware what shows itself in the corner of your eye," the old man, Marehootie, had said earlier. And so he was, moving his head from side to side, and up and down in a steady rhythm. A sudden flash of light or unusual movement of an eddy current would catch his eye. He'd stare directly at it until it dissolved into nothingness or showed itself to be a log breaking the surface, waiting in ambush.

The journey had not begun well. The old man had marked the backs of the boy's hands with white ashes and clay so that he could signal the men to go right or left, around fallen trees, submerged brush or rocks and shoals in their path. But when the canoe suddenly came upon a bank cave-in, where the water shallowed, the boy mistakenly pointed directly at it. The men steered to where he pointed and the canoe ground against the limestone rubble and came to a sudden stop.

The man in the back, the one they called Nihoto, perhaps because he was deaf and could not hear even himself, growled his angry complaint. The others were silent, working their paddles backward in the water. Moments later they were free and moving forward once again. Even in the darkness, the boy could sense their disapproval.

From then on the boy concentrated on pointing the way he wished the canoe to go, his gestures for change in direction smooth or emphatic, depending on the nearness of the approaching hazard.

The mission priest had baptized him as Juan de Coya, honoring the village of his birth. When these men spoke to him, as they rarely did, and always in hushed tones, they called him, simply, Coya.

On they went, hugging the shoreline on the east side where the oncoming current was slowed and where the overhanging hickory and cypress afforded a blanket of seclusion from the moon that lit the middle of the river.

They had not planned to escape under a full moon, but the timing was not theirs. It was the soldiers who had chosen this night to amuse themselves by burning a crippled old man at the stake.

"The Spanish will never catch us now," Crying Bird said once they were safely away from the island and the soldiers. "The current is not swift here and by the time they begin their pursuit tomorrow, we will be half way to Utina."

"And they may find it difficult to chase us," said Chief Tacatacura of the Mocama Timucua. He was cloaked in his regal match coat of turkey feathers and sea shells, and was the only man in the canoe whose hands were empty. Because of his royal blood, he was not expected to help with the paddling.

"I have spoken to the canoeists," Tacatacura continued. "There are many dead-end sloughs and creeks that can be mistaken for the main channel. I suspect the Spaniards will find themselves doing more exploring than pursuing."

"That was well planned. It is good to travel with a companion who has such influence," Crying Bird said.

"The Spanish threaten my people to get their cooperation," Tacatacura said. "But I am still their chief, at least over those who live away from the mission. The canoe people will do as I say."

The old man, Marehootie, spoke. "It may be that the beautiful pearl I used to bribe the canoe boss may confuse his sense of direction, also."

"If you are done praising yourself for your clever planning, my brother, perhaps we need to talk about the dangers that still face us," Crying Bird said. "We are four days from home, and unless the Spirit blesses our journey and blinds our enemies, none of us will reach Wekiva."

The others fell silent while Crying Bird spoke of what lay ahead. Nihoto, the deaf one, hummed an ancient Muskhogean chant and continued to paddle as the war canoe moved steadily southward through the blackness of the river night.

"We will travel without stopping tonight, tomorrow and the next night. During the second night we will enter the most dangerous part of the journey, the land of Utina. From that point we will hide during the day and move on the river only when it is dark. It would be foolish to travel the river in the daylight.

"There is only one remote village in all of Utina where we may be welcomed," Crying Bird said. "If the people appear friendly, we will stay there for awhile and talk to them until it is dark and time to go."

Crying Bird dipped his paddle into the water, his powerful arms and shoulders like limbs of a mighty oak. Nihoto worked in the back keeping the canoe straight in an eddy current.

"If we are discovered by anyone on the river, even a child or an innocent fisherman, they are our enemy and must be stopped from giving us away," Crying Bird said.

Coya turned to look at Crying Bird, unsure of his meaning.

"That is why we should take care in not being discovered," Marehootie said, looking at the boy. "If we are seen by people of any other Utinan village, the word will be spread up and down the river and we will be hunted until we are found and butchered."

Coya lay on a bed of palmetto leaves, his head cushioned by a clump of the moss that hung everywhere from the trees like long gray beards. He had not slept for two days and his imagination had played tricks on him as he tried to concentrate on his lookout duties. Twice he signaled warnings of obstructions that dissolved into nothingness before his weary eyes. Before daybreak, a huge alligator rose out of the water, its mouth an open maw of blood-stained teeth, poised to attack the canoe. The boy screamed, and in the blink of an eye, the alligator was gone, leaving not even a ripple in its wake.

Crying Bird had decided it was time to rest. "There is no need to exhaust ourselves. We have come a long way, further than I had expected. We will eat and sleep now."

They guided the canoe into a slough that led off the main channel, covered the dugout with a camouflage cloth, and then waded to a hammock of hickory and pine trees. Crying Bird carried his crippled brother, Marehootie, on his back.

The deaf Indian, Nihoto, climbed a tree as swiftly as a raccoon and watched up and down the river while the others slept or simply rested. In time he would be relieved by Crying Bird. Marehootie, who could not walk, much less climb a tree, and the boy had no lookout duties. Chief Tacatacura, of course, was not expected to stand guard.

As they rested, the sun rose over the river and shot its first golden arrows through the trees. Marehootie produced a small glass bottle of mosquito medicine and they all rubbed it onto their faces, ears and limbs. Mosquitoes, intent on one last feast before the heat of the day, brushed against the boy's arms and forehead and then were gone.

At first, sleep would not come to Coya. He thought of what must be happening at the mission. The remaining five students would have awakened by now in the convento, washed and dressed for the day, and gathered in the mission church for Father Pareja's morning prayers.

The boy could hear the words of the priest, the familiar verses of scripture that he might recite, and the way his soft and comforting Castilian accent moved seamlessly between Spanish and the Timucua tongue, and even the language the boys were not required to learn called Latin.

Prayers done, they would disburse to their morning chores of sweeping the mission yard, policing the friar's garden for weeds, or helping the cooks. One unlucky boy, whoever spent too much time playing and too little time studying the catechism, would clean the convento and Father Pareja's apartment. He would also have the unpleasant duty of emptying and cleaning the chamber pots, including those of the soldiers in the barracks.

His memories of Father Pareja had begun to comfort him and make him drowsy. But Coya was suddenly fully awake when he remembered that in the night, just before the escape, he had started a fire in the barracks. If the fire had been successful, perhaps there were no soldiers' pots to clean. Coya felt his guilt, and prayed that no one was hurt. He rolled onto his side facing away from the morning light.

What must Father Pareja be feeling now that Coya had run away from his home with these pagans? What betrayal must he feel that his favorite, his altar boy, should flee from the Word of God? Tears welled in the boy's eyes and ran down his cheeks.

What else was there for him to have done? The Spanish sergeant had announced his intention to burn the old Acueran, Marehootie, at the stake, and had written a warrant for his death on fine parchment. Yet, Father Pareja had done nothing to stop the impending murder, and the boy could not understand how a man of God would allow an innocent Indian to die to satisfy the evil in a soldier's heart. The tears were for the priest whom he loved, but who had betrayed him, and whom, in turn, Coya had betrayed by running away, and for himself.

Marehootie was hopelessly crippled by the sergeant's beating, but alive, and now in the protection of his kin. The priest would surely die of a broken heart. Coya would be an outlaw in the eyes of the Spanish, a renegade Indian fled from the Word of God, a *cimarrone.*

Eventually Coya slept soundly and awoke when the sun was high overhead. The others were gone, except for Marehootie who lay naked in a place where the sun bathed his leathery skin.

"I had almost forgotten how the sun warms the bones," he said when he heard the boy stirring about. "My prison had only one tiny window, but no sunlight to speak of."

"I was there. I saw what it was like for you," the boy said.

"If they lock me in a cage again I will insist on a larger window. I have learned to survive without freedom, but without the sun to warm my bones I would not live long."

"They will never lock you in again. I promise you that," the boy said. "They will have to kill me first."

Marehootie chuckled. "Do you think they would hesitate to kill you, now that you have fled the mission and joined a band of criminals?"

The boy had not thought of it that way, and did not answer. He arose from his bed of palmetto and moss and walked around. "Where have the others gone?" he asked.

"They went to scout a village that is nearby."

"Are we still in the land of Utina?"

"Tomorrow night we will leave Utina. Unless we run into trouble we will be home in two days more," the old man said, his voice trailing off.

"Then we will be at Wekiva?"

"Perhaps. Some of us may reach our home. Maybe all of us will. We have come a long way already, but there are people on the river who wish us dead."

The boy considered what Marehootie had said. "If we are in danger, should the others be showing themselves in an Utinan village in the daylight?"

The old man did not answer. Instead, he shielded his eyes with a palm leaf. Soon he was asleep again, snoring quietly.

Later, the boy was startled when Nihoto suddenly appeared without sound or warning. He spoke the indistinct tongue of one who is deaf to all sounds, even his own voice.

Nihoto helped the old man to his feet and lifted him onto his back. The deaf man was a head shorter than Marehootie, but so powerfully built that he carried the old man easily. Coya followed as they made their way back to where the canoe was hidden.

"We will see the others soon," Marehootie said before the boy could ask. With Coya paddling in front, the canoe entered the river in the late afternoon and turned once again to the south.

Soon they were hailed from the shore. Chief Tacatacura stood among a group of smaller two- and four-man dugout canoes, waving his arm and shouting. It was the embarcadero of a village on the eastern shore.

A narrow slough bled into the river at this point, and Coya directed their canoe into it. The water was soon too shallow to go farther. Two men were there to help Marehootie to shore. Six others quickly lifted the canoe out of the water and hauled it into a thick jungle of briars and vines. The air carried the scent of smoking meat.

"Do you know where you are now?" Marehootie asked.

The boy had tears in his eyes, but blinked them away. "I have not been to this place since my fourth summer. That smell is from the barbacoa that stands near the entrance to the council house."

Coya led the others as he strode purposefully down a well-worn path that led through a copse of elderberry bushes, between two clusters of small, round thatched houses, past the rack where alligator meats, fish, birds and venison were being smoked and preserved for future meals, and directly to the door of the council house of the Utinan village of Coya. His home.

Marehootie spoke quietly, as people were standing around watching the strangers. "Stay here. Nihoto will be with you. You may be invited in. If so, walk in proudly and stand straight. I or Crying Bird will speak for you. If no one comes for you for a long time and you hear me cough loudly you must enter boldly, even if a guard tries to keep you out." Before Coya could protest, the old man hobbled into the council house, supporting himself unsteadily on his crutch.

The boy stood outside the doorway. He heard muffled talking inside, sometimes loud and sometimes quiet, but he could not understand what was being said. Above all the voices, Coya heard Crying Bird's resonant tones, like the deep growl of a bear. Another voice was somehow familiar and comforting, though Coya could not place it.

Coya was aware of the eyes that watched him. A tiny boy-child peeked from inside a nearby hut, making gurgling noises, a finger massaging his gums. Two boys, about Coya's own age, ventured toward him, trying to appear bigger than they really were, but they lost their nerve and retreated when they saw the scowl on Nihoto's face.

Women congregated a short distance away, at first four of five of them, then more, watching him closely. One began to make high, chattering bird calls, sounds that Coya had heard in the villages near the mission when uncivilized people came to the town. Soon they were all making the same sound. At first it was unsettling, but as Coya watched their faces he saw it was excitement and not anger they expressed.

A young woman carrying a baby approached and reached out a hand to touch Coya, but retreated when Nihoto raised his arm as if to strike her. The noise of the bird calls rose quickly and soon became deafening. Only Nihoto, who could not hear, was unfazed. Coya faced them and struggled to appear comfortable and unafraid.

In an instant it was over, and all was silent in the village. The women stood quietly, covering their mouths with their hands. Coya sensed someone behind him and he turned.

A tall man stood in the doorway of the council house. He had only one arm, the left. His face bore the red and black markings of high office.

"Welcome to your home, nephew. I am Acoto. I am *inija* to our chief. He will see you now."

The man embraced him with his one arm and led him through the doorway.

Chapter 2

Convento de San Francisco
San Augustín

The message from the governor said the patient would arrive by midday, which meant that Father de Avila had sufficient time to make room for an extra bed in the crowded, six-bed hospital. His plan was to remove his own belongings to the new convento across the square, and to dispose of the bed rolls and personal effects of the deceased patients that accumulated so quickly and were stacked like cordwood along the back wall.

When the monastery had burned to the ground two years earlier, Governor Canzo was quick to offer Our Lady of Solitude as the Franciscan headquarters, since there were no funds available either in the government *situado* or church accounts for new construction.

It was a trap, and Father Marron had fallen into it. In its three year existence, the hospital had been managed by the government, and because most of the patients were soldiers, the sergeant major was required to provide men to tend to the sick and injured. Priests had only been called upon to hear confession, administer last rites, and bury the dead.

Now, because they were on the premises, the governor required the Franciscans to do it all. Healthy soldiers hardly ever entered the hospital, even to visit their fallen comrades, for fear they might be pressed into service by the priest.

The only doctor in San Augustín had been a civilian who refused to attend the soldiers. He limited his practice to the merchants, governmental officials and the clergy of the town. He would, on occasion, answer the priest's questions on how to treat burns, bowel irregularities or wounds. But the good doctor hoarded the meager supply of medicines that came his way, and would not share them. The doctor had died during the winter, of an illness that he himself failed to diagnose or treat effectively. "God's retribution," the priests said among themselves.

Men from the garrison used to appear at the front door of the hospital, two or three every morning, complaining of a variety of digestive problems, severe headaches or other inexplicable maladies. Some sought medicines. The priest usually had none to offer. All of them asked for a note excusing them from whatever daily duties had been assigned to them.

In time, de Avila had come to require an hour of the soldier's help in return for the work excuse. Some of the men decided that whatever it was, their assignment for the day was preferable to an hour in the hospital, cleaning the waste left by a dying comrade, or washing their bodies for burial. Now, few men appeared for sick call.

When the brigantine from San Juan del Puerto dropped anchor shortly after daybreak, and the injured man was brought ashore by the soldiers, the priest was not ready. He ordered the soldiers to leave the man outside in the shade of a sweet gum tree until a place was available. Two Indians assigned to work in the mission and hospital by Chief Soloy removed de Avila's meager possessions and took them to a room at the convento. A solitary private made repeated trips to and from the garrison carrying the belongings of his deceased comrades.

While they worked, de Avila went to inspect the injuries to the new patient. He had been told that the man suffered concussion wounds and burns from an explosion. Hardened as he was to the sight of physical injuries and the ravages of illness, he felt he was prepared for the ugliness of the wounds described. But the priest shuddered when he removed the cloth draped over what remained of the man's face.

The left eye was sunken into its cavity, sightless and cocked at a strange angle outward, as if looking for his ear, which was no longer where it belonged. The bulbous tip of the nose had been ripped and hung by a shred of tissue, tinged by gangrene. His nostrils, thus exposed, gave him a porcine look. The left side of his scalp had been blown away, leaving only a fuzzy tuft of scorched hair above what was left of his ear, and the remainder of the face was either red or charred black.

"God have mercy," de Avila said as he began the examination. A familiar despair settling in, with the certainty that he had neither the medicines nor the training to save the man's life.

Not one of the sixteen patients who had been in the hospital under de Avila's care had survived to walk out of it. Fifteen had died of their fevers, from loss of blood, or for no reason that was apparent to the priest. The other was a fifteen-year-old soldier from Malaga, a boy who missed his home and had developed palsy. He feared each day would be his last, and wanted to confess his venal sins to the friar almost every day. The memory of that boy was the hardest for de Avila to bear, for he feared that he had failed to save not only his life, but also his soul. One morning de Avila was awakened by the cries of another patient. He leapt from his bed and ran into the ward, only to find the boy was hanging by the neck from a support beam.

De Avila was no stranger to suffering. He was there at the time of the insurrection in Guale when five of his fellow Franciscans in neighboring missions were murdered by the Indians and their bodies dismembered. For reasons known only to God, de Avila was kept alive by the Indians, and made a slave. He had been stripped naked, and the Guale would neither clothe nor feed him, but left him to fashion his own clothing from rags and palmetto leaves, and to eat only berries and nuts that grew wild and such small animals or birds as he could snare. Once, he was whipped for trying to dig tubers from an old garden.

For six months he was held captive, filthy, cold and starved, until the day the Indians had miraculously had a change of heart and left him on a well-traveled trail where the Spanish soldiers could find him, with so much food that he became ill trying to sate himself.

That was a nightmarish time that seemed to never end, but in a strange way he had understood his place in it. If he perished it would be in God's name, and his suffering would make him a martyr, as the others had been martyred before him.

When he was returned to the care of the Franciscans in San Augustín, his nerves were shattered, and he was deemed unfit to return to mission work. Father Marron, de Avila's good friend Father Francisco Pareja of San Juan del Puerto, and even the diocesan priest of San Augustín prayed with him, listened to him, and consoled him for the guilt he felt at having survived while the others perished.

Then he was assigned to work here in Our Lady of Solitude. After two years of futility, witnessing daily suffering and with death his constant companion, he sometimes dreamed he was back in Guale where he might die happy in God's service. For this failure, his inability to save either lives or souls, there would be no absolution.

De Avila looked for a place to touch his new patient with the backs of his fingers, to see if he was fevered. The right forehead and cheek were unburned, so he touched him there and felt the heat.

The man was unconscious and could give no complaints of pain to help de Avila in his examination. Moving the head and neck might actually harm the man more if he had a spinal injury. Besides, the priest did not want to touch the left side of his head at all.

The man was naked under the sheet, except for the right arm of his tunic which remained after the rest of his clothing had been blown away.

The priest gently manipulated the arms and fingers, and then the legs. He found no sign of fractured bones. There was no way to determine internal wounds or what injuries there might be to the spine. He forced open the man's mouth and saw no sign of accumulated blood.

The soldier was apparently barefooted at the time of the accident, or perhaps his boots were later removed. The feet and toes appeared uninjured. Other than the wounds to the man's face and head, and burns on his left shoulder, no injuries were apparent. Apparently the soldier had turned to the right at the instant of the explosion. Two men standing to his left were decapitated, one of the witnesses had said.

De Avila lifted the man's wrist, feeling for a pulse. It was hard to find. He felt for the heartbeat and found it was faint, but slow and steady.

Suddenly the man grasped the priest's arm in his fist, and pulled himself to a sitting position, his right eye now open wide and looking at de Avila. His mumbled curses were profane, but mostly incoherent.

De Avila jerked backward, falling onto his side, but could not retrieve his arm from the vice-like grip of the dying man.

Chapter 3

The day was warm and the hearth in the center of the council house remained unlit. Even so, the air inside bore the comforting hint of burned cedar, familiar and sweet to the nose of the boy.

Coya stood before the principal men and elders who sat on benches to the right of the door. To either side, other men sat, according to their rank and clan on lower seats. They all talked quietly to each other, looking at Coya as if studying his features, judging his strengths and weaknesses. Acoto, the one-armed man, stood beside the boy. When Acoto began to speak, the others fell silent.

"We welcome home a son of the village of Coya, the child of a mother of White Deer Clan who was sister to us all but is now in spirit. She was one we all loved dearly in life and respected for her strength of character and beauty." Coya stood straight at the mention of his mother.

"Eight…" Acoto paused, and then began again. "Nine summers ago, his mother was taken from us in a cowardly attack by our enemies."

A murmur ran through the room as old memories stirred emotions that discipline and respect could not suppress. After a moment of indulgence, the chief, sitting in the center and higher than the rest in his own walled cabana, rapped the boards twice with his stick, and immediately all fell silent.

Coya, for a moment, could picture his mother's smile. It was a memory time had not erased.

"When his mother passed into the world of spirit, so well loved was she that all of her White Deer brothers and sisters offered to raise the child as their own," Acoto said, resting his hand on Coya's shoulder.

To Coya's left, Marehootie and his companions sat in seats of honor, raised above the level of the common people, but much lower than the seat of the Chief of Coya. Acoto faced them as he spoke, positioned also to see the chief.

"Our Paramount, Olate Ouai Utina, spoke to his brother Honoroso and said that the boy should be an offering to his friend, the Spanish governor, who –"

Again, the men reacted, carried by their anger and memories. One spit into the dirt and swore loudly. Another stood to speak, but was grabbed by the man sitting next to him and pulled back onto his bench. Two men in the second tier began to argue and push each other, and would have exchanged blows had the chief not banged his stick again, this time more violently.

Acoto spoke. "There may be some among us of such weak character that they would insult our guests and embarrass our chief. Those who listen quietly may remain, but any who would show disrespect must leave now or be whipped and expelled."

Four guards, stronger and larger than the others, walked from their station near the doorway and faced the crowd.

Coya looked at Marehootie and saw the old man was smiling, as if he was enjoying himself.

Shouts of approval spread through the room, and then all was quiet once again. Suddenly, one of the men who had almost fought his neighbor left his place; roughly pushing aside those in the row below him, he stalked toward the door, cursing. He wore suspended from his neck a bear claw, the sign of Bear Clan. On his right shoulder there appeared a white stain, as of clay, in the shape of a quarter moon. Coya had seen a great variety of bodily markings worn by members of the many clans among those who shared the Timucua tongue, but this one was unfamiliar.

The man's path took him past Coya, but before he could approach the boy, Crying Bird jumped to his feet and blocked the way, extending a hand into the man's chest, knocking him backward. For a moment no one moved or spoke.

"He means no harm to the boy" the one-armed *inija* said, softly. Crying Bird stood his ground but allowed the man to gather his dignity and leave the house. Whistles of derision by some of the men followed him out. Others remained silent.

The chief rapped his stick once again, and gestured to his *inija*. Acoto stepped up to the chief's box. The two spoke privately for some time. Acoto moved to the floor and said that everyone should go to his house and attend to his family until summoned back to the council house for the evening meal. At that time, the guests would be called upon to address the council and answer questions put to them by Chief Honoroso.

Tacatacura was invited to visit in the home of Chief Honoroso, and the two of them left the council house together. Before the rest could follow their chief single-file through the doorway, the four large warriors positioned themselves so that no one could approach Coya.

When they were all gone, Marehootie leaned on his crutch near the doorway and spoke quietly with Acoto. After the one-armed *inija* left, Marehootie returned to the bench where the others waited, a wry smile creasing his cheeks. His eyes, however, were sad and tired. Nihoto remained by the door so they would not be disturbed.

Three women came into the council house, one carrying a clay container of red coals and the other two a large earthen pot. Before long the hearth was ablaze, and from the pot the tantalizing smell of roasting holly leaves filled the house.

"This is not good." Marehootie spoke softly to Crying Bird, so as not to be overheard by the women. "Acoto and the chief are concerned for the boy's safety. There are still those in this village who follow Olate Ouai Utina, and who favor his son, Osprey."

Coya looked into Marehootie's face, and into that of Crying Bird. "I don't understand what is happening. This is my home. These are my people. Why should I be in danger?"

"Your home? Your people?" Crying Bird asked, his eyebrows arched. "I doubt that you could name even one of the men you saw here. The chief of the village is your own uncle, Honoroso, but you did not recognize him and you did not even bow in his direction to acknowledge him. Your manners are poor, and you have much to learn."

Marehootie started to speak, but closed his mouth, slumping on his bench. Coya stared at the dirt floor at his feet.

Crying Bird turned to Marehootie. "You should have taken more time with the boy, teaching him respect for his elders."

"There was so little time at the mission," Marehootie said. "I could not teach the boy all he needs to know. It took seven days before he learned to show respect even for me."

"Two days!" Coya shot back. "It was only two days before you had me saying '*Nariba*' to show you respect and '*paqe-paqe*' to apologize for my bad manners."

Marehootie turned to face the boy. The wrinkles around his eyes deepened, his mouth spread wide, and he laughed out loud, almost losing his balance on the narrow bench.

"Two days. You are right," he said. "It is my memory. I have lost it." Again, the old man started to laugh, but stifled it by covering his mouth with his hand.

Crying Bird scowled at the women who stood nearby, listening. They moved away quickly to the other side of the council house fire.

"There is much you need to know," Crying Bird said to the boy. "There are those even in this village who want you dead. It is bad enough that other villages in Utina will oppose you. We thought that at least you would be safe here."

"Dead?" Coya asked. "Why would anyone other than the Spanish want to harm me? And they, only because I burned their barracks. And perhaps because I came with you, and am now a *cimarrone*."

Crying Bird and Marehootie exchanged a long look. Finally, Marehootie turned to address the boy.

"There are only two things you need to know and remember tonight," Marehootie said. "First, there is the story of what happened here. The chief, your Uncle Honoroso, refused to join with Olate Ouai Utina and the Spanish in a war against the Potano people. That was years ago, but Utina never forgot nor forgave his brother for withdrawing this village and three others from the Utinan federation.

"Because Honoroso is of the White Deer Clan, and Utina's younger brother, Utina could not kill him nor harm him without offending the spirits of the ancestors. That would be the end of the federation, and Utina knew it. So he struck back the only way he knew how.

"He chided Honoroso for his disrespect, and demanded to know who among the leaders of the village advised him to refuse to fight. That was an insult, and Honoroso refused to answer because his word is law in this village, and what advice he received in reaching his decision was none of Utina's business.

"Utina asked him directly if his *inija,* Acoto, was one of the cowards who would not kill Potanans. Again, Honoroso would say nothing. Finally, Acoto rose to defend his chief and said to Utina that he and all the elders agreed with Honoroso, that what Utina was doing in joining with foreigners to attack the other people of the river was dishonorable.

"It was a brave thing Acoto did, speaking up like that, but it was an insult that Utina could not let pass and still save face. He seized the *inija* and ordered his men to hold him down on the hearth," Marehootie said.

"I was not here, of course. No Acueran was ever allowed into an Utinan council, as we would not allow them into ours. But I was told the story many times by traders and other people, and every time the same. It is the reason Acoto is one-armed.

"Utina used his battle axe to chop off the arm of Honoroso's *inija*, right over there," he said, gesturing toward the stone floor by the fire. Coya's eyes moved to the hearth. He tried to imagine what it must have been like.

"While the *isucu* worked to save Acoto's life, Utina said to Honoroso, 'Your *inija* was your right-arm man. Now he has only a left arm. You should get yourself better advisors.'"

The heat from the fire had become uncomfortable, and Coya felt as if he wanted fresh air to breathe.

"Utina left the village of Coya that day," Marehootie continued, "and from what I have been told he never returned. He took Acoto's severed arm and hung it in a tree where the main trail enters the village. He warned that if anyone removed it from the tree he would return and leave a village of people with only one arm. And no one ever buried that arm. It withered and dried in the sun. Eventually the rope that held it fell apart and the bones of the arm and fingers fell to the ground. It shamed Acoto and the members of his clan, as it did all the people of Coya."

"A wild cat dragged the bones away one night, or so the story goes," Crying Bird added. "Many in this village will never forget the cruelty of Olate Ouai Utina. Perhaps, even now that he is dying, he is still respected and feared by some people here."

The boy sat back on the bench thinking about what had been said.

Presently, Crying Bird reached out his hand and tapped Marehootie's knee. "And the second thing?" he asked.

"What do you mean?" Marehootie said.

"You told the boy there were two things he should remember."

"Ah, yes, I almost forgot. Coya, you have heard that Olate Ouai Utina is dying. His sickness is the one that follows the soldiers. Wherever they go, people get sick with sores all over their bodies. Some people say it is almost funny, that Olate Ouai Utina should die this way, but death is never something to laugh about. That's why I say it is 'appropriate,' the way he is dying."

Crying Bird interrupted again. "Is that all you want to tell him, the way Utina will die?"

"Patience," Marehootie said. "You need to learn patience, brother. A well-told story cannot be rushed."

The old man turned once again to the boy. "The question is who will succeed Olate Ouai Utina when he is dead. His heir must come from White Deer Clan. Everyone understands that. All chiefs, everywhere, are White Deer, and must be born of a White Deer woman.

"He has no White Deer uncles still alive, and none of his brothers are young and strong enough to be *Holata Aco.* He had three White Deer nephews, children of his sisters. By rights, the eldest of the three should become Chief of Utina. But they all died of the Spanish sickness last winter, one after another, within days of each other.

"Go on with your story," Crying Bird said," but make it quick. The others will be coming back soon."

Marehootie straightened his tunic at the shoulders. "The problem, of course, is that he has no living White Deer nephews or nieces, and so there are no direct successors to the chiefdom. There is no one the elders could find who is suitable.

"Finally, Utina shocked everyone by naming his own son, Osprey, as the next Chief of the Utina. You can imagine how upsetting this is to the elders. Osprey's mother was of the Bird Clan. Does this mean that in the future all chiefs come from Bird Clan? They are too stupid to lead. Everyone knows that. And when Osprey dies, is the next chief to be his son, who might be of the Buzzard, Earth, Bear, Turkey, Panther or some other clan? You can see how confusing it would be," Marehootie said.

"All these questions were put to Utina by the elders," Crying Bird added. "His only answer was that it works well for the Spanish. So that was it. The Spanish consider a child to be the heir to his father."

From outside the council house a whelk shell sounded, summoning the men. Soon they began to file in, each moving to his assigned bench.

"Many Utinans forgot that there remains one legitimate heir to Chief Utina," said Marehootie. "But not so here, in the village of Coya. They remembered, and the elders asked that he be brought forth so that his legitimacy could be attested, and his character and strength measured."

The boy reached out and touched Marehootie's lips so that he would be silent.

"And you came for me. You came to the mission and became my friend, intending all along to take me away." The boy's eyes were now moist. "And you risked your skin to bring me here so that I might become Chief of the Utina."

Marehootie reached out his arm and pulled Coya close. "I told you he was a bright boy," he said to Crying Bird. "He is soft from eating mission food, but we can toughen him."

Chapter 4

Convento de San Francisco
San Augustín

Father Francisco Pareja, Doctrinario of Misión San Juan del Puerto, arrived at San Augustín shortly after noon on the third day of the journey southward. The well-marked, interlaced Indian trails were easy to follow for the priest and his companion, a soldier assigned by the sergeant major to guard him.

Pareja had objected when he was told of the arrangements. "I have traveled back and forth two dozen times without a soldier to guard me, without one incident or threat," he argued. Gonsalves would not hear of it. In light of the deaths and strange happenings at the mission, he forbade Pareja to travel without armed guard until the governor decided otherwise.

The priest had hoped to travel in the company of the *inija* of the village of Alicamani, and two religious students who had never been to San Augustín. When the Indians learned that a soldier would be with them they decided to stay at San Juan.

The friar and soldier entered San Augustín from the northwest. Pareja dismissed his escort and went directly to the hospital, rather than stop first at the friary to bathe and rest from the long journey.

"Francisco! Praise God! I heard that you were coming." Father de Avila had been sitting on a bench in the shade of an oak tree, and now rushed into the sunlit yard to embrace his old friend. "Tell me why you are here. How long can you stay? Have you spoken to Father Marron yet?" De Avila spoke rapidly, tears of joy wetting his thin, pallid face.

"Slow down! At least let me catch my breath. I have been on the trail three days, and now you wear me out with your questions," Pareja protested, hugging his young friend.

"Join me here, in the shade," de Avila said, directing Pareja to the crude wooden bench that was long enough for two to sit comfortably.

"To try to answer you, I am here for two reasons. Father Marron had sent word to me to come see him. I had put it off because of a certain – problem, you might say, that we had at the mission, which accounts for my second reason to be here."

"We have heard of your problems," de Avila said. "I fear that one of your burdens has become my own."

Pareja's brow furrowed as he looked into de Avila's dark eyes.

"I speak of the sergeant, Suarez. He was brought here five days ago, half dead. I'm afraid my poor ministrations have not helped. He is comatose most of the time, and fevered. He cannot last long. Perhaps God will claim him today or tonight. I doubt that he will last until the Sabbath."

Both priests crossed themselves. Pareja leaned forward, holding his head in his hands. "I'm sorry this has fallen on you, my friend."

The two Franciscans were quiet for awhile. Finally, de Avila spoke. "He was lucid, two days ago. I offered to hear his confession."

Pareja waited, but when the younger priest did not say more, finally he asked, "Has he confessed his sins?"

De Avila wiped his eyes with a kerchief and sighed. "He cursed me."

"God certainly has a way of loading us down with interesting burdens, wouldn't you agree?"

"I don't recall this precise moral dilemma being put to us in Seminary in Seville. There the answers were self-evident.

Here, in this place, the answers, and sometimes even the proper questions, elude me."

The older priest put his hand on the knee of the young friar. "You and I face the same predicament where this man is concerned. We both have reason to feel ill-will toward Sergeant Suarez. You, because you know he is guilty of fomenting the revolt at Guale five years ago. We both lost dear friends, and you suffered terribly because of it. It must have been galling for you when Suarez was given credit for your rescue from the Indians there."

"That is true," de Avila said. "I struggle every day with my abhorrence of the man and my duty to minister to him with love. I am not a saint, only a poor priest. I suspect you also have reasons to dislike the man."

When Father Pareja did not immediately reply, de Avila went on. "Will you tell me what happened at San Juan?"

Pareja took a deep breath and turned to face his friend. "Once upon a time, you confessed to me. Will you now hear my confession?"

Again, de Avila crossed himself. "If you need to tell me something in the sanctity of confessional, I am willing to listen," he said solemnly.

Together they uttered the Prayer of Confession. The mission yard was empty. There was no one nearby to hear.

"Bless me, Father," said Pareja, "for I have sinned."

Pareja gathered his thoughts before he continued. "As you know, the old Acueran man who calls himself Marehootie was suspected by the sergeant of having been involved in the murders at Guale. The sergeant tried to beat a confession out of the old man. Marehootie stood up to him and spit in his face. I was not there, or I might have prevented it. I was told by my altar boy, Juan de Coya.

"I grew quite fond of the old man. He is an excellent linguist and had been essential to me with my studies of the Timucua tongue. Juan served as interpreter and worked closely with us on translating catechism into the Indian language.

"I learned to love and respect the old man. His is a gentle soul. I could not imagine he would harm a priest, or anyone, for that matter. I stood up for him, at least in the beginning. I'm sure I made things difficult for the sergeant.

"When I was here that last time, Suarez took advantage of my absence from the mission. He beat the Indian, again. In fact, he broke both of his feet and crippled him."

Pareja took a kerchief from the pocket of his robe and wiped the moisture from the corners of his eyes. Then he blew his nose with the same rag, folded it and put it in his pocket.

"He also beat the boy," he said, "and cut his ear so badly I had to sew it on for him."

De Avila shook his head slowly.

"I confronted the sergeant, of course. He admitted he had insufficient evidence to convict the Indian of the deaths at Guale. Then he made an outrageous accusation. He said that the old man was what the French call a *berdache*. We might say homosexual."

A soldier walked across the yard, past the priests where they were talking, and into the hospital. Pareja waited until he was out of earshot before speaking further.

"Suarez claimed the legal authority under military law to burn the old man at the stake."

"I never heard of such a thing," de Avila said. "Preposterous!"

"Perhaps. I know nothing of military justice, or of man's law, for that matter."

"But surely, as *Doctrinario* of the mission you could have forbade him and appealed to the governor to put a stop to it."

Father Pareja again lapsed into silence. "It was not that simple," he finally said. "Sometimes even the most earnest prayer will not produce the right answer to a moral dilemma."

"To me it is clear." De Avila was standing now and facing Pareja. "I cannot imagine a reason for not saving the life of the Indian, Marehootie."

"If I speak it, you must never repeat it to anyone," Pareja said.

De Avila sat down again. "Everything you say today is in confidence. You need not hold back for fear I will repeat it and violate the sanctity of the Confessional."

"I did not mean to suggest that you would do so. It is just so hard for me to say it. Give me a moment." Pareja fell silent again, collecting his thoughts and feelings before speaking again. "Sergeant Suarez told me that he believed that the boy, de Coya, was the old man's lover. If I insisted that the old man be tried on the charge in San Augustín, Suarez intended to charge the boy as a *berdache* also. He said that they would both die for their sins."

De Avila slumped on the bench, leaning against the tree. He exhaled deeply.

Father Pareja continued. "I didn't believe it. Of either of them. I erred by not calling the sergeant's bluff, and my weakness is the cause of all that happened later. The guilt is mine. Those deaths need not have happened. I confess it."

"There's more?" de Avila asked.

"The last night was very confused. I did not see a lot that happened. I was in my apartment praying to God for guidance on what I should do. Suarez had his men prepare the execution site outside the mission, behind the garrison. At about eleven o'clock the church bell began to ring. I ran out into the yard. There was a fire beyond the barracks. I saw Juan de Coya near the prison cell where they held the old man, but Marehootie was gone."

Father Pareja bowed his head. "The soldier who was guarding him, a boy of about fifteen years, was dead. His throat had been cut.

"The barracks soon were ablaze. I thought the fire had spread, but then I realized that the barracks fire came from inside Suarez' apartment. Then the powder magazine exploded. The Indians took their time putting out the first fire. They made no effort to save the barracks. By the time the fires were out, four soldiers were dead and the sergeant mortally wounded.

"De Coya also disappeared. I assume he and the old man are together, somewhere. The sergeant major does not know it yet because I did not tell him, but Chief Tacatacura was also missing from his village. None of his people seem concerned by his absence. Perhaps he is with the others.

"My biggest concern is the boy, de Coya. I fear he may have killed the guard. Juan is twelve years old, an innocent. His guilt is mine alone."

Father Pareja stood and prepared to walk across the yard to the monastery. "Thank you, Francisco, for listening to me. As they say, 'confession is good for the soul,' and at least it has lifted my spirits."

"Answer me one question, if you will," de Avila said. "Why did you not tell Gonsalves that the chief and the boy were gone from the mission?"

Father Pareja looked at the clouds building in the west. There would be a late day shower.

"Perhaps it is because I pray that they never be caught," he said.

Chapter 5

Before they set out, Crying Bird spread the camouflage fabric in their dugout to cover light-colored bundles that would reflect moonlight. Once on the river, they hugged the shoreline, keeping to the shadows of overhanging trees and avoiding the bulrushes and river reeds in which they would be easily heard and seen.

"What was said that caused us to leave so quickly?" Coya asked.

For awhile no one answered. Finally, Crying Bird spoke in low tones. "Chief Honoroso suggested we not tarry, but get as far away as possible before daybreak. The man who caused the disturbance in the council house is a friend of Osprey. He went looking for him to tell him where we were. Honoroso sent us away for our own protection."

Chief Tacatacura, who seldom offered his opinion, spoke out. "I wonder if we were asked to leave for our own safety, or if our presence in the village was a danger to the Coyans."

Coya's eyes were accustomed to the dark and he knelt in the bow, alert to anything in their path. The others had come to trust his judgment when he was well rested. It was second nature by now, the silent hand-signaling that directed the movement of the war canoe through the shadows.

"Why would they fear one man? Is Osprey so powerful that he frightens an entire village?" Coya asked over his shoulder.

"You are too loud," said Crying Bird. "I will answer you this time, but after that there will be no more talking until I say it is safe.

"Osprey is not much more than a boy. He is three years older than you, but he is already as tall as his father. He has been to the village of Coya twice within the past ten days, showing off the musket the Spanish gave him, and trying to convince the young men to join him. He shot a deer and a bear in the same day, and dragged them into the village. The hunters had already laid by enough meat for the winter.

"Honoroso says Osprey has become more belligerent now that he has the weapon. He taunts people and insults them. Osprey may be looking for an excuse to shoot the gun at a person, to prove he is a man and strong enough to be chief."

No one spoke for a long time. In the middle of the night Nihoto made a sound, and when the others turned toward him the Indian pointed to his nose, and then into the dark sky. Soon they could all smell the thin smoke of a dying campfire. The river here was wide, and Crying Bird gestured that they should move to the other side to avoid a small village ahead. They glided across the river and found seclusion in the shadows of hickory trees. Other than the cry of a baby, there was no sound or movement from the village.

The moon hid behind a cloud, but Coya kept the canoe under the outstretched trees that crowded the shore. A growth of willow hung low over the water, and rather than direct the dugout away from shore, Coya motioned that the others lower their heads to avoid the branches. They all understood his gesture, except for Chief Tacatacura who had dozed off into a light sleep.

Marehootie grasped a limb to lift it up over the chief's head. The movement dislodged a snake that fell into Tacatacura's lap, awakening him. The chief blinked away the sleep in his eyes and watched the snake undulating, as if trying to determine how it came to be in a canoe, and not in its tree.

Tacatacura slowly moved his hand, grasped the moccasin behind the head and dropped it into the water.

No one remarked about the snake until much later, but even as he continued to guide the canoe up the river, Coya worried that he had been responsible for exposing the chief to danger. He wondered if there was any truth in the superstition that a snake in a boat foretells disaster.

They moved into a small creek and tied up to a bush. After they relieved themselves on shore, the men sat in the canoe and passed around a basket of food Honoroso had given them when they left the village of Coya. Crying Bird studied the stars and the moon, calculating how much time remained before the sky would lighten.

He looked at Marehootie. "There is more than one way to enter the lake with the water as high as it is. I know of a hidden slough that may be passable, although we might need to get out and pull. If the Utinans are looking for us on the north end of the lake, they will block the main channel."

"I agree," said Marehootie. "My only worry is whether we will reach the spring run before it becomes too light. This time of year the fishermen are out on the lake early, looking to spear the bass."

"Then we need to go right now," Crying Bird said.

The others quickly filled their mouths with corn cakes and picked up their paddles.

The slough held enough water to float the canoe, so no one got wet. If there were people looking for them, they were not watching the slough, and at the darkest time of the night the canoe emerged into a huge lake. Crying Bird knew the lake well, and sat in front, paddling and directing the canoe along the western shore. Coya sat behind him, using Marehootie's paddle. Nihoto was in his usual place in the rear.

The men worked hard, racing against daylight and discovery. Coya watched Crying Bird's muscular arms and shoulders as he effortlessly but powerfully propelled the dugout through the water.

The shoreline swung once again to the south. Here there were no overhanging trees, only intermittent banks of reeds and river cane. The moon had moved well to the west, but it was still bright and the canoe would have been visible to anyone awake on shore.

To Coya, the paddling seemed easier than expected, and the canoe glided smoothly through the shallows despite its size and heavy burden. The old Acueran, Marehootie, had bragged to Coya that the canoes designed and built years ago in his home village of Ibitibi were the best to be found on the River of the Sun.

Crying Bird raised his hand as he studied the shoreline. Coya and Nihoto rested their paddles, awaiting a further signal. When Crying Bird gestured to the right, Coya dipped his paddle on the left side and gave the most powerful stroke his twelve-year-old arms could provide. Nihoto gave one strong stroke and then canted his paddle, swinging the end of the canoe sharply to the left as they glided through the reeds and into a small creek. It was just getting light.

They had not gone far when Crying Bird again raised his hand. The current here was swift, trying to push the canoe back toward the lake. Crying Bird tied the canoe onto an overhanging branch to hold them in place. In the breaking daylight, Coya could see a small round pond ahead. On the far side, a sloping hill rose to a knoll that was flat across the top, without trees or vegetation.

Tacatacura was fully awake, and stood up to get a better view. “What is this place? It looks like an old ceremonial center, with that flat topped hill.”

Crying Bird answered him. “That is what it is: a holy place. The *Jarva* of Acuera says it marks the entry into the underworld. The Utinan Shaman tells it the same, and they are afraid to come here. The spirits of the ancestors are strong here, and they do not welcome company. See how the waters try to push us away?”

“It is a powerful spring,” Marehootie added. “Its waters feed the lake. It will not allow us in unless the ancestors hear our prayers and welcome us.”

There they waited. Time passed and the moving waters gently worked the canoe first one way, and then another. Behind the boy, Marehootie broke the silence softly, and Coya turned to look at him. The old man's eyes were closed and his lips barely moved, his words in the Acueran tongue, so muffled and indistinct that the boy could understand none of them. There was a rhythm to his utterings. It was a song, an ancient chant, meant only for the ears of the spirits to whom it was spoken. Coya had heard the old man sing many times when he was held prisoner at the mission.

As suddenly as he began, the old man fell silent. More time passed, and the only sounds were those of the night: an unseen whippoorwill, a dim chorus of frogs and the gentle whisper of the spring water against the hull of the canoe.

Crying Bird sat hunched over in the front, his shoulders rounded. He moved as if to stand, but settled back on his haunches, his face and arms now raised to the coming light of day.

His song was huskier and louder than his older brother's, but no more intelligible to the boy's ears.

"*Oh yaa tan a-na-ya-no-ibir-ho-hiro*," he chanted, followed by speeches that went on and on until once again he returned to the original phrase and fell silent.

Coya was reminded of the songs of praise that had been taught by Father Pareja before the boy even understood the Spanish language, haunting and beautiful music even without meaning to the words.

Were these hymns that Crying Bird sang, and the repeated phrase the chorus? Coya listened and wondered. No, this was different. No hymn he had ever heard contained long silences. They were also unlike the chants of the priest at the Mass of Holy Eucharist. Still, for some reason, he found them familiar.

Where had the boy heard these chants, the chorus so familiar that he could repeat it perfectly? And, when? Coya had heard the ancient prayers of the old man in his cell at the mission, but this was different, unlike those short murmurings.

"*Oh yaa tan a-na-ya-ma-no-irir-hi-hiro*" settled into the boy's mind where it was comfortable and welcomed.

The current slowed and soon the dugout rested quietly in still water. Crying Bird turned and smiled at his brother. Then he untied the rope from the tree that held them in place. Paddling alone, Crying Bird moved the canoe forward into the spring pool.

Coya was awakened from his sleep by the sound of people talking. He lay on his pallet in the clearing where they had made their camp beside the spring. His dreams were of the mission and of Father Pareja, and Coya wished to go home. He did not open his eyes to the daylight.

"We will stay here until nighttime, praying to the spirits for their blessing and protection." It was Crying Bird, speaking to Chief Tacatacura.

"Leaving the lake and reentering the river will be the most dangerous time for us," Marehootie added. "There are two Utinan villages, one on each side of the mouth of the river. They will be waiting for us there."

"We will do whatever is necessary to avoid them," Crying Bird said, "even if we have to abandon the canoe and walk through the swamp."

"The traders have tried that. They say it is impossible," Marehootie said.

"Nevertheless, we will do what we must," Crying Bird said.

The boy listened and wondered how they could possibly wade through alligator infested swamps at nighttime in the heartland of the enemy, carrying a man who could not walk. And having left the canoe, where would they find another if they lived to discover the river again? He knew it was not his place to question Crying Bird, the powerful *Atichicolo-Iri*, Spirit Warrior of the Acuera.

Soon, weariness overcame worry, and Coya was once again with the priest.

In the afternoon, their rest was disturbed by the sound of voices and laughter from the lake. They were Utinan fishermen.

Crying Bird and Coya peered through the reeds from the spring run. "Olate Ouai Utina claims sovereignty of the lake," said Crying Bird. "He says the Spanish awarded it to him, but it was not theirs to give."

Here the lake was so wide the eastern shore could not be seen. Two canoes of men fished the shallows to the south, working the shore line. To the northeast, where reeds grew into the lake, duck hunters hid from view, shooting arrows at birds that flew by or dabbled in the water. Some ducks were killed, and a small boy waded out to collect them along with the arrows that had missed their targets but which floated in the water.

"When my brother and I were children," Crying Bird said, "before the Spanish came, the lake was shared. Utinans fished the northern shore, and to the east. We Acuerans fished and hunted the west side and even the Mayaca controlled what happened to the south. There were disputes, but no one died. But now Utina controls it all. Mayaca and Acuerans are now forbidden. Some have been killed by the Utinans for trying to catch fish to feed their families. Even the traders who make their living up and down the river are stopped at the villages and their canoes are searched. The Utinans steal from them and require bribes to let them pass."

As the sun approached the horizon, Marehootie and Crying Bird left their camp beside the spring-fed pond and circled to the base of the slope. The older man draped his arm over the shoulder and neck of his brother and used a crutch fashioned from a sapling hickory. They ascended the hill slowly, haltingly. The sun now cast long shadows beside them. Four figures moved up the hill. Coya lay on his side, watching and wondering why Crying Bird's shadow appeared taller than Marehootie's.

Marehootie stopped well below the brim of the hill and stood on his crippled feet, bracing himself with the crutch. Soon, Marehootie turned and looked back toward the lake. To the west and north, the faint sound of thunder could be heard, and dark clouds lifted their heads above the horizon. Crying Bird continued to climb until his shadow, cast by the setting sun, reached the top. He went no further.

At a distance, Coya awaited what would happen next. He could not be sure exactly when the prayers began, but as their volume increased and the sound flowed down the hillside and across the waters of the spring pond, his own lips began to move.

"*Oh yaa tan-a-ya-ma-no-ibir-hi-hiro*," Coya chanted softly, but without error, mimicing Crying Bird's prayer.

Behind Coya, sitting with his back to a tree, Chief Tacatacura watched and listened. Nihoto, the deaf one, still weary from the exertions of three days and nights of hard work, slept through it all.

Chapter 6

Misión Nombre de Dios
San Augustín

Father Francisco Marron, Custos of Missions of La Florida, sat huddled in a chair in his tiny friary apartment. Late afternoon sunlight streamed through an open window, providing warmth and illuminating tiny dust motes when he adjusted his shawl to draw it tighter round his neck.

He did not rise to greet his guest, but smiled and extended a bony hand. Father Pareja knelt and kissed it, his lips warm against the cold fingers. The friar could tell the custos was ill.

"I would have come sooner," said Pareja, "if I had known…"

Marron waived his hand, dismissively. "You came as soon as you could, I'm sure. Sit down. We have important matters to discuss."

Pareja took a seat on a small wooden stool. From where he sat, Marron was back-lit by the window, and it was difficult to make out the expression on the superior's face. Pareja moved his seat so he could see him better.

"I suspect you will want a full report on the disaster at San Juan, and I am prepared to write one if you require it," Pareja said.

Father Marron fixed Pareja with a doleful look. "It is my understanding that there was a fire at the mission and that several soldiers died as a result. Why might I not require a full written report of such an occurrence?"

Pareja shifted uncomfortably. He crossed his right leg over his left under the heavy woolen robe. "Sometimes there can be reasons why the greater good is served by silence."

Marron sighed. "I do not make a habit of keeping secrets from the governor. He will expect a full report. Canzo may also require your testimony at an *audencia* on the subject of the conflagration at San Juan. Gonsalves has told him that the fire was caused by the carelessness of a sergeant, and that if the man survives, he may be prosecuted for it."

"They call it 'carelessness' when it describes the neglectful manner in which a man is to be burned to death?" Pareja said.

Father Marron looked at the younger friar. "I see I have upset you. The word was mine, and not the governor's. He was troubled by the planned execution, as well as the manner in which it was to be carried out."

When Pareja did not respond immediately, the older priest went on. "The governor is also curious about the death of one of the soldiers who was some distance from the fire, and who suffered a wound to the neck." Marron's manner was now more animated, and he watched Pareja closely.

"If it were simply a question of testifying against the sergeant, I would have no hesitation. I know none of his secrets. He has never confessed to me, nor have I ministered to him. As you know, God forgive me, I could never tolerate the man. His blasphemy and profanity were beyond anything I have ever heard – totally out of place in a Catholic mission where there are souls to save and little children listening. He delighted in marching his soldiers right outside the church door during Mass. His curses sometimes drowned out the beauty of the Gospel, I'm afraid.

"But it was his cruelty toward the Indians I could never abide. I know the governor feels responsible for our safety, but we pay a heavy price for whatever protection the soldiers provide. It seems sometimes that while God works through the friars, Satan himself works through the soldiers." The priests crossed themselves.

"And I have other concerns," Pareja said. "As in many matters, it is not as simple as it might appear."

"Your dedication to the Indians has been apparent from the beginning, and their love for you, I might add," Marron said.

Pareja's fingers explored the seam of his robe, where it had begun to unravel. He had two robes when he came here, seven years ago. The first was now in tatters, and he used the cloth to patch the one that remained. There would be no replacement robe if it fell in shreds. He had learned to make do, just like all the friars who had ever come to La Florida.

"You say it is not so simple, by which, I assume, you mean that you have very good reason why you are reluctant to write a report or testify against Suarez," the superior said.

The friar continued to look down.

The older man reached out and patted Pareja's clasped hands. "Francisco, talk to me."

Tears flooded Pareja's eyes and he fumbled in his pocket for his kerchief. Finally, he breathed deeply and looked into the face of his superior, the man he had followed here from Spain.

"If I were to testify, great harm might befall my people. They are innocent of setting the fire, but there are certain matters – certain accusations that might be made by the sergeant against some of the people who attend the mission."

"And to speak of such matters would violate their trust in you?"

"And my vows of priesthood. Also, I could not face my people if I betrayed them."

Slowly, the custos of missions rose to his feet and stepped across the room to a crude table that stood against the wall.

"Francisco, how long has it been since you tasted good Spanish wine?" he asked.

"The only wine in San Juan is the Blood of Christ. There is so little of it, and so many take Communion, I confess I have to water it down so everyone can partake."

"Water into wine would be a good trick," Marron said.

Pareja smiled, relieved at the change of subject. "Our Blessed Savior taught us that it could be done. Chapter two of the Gospel according to St. John. The wedding feast at Cana."

"There you have made an ecclesiastical error," Marron said. "What you are doing at your mission is turning wine into water, not water into wine. Nevertheless, as custos, I enjoy certain prerogatives. One of which is an occasional bottle of red Spanish wine. I keep it here, for distinguished company."

Marron carefully lifted a wine bottle from a basket and placed it on the table. His hands shook as he poured a small amount into two tiny cups, and handed one to Pareja.

"We are so blessed by the spirit here," the superior said after he took a sip. "We do God's work on Earth. This is a life worth the living. And the dying."

Pareja lifted the cup to his lips. It had been eight years since he had tasted undiluted Spanish wine.

"You certainly do seem to enjoy your prerogatives," Pareja said, turning the shiny goblet in his hand, studying the smooth glazed bowl and the artistry of its form. "I have seen nothing so beautiful since our departure banquet at the monastery in Seville so many years ago."

"Fine Iberian crockery, wouldn't you say?" Marron asked.

"Or maybe even French. I am no expert on tableware, but it does make me homesick to hold something so fine in my hand once again."

Marron sat down and pulled the woolen shawl snug around his shoulders. "I'm afraid I have fooled you, Francisco," he said. "The cups were crafted here at Nombre de Dios by the women of the mission. We use them for barter with the people of San Augustín to support our work here."

Pareja again studied the cup, holding it up to the light filtering in through the open window. "A talented people. What other surprises do they hold for us, I wonder?"

Marron cleared his throat. "I will have to think about requiring a report from you. We could claim clerical immunity to a subpoena from the governor. We did that once before, when Father de Avila returned from Guale and refused to testify against the Indians. As I recall, it made Governor Canzo very angry. He did not speak to me for more than a month, but I considered that a blessing at the time."

Father Marron turned to look out the window. The sun was setting and the gulls and pelicans were flying to wherever sea birds go for the night.

"There is a delicate relationship between custos and governor. He controls the purse, and we are at his mercy for the supplies we need to do God's work. Still, he would have to honor the principal of clerical immunity or risk the wrath of the bishop." Father Marron turned back to face Pareja. "The bishop might require such a report. Perhaps when I speak to him and explain the circumstances, he may overlook it."

Pareja looked up. "You will be seeing the bishop?"

Marron was now smiling broadly. "Yes, and that is the reason I asked you to come see me in the first place, even before the events at San Juan. Perhaps you saw the three-masted ship in the harbor. In two days it sails to New Spain. I will be on board. The bishop has asked me to join him in Mexico."

Pareja stood and stepped quickly to the superior. He knelt and kissed the hand of the older man. "I cannot imagine what life will be like here, without you," he said. "When I or the others become depressed and overwhelmed, we always know that you are here in San Augustín, that you will listen to our troubles, pray with us and send us back reinvigorated by your strong spirit and counsel."

Marron withdrew his hand and placed it on the top of Pareja's head. "When I am gone the work will continue here, as before. And it was not my counsel or prayers that made the difference, anyway. It was, is and forever will be our Blessed Savior who directs our efforts here in La Florida. And I am leaving another in my place to serve as custos. He is one of great intellect and ability. He will bless the mission work here in La Florida. He has the youth and stamina to stand against a battalion of profane sergeants. He also has the spiritual strength and character, I believe, to stand against a bullying governor, if need be."

Before Pareja could reply, Marron reached into the pocket of his robe, withdrew a document and handed it to the younger priest.

"I have here, in this dispatch from His Eminence, the Commission of Custos, effective the day of my departure."

Pareja took the parchment into his hands, removed the ribbon that bound it and unrolled it. At the bottom was the seal of the Bishop of New Spain, along with his flourished signature. At the top, the name Francisco Pareja appeared in bright red ink.

Chapter 7

When darkness neared, Crying Bird waded down the creek to see if any fishermen remained on the lake. He came back to camp and said that they were gone, that they had fled to escape the storm that threatened. In his absence, Marehootie had directed that the canoe be loaded carefully, with the heavy bundles distributed evenly.

The spring current thrust the dugout swiftly into the lake. The night was dark, and a heavy cover of clouds hid the moon. They had not gone far when the wind picked up, disturbing the water. Thunder rumbled to the west, and an occasional bolt of lightning zigzagged between the clouds.

In a short while, conditions worsened and as they made their way to the south, the sturdy war canoe was rocked by the action of the waves. Everyone but Chief Tacatacura paddled now, and as the shoreline moved back to the east, the waters splashed over the side into the canoe. Crying Bird directed the men to shore.

"We will wait here for the rain," Crying Bird said when they were again on dry land. "If we are lucky it will be a powerful storm."

Coya looked back at the lake waters churning white with foam. He wondered why Crying Bird and the others prayed for violent weather, and appeared jubilant as it became more dangerous and threatening. He also knew it was not his place to question them.

It was, indeed, a violent storm, and at its height they launched the canoe into its teeth. Marehootie and Crying Bird whistled shrilly as they paddled. Wave after wave of windblown water broke over the sides, drenching the men and their bundles and stinging their eyes.

Coya and Marehootie used large gourds to bale the water accumulating in the bottom, while the others paddled. Overladen with the extra load, the canoe became heavy and difficult to maneuver. With each wave that crossed them, Coya was certain the boat would founder and sink.

On Crying Bird's command, four paddles worked hard on the left side, and the canoe again turned to the south, propelled now more by the wave action and wind behind them than by the strength of the paddlers. Head-long the canoe sped with a lurch, and then slowed with a sickening wallow, only to speed ahead once again on the crest of another wave.

Chief Tacatacura joined Marehootie and Coya in baling the water. Crying Bird in the front and Nihoto in the rear continued to paddle fiercely to control the direction of the sluggish craft.

Coya felt a hand on his shoulder. It was the old man. Marehootie pointed to the left, at the high bank where the river met the lake. There was a village, a large one, from what Coya could make out through the darkness. Three campfires glowed, but smoldered and smoked as the rain sought to quench their flames. The shadows of men could be seen darting about, erecting palm frond barricades to protect the fires from the blowing water.

A second village, directly across the river from the first, was already in darkness as the stinging rain had extinguished the camp fires.

Later, after the storm had blown its course and the canoe was safely in the river away from danger, the men rested.

"I have never been more frightened in my life," Coya began, then corrected himself. "Except for the day the sergeant tried to kill both of us, I have never been more afraid of anything."

"You had good reason to fear the Spaniard's evil intentions, but the storm was an answer from the spirits to our prayers at the holy place," Marehootie said. "The Utinans waited for us and would have killed us, whether we tried to pass during the daylight or at night."

"Their guards were so desperate to keep their fires burning that they abandoned their posts," Crying Bird said. "The spirit blinded them to our passage."

Well before sunup they passed the sleeping Acueran village of Apo on the west side of the river. No fires were lit and no one was awake to greet them, so they continued to the south. The men and the boy relaxed their vigilance and spoke more freely.

"We are well away from Utina territory now," Crying Bird said. "We could easily reach home by sundown."

Marehootie spoke to Coya. "Most of the Acueran homeland is to the west of here. The Mayaca are east of the river, and south, although they move back and forth from here to the ocean as the seasons change."

"I remember you said that the Mayaca burned your village years ago, claiming it as their territory," said the boy. "Will you show me where Ibitibi stood?"

"We have already passed it. There is nothing to see. The Mayaca wanted Ibitibi so badly they would go to war and kill for it. When they won, they didn't want it any more."

"Do you still fight the Mayaca?" Coya asked.

Crying Bird answered. "We had some good wars between us when we were both strong. There have been so many people on both sides dying from the Spanish disease, neither Mayaca nor Acuera want to fight each other. Perhaps we are still strong enough to fight a common enemy."

In the middle of the day, they followed a narrow creek off the main channel to a sandy area where they could bathe away the sweat and smoke of the council house and relax in the shade of willow and hickory trees. A cooling breeze tamed the heat of the day. Crying Bird suggested they try to sleep so that they might be refreshed for their homecoming.

No one slept, however. The anticipation of their arrival at Wekiva and the adventures they had experienced on the journey from the mission left them wide awake. So they talked, except for Nihoto who climbed a tree to act as lookout.

All but Coya and Tacatacura lived in the communal village on the Wekiva River. Coya had heard Marehootie's stories of the river and of the village when it was just a fishing camp, but he learned more as he listened to Marehootie and Crying Bird describe it for Tacatacura.

"A beautiful, cool, spring-fed river, where the water is cleaner than the air itself," Marehootie said. "The fish and turtles and snails and shell fish and birds are so abundant that no one need go hungry."

"Best of all," Crying Bird added, "it offers seclusion from the Spanish soldiers who search for us on the River of the Sun, but who have never discovered Wekiva nor charted its existence. It has a narrow mouth hidden under the shadowing willow trees."

After some coaxing by Tacatacura, Crying Bird began to describe the village of Wekiva, a place that was little more than an Acueran fishing camp years before, but, with the coming of the Spanish to the River of the Sun, had become a hiding place, a sanctuary village of more than two hundred people from different chiefdoms.

"We all live together despite our differences in custom and religion," said Crying Bird, glancing at Coya who was scraping a painful callus from the ball of his right foot. "If we fought among ourselves or even came and went as we pleased, it would not be long before we would be discovered. Not even the Utinans know its location.

"There is a family of Potanans with us. They have a crippled son, and nowhere else to go since their village leaders were murdered by the Utina and the Spanish. They are no trouble, and they honor me as their chief," Crying Bird said.

"There are ten or eleven Mayaca who have sought shelter with us. In the beginning, they may have been common criminals hiding from the justice of their chief, but they are honest people who work hard and so are welcomed. They have even learned to speak the tongue of the Timucua people, and most of us now understand what they are saying when they talk to each other as Mayaca.

"The people of Potano brought us corn and cleared a small field to grow it. The Mayaca sometimes bring oysters from their relatives on the coast. They also showed the women some good ways to prepare clams. We eat well. It is an advantage living with people who are different from us."

"I am surprised you have not grown fat," Tacatacura said.

"We work and play hard. Because we may be attacked at any time, we will not tolerate lazy people who cannot run and fight."

"Are you forgetting your *inija*?" Marehootie asked.

"Ah, yes, Yano," Crying Bird said, chuckling. "I had almost forgotten him. He walked into Wekiva years ago asking for sanctuary for himself and his people. His village had been attacked by Utinans, he said, and they had no place else to hide."

"Yano is about my age," Marehootie said, "and a little strange. Sometimes he gets confused. He still waits for his people. They did not follow him, but he has not given up hope, and he sometimes wanders deep into the swamp looking for them. My brother has honored him by calling him *inija*, but he is worthless."

Crying Bird laughed out loud. "Not always worthless. On his good days he is as smart as any man at Wekiva. He can be an eloquent speaker. I even use him to settle disputes among the others."

"But on his bad days?" Marehootie asked.

"On those days he is as worthless as he is toothless," Crying Bird said.

"He was ill when he joined us," Marehootie said. "Day by day he began to lose his teeth until they had all fallen out except for the back teeth. He doesn't seem to be embarrassed by his looks. Yano doesn't bother to close his lips when he laughs as some people do when they are missing a tooth."

Tacatacura interrupted. "What a strange name. I have never known a man named Yano."

"That's not his real name. In the dialect of Acuerans 'yano' means 'no people,' Marehootie said. "The young men teased him, calling him Yano, and he began to answer to that name."

"Marehootie, can you remember his real name?" Crying Bird asked.

Marehootie was silent for a while. "No, I really can't remember."

"Neither can I," Crying Bird said.

There was silence for a time, then Crying Bird continued. "A clan of Ocales joined us, fleeing an illness that destroyed their village. One of them, an old woman, was dying with a strange disease, and we refused to allow them into our village. We turned them away. In four days they returned, saying that the grandmother who was ill had given her life so that the rest might gain sanctuary."

Marehootie spit a palm berry seed into the water. "The next spring I was looking for special herbs and medicines at a place we call Black Water Creek. I found a crude charnel house with the remains of a woman wearing Ocale clothing. The bones had been scattered by animals. The woman was left there to rot. It was an evil place. Someone had carved a wooden owl to frighten people away, and I left immediately."

Marehootie looked at Crying Bird. "We should have chased the Ocale out of our camp for showing so little respect for their dead, but my brother was chief and said that we must tolerate them."

"My council includes at least one person from each tribe and clan," Crying Bird said. "It is an unusual arrangement, with people who are not White Deer Clan advising the chief. With someone there to explain our differences it is easier to be tolerant and keep the peace. It seems to work well for the people of Wekiva."

Marehootie scoffed. "There have been many disputes. One time the Potano storyteller was telling all of the children the Story of Bread. She got it wrong, and I corrected her in front of the children. It's important that the stories be told perfectly at each telling, or in time they will be full of errors and no better than fanciful legends."

Crying Bird chuckled. “Tell them what happened next.”

“Go on with your description of Wekiva,” Marehootie said.

“If you won’t tell it, I will,” Crying Bird said. He waited for his older brother to continue, but Marehootie remained silent. “The storyteller’s name was Osonga,” said Crying Bird with a glint in his eye. “She said she would kick Marehootie’s butt for embarrassing her in front of the children.”

The others laughed at the thought of Marehootie being threatened by a woman. Even Chief Tacatacura, who seldom smiled, chuckled out loud.

“And she could have done it, too,” Marehootie admitted. “I had a name for her. I called her Woodpecker Lips, because it described her toughness. She did none of the women’s work, but led the men in their war games. She was young, athletic, spirited…” Marehootie fell silent.

“She was one powerful woman, and beautiful,” Crying Bird said. “So beautiful that my brother married her to avoid having his butt kicked.”

Another burst of laughter rose from the group. When it faded, Coya asked, “Will I meet her, this warrior princess?”

Marehootie cleared his throat. “That was a long time ago. We were together three years.”

When the older Indian fell silent, his brother finished the story. “Osonga died giving birth. The child also died.”

A zephyr breeze rippled across the water cooling the travelers.

“I’m sorry,” Coya said. “*Paqe-paqe.*”

Marehootie was quiet for a long time. As the sun set, they launched the canoe back into the river and proceeded south.

They slowed, timing their arrival at Wekiva for full dark to avoid being seen. When they were near their destination, the war canoe stopped under a stand of sweet gum trees along the west bank of the River of the Sun.

Crying Bird and Marehootie studied the darkened shoreline on the other side, whispering quietly. Coya also watched. After a long time he saw something, a quick movement at the very edge of the water, and he pointed it out to the men.

A nocturnal raccoon moved back and forward along a fallen log, fishing in the shallows for an evening meal. Eventually she snagged a small perch and leapt back to the shoreline, collected her children and moved away through the palmetto scrub.

When the men were satisfied that they were alone, they prepared to enter the mouth of the Wekiva River. The entrance was narrow and swift, and covered over by the long, intertwined arms of two willow trees that lined the bank.

Nihoto slipped quietly into the water and grasped the fiber rope at the bow. Crying Bird prepared to join Nihoto in the water to push, but Chief Tacatacura slid over the side first, and took his place at the back with his muscular shoulder braced against the stern.

Slowly the canoe moved forward until it was next to the stand of willow. Here, the current from the side was suddenly strong. As Nihoto bowed his back to drag the canoe under the trees, Tacatacura allowed the stern to swing outward into deeper water, so the dugout could more easily enter the narrow opening.

Sitting in the rear, Coya looked back at Tacatacura as he struggled to get his footing on the sandy bottom. Slowly the canoe moved forward again. Nihoto had already disappeared under the trees. Tacatacura was breathing hard from the exertion.

Coya turned again toward the struggling chief with words of encouragement. Suddenly a flicker of light flashed in the darkness of the other shore. Then it was gone, like a dying ember that has jumped from a camp fire. Before he could speak of it a bright blue flash lit the darkness reflecting a cloud of smoke and the indistinct image of a man holding a weapon at his shoulder.

In the middle of the night, in the house of Chief Crying Bird, the elders of Wekiva again questioned the boy on what he saw and remembered.

"That's all I can tell you. There was a man with an arquebus, or maybe it was a musket. It was just a flash of light. I can't be sure. Then the sound hurt my ears. Chief Tacatacura was laying face down in the water. The water there was clear, but it was stained with his blood. I reached for him and grabbed him by the hair. Then Marehootie threw himself on me, and I was in the bottom of the canoe."

"You said that you saw a flicker of light, just before the flash?" Crying Bird said.

"It's hard to describe. It was like an ember that pops out of the fire. You know, it will flare up a little just before it dies," Coya said.

"Musket," Marehootie said.

Crying Bird nodded.

"This man you saw, describe him for us once again," Marehootie said.

The boy closed his eyes tightly, but the picture would not come. "Just a man. I don't remember."

"Spanish? Was he a soldier?" Crying Bird asked, rising to his feet and standing over the boy.

"Maybe Spanish. Maybe Indian. I can't remember."

"Tall? Short? Thin? Fat?" Crying Bird insisted.

"Leave the boy alone," Marehootie said. "He's doing the best he can to remember."

"Maybe he was tall," the boy offered.

"Not good enough!" Crying Bird said. Then he turned and ducked through the door and into the blackness of the Wekiva night.

The boy and the old man sat quietly in the chief's abode. One by one, the elders of the village left for their own houses. A smoldering smudge fire under a bed smoked the air, irritating the boy's eyes. He wiped away the tears with a piece of deer hide.

"Why would someone want to kill the Chief of the Tacatacura?" Coya said. "Surely he has no enemies this far from his home."

Marehootie was slow to answer. “A man without experience with a musket might aim too low, especially at night. The farther away, the higher he must point the weapon to hit his target. I believe the musket ball was intended for you.”

Through the thin walls of sapling poles, palmetto fronds and thatch, they could hear the sounds of the night creatures, the owls, frogs, and whippoorwills.

They could also hear clearly the sound of a whip slapping skin as the grieving chief of the village lashed himself.

Before daybreak, four warriors and trackers, led by Crying Bird, ventured down the Wekiva and across to the other side of the River of the Sun. A shower had fallen during the night, erasing any sign of the murderer or any clue to his identity.

Chapter 8

Presidio, Office of the Sergeant Major
San Augustín

The Governor's Summons commanded Father Pareja to appear at the Government House in the town of San Augustín, and there to give testimony under oath regarding the circumstances surrounding the deaths of four of the King's soldiers at Misión San Juan del Puerto. The friar's written response was polite but firm; the governor had no authority to command anything of Pareja who answered only to God, the Pope, and the Bishop of New Spain, in that order.

After two days of delicate negotiation with the sergeant major, both parties agreed to meet in the presidio office. It was hardly a neutral venue for such a meeting, but the governor had flatly rejected Pareja's suggestion that they meet at the hospital or convento, and Pareja refused to appear at Government House. With Father Marron's departure for Mexico, Pareja was left to his own devices in dealing with the government.

Sergeant Major Gonsalves had surrendered his seat behind the massive mahogany desk to Governor Canzo and stood at the balcony window looking out onto the busy dirt street one floor below. A scribe sat cross-legged on the floor, preparing to record whatever he heard on a tablet of parchment using a turkey quill pen. An Indian boy stood close to the governor, fanning him with a woven palmetto frond against worrisome flies and the stifling heat of the San Augustín summer day.

Father Pareja sat impassively in a chair facing the desk, his arms folded over his chest. Sunlight filtered through the window, without an accompanying breeze, focusing light and heat on the priest's face.

"I have asked you here to talk with me today about the death of one of the four soldiers fourteen days ago at San Juan. I have received Sergeant Major Gonsalves' report concerning the explosion and fire that killed and injured the others and destroyed the powder magazine and garrison. In addition, I have read the statements of the surviving soldiers, and am satisfied that the culpability for the disaster rests squarely on the shoulders of Sergeant Suarez. If he survives his injuries, he will be dealt with."

Pareja could hear the scratching of the quill on parchment breaking the silence that followed the governor's words. He said nothing, but unfolded his arms and began to nervously drum the fingers of one hand on the chair arm.

"I am preparing a detailed report for the Council of the Indies," Canzo said. "I will also report to our King, as is my duty when any of his subjects are lost within my jurisdiction. The next ship bound for Spain is scheduled to depart in three days, so you can see the urgency of clearing up these matters and completing my report."

Pareja nodded his head in response.

"Of course, you understand that any factual accounts, other than from my personal knowledge, must be supported by sworn statements."

Pareja spoke for the first time since he was greeted by the governor upon his arrival. "I understand fully what you are asking of me. This is a delicate matter." He extended his left arm, palm up. "On the one hand, you have your duties to fulfill, and reporting to the King is clearly one of them. On he other hand," he said, stretching out his right hand in a similar fashion, "it is my priestly obligation to serve God and those he has placed in my charge. The message I deliver to the Indians is one of God's enduring and undying love and forgiveness of sin, not one of earthly retribution or punishment. Perhaps that is why the charter granted by the King to the Franciscan Order grants us the privilege of immunity from compulsory legal process."

Governor Canzo stared unsmiling at the priest, then gestured to the scrivener that he stop writing.

"You can't do that," Father Pareja said, rising from his chair. "You can't command your scrivener to write only that which you wish him to record. It must be clear in your records that I have invoked my clerical privilege. Until the bishop commands me to speak, it is my duty to remain silent concerning the events that occurred at San Juan del Puerto."

Canzo slumped in his seat, met the gaze of Sergeant Major Gonsalves, and then turned his attention once again to Pareja, who remained standing.

"I'm disappointed, but I will, of course, honor your decision not to be sworn or to give testimony that you think might harm the Indians. I only hoped that you could shed some light on the death of the young soldier who was murdered the night of the fire. I have numerous statements that two Indians disappeared from the mission that night, one of whom is an old Acueran whom, I understand, you had befriended." The governor watched Pareja's face closely.

"Even more troubling, your own altar boy," Canzo said, sorting through several reports on his desk, "an Indian lad by the name of Juan de Coya, also disappeared from the mission that same night."

Pareja stood stoically, determined to let his face betray nothing as the governor peered deeply into his eyes once again.

"I have, of course, issued warrants for the arrest of both of them, authorizing whatever force necessary for their apprehension. Perhaps you could clear up this matter and absolve them of responsibility with just a word or two, so that I might rescind my orders."

Still, Pareja said nothing.

The governor stood and walked out onto the balcony, followed by Gonsalves. They spoke quietly for several moments.

When they returned, Governor Canzo once again addressed the priest. "The other issue concerns Sergeant Suarez and his culpability for starting the fire that caused all of the damage. My information indicates that he planned to burn the old Acueran at the stake. A nasty business!"

Pareja opened his mouth to speak, but sealed his lips and said nothing.

"I know you complained about him, as did several other priests. Perhaps it was my mistake to place such an uncultured man in charge of the garrison at San Juan."

Pareja straightened his robe and picked up his walking stick. "If there is nothing more to be accomplished here, I will wish you good day."

"I'm afraid that without a statement from you, there will be insufficient evidence upon which to convene an *audencia* to try the sergeant for his crimes, should he survive his injuries," Canzo said as he came around his desk. He walked with Pareja to the stairway that led down to the street.

In the doorway, Father Pareja turned and took the hand of Governor Canzo. "You have your duties and I have mine. May God bless us all."

When the priest reached the street he turned the corner behind the presidio to make his way to the friary. The armpits of his robe were soaked with sweat and felt cool with the breeze that blew in from the water. When he was safely out of sight of the second floor window, he suddenly leaped into the air and clicked the heels of his sandals together as he had seen the Indian boys do so often.

The priest walked slowly past the shops and vendors' stalls that lined Avenida Menéndez. He passed the grand, white-washed home of the governor and the market area that was practically deserted during the time of siesta. Tables displaying corn, vegetables and beans baked in the afternoon sun. On others were bolts of brightly colored cloth.

A girl and an older woman sat in the shade of a tree, waiting for buyers for a small assortment of platters, dishes and cups laid out on a blanket before them. Pareja greeted the women in the Timucua tongue, and stooped to examine the

Indian pottery designed and painted to mimic the Andalusian tableware he remembered from his youth.

"Beautiful work," he said, feeling the smooth glazed texture. The women looked at each other and smiled, but did not speak. They were shy, he thought, certainly less outgoing than the women he knew at the mission.

"Are both of you potters?"

"She is a woman of the sacred clay," the younger one said. "I am her niece."

Pareja turned to the older woman who diverted her gaze downward.

"Have you done this all your life?"

The woman remained silent.

The younger woman answered. "She cannot hear you. She had an illness as a child and can neither hear nor speak. I am her ears and voice. The Spirit has blessed her with the clay."

"Indeed, she has been blessed," the priest said, laying the delicate pottery on the blanket. He stood and prepared to go on his way. Then he paused and looked back. "Have you been saved?" he asked.

The younger woman smiled broadly. "I have been catechized and baptized. I attend the mission at the edge of town, Nombre de Dios."

"And her?" Pareja asked, nodding toward the older woman who had tired of the conversation she could not hear, and worked a bit of reddish clay in her fingers.

"She cannot hear the priest, nor speak the catechism. She does not need God. She has the clay."

As Pareja rounded the west end of the friary, he heard the angry sounds emanating from Our Mother of Solitude, ninety yards away. He lifted the hem of his robe and ran to the hospital. Father de Avila stood in the sunlight outside. Vile threats and imprecations emanated from the doorway and echoed across the square.

"Is that the man to whom you administered Extreme Unction just three days ago?" Pareja asked the young priest, knowing the answer before it was given. How many times had Pareja had to tolerate that same disgusting language at San Juan?

De Avila was red-faced and sweating profusely. “It is he. Apparently God has not yet prepared a place for him.”

“He is Satan’s, not God’s,” Father Pareja said quietly, and then caught himself. “Madre de Dios, that I should say such a thing.”

Father de Avila turned to him, the corners of his mouth betraying his mirth. “It is the heat, Francisco. It gets to us all.”

Both men made the sign of the cross.

“I cannot deal with the man any further,” the young priest said. “I paid an Indian woman to clean him and change his bandages. When she saw him with that one eye and half of his scalp burned away she refused, saying he looked like the Devil himself. I convinced her it was her Christian duty and she went back in.

“While I was attending to other work, thinking he would show a woman more respect than he does me, he attacked her and ripped her clothing. A wounded soldier helped her get away from him, and was battered for his troubles. Let me show you what he has done now.”

De Avila led Father Pareja around the corner of the hospital. The window shutters on the west side were broken out, their splintered remains laying in the yard. Nearby, an iron chamber pot lay on its side spilling excrement into a flower bed.

“We have no more shutters in the store house, and no carpenter available to make repairs,” de Avila said. “If we leave it open, the mosquitoes will have a feast.”

Father Pareja put his hand on the younger priest’s shoulder. He could feel him trembling.

“Go back to the friary and rest. Then you can attend to your other duties. I have dealt with the sergeant in the past, and will reason with him, if that is possible. I’m afraid we will get no help from the sergeant major or the governor. Suarez is our problem until he dies or recovers sufficiently to leave the hospital.”

Pareja took the chamber pot to the river and cleaned it. He returned it to the hospital and placed it between two occupied beds. Four soldiers were there, but only one was well enough to speak. Sergeant Suarez pretended to be asleep and did not respond when Pareja spoke to him.

Later, after Pareja had measured the window and collected the tools, iron nails and pieces of board to repair it, he could hear Suarez and the other soldier arguing inside.

Before nighttime the repair was done. Held in place by four bent nails, the window boards fit so perfectly that no mosquito could enter. In the morning, the nails could be twisted to the side and the boards removed, allowing sunlight and air into the room. Perhaps a carpenter could be found in San Augustín to build a proper shutter.

When Pareja finished with his work inside, the other soldier thanked him. Father Pareja sat beside the boy and prayed with him until it was time to go. Throughout, Suarez lay on his side, feigning sleep.

It was full dark by the time Pareja joined Father de Avila at the friary. The women of the village had provided the evening meal of fish soup and maize cakes, and de Avila kept the food covered to preserve its warmth. The two priests sipped the Indian cassina tea and shared the meal. They talked quietly into the night, so as not to disturb the three novice missionaries-in-training who slept in the adjoining room.

Coya Ayacouta Utina

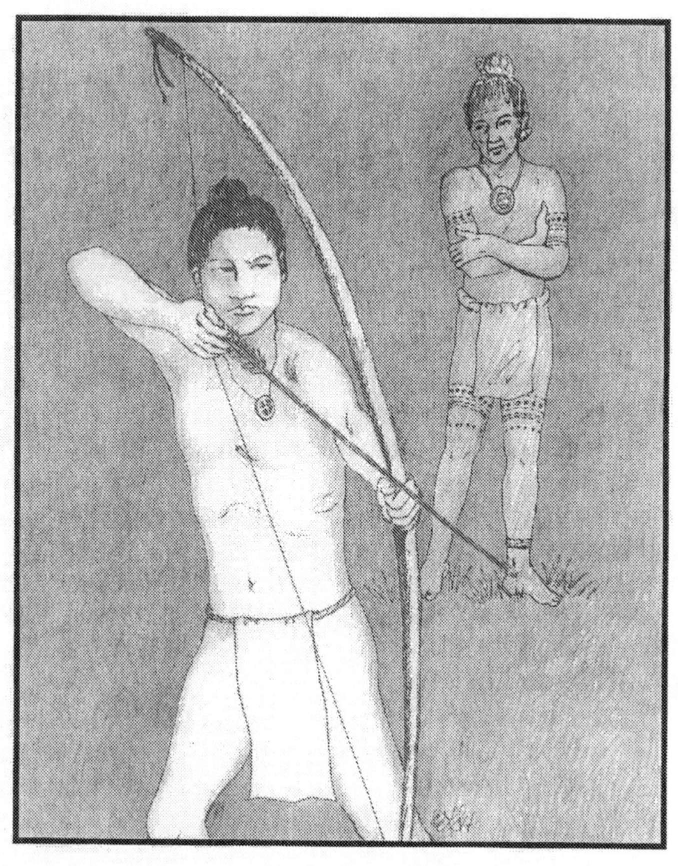

Chapter 9

Summer, 1605

Coya grew tall and lean, a sweet gum tree among live oaks. The mission softness that had worried Marehootie was gone. In its place were taut and lanky limbs, and broad shoulders. The roundness of a child's face was now sculpted with high cheek bones and the hawk nose typical of men of Utina White Deer Clan. Only the occasional crackling of his voice remained of the gangling boy of three summers past.

The old man reclined on a woven mat in the tiny structure that served as council house in the village of Wekiva, while Coya sat cross-legged before the fire, heating chert to knap into arrow and spear points.

"There is something I need to say to you." Marehootie spoke after two young men, who had been stringing a long bow, finished their work and left them alone. Coya wiped the sweat from his forehead with the back of his hand and stood up. He stepped to Marehootie's resting place, knelt, and handed him the points he had fashioned.

The old man inspected the arrow heads, holding each one up to admire the smooth sharpness by the light of the fire. "You got all these from that one piece of rock?"

Coya returned to his place by the hearth. He retrieved a piece of chert from the edge of the fire, held it in the palm of his leather glove and began to apply pressure on it with a sharp antler tool he held in his other hand.

"Crying Bird says you lack heart," Marehootie said.

Coya did not look up, but continued to concentrate on his work. Soon a piece of rock flaked off, and then another. "Why would my grandfather say that?"

Marehootie now lay on his back, looking up to the hole in the thatched roof where the thin white smoke of burning maple escaped into the night. In Wekiva, only maple wood was burned. Crying Bird said it left less of a sign in the sky than other woods like pine that put out a darker, more pungent smoke.

"My brother has been hard on you. I see how he drives you, how he pushes you, and I try not to interfere. You are already the best swimmer in the village and perhaps the best at war games as well. When you put a little meat on your bones, I'm sure you will be as strong as anyone at Wekiva."

"How is it, then, that I disappoint him? From the things he says to me, he is never satisfied with anything I do. Where do I go to find this heart?"

Marehootie sat up and crossed his legs before him. "You know your way around the woods and the swamps as well as anyone, but you won't find it there. If you are someday to become a chief, a leader, it will be for one reason: that your will, your heart, will accept nothing less."

Coya applied pressure to the chert and it broke in his hand. He threw the smaller piece into the fire.

"Where have I failed him, then? Where do I lack the heart for anything he would have me do? Is it my canoe skills that are lacking? Or my ability to survive on what I find to eat in the swamp? Or my skill with the bow or the atlatl?"

"It is your running," Marehootie answered.

Coya scoffed and threw the other piece of rock into the fire. "I can outrun anyone in this village, including Crying Bird. He used to run away from me and hide, because he was so much bigger. Then he would jump out from ambush and slap me with a palmetto whip. That doesn't happen any more. I'm faster than he is."

"Then I suggest you prove it to him. Crying Bird says you are content just to lope along beside him, an old man four times your age. Instead, he says you need to stretch your legs and leave him behind."

"But he's old. I wouldn't have the heart to just–" Coya bowed his head.

Marehootie smiled. "That's exactly what Crying Bird says, that you don't have the heart. When you find it, your lessons will be over, and you will be a man worthy of becoming a chief."

The next day Coya left Crying Bird far behind him on their run. When Crying Bird finally arrived in the village, his face was flushed with the heat, but he was smiling and in a good mood.

"I tried my best. I even took a shortcut," he said to Marehootie, "but I couldn't keep up with that young buck. That's it. I'll never have to run with him again. Coya needs younger legs to test him."

From then on, Coya ran with three other young men, one Potanan and two Mayaca, but even they sometimes became discouraged trying to keep up. Coya never enjoyed their company on the trail as he did that of Crying Bird.

Marehootie was still crippled, but able to walk about the camp using a crutch. Sometimes he would sit under a tree where the trail from the west entered the village, waiting for a glimpse of Coya and his running companions returning home. Every time, Coya would be well ahead of the others, loping along with a graceful stride.

"You are fast, but when I was your age, I was faster," he sometimes taunted the boy.

Sometimes for a day, but more often for several days at a time, Acoto, the *inija* of the village of Coya, visited the boy to teach him what he needed to know about the Utinans and the beliefs of White Deer Clan. At first, because he was Utinan,

Acoto would be met up river and blindfolded and delivered to Wekiva by two men in a canoe. Soon, however, Crying Bird came to trust him not to give away their location, and Acoto was allowed to come and go on his own under the watchful eyes of the guards who were there to meet him and help him maneuver his canoe from the River of the Sun into the Wekiva River.

The history, beliefs and genealogy of the Utinans were explained to Coya. Even the incantations and prayers of the *jarva*, including the ceremony called *Tacachale,* were taught and rehearsed until the boy could recite them as perfectly as any shaman.

Each meeting between the boy and the *inija* took place in a hut beyond the houses of the Potanans, at the very edge of the Wekiva settlement. Out of respect for the secrecy of such matters, Crying Bird ordered that no one try to overhear what was said.

Coya sometimes pondered the differences in customs and beliefs of the Utinans, and of the Acuerans, as they had been taught to him by Marehootie while the old man had been held prisoner at Misión San Juan del Puerto. He reckoned those differences to be small ones, and more of form than substance.

It was sometimes more difficult to reconcile what he had been taught as a Christian with the beliefs of the Indians. According to the friar, Jesus had said, "No one comes to the Father, but by me." Acoto said that with death, everyone passed to the world of Spirit.

Coya remembered how Father Pareja railed against graven images, demanding they be burned in the village square and replaced by the cross as the only symbol of spiritual belief. Everywhere the boy looked at Wekiva, he saw carvings of clan symbols and spirit beings that would anger Father Pareja if he saw them.

The boy could not resolve these contradictions, and sometimes he lay awake late at night, thinking. Perhaps the answers to his questions would come to him when he became older. Meanwhile, each night, and as he arose each morning, Coya knelt beside his bed and recited the prayers the priest had taught.

Only once was he asked what he meant by reciting his prayers. It was soon after he came to Wekiva and it was Crying Bird, with whom he was living, who asked what he was doing. That same night, Crying Bird and Marehootie argued in Marehootie's house next door. Coya awoke, and heard much of what they said.

"The boy walks in two worlds. He is of the people," Marehootie said. "He cannot escape what he is. What he missed as a young child is now being taught to him and he will –"

"But in his heart he is a Spaniard," Crying Bird said.

"You did not let me finish what I wanted to say," Marehootie said.

Coya lay in his bed, listening. When Marehootie again spoke, his words were soft. Night sounds of frogs and cicadas made it hard for the boy to hear more than a word or two, here and there. The older man seemed to say that Coya's knowledge of the Spanish and of their religion were strengths and not weaknesses. Before he could finish what he was saying, Crying Bird cursed loudly. Coya heard the door flap being brushed aside, and then Crying Bird's heavy footsteps as he walked away into the night.

Coya was now wide awake. These two men he loved and who loved each other dearly were being torn apart by his failure to live up to their expectations of him. Or was it that their expectations were different from each other?

Coya felt the tears of a child fill his eyes, and he wiped them away angrily. Tomorrow would be different. Tomorrow he would show the strength Crying Bird required of him.

Acoto kept Crying Bird and Marehootie informed of the boy's progress. After three years of instruction, Coya was knowledgeable in the traditions and ways of the White Deer Clan and could remember the names of the ancestors as far back as Acoto could teach them.

"He tells the legends and stories and recites our history perfectly," Acoto said one day as the three sat together bathing their feet in the chilly water of the spring. Marehootie had brought gaucha cakes of hickory meal and berries, and took a cake for himself before passing the basket to Acoto.

"I don't believe the Utinan Council will find his knowledge or intelligence lacking," the *inija* said.

Crying Bird waved off the basket when it was offered by Acoto. "I don't eat sweet things."

"The boy has an excellent memory," Marehootie said. "Once he understands something, he will never forget it."

Acoto nodded. "That may be part of the problem."

Crying Bird's eyes narrowed as he watched Acoto and waited for him to explain. The Utinan *Inija* used his one arm to pull himself into a more comfortable sitting position against the shoreline cypress.

"I have done what I can. He understands well enough, but sometimes he questions what I tell him, and says to me things he has been taught by the priest. He doesn't reject what I tell him, exactly. Whether he holds our beliefs in his heart is what I do not know."

Marehootie reached into a basket, selected a palm berry, took it into his mouth and chewed pleasurably on the right side where he still had most of his teeth. A trickle of juice hung on his lip.

"We, all of us, know that a man has three souls," Acoto said, "but I'm not sure Coya understands or believes me. When I say the souls reside in a man's eye, in his reflection and in his shadow, he disputes me, saying that the priests say it differently."

"Strange that he cannot comprehend something so simple," Crying Bird said, shaking his head. "Every chief and every *jarva* I have ever spoken to, from whatever tribe, knows of the three souls. It is so well known it should be beyond question."

"Then he asked if I were confusing the souls with three Gods of the Catholics. He called them The Father, The Son and –" Acoto closed his eyes.

"The Holy Ghost?" Marehootie said.

The others looked at Marehootie. "That is it," said Acoto. "That is what he said. 'The Holy Ghost.'"

"What a strange thing for the boy to say," Crying Bird said. "Was he referring to the spirits of the ancestors when he talks about these ghosts?"

Marehootie cleared his throat. "He speaks of one ghost, part of what the priest calls the 'Holy Trinity.'"

Crying Bird rose to his feet, picked up a stick and threw it half way across the pond. "What gibberish! Makes as much sense as a chattering blue jay. The boy will one day face the principal men of Utina, and he will be tested on his knowledge. If he is asked about the three souls and can't answer their questions properly, they will call him stupid. If he chirps on about some three-headed spirit, the Uncle, the Son –"

"The Father, the Son and the Holy Ghost," Marehootie said.

"If he says those things, they will never trust him to be *Holata Aco*. They will laugh in his face and chase us all out of the village."

"Let me take care of this," Marehootie said. "I know some things about the priest's teachings, and perhaps the boy can learn to express himself in words the Utinan Council will understand."

"I hope you are right," Crying Bird said. "We are gambling a lot on the boy. I hope we can make him into an acceptable chief for the people of Utina."

Later, after it was dark, a torch of pine sap lit the faces of the three men and Coya as they sat together in the small Wekiva council house. On Crying Bird's orders, a guard was posted nearby so that they would not be overheard.

"We have not spoken recently about what is happening among the Utina," Acoto said. "Olate Ouai Utina has been dead now for more than a year. He was honored in death, and I suppose that was a good thing for the Utinans, though many of us blame him for our troubles.

"Because we are without a strong leader, our enemies have begun to raid villages that are poorly defended. Four villages along the River of the Sun have been abandoned. The people have moved far away to the west and settled in places the Potanans used to live. We are not only weakened by the lack of a strong chief, we are now divided.

"When Utina tried to convince us that his son, Osprey, should succeed him, the people in the west, particularly those who live near the village of Ayacuta, refused to recognize him because they believe in the tradition that only a nephew of White Deer Clan should rule.

"Antonico was a distant cousin in White Deer Clan and was selected by the supreme Utinan council as an interim chief, to serve during Utina's illness and until his death. Everyone agrees that Antonico is too weak to be chief over more than a village or two. Certainly, he could not be *Holata Aco* of all the Utinans."

Coya's head wobbled as he fought off sleep. Marehootie handed him a cup of hot cassina to help him stay awake.

"Antonico spends most of his time in the Spanish town. He convinced the governor to send a message to Osprey warning him to stop shooting people, or they would take the gun from him. Nothing ever came of it. Osprey still struts about, and Antonico still hides from him in fear."

"Tell me about this village you call Ayacouta," Crying Bird said.

Acoto took a sharp stick from his bundle and, with his hand, he smoothed the dirt floor before them. With the stick he traced the course of the River of the Sun, marked the location of the big lake, and the main villages of Utina. Then he made precise marks to the west and north, in the land once dominated by the Potanans when they were strong.

"It would take three days of fast walking to reach Ayacouta. As you can see, it is closer to the main village of Potano than it is to the River of the Sun. There are seven villages of Utinans there. Several of them are on small rivers. The land is fertile, and some people grow maize and beans. Fishing and hunting are also good, I am told. Best of all, there are no Spanish."

"What news is there of Osprey?" Crying Bird asked.

"He still travels about, claiming to be the legitimate heir of Chief Utina, and waving his musket around to frighten people. Some people say it was Osprey who killed Tacatacura, but he will not speak of it, perhaps because he knows the governor might move against him."

"And perhaps because it was a cowardly act, one that shames him," Crying Bird said.

Acoto looked up sharply. "Do not underestimate Osprey. He is like his father. He has no shame. What he says he will do, he does. He has said that some day he will also kill our young friend here." Acoto placed his hand on Coya's sleepy head. "He knows that only Coya stands in the way of his becoming *Holata Aco* of Utina."

Marehootie spoke for the first time. "And if he was the one who murdered Tacatacura, he knows the way to Wekiva."

The men were quiet, looking into the fire.

Acoto rose to his feet. "I will not be returning to Wekiva. I have done what I can to educate the boy in the Utinan way."

"You are always welcome here, friend," Crying Bird said. He stood and placed his hand flat against Acoto's chest.

The Utinan stepped outside to relieve himself. When he returned, he remained standing. "My ancestors were with me when I came up river this time," he said. "The wind whispered in my ear that I was followed. I moved carefully and backtracked many times, but never saw anyone. There was a fish hawk I saw once or twice. Perhaps it was Osprey. He knows that I am helping the boy. Someone in my own village may have told him, perhaps one of our young men who admire him."

Three days later, the second day after Acoto left Wekiva for the last time, Nihoto rushed into the village, carrying a bundle wrapped in a cloth made of palmetto fiber. Only Marehootie could understand what it was the deaf man tried to say.

"Nihoto says when he went to the mouth of the river to stand guard today, there was a canoe tied to a willow tree. He found this inside."

Marehootie unrolled the cloth on the ground. Inside was an ornately tattooed severed left arm bearing the marks of an *inija.* The rest of Acoto was never found.

That same day, Crying Bird ordered that the village be destroyed. All signs of its existence were burned, uprooted and carried away or covered over. The entire population of Acuerans, Potanans, Mayaca, Ais, Ocale and the others were loaded into canoes for the trip upstream on the Wekiva to a remote area where a new village would be built. Ridge poles from the council house and larger structures were loaded upon a barge pulled by the strongest canoers. It was impossible to reach the new Wekiva village by land from the old. The deep snake and alligator-infested swamp made walking impossible.

Chapter 10

Second Wekiva

The site chosen for the new village was a full day's travel to the southwest. Here and there along the way, the stream shallowed and was more swamp than river, meandering like a dying snake, with little current or direction. In some places an active spring would appear, pumping new vitality and life-sustaining clear water, making it a river once again.

The sun was one hand above the horizon when those in the lead canoe came upon a place where the river straightened and widened for a distance. Here the current was slow, but the water deep enough to be navigable even in the dry season.

The shore on the east side stood well above the high water mark on the cypress trees lining the bank. The land was open and hilly, and rose gradually higher to a half way point from which it again sloped gently down hill to a swampy glade.

The knoll was without trees or vegetation other than thin grasses and clumps of palmetto, and from the river it appeared chalky white, the same color as the clay preferred by potters.

The people left their dugout canoes to stretch their cramped legs and to walk around inspecting their new home. Some time later, as the sun set, Crying Bird blew a call on a whelk shell summoning those who had gone the greatest distance. When they were gathered together and quiet, he spoke to his people.

"The spirit has led us to this place," he said. "And perhaps it has been provided for us, although we cannot know that this soon."

The Chief of Wekiva gestured that the others move about him in a circle, and he knelt down and, with a spade, he dug a shallow hole through the thin, light colored soil that supported the grasses and into what was below. The dirt was loose and he dug his hand into it, reaching down to where only his elbow showed at the surface. He removed his arm and opened his hand that now held shells and sand and bits of broken pottery.

"These are the leavings of other peoples who were here long ago, perhaps beyond memory or legend. Maybe they built the hill upon which we stand. I could say that these were Acuerans, my own ancestors, but there are no legends I have ever heard that describe this place.

"You Potanans have never lived anywhere near here. The same for the Ocale, the Ais, and the rest of you," he said. Crying Bird walked around the circle, showing what his hand held and looking into the faces of the people. When he stood before Chaso, the elder of the Mayaca clan, he raised his hand so Chaso could have a good look.

"You Mayaca sometimes claim other people's land based upon tribal legend," he said. "If your people have lived here before, if this place has been spoken of in your counsels, say it now, Chaso."

The elder Mayaca ran the tip of his finger through the debris in Crying Bird's hand, and he picked out a sherd of broken pottery, no larger than a finger nail. He put it between his teeth and bit down until it broke into many pieces.

"This is inferior workmanship," Chaso said. "Not Mayaca. These are not my people."

"Then it is settled. This place belongs to all of us, or to none of us," Crying Bird said. "I can feel the spirits of the ancestors here, but whose grandfathers they are, I do not know. If we are not welcomed, we will know it soon enough. If the earth does not swallow us, if no one of us dies within the first days and if no child is bitten by a snake, then we will know we are wanted here, or at least that our presence is tolerated.

"Tonight we sleep on the ground or in the canoes. When the sun rises, each group may observe its own rites for sanctifying and purifying the land, and for seeking the blessings of the old people that we might build our village over their bones."

Marehootie stepped to the center, supporting himself on a crutch. "And if we are welcomed," he said, "if none of us is struck down, we will build our houses here. The woods are full of palmetto and young hickory trees. It should take no more than five days for the slowest of us. When we are done we will observe *Tacachale*." A murmur went through the people.

"Coya has volunteered to lead the ceremony," he said.

During the night the two barges arrived, and before the sun was high, the people busied themselves preparing the building sites and beginning construction of their houses. Crying Bird chose the highest point on the hill, and with stakes he marked where the walls would stand. It would be larger than an ordinary house, but small by standards of a council house. It afforded a good view in all directions, and if there were a breeze at all it would be found there. Mosquitoes would be less of a problem at night.

Marehootie and Coya would build their house just to the south, still on the high hilltop, but a little below Crying Bird's house.

A dispute arose almost immediately. The Potanan elder claimed the plot just to the north of Crying Bird, saying that because his people were more numerous than anyone other than the Acuerans, he should be respected and put in a place of honor.

Chaso became angry. He had already begun staking the claim while the Potanans were looking elsewhere. "I have claimed this place for the Mayaca," he said, standing up to the Potanan who was a foot taller.

Before they could come to blows, Crying Bird stepped between them. "I have already set aside this spot for my *inija*, Yano," he said. "As you can see, he is not having a good day."

Yano, the toothless chief without vassals, stood at a distance on a high point, looking and listening for the return of his people, as he often did when he was confused. On Crying Bird's orders, two Potanans and two Mayaca built Yano's house while he wandered about.

No calamitous event occurred, and no one died. No child was snake bit, and no one was swallowed up. As was his duty as chief, Crying Bird spoke to the spirits and then told the others on the fifth day that they were welcomed to the place. They would call it Second Wekiva. *Tacachale* lasted a day and a half, beginning at sundown one day and ending at the second sunrise thereafter. Coya's training had not prepared him for the complexity of it, but Marehootie was there to help in the preparations. There were fewer dancers and chanters than required for *Tacachale*, and some of the traditional story had to be omitted.

The Mayaca, who had no tradition of *Tacachale*, did not participate. They watched from a small knoll, away from the fire, and returned to their houses to sleep when they tired of the dancing, chanting and storytelling of the Timucua.

Even the Mayaca were there at the final event of *Tacachale*, when Coya danced the spirit fire dance, whirling around and around the camp fire while Marehootie beat on a drum fashioned from a hollow oak log. Just before he collapsed in exhaustion, Coya threw the taca potion into the fire, igniting an explosion of blue light so bright that everyone who had not covered his eyes was stunned by it and saw spots floating before them.

As their vision returned, the sun peeked over the pine forest to the east and poured down its blessing on Second Wekiva and its people.

The first village council of Second Wekiva met two days after *Tacachale* in the house of Crying Bird.

Fresh cassina was prepared by the women and passed around among the leaders after they had eaten a banquet of venison stew, frog legs, maize cakes, and sweet turtle. The house was so small it could scarcely contain the twenty leaders and principal men.

When he was ready, Crying Bird stood to speak. "We have found a new home, and have been welcomed to it by the spirits of those who have been here before. Each of us," he said, looking around the house, "each of us has blessed this place and his house in his own way and we will stay here as a village for however long it pleases the spirits.

"We have been together, some of us, for almost forty years. Some came later, but we have all seen children born on this river we call Wekiva, seen them play in the forests and swamps and grow into proud people. Some have died, and we have buried their bones after our own customs. Too many have died, and we grieve for the loss of each one. Many of you have lived here all your lives and may never leave the river. It is our refuge, a sanctuary from the Spanish soldiers and, in times past, from murderous Utinans who chose to be our enemies.

"By staying hidden we have been blessed in two ways. Some of us have been able to make war against our enemies, and then hide where we cannot be found. But what many of you have not seen are the conditions of the villages and people we left behind.

"While we were here, safe, the Acueran nation, the Mayaca, the Potanans, the Ocale and the rest have suffered much more than we who make the river our home. Many villages have been destroyed by the Utinans and the Spanish soldiers. Healthy people have fallen ill and died, and the survivors are scattered to the winds. Some places are so diminished, that even the traders do not bother to visit them any more.

"So we have survived. We are not warred upon because we hide from our enemies. Perhaps because we do not travel about, we have escaped plagues that have killed scores of people who lived in the villages.

"There is one other way we are different from the others on the outside. We are not a tribe, but a group of different peoples living together in peace. Some of us have beliefs that are similar to others. For instance Ocale and Acuera share their understanding of *Tacachale*, while Potanans seem to have some disagreement."

An elder of Potano, raised his hand as if to speak, but Crying Bird motioned that he remain silent.

"Do not deny it. I heard the way you ridiculed Coya for the way *Tacachale* was done, but that is not the point I wish to make. You have your own beliefs that are ancient and revered by your people. They should be guarded against error and taught correctly to your children and their children.

"As Chief of Wekiva, it was my responsibility to lead you all in the spiritual realm, and to intercede for you with the spirits and ancestors. All chiefs have the same duties: to protect the people, to discipline them, to receive their tribute and to ensure they do not fall into spiritual error.

"But I am Acueran. I am neither Mayaca nor Potano. I no longer wish to be your chief, because I do not share the beliefs and traditions of anyone other than Acuerans."

A loud murmer spread through the house as men turned to each other in dismay. Three men asked for the right to speak, but were silenced by one gesture from Crying Bird.

"You want to know who is to be chief? My answer is that each group may select one of your number to carry that title, if you feel it is important. He should be a holy man who can lead your religious observances. Perhaps a *jarva* or a shaman. However –"

Again, angry voices were raised around the fire.

"However, there will be no Chief of Second Wekiva. I will continue to be your leader, and will protect you, receive your tribute, rule over this village and settle your arguments. My word will continue to be obeyed."

"If not chief, what shall we call you?" the elder Mayaca asked.

Marehootie raised his voice. "My brother will be called Governor of Second Wekiva," he said.

It was three days later, in the morning, that a guard patrolling the woods west of the village cupped his hands to his mouth and sounded the call of the red-headed woodpecker. Marehootie was sunning himself outside his house when he heard it, and he went to Crying Bird with the news.

"We have captured an intruder. He is being brought into camp now," he said.

Marehootie followed Crying Bird through the gathering crowd, down the hill, as fast as his crutch would allow.

The guard emerged from the woods, pushing a stranger ahead of him with the point of his spear. By the time Crying Bird arrived, the man was already tied to a tree.

"Who are you, and why do you trespass where you have not been invited?" Crying Bird demanded.

The man was so frightened he could hardly speak, and his voice shook. Marehootie recognized the dialect as that of a Yustagan, a tongue he had not heard in many years.

"What is it he said?" Crying Bird asked.

"He says he is a trader on his way from Ocale to Acuera."

The man spoke again. This time he had more to say, and his eyes darted about, begging for understanding or perhaps for mercy.

"Now he says he comes this way often, along a trail beyond the woods. He does not wish to intrude," Marehootie said.

"Tell him we do not welcome strangers here," Crying Bird said.

By now the man's manner of speech was easier to understand, and Marehootie could tell that he understood what Crying Bird had said, also. Marehootie spoke softly with the man, calming his fears.

"He smelled our fires and he walked a short distance into the woods to investigate. Then he saw the top of your house through the trees and he assumed that since we built our houses on such a high hill where they could be seen, we might welcome a trader.

"I meant no harm," the man said. "Your secret place here is safe with me."

Marehootie approached Crying Bird, and spoke into his ear so the man could not hear what was said. "He has salt and maize seed and metal tools for planting," Marehootie said. "He will trade for deerskin, good quality pottery and yaupon leaves. I think we can drive a very good bargain with this trader. He is convinced we intend to kill him."

Chapter 11

Coya wearied of the questioning. On the second day he heard the same questions he had heard the day before. On the third day it was the same.

"When can I eat?"

"When you can answer perfectly," Marehootie said. The two of them sat in Marehootie's house, facing each other over a smoldering fire that both heated and smoked the air. The door flap was closed against the distractions of a beautiful summer day.

"Tell me once more your understanding of the three souls," the old man asked for what seemed like the hundredth time.

Coya breathed deeply, and then exhaled. "There is the soul that can be seen in a man's eye, the inner light, the one that is extinguished with his death and buried with his bones."

Marehootie said nothing.

"A man's second soul may be observed as a shadow, that tells the truth of him even when he lies. If I strike a man with a club in secret, but someone sees the movement of my shadow mimicking my action, I will be known as a murderer. Worse, my shadow has convicted me as a liar."

"Very good," Marehootie grunted. "Now, the rest of it."

This was the hard part. The old man wanted to hear Coya admit that a man's reflection, whether in a pool of water or in a shiny looking glass, the way he is seen by others, was the soul of the memories that remain behind when he dies. If the boy left it at that and did not add that the priest says only God can look into a man's soul, the old man would be satisfied.

"Do you want to hear what I truly believe?"

"I want to hear the answer that will be expected by the one who will ask it. I will not be with you to explain what you mean to say."

The boy sat quietly. "I understand what they want to hear. They will hear it from me."

Marehootie studied the boy's face closely. "It is time for us to get some fresh air and something to eat," he said.

Crying Bird, Governor of the village of Second Wekiva, sent word that he would meet with his brother and with Coya at his house before sun-up, while the others were sleeping.

Coya did not sleep soundly. For two days his body had been poked with needles of cane by a tattoo man from Ocale who said he had done many Utinan White Deer body designs and knew how they should look. The boy's arms, legs and shoulders stung and burned, seeping tiny blood droplets, making it difficult to find a comfortable position on his bed.

Marehootie provided the red, black and blue dyes he had collected over many years as village herbalist, the *isucu*. He supervised the work as the skin artist meticulously and slowly created swirls and bands of color and zigzag patterns. Before each new design, the man would draw it in the hard sand outside his hut and explain its significance.

He made sure at each step that Marehootie understood and approved what was to be done. "If I make a mistake, you will want to skin me. To correct an error, I will need to skin the boy," the artist said.

The afternoon of the second day, Marehootie tired of watching and went to his house to sleep. While he was gone, Coya had asked the tattoo man to design the sign of a cross on the inside of his right arm, and to blend it in with the other designs so it might not easily be noticed.

The old Acueran, disturbed by Coya's tossing about that night, gave him a medicine made from ground willow tree bark. Some time later, the pain had eased, but sleep would still not come as Coya worried about the summons from Crying Bird.

"Can you tell me why he wants to see us before daylight?" he asked in the darkness. If Marehootie was awake, he chose not to answer.

Coya finally drifted into sleep, but was shaken awake what seemed like moments later.

"Time to go," Marehootie said.

"Chief Honoroso has sent me news of the Supreme Utinan Council. They will meet on the first full moon after the autumn equinox, at the Village of Ayacouta," Crying Bird said, keeping his voice low so as not to awaken Yano, who slept next door.

Coya turned to Marehootie, who sat looking at his outstretched hands, his forehead furrowed, counting on his fingers.

"Don't bother to figure on it," Crying Bird said. "I have done it many times. We have only two moons. Six tens and five more days, to be exact."

Marehootie continued to work his fingers, his lips moving silently.

Crying Bird turned to Coya. "Before Acoto was murdered, he told me you were well-instructed in the Utinan ways and in White Deer knowledge and ceremonies. Marehootie has done what he can to clear your mind of some of the mistakes taught you by the priest."

Coya opened his mouth to speak, but thought better of it and remained silent.

"And I have done what I can to teach you the skills you will need to become a leader of men. But it will take more than knowledge of customs and tribal secrets and herbal magic and making war, and all that, if you are to fulfill your destiny.

"We have taught all we can teach you, Acoto, Marehootie and I. The rest is up to you. What will matter, when the time comes, is what you discover within yourself, and not what we have put there .What you must learn now, you can discover only by yourself when you are far from home with only the spirits to guide your steps."

Marehootie stopped figuring and looked up.

"You will leave here as soon as it is light," said Crying Bird. "You will live alone in the forests and swamps and practice what you have learned. You will take only a knife and this piece of twine." He reached over and handed Coya a coiled palmetto fiber.

"Each morning you will tie a knot. Do not lose it, and do not forget. You may go as far and as fast as you wish, wherever the spirit takes you, but when you count three tens of knots, you are half way through your journey, and you must turn around and make your way back home. You will not stay in a village overnight or depend on the charity of others. Avoid being seen. We did not bring you this far to see you killed by Osprey or his people.

"Perhaps when you return to Second Wekiva in two moons you will know yourself and be better prepared for what you will face." Crying Bird stood and embraced the boy, then walked out of his house into the early gray twilight.

Marehootie tried to speak, but choked on his words. He made no attempt to hide his tears.

The sun, peeking over the tall pines warmed the back of Coya's neck as he waded across the Wekiva River and walked westward, through lands he had never before explored. He wore only his loin cloth and carried only a knife with a blade of obsidian, a ball of twine tucked in his waste band and his medicine pouch that Marehootie had filled with poultices and cures for every imaginable ailment. From the time he crossed the river, he did not look back. Neither did Marehootie nor Crying Bird look which way he went. They were napping in their houses.

Before he left the swamp for higher ground, Coya cut branches from a red maple and tied them in a bundle. The best bows were made of seasoned oak or hickory, but it would take more time than he wished to spend with the carving, seasoning and molding of a powerful and sturdy war bow suitable for bringing down a bear, wolf or panther. For small animals and birds, the green wood of the maple would be good enough. When it broke, it would be easily and quickly replaced.

Before sunset, Coya killed a rabbit that carelessly hopped into a snare the boy had laid along a game trail and covered over with leaves. Starting a fire was more difficult here in the woods than it had been in the village under Marehootie's supervision, where the proper tools were available. He used the lightning shattered trunk of a cedar tree as his fire board.

As darkness approached, the palmetto fiber kindling smoked and flickered to life, and he blew on it and fed it moss and lichens until it was a healthy flame. He roasted the rabbit and nibbled on nuts and berries he had collected along the way.

As he prepared to sleep, thunder rumbled in the west and lightning lit the clouds. Coya arose from his bed of moss, found the rabbit skin, and began to work it with his knife, scraping away the clinging meat and tissue. He scoured the inside of the skin with sand, cleaning it. He separated the sinew, and by the light of the campfire, with a sliver of cane, used it to sew the skin into a pouch. When he was done, he had a soft, round pouch the size of the palm of his hand. He scraped lichens and fungus from a fallen oak log and placed them in the pouch, and then embedded live coals in the center.

The boy hastily cut palm fronds and built a lean-to. Large drops of rain began to fall and were soon driven by the wind. When morning came, the rain stopped, and the campfire was dead. All that remained of it was the rabbit-skin fire pouch, where fungus and lichens still smoldered.

Coya separated some of the rabbit bones that might be useful, and buried the rest. He tied the fire pouch to his belt and put his knife in his scabbard. Before he moved further westward, Coya covered the remains of the fire and tied a tight knot in the end of his twine.

In the days that followed, Coya continued to the west to where the land began to rise and pine trees replaced scrub oak and hickory. Here he felt exposed and in the open, with fewer places to hide than he had enjoyed in the swampy river basin, so he turned his feet to the north and was soon near a river and its creeks.

Sweet turtle meat provided a sumptuous meal. What he could not eat, he smoked and carried with him, wrapped in moss and tucked into the turtle shell which he tied to his waist. He offered prayers for the turtle and thanked God for the bounty he enjoyed.

Coya strung his first maple bow with woven palmetto fiber, and he cut river cane for arrows. Mockingbird feathers fletched the arrows, and he carved small animal bones for the points.

Just after sun-up he would hunt among the oak trees, employing the secrets of squirrel hunting that Crying Bird had taught him. He would stand quietly among the trees, and then throw a stick or rock a distance ahead of him. Many times a squirrel would circle a tree trunk, frightened by the sound. Then it was simple target practice, and soon Coya would have two or three squirrels to roast on the fire and carry with him. The squirrel intestine, when dried and twisted tight, made much better bow strings than those made of palmetto fiber.

He gathered shiny apple snail shells, discarded by the crying birds of the swamp, and strung them into a necklace. He moved at a leisurely pace, stopping to pick hickory nuts, acorns, and berries. Each evening, after he had prepared his meal, and some days when he chose not to travel at all, he busied himself by braiding palmetto trunk fiber into a long rope. He made another using the fiber found among the leaves of the same bush, and it became a cord, as long and as strong as the rope, but much thinner.

While tracking small animals one day, he saw tiny droplets of blood along a game trail. He followed it and found a bobcat feasting on a raccoon under a palmetto.

The cat's skin made an excellent satchel, once he cured it. The raccoon was so badly ripped by the bobcat's teeth and claws that its skin was of no use to him. He offered up his prayers for the sacrifice of both animals. Marehootie had warned him of the stomach agonies that come from eating the smaller cat or its cousin, the panther, so after he removed the skin, ears, fangs and claws, he left the rest for the vultures. But the raccoon was freshly killed, and tasty, and one of its bones made a handy toothpick.

Chapter 12

On the morning that he tied the twenty-third knot on the twine, Coya came upon a well-marked trail and wondered who might be using it and where it might lead him. By his reckoning, he was north, beyond the mouth of the Wekiva and west of Mayaca. Crying Bird had drawn a map in the dirt on the morning of Coya's departure from Second Wekiva, showing where he might encounter different peoples, but Coya was unsure of who lived here.

Coya found a shadowy spot under trees that lined a small creek, near where the trail forked in two directions. He rested and waited. Late in the day he was rewarded for his patience. A party of hunters returning to their village and talking loudly passed by and took the fork to the right. They spoke the Utinan dialect. Still later, a woman with three small children came close, picking berries that grew in profusion along the creek bank. Coya stayed still until they had filled their baskets and were gone.

He emerged from his hiding place and took the other fork, away from the village. Coya looked for cover for the night, where he would not be detected. Here, creeks in briar-covered ravines and hills covered with small knotty trees marked the land. His pace slowed as the going became more difficult and perilous, and he soon learned to grasp onto bushes as he went up and down the steep hills.

Coya tired and looked for a place to make his camp. He stood on the crest of a small hill and looked around. Through the leaves of trees he saw sunlight sparkling on water below the hill and to his right, and he moved in that direction.

As he descended the last chalky hill, his foot slipped and he grasped at a shrub whose shallow roots let go, sending him head first downward. He was falling. Briars ripped at his flesh and his head struck a small tree, knocking him senseless.

When he opened his eyes, he saw the bear. Its mouth was open, and one paw was raised to strike a blow. Coya reached for his knife but it was not in the scabbard. He had lost it in the fall. He closed his eyes and prayed for deliverance. Perhaps if the bear thought he was dead, it would leave him alone.

Presently, Coya opened one eye and studied his adversary. The bear was not a bear, but only a cub. As he blinked away the dizziness from the blow to the head, Coya saw that the cub was not a cub, but a statue in yellowed limestone, knee-high to a man, blotched brown and green with liken and moss, its arm stretching heavenward in greeting.

Coya began to laugh, but stopped when pain welled up in his ribs. "Who gave you the job of guarding this spring, Baby Bear?" he asked out loud.

The boy righted himself and found a suitable place to spend the night. He slept well, despite his injuries. Marehootie's pain potions brought interesting dreams, and Coya wondered if they would work just as well if he were not hurt.

When he awoke, it was morning. His left side was bruised and the reflection in the pool showed a large purple knot on his forehead where he had struck the tree. As he sat beside the bear, he studied the pond before him. It was a spring, not unlike some he had seen on the Wekiva, but this one fed a small creek instead of a river. Sweet gum trees gathered around, shading it and hiding it from view.

When he felt strong enough to move about, Coya scrambled up the hill to retrieve his knife, which had lodged in a crevice. He walked around the spring. Animals had used the waters, and their trail followed the shoreline. Blue-green sparkling water welled to the top, and then spread out, licking the shore line with ripples that never stopped.

The boy waded into the cold water until the sandy bottom dropped away. He retreated to the safety of the shore. The waters were light blue where they mirrored the sky, and green where they reflected the summer leaves of sweet gum. At the very center, the source of the spring, the deep water was the color of indigo.

Coya decided to spend the day in the cool shade of this beautiful spring, with the bear cub as company. It was a pleasant place to recover from his injuries, but the afternoon sun became hot, and there was no breeze. Not even the shade afforded relief. Coya waded once again into the water. It felt much colder now than it had in the early morning. He swam out and when he was near the center, he ducked his head, kicked his legs behind him, and dived into the depths. He saw the spring head, larger around than a man's body and encircled with craggy limestone. Tiny flecks of ground rock or sand spewed upward from the hole, swirling in the water.

He could go no deeper than the spring head, as the water pushed back against him, resisting his efforts to enter. He wondered what might lie below, and whether anyone had been here before him. When he stopped struggling, he was carried to the top like a piece of light wood.

Coya explored the creek bed further down the ravine. He found a strangely shaped limestone rock, large on each end and narrow in the middle. He hefted it and moved it about. It was heavier than it looked, but it would do. He carried it to the spring and laid it on the ground. Coya stretched out his rope and studied its length. Presently he tied the palmetto cord to the end of the rope, then looped the rope around the rock and knotted it securely so it would not slip or give way.

He tied the cord to his waist and struggled into the water with the rock perched on his shoulder. Step by step he eased away from the bank, breathing hard. His foot slipped once, but he recovered his balance. When his foot lost its purchase on the bottom the second time, he heaved the anchor rock further into the middle and filled his chest with air.

The cord was as strong as the rope, and they dragged him into the depths in pursuit of the falling rock. The rock glanced off the limestone rim, and then fell through into the underworld.

Coya felt for the knife. It was there on his hip. The cord was suddenly slack and no longer pulled him down toward the springhead. The rock had found a resting place. Coya grasped the cord and pulled himself down, hand over hand. Soon cord became rope, and he was at the well spring, then through the narrow mouth and into the darkness.

The water that at first rejected him now accepted him and pulled him to the side. It was an underground river, faster than any surface stream. His head cracked against a rock above, and then he was dragged under it and beyond. Coya was dazed by the blow and his lungs screamed for air. He could go no further and hope to live. Too late, he grasped the cord to pull himself toward the spring head and safety.

Coya heard the music. It was at a great distance, but it was unmistakable. The Holy Eucharist, chanted by Father Pareja at Misión San Juan del Puerto. Then it was gone, faded into the past, and in its place the sonorous prayer of Marehootie: "*Oh yaa tan a-na-ya-ibir-hi-hiro*."

Coya was comforted and warmed by the sound, as he had been by the voice of the priest. He relaxed his hold on the cord. He breathed in. The salty water of the spring stung his nose and washed down into his throat.

Coya's mouth flew open, gasping for air, and he found it. A pocket of air below the limestone and above the level of the underground river. Coya's fingers felt a rocky ledge, and he clung to it, keeping his head above water as he coughed and sputtered to rid himself of the water that was now inside him. Coya fought to stay awake and he continued to pray.

He was alive, in a strange underground, underwater world known only to spirits. When he opened his eyes, he sensed the blackness of the cave ceiling only inches above his head. The waters wanted to carry him still further, and he drifted along, his fingers working their way along the thin ledge, until he was stopped by the tethered cord around his waist.

The roof above him had lifted away far enough that he could hold his head and shoulders out of the water, his elbows resting on the ledge. He continued to breathe deeply. The air was stale, but it was as sweet as any flower he had ever known.

The rock ledge was wider here, but still too narrow and the ceiling too low for him to pull himself from the water. His feet and legs dangled below, useless. But there was air, and there was light. Dim shafts of light from somewhere in the upper world of sunshine and breezes and flowers and earth. He clung to the rock, breathing and thanking God that he had been preserved against his own stupidity.

As his eyes became accustomed to a world between daylight and blackness, he looked around. The shelf of rock was half a meter above the flowing stream. Water dripped from somewhere above, perhaps from a fissure in the rock. Coya's fingers felt something wet and slippery, and he picked it up. A leaf. Decaying sweet gum foliage from the world above.

With his right hand he explored further, and he felt something hard, perhaps a stick. It was no stick. It was a bone of a foot, and the skeletal remains of an ancestor laid out on the ledge. A chief's eagle headdress had fallen to the side. An ancient atlatl and spear lay next to him. Near the chief's feet, a bowl of dried maize awaited his rebirth, along with a gourd that may once have held cassina.

Coya crossed himself and said Hail Marys. He prayed for forgiveness for having intruded in this holy place.

The chief had been highly honored in death, and had remained undisturbed for longer than Coya could imagine. In the near darkness, the skull grinned at the pleasure of Coya's company.

Coya breathed deeply from the dank air. When he was ready, he sank below the water and pulled himself by the cord back to the well spring. With his knife, he cut the rope from the anchor rock. He relaxed for the ride as the water propelled him upward to and through the spring opening, and still further upward to the land of the living.

———

On the morning of the twenty-eighth day, Coya decided it was time for him to plan his return to Second Wekiva. He had traveled a long way, but he had taken his time so there was no urgency, but Crying Bird said he should start back on the thirty-first day, and so he would.

If he moved straight east he would meet the River of the Sun in two days, maybe three. From there he could find the village of his birth and perhaps Chief Honorosa would provide a canoe after he visited for a while, and he would arrive home before they expected him. But Crying Bird said that he should arrive on the day of ten sixes. Crying Bird also said he should not accept the charity of others, but live and travel by his own wits.

By taking his time and moving directly south he would see land he had never visited. There was no way to get lost, as long as he kept the River of the Sun to his east. The only danger was if he encountered a village friendly to Osprey.

To fill the lonely time, Coya resolved to practice answering the questions he would face before the Grand Utinan Council at Ayacouta. Without Marehootie to remind him, however, it was difficult to remember the questions, much less the answers that would be required of him.

He found an old hickory and made himself a proper bow, working the wood with opossum grease and stringing it tight with squirrel gut. He repeated the catechisms he had been taught by the priest, and the prayers. When he was sure he was alone and no one was nearby, he sometimes sang the Psalms. Each night he lay under the brilliant stars, the calendar twine clutched in his hand. Before he slept he fingered the knots, counting the days. Soon he began to whisper. "Hail Mary, full of grace, the Lord is with Thee. Blessed art Thou amongst women and blessed is the fruit of thy womb, Jesus."

On the three tens day, Coya moved to the south, avoiding trails where he might encounter strangers. By midday he came to a solid, impenetrable wall of scrub oak so thick it blocked his way. Dense briars and vines stopped him twice when he thought he might get through. Even when he made small progress, swarms of mosquitoes drove him back. The maze of brambles was no thicker than one or two hundred meters, and by backing away he could see the taller pine trees towering in the distance.

Once again he tried, this time on his hands and knees. There was a narrow opening, a game trail under the drooping vines. He stayed alert for snakes and scorpions, and watched for the poison ivy that grew on the ground. A strange odor came to his nose, a sour, unpleasant smell.

Coya judged that he was half way through, when he saw a tawny, golden tuft of hair hanging from a clump of thorns. He had crawled into a panther's lair, so close by he could now hear the deep panting of a sleeping cat.

All of Coya's senses alerted him to the danger. How was it, he wondered, that the panther had not awakened to his approach?

Coya withdrew the knife from his scabbard. Slowly, silently, he crawled backward. He paused, and still there was no sign that the cat was prepared to attack. Coya continued backward, to a place where the path was wide enough for him to turn around, but he continued to back away so he could see the cat if it awoke and decided to charge after him. When he was at last free of the vines, Coya walked away swiftly, but he did not run.

Coya continued eastward, looking for a way around the thicket. He found the end of it, but he stopped to rest in the shade of a hickory tree when the sun was at its highest spot in the sky.

Coya awakened from a nap. He had been disturbed by the harsh, rasping call of a bird. It may have been a jay, he thought. Coya sat quietly, moving only his eyes.

Once again he slept. He dreamed of Crying Bird on his own boyhood journeys in the swamp. He saw Crying Bird the child, thin and weak and ill-equipped to save himself. Marehootie had told Coya the fanciful story of how Crying Bird was saved by limpkins who sacrificed their lives that he might have something to eat and not starve in the wilderness.

Coya was with Crying Bird, and they talked. Again he heard the harsh bird calls.

"Is that a limpkin, Crying Bird?" Coya asked. Crying Bird did not answer, but smiled at the question. His face faded away.

A touch on his shoulder and a fluttering of wings jarred him awake. Coya opened his eyes and saw the bird as it settled on a scrub oak limb.

"Did you awaken me?" Coya asked in a soothing voice. The bird did not answer, but watched him closely, turning its head in a comical manner. It looked like a common blue jay, but without the head crest, and the colors included white and gray feathers in addition to the blue.

"Have you come to save me, Jay? As you can plainly see, I have no need for your puny meat," Coya said.

To his surprise, the bird did not fly away, but continued to study him. Then there was another bird of the same kind, but this time the call was sweet and warbling, a song bird.

"I will pay you for your song, sister," Coya said softly so as not to frighten them away. He reached into his bundle and found the hickory nut meal pouch. The birds were not disturbed by his movement, but curious, and they fluttered still closer, perching on limbs almost within his reach.

Coya scattered a little on the ground, and the birds were immediately on it, snapping up the pieces of nut. Another of the same kind swooped down, landing lightly on Coya's leg, and without even asking permission commenced to feast directly from the pouch.

Coya could not contain his laugh. "You are greedy little people," he said.

Still, there were more, each more aggressive and less afraid of him than the last. One walked up and down Coya's outstretched leg, its tiny toes tickling him and making his leg muscles flinch. Still another landed on his shoulder and pecked at the necklace he wore, attracted by the sun glinting off the shiny apple snail shells. When another landed on his head and walked about as if to make a nest in Coya's hair, he brushed it away with his fingers.

Immediately the birds took to the trees, squawking and cursing and scolding him for his inhospitality. Moments later they were gone, lost in the impenetrable forest of briar and thorn and mosquito.

Chapter 13

The creek was narrow, but the waters were too deep to wade across. Coya was burdened with two bundles that he didn't want to get wet. One was tightly wrapped in animal skin, and contained gifts he had collected for his return home. Some he had fashioned by his own hand, such as the pine knot for Yano, carved to resemble a gnarled old man smoking a pipe. For Marehootie he carried the delicate hide of a fawn that was born dead, but which its mother guarded for three days before she finally gave up and went away. Coya had skinned it and tanned it before he painted tiny child-like animals on the soft leather. He had not yet found a suitable gift for Crying Bird.

The smaller bundle was wrapped in twine, and contained smoked meats and other foods he carried with him, along with arrows, spear points, and rope. The fire pouch, alone, ruled out crossing the river here.

Coya continued downstream and found a spot where the creek widened and shallowed. He waded across, but continued to follow it to the east, wondering where it led.

By evening he crossed a trail, and not wanting to be seen, he continued for a distance until he found a place to camp among live oak trees draped with giant beards of gray moss.

The mosquitoes found him soon after he lay down, and he arose long enough to cover himself with the myrtle leaf mosquito potion Marehootie had packed for him. In the dark, he awoke to the scream of a panther in the distance, placed his knife next to him, and returned to his dreams.

As happened often in the hours before daybreak, Coya was once again at home at the mission with Father Pareja. He smelled the dusky ocean breeze and heard the friar's rhythmic chanting of the Holy Eucharist. The laughing voices of the mission cooks and their children intruded, and soon blended with the sounds of the children of Wekiva running at their play and splashing in the river shallows. In the distance, a dog barked. Marehootie was there, scolding Crying Bird, who argued back and shoved his brother playfully. He jumped back, laughing, before the old man could pick up his crutch to strike him.

Again, the dog barked. It was closer now. Coya was awake, and it was morning. His bundles hung in a tree away from his sleeping place, and he had only his knife and a raccoon skin pillow stuffed with moss.

Coya ran to a live oak tree and rubbed the pillow on the ground around the trunk. He tossed the pillow high into the branches, and it tumbled out and landed at his feet. He threw it again, and the pillow lodged in a fork half way up.

Coya ran back to where he slept, scattered the bed moss about and climbed another tree high into its thick foliage where he hid.

The dog picked up the raccoon smell, and ran around the scented tree barking, snarling, and leaping into the air, as if to climb. Then, another sound could be he heard, people walking quietly in the woods, but sometimes stepping on dried leaves or twigs.

A man with the largest bow Coya had ever seen emerged from the brush, his weapon at the ready. Behind him a young woman followed, stepping daintily to avoid the thorns, a half-filled berry basket in her hand.

The man looked up into the oak, and scolded the dog. "Curro, if you tree one more raccoon I will have you in the dinner pot. We are hunting panther."

The young woman spoke to the man. Coya strained to hear what she said, but her voice was soft, and the barking of the dog drowned out her words. As quickly as they had appeared, they were gone. The dog remained, and sniffed about until he found where Coya had slept. He began again to bark. His master's shout echoed through the forest, and the dog reluctantly obeyed and ran into the woods after him.

Coya descended to the ground and followed after them at a distance, darting from tree to tree, trying to stay close enough to hear but not be seen. He had left his bundles, but they would be there when he returned. Once, the tall man looked behind him as if sensing that they were followed. Coya lay flat on the ground behind a palmetto bush until they moved on.

From a stand of sweet gum trees, Coya looked down into the small village where the man and girl had gone. There were twenty or more houses, a storage shed and a barbacoa that smoked continuously, scenting the air with the smell of roasting venison. In time, Coya's stomach rumbled in discomfort.

The young girl sat cross-legged outside the largest house, working the berries with a small mortar and pestle, preparing them to be cooked into a jam. The man with the long bow lived in that same house, but Coya sensed from their gestures that they were brother and sister and not lovers. An older man, with the resplendent tattoos of a chief, lived there also, along with his wife.

Late in the day, Coya returned to his camp site, but came back to the stand of sweet gum when it was dark. It was a quiet village, and Coya could see that no one carried a weapon. Perhaps they need no guards, he thought. He watched as the people went to their houses for the night. Soon, no one at all appeared to be awake, other than the hunting dog that lay outside his master's house.

The dog worried Coya. How could he carry out his plan without the dog alerting the men of the village that there was an intruder? Coya thought of one plan after another. None of them seemed likely to succeed. Coya had decided to go back to his camp and give up his plan when a lightning storm moved over the village.

Soon the dog began to whine and bark, made nervous by the flashes of light and thunder. The door flap opened and the dog was invited inside the house.

Coya moved stealthily, from shadow to shadow, until he was in the center of the village.

When the sun came up the next morning, Coya watched as the younger man stepped out of the house. He did not look down to discover the surprise Coya had left there, but went to join several other men in the shadow of a tree, throwing stones and gambling.

Perhaps these were Osprey's people, and this was a dangerous game. Coya certainly gambled more than the men under the tree, who had only cowry shells to lose, and not their own lives. Coya wondered if he was being foolish, risking so much to speak to the girl.

The older man stepped out of the door, and stretched his arms to awaken himself fully. He also kept his eyes up, and did not look down. He carried himself erect and with great dignity. His shirt was of brightly colored Spanish cloth, the kind Chief Tacatacura had worn. Another man joined him, bowing and treating the first man with great deference. This would be the *inija*, Coya guessed.

The two strolled over to where the gamblers sat. The others made room, and when the chief was seated, they handed him the stones. It was his time to throw them.

Coya awakened to screams of excitement. He had not slept during the night and had dozed off in his hiding place. The girl stood outside the house, holding the berry basket filled to the brim with elderberries, and the necklace of shiny apple snail shells he had left there. She shouted at her brother, accusing him of having played a trick on her.

The men gathered around her, confused about the unexplained appearance of the gift. Before they could decide what they should do, Coya walked into the village with a pleasant smile on his face and his palms raised, showing he was unarmed and meant no harm.

"Coya?" Chief Chilili fixed the boy with a suspicious look. "I know a village by that name."

"It is where I was born," Coya replied.

Coya sat in the dirt, directly in front of the chief. The others stood in a half moon circle, the gambling forgotten for the moment in light of the interesting visitor. People came from their houses to share the excitement. Coya looked around hoping to see the girl, but she had gone back inside her house.

"How is it you are named after a village and you are not its chief? I know the chief of the village of Coya. He is Honoroso and he is my brother."

"I was given the name by the Spanish. While I was a child I lived at a mission. Now I have come home."

"Ahhhh! I see," Chilili said, covering his mouth with a hand, his eyes wide and intense. "And where is this home of which you speak?"

Coya thought of how he should answer the chief's question. He could say nothing of Wekiva. "I live in the woods. I travel about," he said.

"If you are a vagrant, a *cimarrone*, you must be very good at it because you appear to be well fed." There was laughter among the young men. From the corner of his eye, Coya saw the girl was now standing outside her house, listening. When she saw him glance her way, she ducked back into the house.

"I have a village where I stay most of the time," said Coya. "My chief is called Crying Bird."

Chilili, his *inija* and the other principal men stepped away and talked among themselves excitedly. Coya heard them speak the words "*Atitchicolo-Iri*" and "Acuera." Presently, Chilili stepped back to where Coya sat.

"No one here will ask you how we could get to your village. If you are who you say, you would not tell us even if we demanded to know."

Chief Chilili spread his arms so as to encompass the entire village. "You are welcome here, Coya. You will find no Osprey people among the Chilili."

Coya accepted Chief Chilili's invitation to stay for five days. Each evening as he had promised Crying Bird, Coya returned to his own camp in the woods and dreamed of the Chief's daughter who was called Mora. The girl ignored him during the day and would not return his smile when they passed each other in the village.

Coya learned to gamble with the men and went on a hunting party with Mora's brother, Big Bow. Coya felled a large buck with the bow he had made, but his bow was half the size of his host's.

On their way back to the village, Coya walked beside Big Bow. "I saw you walking in the woods with Mora and your dog. I followed you back to Chilili. I spied on you because I am smitten with your sister."

"You must be a very good tracker. I knew we were being followed, but I thought it was a panther."

"Are you troubled by a panther?" Coya asked.

"A panther spirit. It is very old and slow. Maybe it has lost its eyesight, or its hearing. It can no longer catch deer or foxes or turkeys, so it preys on children. One child from Chilili died, and one from another village. Even women who pick berries need someone to protect them. That is why I was with Mora that morning."

"Why do you think it is a spirit, and not a real living panther?"

Big Bow turned to face Coya. "You can hunt a panther; you can tree it with dogs or track it to its lair. This one just kills and disappears until it kills again."

Coya did not speak again until they neared Chilili. "Do you think your father would consent to me marrying Mora if I rid you of this panther spirit?"

Big Bow laughed out loud. "If you can kill the panther with that puny bow you carry, I will marry you myself."

Chief Chilili planned a feast for the last night before Coya's departure. He ordered that the council house be decorated for the occasion, and that the cooks prepare a meal of the best the storehouse had to offer. The *jarva* said his blessings and spread corn pollen at the doorway to the council house.

When Coya did not come to the village on the fourth day, Big Bow went looking for him. On the morning of the fifth day, Chief Chilili ordered that a search party find him. Before the search party was ready to go, Coya walked into the village. He carried the tawny skin and head of a panther.

Coya's right shoulder and back bore the signs of the panther's claws. His left arm had been badly bitten, and blood still oozed below the bandage Coya had applied.

The mother of the child who had been killed wailed her grief and pounded the animal skin with a club. She fell exhausted on the ground and crawled to where Coya stood with the chief. She kissed Coya's feet.

"How did you kill it?" Big Bow wanted to know.

"I found its lair, and paid it a visit. You were right, my bow was useless. It was so crowded in the panther's house, I could use only my knife."

Coya presented the panther skin to Chilili, who accepted it gratefully. "I would be even more honored, if you give the head of this cat to Crying Bird. I have a woman who can make it into a beautiful headdress," Chief Chilili said.

Big Bow examined Coya's knife, holding it up and marveling that light shone through the glassy blade.

Coya carried one last gift, covered with a woven palmetto fabric. He went in search of the girl. He stood outside the chief's house and called her name. In a while, Mora stepped outside, acting annoyed and shielding her eyes from the rays of the setting sun.

"I have this for you," he said. He pulled back the cover. It was a house for birds, built of thin twigs and the bark of a cedar tree. Inside, three docile jay birds blinked at the light.

"If you will go with me tomorrow, I will show you where they are to be released. They will stay nearby as long as you bring them food. That way, you can play with them every day."

One of the birds had its eye on the necklace of shiny apple snails suspended from Mora's neck. The girl said nothing, not even a word of thanks, but she smiled at Coya before she turned and took the birds into her house.

It had been many days since Coya had eaten food prepared by women, and it was a wonderful feast that included fish, quail, and a soup made of venison.

The feast was followed by entertainment and dancing, but Coya was impatient for it to be over. When the others were gone, Coya and Chief Chilili remained in the council house.

"Is your *jarva* skilled in his arts?" Coya asked.

"I hope he is, but with magic sometimes it's hard to tell. Why do you ask?"

"I gave him all I had to trade to cast a spell on Mora, so that she would love me." Coya watched the chief's face to see if he became angry. "He said he would use a coco plum potion and that it always works on young girls."

Chilili fell back on his bench, laughing. When he could speak again he said, "And I paid the *jarva* a small fortune to smoke my daughter's skirts with herbs, and to say the prayers to make you take her with you."

Late that night, when Coya made his way toward his camp in the woods, Mora was with him. He carried her few possessions. Mora carried the birds.

"We will release them where you found them," she said.

While they lay together looking at the stars, Coya spoke. "I was sure you didn't like me. Was it the *jarva*'s spell that changed your heart?"

Mora laughed and rolled to her side, placing her hand on Coya's chest.

"How could I not love a man who charms the birds from the trees?"

Chapter 14

On the morning of the six tens day, Coya and Mora waded into the shallows and looked across to the village on the hill. It was the same as when he'd left, Coya said, except for a house far to the south where the thatched roof had fallen in. An Ocale woman had lived there alone, but it now appeared abandoned.

Summer rains had swollen the river, but it was a safe crossing with Coya holding the bundles above his head and Mora with one hand on his shoulder.

Before they reached the shore, Crying Bird and Marehootie were at the water's edge waiting to greet them. Even with his crutch and Crying Bird's arm for support, the descent was difficult for Marehootie, and he stumbled, but managed to stay on his feet. People came from their houses and gardens to witness Coya's return.

Tears of joy streaked Marehootie's leathery face. "Spirits bless us! Look, Brother, at what the boy has found in the woods." The old man wrapped his bony arms around Mora, squeezing her up and down.

Nihoto was there to take the bundles from Coya. Crying Bird grasped Coya by the shoulders. "I was afraid you would starve to death, but you are taller and stronger than when you left us."

Crying Bird released his grip and looked at the fresh scars on Coya's shoulder. "It looks as if you allowed a cat to sneak up on you."

"It was my husband who sneaked up on the cat," Mora said.

"That is a story we will all hear today at the council house," Crying Bird said, "along with the tale of how he lured this princess away from her family."

They moved up the hill, with Marehootie's arms around the shoulders of Crying Bird and Coya who carried him. Mora followed behind with the old man's crutch. The climb was easier than Coya remembered. He saw that in his absence, the slope had been terraced so that there were easy steps to the top.

"You shall have my house," Marehootie announced. "I have been living with Crying Bird since you left us, and I have come to enjoy his snoring."

Coya protested, saying that he should build a new house for Mora or perhaps rebuild the one that was now falling down.

"No. I am Governor and I decide such things," Crying Bird said. "Marehootie is right. You should be close by for the sake of safety."

Coya looked at Mora for a response. They had talked earlier about having a house away from the others, for their privacy. "As long as our lovemaking doesn't keep them awake, I suppose it will be all right," she said, smiling sweetly.

Marehootie howled with laughter. Crying Bird chuckled, and Coya's face turned bright red.

The day was warm, but as soon as Marehootie joined them, Crying Bird closed the door flap. Mora busied herself next door, cleaning Marehootie's house and storing her possessions. Nihoto, the deaf Indian, stood watch outside Crying Bird's house so that no one approached to listen in.

"We told you to return today for a reason," Crying Bird said. "I thought you would tire of being alone in the woods and come back sooner, or perhaps get lost and come back later than the day I selected. Marehootie and I had a bet. He said you would be here today."

"The boy was trained by a friar. They always know exactly what day it is," Marehootie said.

Crying Bird coughed and wiped his mouth with a piece of cloth. "We wanted you here now so there would be time to get to Ayacouta by the full moon after the equinox. We had a visitor while you were away, a messenger from Chief Honoroso, and he said the council will not be held, that so many of the chiefs and principal men of Utina are ill that they decided to postpone the council until the winter solstice."

"Did you know this messenger?" Coya asked.

Marehootie spoke. "My, aren't you the suspicious one! Are you suggesting the messenger may have come from Osprey and not Honoroso?"

"It crossed my mind," Coya admitted.

"That was good thinking," Crying Bird said. "Osprey is a trickster, and he might try to become chief by keeping you away from the council. But the story is true. I sent my own messenger to Honoroso and he confirmed it."

"It makes sense to me," Marehootie said. "There is always more illness this time of year. Sickness has even struck Crying Bird. In the winter it will be easier to travel."

"Tell me, did you encounter Osprey while you were away?" Crying Bird asked.

"No. I stayed away from people most of the time, avoiding the hunting trails and the river where many of the towns are located. I stayed west of the River of the Sun the entire time. The only village I was in was Chilili, and I only went there to win the heart of Mora. Chief Chilili said they were no friends of Osprey, and I believed him."

Crying Bird coughed again, this time more violently. Marehootie crawled on his knees to him and gave him a sip of cassina mixed with honey. Presently he was again able to speak.

"Osprey has been here. Not at Second Wekiva, but at our first village. We still keep a guard where the rivers meet. He saw Utinans at the old village, walking around and digging in the dirt. He said the leader carried a musket. They tried to move up river, but we had felled a large cypress across the river and they were too lazy to walk. They will find us, though, sooner or later."

"More likely, they will hear traders talking about the new village on a hill," Marehootie said. "Osprey is smart. He will figure it out, and attack us from the west or south."

Coya rubbed the scar on his right ear, the one he'd received protecting Marehootie from the soldiers, as he sometimes did while thinking. "You do not fear Osprey. We have men who can fight. Perhaps we will lay a trap and deal with him once and for all."

"Osprey only wants two things," Crying Bird said. "He wants to kill you, and he wants to be *Holata Aco* over the Utina Nation. He was trained by his father, Chief Utina. He may lay a trap, but he is too much of a fox to step into one laid for him."

"And we cannot risk a fight in which you might be killed," Marehootie added. "That is one reason we sent you away, in case he came looking for you."

Marehootie crawled to the side of the house while he spoke, and rummaged through bundles of Crying Bird's possessions. He returned and laid a packet wrapped in animal skin before the boy. "Open it," he said.

The leather bindings were tied tight and Coya worked to loosen them. He rolled open the deer skin, and spread it out. A satchel of finely woven palmetto fiber was inside. He opened it. Crying Bird handed a torch to Marehootie who held it so that the boy could see.

Pearls, more than could be held in two hands, some as large as snail shells, shone in the light, reflecting amber, blue, and pink.

Coya breathed in deeply, and then let his breath out. "I have seen the pearls Marehootie wears, and I know the story of the Cofitachiqui wealth that was used to fight the soldiers. I just did not know there were so many, or that they were so beautiful."

"There were twice this many pearls forty years ago," Marehootie said.

Crying Bird started to cough. He sipped his drink and his lungs relaxed. "Osprey also knows the story. He knows we used pearls to pay the Yammassee to fight Utina twenty years ago. If he gets his hands on them, he will buy enough influence on the council to become *Holata Aco* of the Utina nation."

The homecoming feast was a disappointment. The Ocale widow had been head cook, but had gone to live with a trader. No one could cook as well as she.

Coya's stories disappointed no one. He told of the tame birds, of how they ate out of his hand and sat on his head. He told about how he first saw Mora, and how he loved her, and how he crawled into the lair of a panther to win her affection. He spoke of the spring and the cub that guarded it and how he almost died in the underwater cavern.

As Coya described the watery underworld, he noticed that Marehootie and Crying Bird eyed each other, communicating without a word, as brothers sometimes do after sixty years of companionship.

Marehootie took Coya and Mora to the small grassy knoll overlooking the river as the sun played hide-and-seek with a bank of thin clouds.

"We have the most beautiful sunsets here, this time of year," he said. "It reminds me of my childhood at Ibitibi. We had a shaman, an old blind *jarva*, who said that all sunsets are equally beautiful, but that sighted people were blind to the beauty that is there every day."

"Tell me about your people, the Acuera," Mora said. "In my childhood we Utinans feared you. I was told you were all cannibals and murderers. I know now that those were only stories."

"Don't get him started!" Coya said. "Unless you want to hear a story with no ending."

"Let me tell a little," Marehootie said. "I promise I won't bore her or keep her from your bed."

Marehootie wore a soft shawl on his head and shoulders to protect him from the cool air of the approaching night, but folded it back so his face could accept the last warming rays of the sun. "I am very old, as you can see. I have been many places, met many people, and bedded many beautiful women. I loved only one." He fell quiet for a while.

"I am White Deer Clan. My mother died when Crying Bird was born. My father was Alligator Clan. I don't know what happened to him. I assume he is dead by now."

Coya laughed. "If he is still alive, that would make him more than one hundred years old."

"Don't laugh. With the Acuera, that is possible. The *jarva* I've mentioned, who was blind, lived to be two hundred years old."

"You told me of Blind *Jarva*, but you said he died in his one hundredth summer," Coya said, giving Mora a quick smile.

Marehootie ignored what Coya said, and went on with his story. "Crying Bird is my only brother. I have one sister. Her name is Amita. I have not seen her for many years."

Mora spoke. "My husband has told me of your travels. He says you have been everywhere there is to go without taking a ship to get there."

It was Marehootie's time to laugh. "Not everywhere. There is one place I have always feared to go."

"Where would that be?" Mora asked.

"It is where my sister was heard from last. If she still lives, it is among the Spanish in San Augustín. I have decided to go there before I die and look for her. At my age, and feeling the way I do with these aches and pains, it must be soon."

"That is a dream, old man," Coya said gently as he leaned to the side so that his arm brushed against Mora's bare shoulder. "You could not get there by yourself."

"Oh, I will not be alone. Nihoto has said he will go with me," he said.

"I would like to see that, a cripple riding the back of a man who cannot hear. How will you tell him which way to turn?"

"Nihoto and I have overcome much worse in the last forty years." Marehootie gazed far off to where the last light illuminated the golden top of a towering cloud.

Two nights later, after they had made love, Coya told Mora that he must leave the village for a few days. She wept softly. Coya went to the house of Crying Bird and Marehootie, and they talked quietly into the night.

When the sun rose, it lit Coya's path to the northwest. He carried with him only his knife, a few hickory cakes, a satchel containing a great length of rope and a tightly bound leather packet.

When he returned three days later, Coya went looking for Marehootie and Crying Bird. He found the Governor of Second Wekiva working alone in the council house fashioning spear points from stone.

"Have you done what you promised?" Crying Bird asked as Coya entered through the low doorway. Somehow the greeting seemed brusque, even for Crying Bird.

"Yes, it is accomplished," Coya said.

Crying Bird grunted, but continued to look down, concentrating on his work.

Coya moved back toward the door. Perhaps his other grandfather would be happy to see him, he thought. He turned back to face Crying Bird. "I looked for Marehootie and couldn't find him."

Crying Bird spit toward the fire, and his spittle landed on a flat piece of heated rock. "He is not here."

Coya waited for Crying Bird to say more.

Finally, he spoke. "I could not stop him. You know how hard-headed my brother can be when he makes up his mind to do something stupid." Crying Bird turned to face Coya, letting the half-finished spear point slip from his fingers.

"You will never see him again," Crying Bird said. His voice cracked with emotion. "He has gone with Nihoto looking for our sister in San Augustín. If he survives the journey, the soldiers will know who he is and kill him."

Coya came back to where Crying Bird sat, and knelt next to him. He looked into the old man's face, expecting for the first time to see tears. He saw only hardness and deep anger.

"He told me that he wanted to travel to San Augustín, but I had no idea he would actually go, or that he would leave so suddenly without telling me goodbye," Coya said.

"He thought it would be easier this way, for both of you." Crying Bird picked up the piece of chert and began to work once again.

Chapter 15

The village of Tocoi sat at the crossing of two trails. One was traveled by dugout canoe and the other by foot. The River of the Sun, or as the Spanish came to call it, Río de San Juan, stretched from the land of the Ais, far to the south, to Misión San Juan del Puerto and the ocean to the north. The other trail, perhaps as ancient as the river, ran east and west from the coastal village of Soloy where the Spanish had established San Augustín, to Tocoi, and then beyond the river and into the heart of Potano and the Western provinces, all the way to Apalachee.

In all of his sixty-six years, Marehootie had never set foot in Tocoi. Never, in fact, had he seen the village in the daylight after twenty or more journeys up and down the river. There was always a reason to travel at night and avoid being seen. But the sun shined brightly as his canoe slid ashore at the embarcadero.

A solitary Spanish soldier, in his woolen uniform and carrying a musket, walked among the Indians, trying to stay in the shade to avoid the heat. He carried a metal hat under his arm and his head was wrapped in a kerchief of Spanish cloth. He took no note of the old Indian and his deaf companion who helped him out of the canoe and ashore.

Marehootie's feet ached after two days of no use, and he leaned on the strong arm of Nihoto who half-carried him to where a fallen log served as a bench for people waiting to be ferried across the river.

Two boys descended on them. "If it is for sale, I will buy your canoe," one of them said. He waded into the water and circled the canoe looking for cracks or other signs of damage. "I will pay fifty cowry shells for it." He spoke the Mocama dialect.

The second boy, taller than the first and dressed as an Utinan, stood back studying Marehootie and Nihoto. "I will give you fifty plus five for such an inferior canoe," he said.

Marehootie crooked his finger to him, inviting him to come close. "What do you know of canoes? Do you see the marking on the bow? Do you know what it means?"

The boy rubbed his chin with his thumb, studying the canoe. "All right. I will give you fifty and seven shells for it. No one here will give you more."

"Fifty and eight," the boy in the water shouted.

A middle-aged Indian with a fat belly had been watching from the shade of a hickory tree, and he stepped into the sunlight. "Do not do business with these children and their shells. I have dealt in canoes all my life. This one is made of the finest yellow pine. It comes from an Acueran village that burned down many years ago."

"You remember Ibitibi?" Marehootie said. "If so, you know this canoe is one of a kind. There could never be another."

While Nihoto guarded the canoe and the bundles, Marehootie and the man sat under the tree discussing their differing opinions on the canoe's worth. Marehootie had no idea of the value of the Spanish silver coins the man dealt in, but when the man offered three coins, the Acueran was sure it was not enough. Perhaps one coin was as good as to fifty of the shells, he thought.

The sun moved across the sky as the two men continued to argue. When Marehootie demanded six coins and said he would not accept less, the man became angry, and stood and walked away.

Before long he returned and sat down and was pleasant once again. "Ibitibi did a beautiful job on your canoe, but I deal with river traders and they require war canoes large enough to carry twenty arrobas of maize and fifty or more deer skins on the same trip."

"Then find yourself other customers. Some chief would pay dearly for the privilege of being seen in this one-of-a-kind Ibitibi."

"It appears that you have two problems, Marehootie," the man said. "You need to sell this fine canoe, for which you have no more use, and you are too crippled to make it on your own to the Spanish town with all your bundles."

"Nihoto is strong. He will carry me in the rough spots."

"But I have studied your bundles. They are the size of arrobas. Nihoto may be strong, but he cannot carry all that. If he leaves the bundles along the trail, to carry you over the rough spots, as you call them, the bundles will be stolen before he returns. Marehootie, there are bandits and thieves all around us. I am your friend, you must believe me."

"I know a thief when I see one," Marehootie said, looking directly into the man's face.

Ignoring the insult, the man went on with his thought. "I will send those two boys with you, to carry your bundles. I have been admiring your necklace. Those are fine pearls. Give me two of them, one for each bearer, and I will pay you the six coins you ask for the canoe. I will be losing value, but I like you. You have the look of an honest man."

"You will give each boy a pearl?" Marehootie asked.

"They will be paid, but they like to deal in shells. It is a long difficult trail to the Spanish town, but they will do it for twenty shells each."

"Give the shells to me. I will pay them at San Augustín," Marehootie said. He took his necklace from around his neck, and removed one of the larger pearls, again tying the strand. He handed the pearl to the man.

"This is only one," the man said.

"That is all those boys are worth," Marehootie answered.

At the end of the second day they arrived at the village of Soloy, and the boys argued that they had been promised thirty cowry shells each. Marehootie gave them only what he had agreed to pay, twenty for each boy. Grumbling that they had been cheated, the boys ran off to San Augustín where they could spend their money and then find work carrying bundles back to Tocoi.

"These children are more Spanish than Indian," he said to Nihoto, using his hands and fingers to make the signs the man understood. "Perhaps they have no uncles to teach them right from wrong."

"I am looking for my sister," he said, speaking to the friar at Misión Nombre de Dios the next morning. "Her name is Amita, and she was born in Ibitibi in the land of the Acuerans."

"She must be very old," the priest said, looking at Marehootie. "Do you know that she is still alive?"

"I wouldn't be asking for her if she was dead."

The priest opened a ledger on his desk, and ran his finger down a column of names. When he reached the bottom, he turned the page, and then another.

"Ah yes! I know this woman. She attends Mass almost every Sabbath. She is called Amita Carrera. In parenthesis it says 'de Ibitibi.' It must be her. She is married to a soldier, I believe, but I have never seen him in church. You will find his house in the compound near the barracks."

Marehootie thanked him for the information. "I used to know a priest from Misión San Juan del Puerto, a Father Pareja. Do you know of him?"

The friar smiled broadly. "Of course I know him. Father Pareja is our custos of missions. If you are looking for him, he can be found at the new monastery down by the water."

Chapter 16

The house was small, compared to the others Marehootie saw as he walked through the streets of San Augustín. It was not really a house at all, but a squat wattle and daub structure among others of the same kind, lined up beside each other with wooden plank doors facing east toward the plaza the soldiers used for their exercises and parades.

Earlier, he had watched a Spanish woman looking foolish rapping her knuckles on a door, as if she were a woodpecker with no voice to announce her presence.

"Amita?" Marehootie called from outside.

He called again, and when he got no answer, he walked to the side of the house and looked in an open window. An old woman, dressed as a Spaniard but with the black hair of a Timucuan, sat on a stool at a potter's wheel, working the clay.

When she heard him call her name, she stood up and moved haltingly toward the window. She was small, and her back was hunched over from a lifetime of hard work.

"It is you, my brother?" Her hands shook as she reached through the open window and felt his face.

In an instant she was gone away from the window. A moment later she rounded the corner of the house to where Marehootie stood, leaning on his crutch. She grasped his arm and pulled him so roughly Marehootie lost his balance, and fell to the ground.

Amita half-carried him into the house, and then went back outside. In a moment she returned, carrying the crutch. When she closed the door, they held each other, each shedding tears of happiness.

"I am content with my life here," she said later as they sat together on a woven palmetto fiber mat that covered much of the dirt floor. The house was furnished with a small table, two wooden chairs and a low bed. All of the houses for officers and their women were the same, she said.

"My husband is good to me. He does not beat me, as many soldiers punish their wives for disobedience. And did you notice this pottery wheel? My husband won it gambling with a merchant. Let me show you." Amita sat on a stool and moved her foot up and down on a wooden pedal. The wheel began to move and her fingers gently shaped the sides of a clay bowl as it turned before her.

"The other women do it the old way, coiling the clay before they smooth it. I can make twice as many pots, and they are more sturdy and do not break as easily in the oven. I sell my pottery at the Saturday market."

"Let me try," Marehootie said. Amita stood behind him, telling him what to do. Marehootie's legs were too long, and he moved the stool away from the pedal. The movement required of his foot was soon very painful, and he gave it up.

"That's harder than it looks," he said as he lowered himself from the stool and sat with his back against the wall. "You must be very proud, being a good potter and creating such beautiful things. Our mother was a potter. Do you remember?"

"I remember well. I'm very lucky. Perhaps I got my talent from her." Amita was smiling, but Marehootie could see her eyes were once again red.

"Tell me about your life here among the Spaniards."

Amita prepared cassina from roasted yaupon, and they sipped it together. With the door standing open, a breeze came in and left through the window, making them very comfortable despite the hot day.

Amita had been a gift to a soldier from her uncle, the Chief of Acuera.

"He was cruel to me, and I did not cry when he left on a ship for Spain. We have a child, a girl. He wanted a male child, and I disappointed him, so he changed his mind about marrying me and went back to his other family.

"Before he left, he gave me to Señor Barcon, the man I live with now. My daughter lives with another soldier. Louisa and I work at the market together on Saturday and we attend Mass at the mission on the Sabbath. Perhaps you will meet her while you are here."

"Where does Louisa live?" Marehootie asked.

"Just two doors from here."

Marehootie's brow wrinkled. "Why don't you see your daughter every day, living so close?"

"We have our work to do to earn money for our men. She sews the soldiers' uniforms and I do my pottery. Louisa's husband drinks wine and gets angry sometimes, so she is afraid to have company or to be away from his house."

"Amita, you were a Princess of White Deer." Marehootie was immediately sorry for what he'd said when he saw the sadness in her eyes.

"Not here," she said. "Only in the villages are we honored for our clan. Here it doesn't matter. White Deer is no better than Buzzard, or Earth, or Fish clan. They call Louisa 'mestizo,' which means she is a half-breed. At least, we are respected more than the black slaves."

"Why do you stay?" Marehootie asked. "You could come with me and see Crying Bird again. We could be together, as when we were children."

Amita glanced out the window. Palm fronds on the tall trees that circled the parade ground flapped in the strong ocean breeze.

"Perhaps I stay because I have no place to go. I only lived one other place in my life, and that was Ibitibi. Besides, Louisa is here, and I am happiest when we go to Mass together."

Amita reached out and took Marehootie's hand in her own. "I have lived my life with my memories of you, my handsome and witty brother. And of Crying Bird, so powerful, but so intense it was sometimes frightening. And I see myself there with you, in Ibitibi."

Amita kissed Marehootie's fingertips. "I stay because I love my husband, and because he would starve to death if I did not look after him."

"Perhaps our memories are all we have left," Marehootie said.

Amita opened her mouth as if to speak, but closed it and said nothing.

Marehootie looked at her expectantly.

"Is that the way you remember me," she asked, "as a princess?"

When Father de Avila returned from siesta, he took no notice of the Indian sitting in the shade of a tree outside the monastery. The priest unlocked the door and stepped into the room and then went to open a window for ventilation.

As he turned back, he was startled to find the Indian standing close behind him, leaning on a crutch.

"Good afternoon," de Avila said in the Timucua tongue, taking a step backward. "What is it you want?"

The Indian did not answer, but starred into the face of the priest.

"Are you looking for food? The friar at the mission will give you soup if you are hungry."

The Indian finally answered him in Spanish. "I come to see the priest, Pareja."

Father de Avila asked the Indian to sit on a chair, and then he went through another door into the office of the custos where Father Pareja was napping on a pallet, as was his custom during siesta. He woke the older priest gently.

"There is an old Indian to see you," de Avila said.

Father Pareja rolled to his side and placed his feet on the floor. "Francisco, this is Thursday. Today I work on my sermon. Have him return tomorrow morning." He stood, stretched and moved to his desk.

Father de Avila stood with his arms crossed. "I think you will want to see this particular Indian," he said.

Father Pareja walked past his assistant and cracked the door wide enough to see into the other room.

"Is it…?" de Avila asked.

Father Pareja closed the door and leaned against it, rubbing his face with his hands. "It has been five years, but I believe it is he. I believe it is Marehootie."

"Why have you come?" Pareja asked. He had not offered to embrace the Indian, but gestured for him to sit in the wooden chair in front of the desk.

Marehootie looked around the room, at the stacks of books, the rolled manuscripts and religious icons that decorated the whitewashed walls.

"I have come to the Spanish town because I am old, and because my sister is here. Neither of us has many years to live, and we have not seen each other since we were children."

"I can understand that," the priest said.

"And to repay a debt to a man who was once my friend."

Pareja looked at Marehootie, his hair grown gray and his cheeks more hollowed than the priest remembered.

"You owe me nothing, other than an explanation."

Marehootie leaned forward in his chair, locking his eyes on those of the priest. "You Spanish require an explanation for why a man would prefer to run away than have his flesh burned from his bones?"

"Not that," Pareja said. "Not the running away. I bear my own guilt for what they would have done to you. I could have prevented it, but I did not. I thank God that you escaped. I could not have borne it if they had killed you."

"Nor I," Marehootie said, the hint of a smile creased the corners of his mouth.

"What bothers me almost as much as my own weakness was that you took Juan de Coya with you. You had no right to do that." The priest's words were harsh, but even as he spoke his lower lip quivered. He pulled a kerchief from the pocket of his robe and wiped his eyes.

"I did not force him, or even ask him to go with me. It was his decision."

"But you lured him away with your stories. You took him from the church, for your own purposes. Juan de Coya was baptized. His soul belongs to God, and you spirited him away to be a – a – *cimarrone.*"

Marehootie sat quietly while the priest again wiped his face. When the Spaniard seemed to have composed himself, the old man responded. "I cannot speak for who owns the boy's soul. I can tell you this much, that Coya still prays the prayers you taught him, and he has grown into a man of great strength and character."

Father Pareja walked to the window and looked out, his hands clasped behind his back. "I wonder," he said.

"What is it you wonder about? Is it about the guard outside my cell, and who killed him? You can rest your mind. Coya was not there; he did not do it."

Pareja turned back to face the Indian. "If that is so, I do not care to know who did kill him. I refused the Governor's Summons to tell what I knew. I only pray that whoever killed that young boy confess it and seek forgiveness of his sin."

"I do not come here to confess, Father. I come only to say the boy is safe, and to see an old friend."

They talked through the afternoon. Marehootie spoke of his hope that Coya would some day become a great chief, *Holata Aco* for all the Utinans. He would not say where they lived, nor did he mention his brother, Crying Bird. The priest did not ask him about what happened the night of the escape from Misión San Juan.

Father de Avila sat quietly, listening as Marehootie and Father Pareja remembered their time together at San Juan del Puerto.

Pareja spoke of the success of the missions, and the continuing hardships of the priests. "It is difficult to attract the best priests to La Florida. Some have returned to Spain and told wild stories to justify their own failure here. And still, the Indians come to San Augustín. They ask the governor to send priests to teach them the Word of God. Sometimes they have already built a church. So far, we have had neither the funds nor the friars to satisfy their needs. But perhaps, now that the monastery is built and more friars are coming from Spain, we can make better progress."

Pareja stood and began walking about, becoming animated. He spoke of his vision for a school for interpreters at the monastery, where religious students could be prepared to accompany new priests to their missions. "The brighter boys could help me interpret scripture into their tongue, so that even the unlearned could be touched by God's Word."

The sun was already setting when they both tired.

"Perhaps I will see you tomorrow," Marehootie said. "On Saturday I will be meeting my sister and her daughter at the market."

"Not tomorrow," Pareja said. "I will be busy all day preparing for Sunday Mass. Perhaps you will attend Mass and we can talk after that."

Father de Avila was suddenly on his feet. "Father, forgive me," he said. "Haven't you forgotten the archivist?"

Pareja stood up. "God forgive me! I did forget. Marehootie, you must leave San Augustín immediately. You are in great danger. The Sergeant at San Juan, Suarez, is still alive. He survived his injuries and has been given a job as the governor's archivist. He is more evil that ever, if that is possible."

Marehootie stood slowly and stretched his back. "But I am not finished with my business here."

"There is a warrant for your arrest issued by Governor Canzo. He is gone, along with his sergeant major. Governor Ibarra is new and will have no knowledge of the order. But if Suarez sees you he will find that document and have you arrested and thrown in prison."

Marehootie embraced the priest and kissed him on the cheek. "You worry too much, Father. Perhaps I will see you at Mass on Sunday."

Chapter 17

Five days before the day set for the Utinan Grand Council, Chief Honoroso and his companions arrived at Second Wekiva from the east. Two other village chiefs accompanied him, each with his wife, *inija* and *paracousi.*

One chief had three wives, but only two were with him. "These two travel well together. The other one always makes trouble," he said when he was introduced by Honoroso to Crying Bird and Coya.

All of the war chiefs had warriors with them to provide protection on the journey. Most of the time the heavily armed men, with their faces painted red and fingernails long and sharp, stayed out of sight, scattered in the woods on all sides of their leaders.

By torchlight, Honorosa, Crying Bird and Coya squatted around a deerskin map of the route from Second Wekiva to the village of Ayacouta. At the end of the first day they would reach an old trail that led toward the northwest, and they would camp there. The next day, they would go from trail to trail in a zigzag pattern; it would be three days to their destination, Honoroso said.

Coya studied the map. He took a stick and pointed to a place where two trails crossed. "When we reach this crossroad, Crying Bird and I will go a different way. In a day's time we will join you here," he said, poking the stick into the map where the path crossed a small stream.

Honoroso exchanged a look with his *paracousi*, who was frowning.

"We trust our brothers, but it would be better if we all stayed together. That way, no one will get lost and delay our arrival at Ayacouta."

"Coya has an important errand to accomplish," Crying Bird said. "Only the two of us will leave you, and only for a day."

Honoroso stood. "The country to the east of the trail is wild. No one at all lives there except snakes and wolves."

"I know that land well, having traveled there recently," Coya said, an edge to his voice. "We will not get lost in the woods."

"I was only thinking of the safety of your wife, Mora. She would be more comfortable if she stays with us on the well-traveled trails."

Coya stood up and stretched his back. "Agreed," he said, grasping Honoroso by the arm.

On the morning of the second day, Crying Bird and Coya separated from the others and moved northeast through a thick forest of sweet gum and grapevine. The land gradually dropped off into a bottomland of river swamp, and then rose again on the other side. By midday they were among chalky hills and ravines, with no trails to guide them.

Coya moved so swiftly that Crying Bird had difficulty keeping pace. They arrived at a steep ravine where sunlight glinted on water below.

Coya handed Crying Bird a rope and asked him to tie it around his waist. He looped the other end around a tree. As Crying Bird backed down the hill, Coya gradually released more rope until Crying Bird shouted that he was at the bottom and had not fallen.

Coya lowered himself in the same manner, leaving the end of the rope tied to the tree at the top. "It is our way out," he explained.

Crying Bird was admiring the rock bear. "I thought it was real."

"The cub guards the wealth of Cofahiqui." Coya brushed away fall leaves that had settled on the bear's head.

Here on the sloping bank of the spring, as above, there were signs of the heavy summer rains. Scrub oak and sweet gum leaves had fallen, and were matted together on the ground. Tiny rivulets were cut into the soft earth.

Coya was confident of what he should do, and had planned carefully. He carried a second rope, which he looped around a rock and then tied securely. With Crying Bird watching, he waded as far as he dared.

"There must some safer way –" Crying Bird said.

Coya saw the look of alarm on Crying Bird's face. He smiled at him and then heaved the anchor rock into the spring.

As before, Coya was dragged down against the powerful upward flow of the spring, through the cave opening and into the black underworld. He thought of the dead chief and wondered if he had been transported by his family to his resting place in the same way.

The ancestor was there, as before. In the faint light that filtered down from above, he looked directly at Coya, his jawbone open in a smile, or perhaps a grimace.

The underground stream was at the level it had been before, well below the ledge where the dead man lay next to the leather satchel Coya had put there. The ledge was wet, and small puddles could be seen and felt in low places on the rock. Leaves of scrub oak and sweet gum had washed down through cracks in the rocks above and settled on the ledge. Coya reached out and grasped the leather packet. It was wet to the touch. Water dripped from the rock fissure above onto his hand.

"These will make wonderful gifts for the chiefs of Utina," Crying Bird said as the two of them sat beside the stone bear and unwrapped the bundle. "We have used the wealth of Cofahiqui to fight the Utinans and the Spanish for forty years.

Now it will be used to make peace between Utinans and Acuerans. Perhaps together we can resist the Spanish."

Crying Bird's long, sharpened fingernails struggled to untie the swollen leather binding which was wet and slick with dirt. The sinewy deerskin was wrapped tightly and folded back upon itself so intricately and securely that it took time to open. Finally, Crying Bird reached the inner layer of thin, soft rabbit skin and unwrapped it carefully, disclosing its contents. Even here the inside of the skin was moist and covered with mold.

Crying Bird dipped his hand into the pouch, and then he stood up and moved to where he was sunlit and out of the shadows. He opened his hand to find that the pearls were no longer pearls, but more like small river pebbles of mottled gray and brown. Their luster was gone.

Coya could not speak. There was nothing he could say. He had been entrusted with a fortune, and had lost it by his own carelessness and stupidity. But what did he know of pearls and how they should be cared for? He had done what he thought was right.

Crying Bird continued to inspect what remained.

"I left them in a safe place," Coya said softly. "They were on a ledge above the spring river next to the bones of an ancestor who has not been disturbed in his sleep. I'm sure the water of the spring did not come up to the ledge. Perhaps water from the surface…"

Crying Bird made no reply, but continued to examine the pearls. A few of them, not more than five or six, were not yet discolored, and he set them to the side on a flat limestone rock in the sun.

"Perhaps they will dry and become beautiful again," Coya offered.

Crying Bird's fingers sifted through what remained. He sat back on his haunches and wiped his hands on his loin cloth. "Leave me," he said.

Coya got to his feet and moved carefully up the slope to the trail above, grasping the rope hand over hand. He reached the top and turned and looked back down to where the sunlight reflected the silver of the old man's head.

Crying Bird picked up the pearls he had set aside and placed them with those that were spoiled. He wrapped the bundle much less carefully than when he had unwrapped it. He took the knife from his waistband and held it in the air, reflecting the sunlight.

Coya could hear the prayers the old man offered up, kneeling there beside a secret spring guarded by a bear. They were Acueran prayers, guttural, coarse and unfamiliar to Coya's ear. When Crying Bird was done with his prayers, the knife came slashing down into the leather packet. Over and over he stabbed the deer skin until it was shredded and his fury was spent.

From above, Coya watched as Crying Bird grasped the packet and flung it to the center of the spring pond. The eddying currents swirled the bundle about in a circle. Gradually, as it filled with water, it began to sink slowly. Rising jets of water toyed with the pouch, lifting it momentarily and spinning it about, then releasing it to sink further into the depths, until the next upward stream buoyed it up, shaking the leather bundle once again, loosing and scattering the pearls which sank further down until they were lost from sight.

Eventually, after they had traveled into the nighttime, Crying Bird spoke.

"They were once of great trading value, and when blessed by the *jarva* were powerful magic. Some men died with a pearl in their medicine pouch. I always believed that the pearl made me invisible to my enemies. How else could I have survived so many battles through forty years?

"In time, some of the warriors began to ask for two pearls, or four of them, or more before risking their lives. But as time passed, we all had bits of silver and copper breastplates and mirrors and Spanish beads with which to adorn ourselves. One day, no one at all wanted a pearl.

"Only in the memories of old men who live in the past, like me and Nihoto and Marehootie, did they still hold magic."

Chapter 18

Ayacouta, Utina territory

Ayacouta was overrun with people. More than twenty chiefs, along with their wives, children, and principal men had come from all directions. While the women and children went directly to the river to bathe and refresh themselves from their journey, the men looked for old friends and decided where they would sleep for the night.

"Now I can see why Ayacouta was selected as the site for the Utinan Grand Council," Crying Bird said to Chief Honoroso as they stood inside the massive council house. "There must be seating for five hundred here."

Like all council houses, this one was round, with a fire pit in the center. The royal box, or cabana, stood ten steps above floor level, against the wall directly across from the doorway. Other cabanas at various heights, depending on the rank and importance of its intended occupant, lined the wall. Two separate inner circles of low benches had been built between the cabanas and the fire pit, to accommodate all the men expected to attend.

Crying Bird and Chief Honoroso had walked into the village together, leaving Coya and the rest of their party outside until Crying Bird determined it was safe for them to enter. They had gone first to the grand house of the Chief of

Ayacouta, which stood on a hill in the center of the village, to pay their respects to the chief, and then to the council house to decide where their group would stay the night.

"Osprey got here first," Honoroso said. Crying Bird could see that the royal box was occupied by a tall, muscular young man with fearsome black and yellow markings on his face, dressed in a deer skin match coat. He was surrounded by guards, each wearing the mark of a white quarter moon on his shoulder.

Crying Bird chuckled. "That is what I call an arrogant gesture. Sitting in the royal cabana is his way of telling everyone that it is where he belongs."

"Chief Ayacouta told me that Osprey has been there for two days," Honoroso said. "To avoid a confrontation, Ayacouta invited the interim chief, Antonico, to sleep in the chief's house. Osprey may sleep there tonight, but he will surrender the cabana to Antonico before the council begins tomorrow."

Osprey had fifty men with him, including three chiefs who had been vassals of his father. Others came from the river villages, loud and uncultured and well-armed. "They are the dregs of Utina, the worst of the worst," Honoroso said in a low voice, so as not to be overheard. "Some are criminals and outcasts from their own villages."

"I do not see that he has a musket with him," Crying Bird said.

"The village chief forbade Osprey from carrying the weapon. Osprey does not want to anger Chief Ayacouta, since he is an influential voice on the council. Osprey has a camp nearby and he probably left the musket there."

"He resembles his father," Crying Bird said. "The way he sits there, trying to look regal with his chin high."

"Arrogant people sometimes make strong leaders," Honoroso said.

Other chiefs chose to stay at a smaller council house in a nearby village, and thus avoid Osprey's bullies. Honoroso suggested to Crying Bird that they do the same.

"This is a fine council house. There is room for two hundred or more people to sleep comfortably here. This is where we will spend the night," Crying Bird said.

When Coya arrived with his guards and the rest of the party from Wekiva, they selected low benches to lie on, choosing warm comfort near the fire over the chilly status of high cabanas. Two men were chosen by Honoroso to remain awake while the others slept. Mora and the other women and children went to stay with the women and children of Ayacouta in their houses.

Osprey sat on the highest bench, staring intently across at Coya, who ignored him and rested comfortably on the other side of the fire.

In the middle of the night, Osprey sounded the shrill bird call of his namesake, to the delight of those of his gang who were still awake, and to the terror of some on the other side. Crying Bird slept so soundly he did not hear it. Coya rolled to his side, pulling the deerskin close around his shoulders, his back to Osprey. He found it difficult to get back to sleep.

The Grand Council of Utina began at midday. The house had been cleared of the sleeping men at sun up, and cleaned thoroughly by the women. A cooking fire was lit in the hearth and yaupon leaves were roasted and then boiled for cassina. Honoroso suggested to the village chief that the leaves brought by the guests from Wekiva be used to make the ceremonial brew. "Our former enemies honor Utina with the best they have. It would be impolite to reject their offer of friendship," he said.

Crying Bird, Coya and the others from Wekiva were shown where they should sit, on the lowest benches, nearest the hearth. They were not the best seats in the house, close to the women working the cooking pots and far from the cabanas of the highest chiefs.

As the royal procession began, the *inijas* entered first, each of them strutting into the council house wearing colorful costumes and bodily ornaments of shell and beads and shiny copper. They circled completely around the hearth before climbing to their assigned stations.

Paracousi were next, entering to the sound of beating drums, they circled about the house in a whirling war dance, with fiercely painted faces and headdresses of panther, fox, and wolf skins.

When Osprey entered he was by himself, and he walked slowly around the circle to the beat of a single deep drum, his arms held high in greeting. Here and there, people rose to their feet and saluted him with bird calls and upraised fists.

Crying Bird leaned toward Coya. "He is honored as The Beloved Son of Olate Ouai Utina," he said.

When his stately parade was finished, Osprey climbed slowly to the top, to where he stood by the highest seat of honor. He gestured as if to sit down, then turned and spread his arms wide, as if asking consent. The young men roared their approval. When the din stilled, Osprey took one step down and to the side and seated himself in the second highest cabana.

One by one, twenty-seven chiefs made their entries, each receiving, in turn, a boisterous salute. They wore winter match coats of fine deer hide, painted with the images of small animals and birds and decorated with beads and jewels and all manner of colorful feathers. One wore a collar of a fat rattlesnake, and he flicked it with his fingers making it rattle.

Honoroso, chief of the river village of Coya, made a dignified entry and was saluted respectfully. Chief Chilili strolled by Coya in the procession. When he was directly in front of the young man, he paused and embraced him. Derisive catcalls were drowned out by boisterous shouts of approval.

When the chiefs had taken their places, they remained standing. Antonico's entry was subdued, but dignified, compared to the others. His face was both tattooed and painted bright red, and his lips dyed the color of the sky. He wore a resplendent cape of turkey feather. His hair was embroidered with sea shells and the feathers of sea birds.

As the Interim *Holata* of Utina ascended to his place, he received a howling salute. Only Osprey looked away and would not rise or acknowledge him.

———

The cassina ceremony was followed by half a day of speeches. The chief of the village of Ayacouta greeted the men. He noted that this was the first Grand Utinan Council in more than thirty years.

Each visiting chief was introduced in turn, and they all presented the greetings of their people. They reported on important matters, such as recent deaths in their villages and whether they had experienced good rains and bountiful crops. When they were done, Antonico remarked that it was the first time no one complained of being warred upon by their neighbors.

Coya, having not slept well the night before, struggled to stay awake. When his head nodded, Crying Bird gave him cassina to drink, and Coya was soon alert and listening.

A banquet of turkey and maize was served by cooks who delivered the food to the boxes and benches where the men sat. As a special treat, Honoroso had brought smoked manatee from the river. It was a delicacy many of the western Utinans had never tasted.

The sun was setting as the men walked around outside while the council house was again cleaned, and the food removed. Before they could reenter, the *jarvas* held a secret ceremony, purifying the house and summoning the spirits of the ancestors to attend and bless what was to occur.

When they were again assembled, the Supreme *Jarva* of Utina was the first to speak. The house was silent as his voice boomed from where he stood beside Antonico's cabana. The *jarva* told first the story of creation, of the Utina's entry into the world. Other *jarvas* and shaman nodded their agreement as he related ancient stories of spirits who created, blessed, and led the Utinan Nation.

He spoke of the revered ancestors, the soul of the Utina. He reminded them of wars, and princely chiefs, and of their greatest leader, Olate Ouai Utina who watched over them from the other world.

"Now we come together in the presence of our ancestors, and with their guidance, to choose *Holata Aco,* Chief of all Utina. The wisdom and blessings of the spirits abide with us. Before the sun rises again, we will have chosen rightly." he said.

Antonico stood. He spoke in a quiet tone, but so resonant was his voice that everyone could hear what he had to say. He reminded them that the questioning of a future chief was to be done in a respectful manner, and that once he was chosen by the council, the *Holata Aco* would never again answer to any man. His will and his word would be law.

A quiet descended upon the house. Antonico reminded the assembly that only a very few living men had ever attended such a council. Even here, only the chiefs, the paramount *inija*, and the most experienced and eldest *jarva* could speak or ask questions.

"The Great Chief of the village of Coya has asked for the opportunity to share his wisdom with us," he said.

Chief Honoroso stood in his place in the second row of cabanas. His voice was not as strong as some, and he forced his words out so that he might be heard by everyone.

He spoke of the birth of a child to a sister of Chief Olate Ouai Utina, in the village of Coya on the River of the Sun, sixteen summers past. He said that the child had been orphaned when his mother passed into the world of spirit, and that it was the wise decision of his uncle, Olate Ouai Utina, that the child be delivered to the Spanish governor, that the Utina might learn the ways of the Spanish people, and to establish a firm bond of kinship and trust between the two peoples.

"Now, as divinely predestined, he has been returned to the bosom of his people, wise and cultured beyond his years and learned in the ways of the Spanish," he said. "It is the greatest honor of my life to stand before this great council and sponsor him that you may question him and find him worthy, or not, as your collective wisdom, and the spirits of the ancestors who are with us, may determine."

"Do not try to remember what you have been taught," Crying Bird whispered. "Be slow to answer, but speak plainly and from your heart."

Coya stood, and walked slowly around the hearth.

"He walks like a chicken!" someone said out loud from the lower benches as Coya passed by. Laughter broke out among some of the young men. Antonico's stick crashed against the boards and the laughter stopped.

Coya continued to his place directly in front of the *inija.*

"What is your name?" the *inija* asked.

"I am called Juan de Coya by the Spanish. I am now called Coya, after the village of my birth. I am the nephew of Olate Ouai Utina, the only child of his eldest sister. The genealogy related by Chief Honoroso is correct. I am White Deer. I do not remember my father, but I am told he was Earth Clan."

A murmur passed through the house. From above, Antonico rapped the boards of his cabana with his attention stick. "Quiet!" he commanded, "that we may hear his every word."

"I ask now what many have asked," the *inija* said. "Are you Spanish or are you one of us?"

Coya paused. What was it Crying Bird had said? *Speak the truth. Speak from the heart.*

"I am as Utina as any man here. The spirits of the ancestors dwell within me, and speak to me." Coya paused, and looked into the faces that surrounded him on every side. "But I am different from some of you. I was taught by the Spanish priests. I speak their tongue and, as much as possible for any Indian, I understand their ways." Coya paused once again, then spoke further.

"There is more you should know. I know the Spanish God. I speak to him, and in my heart he speaks to me." A gasp went through the house at the amazing things that had been said. Crying Bird's face was a mask, as if nothing had come as a surprise. When Antonico's stick brought no silence, every *jarva* in the house banged their sticks until quiet was restored.

"And does this spirit, this Spanish God, give you special powers?" the *inija* asked.

Coya looked toward Chief Chilili, and motioned for him to stand. "Chief Chilili wears the cloak of a panther I killed. How many of your young men have done that alone, and with only a knife for a weapon?"

Every eye turned to gaze at Chilili, who stood proudly displaying his coat.

"And I have been known to charm song birds from the trees," Coya said.

When the *inija* finished, the *Jarva* of Utina had questions to test Coya's knowledge of the spirit world, and of the traditions of the Utina. He would not ask questions of White Deer Clan beliefs, since there were people present from other clans.

Coya answered every question as he had been taught by the one-armed *jarva* of the village of Coya before his death.

"What is your understanding of the soul?" the eldest *jarva* asked, finally.

"Which do you mean?" Coya said. "The soul that dwells in a man's eye and goes to sleep but stays with him in death? Or do you ask of the soul that is seen in a man's shadow? Or do you want me to explain the soul that shows itself in a pool of water, the one that resides in the memory of others?"

The *jarva* spoke to other *jarvas* clustered around him, and then turned to Coya once again. "You have answered every question correctly," he said, taking his seat.

Coya let out a long breath, relieved that he had passed the test.

The *inija* rose to his feet, saying he had one last question to ask. "What do the Spanish priests know of the souls, if anything?" he asked.

"They say it differently," Coya responded. "The friars speak of a man as having but one soul, and that one can belong to their God or to his opposite, whom they call the Devil. And yet a man can have three spirits dwelling in him. They are called The Father, The Son, and The Holy Spirit."

The *inija* waved his hand back and forth in front of his face, as if swatting away mosquitoes. “Too much for me. Too much for me. In the future I will leave that sort of questioning to a *jarva*,” he said, laughing as he retook his seat.

So it went through the night. When they had no further questions for Coya, he sat, and Osprey strolled down the benches, and around the floor, gesturing to his friends. As he passed where Coya sat, Osprey playfully swatted at his face and would have slapped him if Coya had not reached out and grabbed his wrist.

In an instant, their eyes met. Others might have seen the smile on Osprey’s face. Coya saw only the angry redness in his eyes. Coya held Osprey’s arm a moment longer than was necessary, then released it.

A chief from a river village invited Osprey to relate his many experiences in war, and Osprey talked for a long time about battles the Utina and the Spanish had fought against the Potano, the Mayaca and the Ais. He bragged of the men he had killed and how he ignored their cries for mercy.

Chief Honoroso stood and was acknowledged.

“What we all want to know,” he said gesturing so as to include everyone, “is what claim a Bird Clan member can make to leadership. My good friend Chilili is White Deer, as is Coya, and Antonico, and your own father, Olate Ouai Utina, as well as every chief here, and their *inijas*. Meaning no disrespect, but Bird Clan are suited to the work of great hunters and many are fearless warriors. Since the beginning of the third world, the wisdom of leadership has resided only among White Deer. It is into the ear of White Deer that the Spirit of Thunder speaks.”

Throughout the house, many men leaned forward listening closely. Some of Osprey's people exchanged worried looks.

“It occurs to me,” Honoroso said, “and I have heard others say that you would be better suited to be *Paracousi* of Utina. That would be Coya’s decision, but I for one, could recommend it to him if he asked me.”

“My father nullified that rule,” Osprey said in a loud voice. “The Spanish men pass power to their sons, not to their nephews. That is a good rule, and my father Olate Ouai Utina was wise to adopt it as our rule also."

Murmurs passed though the council house, particularly among the western and northern Utinans, who sat together.

Chief Chilili was next to question Osprey. "What do you say of the Acuerans? They have been our enemies, but now they talk of peace."

Osprey hawked deeply in his throat and spit on the floor.

Chilili spoke again. "They are here with us now. What do you say to Crying Bird, the one they call *Atichicolo-Iri,* the Spirit Warrior? He now comes as a friend of Utina."

Osprey turned around, so he could see Crying Bird, where he sat next to Coya.

"I say this to Crying Bird and to his band of murderers and to the phony Spanish town Indian he carries about." He spat again, not nearly far enough. His spittle reached only the coals of the fire where it sizzled and was gone.

Two chiefs rose to speak for Osprey. They argued that he was a strong leader, valiant warrior, and a suitable successor to Olate Ouai Utina whose name they invoked frequently in their arguments.

Chief Honoroso stood to recommend Coya, who, he argued, was the only one qualified, the only White Deer, as tradition required.

Chilili also spoke for Coya. "I am his father-in-law, but more than that, I would be his vassal."

Others spoke of the tradition of White Deer leadership, and its importance to Utinan society. Before daybreak, the decision was obvious to everyone. Only two chiefs had spoken against Coya, and they were from the lower river, where Osprey's influence was greatest.

The son of Olate Ouai Utina slipped out of the council house with four or five of his companions, almost unnoticed.

Antonico invited Coya to come to his cabana and handed him his royal staff. Antonico then stepped down and slowly walked to the doorway, his responsibilities ended. As he opened the leather door flap to go outside, the first rays of a new sun entered the house.

The two chiefs who had spoken for Osprey came to Coya after the council ended, kissed his hand, and pledged their support.

Too excited to sleep, Crying Bird and Coya walked together in the woods behind the council house. "Tell me once again about the birds you charmed from the trees," Crying Bird said.

"That was the strangest thing. They were attracted to me. One even landed on my head."

"What kind of birds were they?"

"They looked like blue jays, but the coloring was different. They have no top knot like a blue jay. Sometimes they sound like a blue jay, sometimes like a warbler. Why do you ask?"

Crying Bird stopped the boy and looked him in the eye. "Find something else to brag about, Coya. Those birds are called scrub jays or camp birds. Many people have seen them. They will come out to play with anyone other than a fox or a bobcat."

Chapter 19

San Augustín

Marehootie did not sleep well in the council house at Soloy. Traders conducted their business into the night, selling deer hides and curing herbs to soldiers and the people of San Augustín who sought them out. When there were no customers, the traders gambled among themselves, making it impossible to sleep.

Nihoto, blessed with deafness, slept peacefully until Marehootie shook him awake. At daybreak, the traders had left for the Saturday market where they would display their goods alongside those of the Indians who lived in the village.

When they were alone, Marehootie spoke to Nihoto, using his lips and hands. "Are you excited today? This is the day you begin your journey home."

Nihoto made a sour face. "Forty years my home has been with you. No one remembers me at Cofahiqui."

Nihoto's manner of speaking was mumbled and indistinct, because he could not hear his own voice. To Marehootie, who was with him every day, it was just another language and he understood well what Nihoto said.

"You have children and grandchildren. The traders who come from Cofahiqui have told us of them."

"I left them when they were babies. They will not know me, or even remember my name," Nihoto said.

"Still, you are more fortunate than I. You have children, even if you do not know them, and you have a village where you can go to die. I have no one at all, no heirs and no village. My sister Amita and her child are here. I will ask them if they will bury my bones when I have gone to the spirit world. My place is here with them. Your place is with your clan."

Nihoto shook his head. "You are my clan. When you die, it should be me who buries your bones."

"Then, who will bury Nihoto?" Marehootie asked.

A trader from the north who was done with his business at the Spanish town agreed to take Nihoto with him, at least as far as the trader's village in Guale. From there it would be only two days travel by river to Cofahiqui.

Marehootie offered the man six pearls from the strand he wore around his neck if he would assure him that Nihoto would be delivered home.

The trader looked at the pearls. "Where I am going, these pearls are common. Do you have coins?"

Marehootie reached into his pouch and withdrew three of the reales he had gotten for the canoe. "I have these," he said.

"That will be enough to buy your friend passage to Guale." The trader reached to take the coins, but Marehootie's hand snapped shut.

"Two of the coins are for you. The other is for the man who delivers him to Cofahiqui."

"You can trust me on that," the trader said.

"I don't have to trust you. If you think Nihoto is simple-minded you would be making a mistake. He understands everything, and he has killed more men than you could count. And you will notice that he sleeps with one eye open."

The trader watched as Nihoto picked up two heavy bundles as if they were feathers, and placed them in the canoe.

The old Acueran and the Cofahiquan embraced for the last time. Marehootie was emotional, and fought against his tears. Nihoto was merely angry.

Marehootie turned away from the river with a heavy heart, and struggled on his crutch up the sloping hill toward the town. The bell in the tower of Misión Nombre de Dios announced that it was midday, the time he had agreed to meet Amita and her daughter in the market.

The door of the archive remained closed, even while the attendant was on duty. A small window offered little light. Only a solitary oil lamp provided enough illumination for Suarez, with one eye, to study the military and government records entrusted to him by the offices of the sergeant major and of the governor.

He took the copy of a dispatch that had been sent to the ensign of a coastal vessel, containing the manifest for the Tuesday sailing, folded it and put it in its packet. Suarez walked along the narrow passageway between stacks of leather trunks and wooden boxes, some reaching above his head and wedged into place against the ceiling.

Each box was inscribed on its side with a code, signifying the nature of its contents. Nowhere was the code recorded, except in the memory of the archivist.

Governor Canzo had dealt harshly with Suarez in the aftermath of the events at San Juan del Puerto. Without evidence to charge or prove dereliction of duty, the governor had, nonetheless, stripped him of his rank and dismissed him from the Army of the King of Spain.

It was the worst time of his life. With no income and no commissary privileges, Suarez walked the streets of San Augustín after he left the hospital. One eye was removed by the priest, de Avila, and Suarez wore a black patch to hide the horror of the hole that remained. The patch could not hide the burn scars that covered half his face, the charred stump of a missing ear, nor the pig-like nose.

The sight of him frightened the children, and they hid behind their mothers' skirts in the market where Suarez begged for food. Later, when the children had lost their fear, they sometimes pelted him with rotten fruit and taunted him with laughter and insults.

The priest at the cathedral of San Augustín fed him, placing a bowl of soup or stew and sometimes a piece of bread at the back door of the church in the evening. On rainy days, the priest left the door unlocked so that Suarez could take shelter from the weather. Soon, he began to sleep inside the church.

When the priest caught him stealing from the poor box, he ran him out and chased him down the street. From that day on, there was no more church food for Suarez, and the back door was securely latched.

Suarez stood on a three-legged stool and removed two boxes from a stack. Beneath them was the box marked with a code signifying that it contained naval orders and manifests. When he'd filed the dispatch in its proper place, he closed the box and restacked the other two on top of it. He went back to his desk and inspected the next document to be analyzed and filed away.

Suarez' luck had changed when Governor Canzo returned to Spain along with Sergeant Major Gonsalves, and with the arrival of Governor Pedro Ibarra. The man who had been archivist was murdered the first week after Governor Ibarra took office. No one was charged with the killing. Suarez presented himself for the position and when no one else was found who could read and write, or who could be spared for the job, he was made archivist.

Suarez was now allowed to take his daily meal at the commissary with the soldiers. He was also paid a pittance for housing. Instead of using it, Suarez slept on the floor of the archive. He saved his housing allowance in hopes that he would one day have enough to buy passage to Spain. He calculated that it would take six years.

The bell sounded from the mission church. It was time to eat. He folded the document, stacked it with the others, and locked the door on his way out.

Marehootie found Amita with her blanket spread under a tree, displaying glazed and painted bowls and pots. The young woman with her sold sun bonnets and clothing. She was dressed neither as an Indian, nor as a proper Spanish lady. She was in Spanish attire, but her blouse was cut low in front and the tops of her breasts could be seen.

Marehootie hugged his sister, and they kissed each other on the cheek. When he took Louisa in his arms Marehootie smelled flowers. Acueran women smoked their skirts with sweet-smelling herbs to attract men, but this sweetness was much stronger. "You smell as sweet as your mother's spirit," he said.

Marehootie laid aside his crutch and sat between them. One woman stopped and felt of the material Louisa had and asked her how much she would charge to make a gown. Another could not decide if she should buy a pot, and finally walked away. Only the merchant selling a few vegetables had success. He soon sold all he had and left.

"After siesta, the people will come back to buy," Louisa said.

"I hope some day you meet our brother Crying Bird," Amita said to her daughter. "He was always so handsome. He never married, did he, Marehootie?" she asked.

"No. His life was much too busy. He was greatly honored in Acuera all his life."

Louisa appeared bored with the conversation of old people and looked about at the shoppers and passing soldiers. During a lull in the conversation, she turned to Marehootie. "The only Acueran who is talked about here is called *Atichicolo-iri*," she said.

Marehootie looked at his sister, and then at Louisa. "What do you know of *Atichicolo-iri*?"

"All the soldiers know of him. They say he is a murderer who moves like a ghost and can never be caught. They also say he has a brother who is just as bad."

"That would not be my brother. He is a great shaman, not a warrior." Marehootie struggled to his feet, using his crutch. "I have Spanish coins, but I do not know their value. You must help me buy gifts for my beautiful sister, and for her sweet-smelling daughter."

Louisa looked at the three coins Marehootie carried. "Enough for gifts for us all," she said.

They walked across the road to where a merchant displayed brightly colored Spanish fabric. Louisa bargained with him for a bolt of yellow cloth, and when he lowered his price to one Spanish reale, she handed him one of Marehootie's coins. Amita cried when she saw that Louisa meant the cloth for her.

Louisa refused to allow Marehootie to spend his money on her, but changed her mind when the merchant showed her a colorful scarf from Mexico. He also displayed knives with blades of green obsidian that interested Marehootie.

"They also come from Mexico," the merchant said. "These came in by boat three days ago."

Marehootie examined the blade in the sunlight, turning it about. "How much is this worth?" he asked, turning toward Louisa.

Before she could answer, there was a loud commotion and shouts of alarm from people standing nearby. A man rushed toward them holding a knife in his hand. Marehootie pushed Louisa out of the way.

Marehootie recognized the attacker as soon as he saw him. The man was now grotesquely ugly, but it was he, the sergeant called Suarez.

Marehootie's crutch leaned against the vendor's stall. He had only the obsidian knife to defend himself, and he turned to meet the charge. Suddenly Suarez was knocked to the ground.

Nihoto was upon the Spaniard and began beating him about the head and face. The knife had been jarred loose from Suarez' hand in the fall and he groped about for it with his right hand while trying to stave off Nihoto's blows with the other. Without his crutch, Marehootie moved forward, determined to kick the knife away from Suarez. Nihoto stuck his thumb in the man's good eye, but the Spaniard had found his knife and he plunged it into the side of the deaf Cofahiquan.

Marehootie fell on them both, and the green blade in his hand ran red with Spanish blood.

Marehootie felt the kick from a soldier's boot, and he did not resist as the knife was taken from him. He lay on his side, looking into the open, lifeless eyes of Nihoto. He looked up into the angry faces of the soldiers and bystanders. He saw Amita, her hands covering her face as she cried, and Louisa comforting her.

Among the faces in the crowd he saw Father de Avila. As he was dragged away by the soldiers, Marehootie shouted to him, "Tell the priest. Tell Pareja how it happened. He will protect me. And get my crutch. I will need it."

Chapter 20

Ayacouta

Coya soon learned that becoming *Holata Aco* of Utina was easier than being *Holata Aco* of Utina. He was trained to pass the test, to gain approval of the Grand Council, and in that he succeeded. But nothing prepared him for, and he had given little thought to, what would follow.

Who would become *Inija* of Utina, his second in command? Who would be *Jarva* of Utina and who would be *Paracousi*? He had no power to remove village chiefs or to replace them. That was for White Deer Clan of each village to decide. But who would be his vassal chiefs to rule over the provinces?

"First, the people want to know where you will make your home," Chilili said as Coya sat with the elders in the house of Ayacouta's Chief. It was the morning of the second day of his reign, and Coya had not slept.

Honoroso disagreed. "I think the first thing to decide is by what name we shall call you."

Coya looked into their faces. Crying Bird was not among them. He was Acueran. This was Utinan business.

Through the morning and afternoon and the night that followed, shamans and *jarvas* and medicine men from across Utina danced outside the house, chanting prayers, scattering secret pollens and other magical talismans, and invoking the attendance and blessings of their ancestors. The eldest and wisest *jarva*, his face hideously stained red and black and wearing the ears of a great horned owl on his head, waved a broom about to chase away evil spirits.

After he had listened to his advisors and given the matter deep thought, Coya made his first decision. "I will be called Coya Ayacouta Utina," he said. "The name honors me, tells where I will reside and commemorates the greatest of all chiefs, Olate Ouai Utina."

By midday Coya had announced that the senior *Jarva* of Utina, who had a powerful understanding of the spirit world, should be retained. There were six other *jarvas* who coveted the position, all younger and more energetic. Unfortunately, only the oldest man had ever conducted *Tacachale*, and by custom the ceremony had to begin on the tenth day after the new chief was chosen.

The other *jarvas* had gone away seemingly satisfied with Coya's decision. As they left, Chilili leaned over to whisper in Coya's ear. "None of them wanted to lead *Tacachale* as their first act as *jarva*. Let the old man do it. If he makes a mistake, they will tell you about it."

The sun was setting as word went out concerning other appointments. Coya chose only men he knew and trusted. Big Bow would be *Paracousi* of Utina. Honoroso would be Coya's vassal chief over the fifteen villages near the River of the Sun. For the upland and lake province, Chilili would be the leader, with twelve village chiefs reporting to him.

For half a day they discussed what must be done to prepare for *Tacachale.* Four hundred leaders had come to Ayacouta for the council meeting. For *Tacachale,* since everyone would come with their wives and children, there might be five times that number.

There was no council house ever built that could accommodate that many people. The ceremony would take place outside, at the ball field.

Chiefs and their principal men would sleep in the council house, Coya decided. The four hundred *jarvas*, singers, dancers and musicians would have a shelter prepared for them beyond the ball field.

"I will ask the Chief of Ayacouta to locate camp grounds outside the village for all the others, and assign them to people as they arrive. I will not tolerate arguments or fights over who will sleep where."

The old village chief said he understood, and promised to have his people lay aside sufficient fire wood and kindling, although it would require great effort.

"There is one thing else for us to accomplish," Coya said. Two of the chiefs had already risen and prepared to leave. They sat down immediately.

Coya remained deep in thought, his head down. When he had their full attention he looked up.

"Three years ago a great chief was murdered. You have heard of him. His name was Tacatacura, and he was shot with a Spanish musket when there were no soldiers here. One year ago, Honoroso's *inija*, Acoto, was killed in a brutal manner. His murderer was the same man who killed Tacatacura."

Two of the elders exchanged a look of concern.

"Send out the order throughout Utina. Bring the murderer to me to face justice. Whoever brings him to me, whether he is dead or alive, that man will be my *inija*. Bring me Osprey."

On the day *Tacachale* was to begin, nothing had been heard of Osprey. Three parties of hunters had gone looking and had come back with nothing to report.

"Perhaps he has gone to the Spanish town to enlist soldiers to help him," Honoroso said. "Or it may be that he has killed himself."

Neither explanation seemed likely to Coya.

The village was overwhelmed with people. By midday, there were many more than three thousand, and still they came. Never before, even in the early days of Olate Ouai Utina, before the sicknesses had begun, had so many Utinans congregated. Everywhere Coya walked, he was surrounded by a guard of Big Bow's men who protected him against the crowd of well-wishers and those who would ask favors, or simply wanted to see him up close and touch his match coat.

Crying Bird came with people from Second Wekiva, including Yano, the toothless chief of no vassals. Yano was still strong, despite his years, but sometimes wandered away and got lost.

Crying Bird had also brought with him the nephew of Chief Potano as a special guest. He was the first of his tribe in forty years to walk into an Utinan village, other than those who had come chained as slaves. Coya ordered Big Bow to provide three strong guards to protect the Potanan from harm.

Coya rested during the afternoon. He lay in the fine new house that had been built for him, with his wife beside him. Mora's face had been painted by the beauty women, and she had bathed in flower water. Her head was encircled with flowers, and her eyelids and lips were painted the color of the sky. There would be time to repair her face and to dress for *Tacachale* after being with her husband.

When they had made love, Coya laid back and closed his eyes. The excitement of the past ten days and the lack of sleep had sapped his strength, and he needed to rest for awhile. He heard the voices of the men outside as they prepared for the ceremony, carrying wood for the fire and benches from the council house. The soft sound of chanters rehearsing beyond the ball field drifted into his consciousness and blended there with wind rustling through a forest of trees.

When he cried out, Mora went to him. "You were dreaming, my love," she said. She sat next to him and held him in her arms.

Coya's shoulders shook and he breathed heavily. When he was fully awake, he spoke. "I was in a dark forest and alone and could not find my way. I was on a trail, and the light through the trees showed me only where to take my next steps.

I feared I might be walking into an ambush or a trap, and had no one to ask, so I stopped. But then there was another trail that crossed the one I walked. I knew I could not go back, but must decide which way to turn, or whether to go straight ahead."

Coya stood and walked to the door and threw back the flap, looking out at the activity in the village. He turned back to face his wife.

"Down the trail to the left I could hear the sounds of Catholic prayers, and I could see Father Pareja there, weeping. I knew it was for me he suffered. I wanted to say, 'forgive me Father, for I have sinned,' that he might hear my confession and absolve me. But all I could say was, '*paqe-paqe,*' as an Acueran might in begging forgiveness. He did not understand me, and he looked away."

"It was just a dream. You –"

"Wait, there's more," Coya said. "A man stood in the middle of the trail to my right. He was in the shadows and I could not see his face, but he held his arms up to the sky and prayed."

"Let the dream fade from your memory, or you will never escape it," Mora said.

"I know the prayer. It was in the Acueran tongue. It went like this: '*Oh yaa tan-a-nay-a-ma-no ibiri-hiro.*'"

"Stop it! You are frightening me," she said, placing her hand over his mouth.

He gently took her by the wrist and pulled her hand away. "Hear me out. Ahead of me on the trail there was another spirit who beckoned to me and spoke softly. I recognized him as soon as I heard his voice. It was Marehootie, and he was telling me something important. I tried to hear him, but his voice was drowned out by another voice, repeating, '*Oh yaa tan-a-nay-a-ma-no ibiri-hiro,*' over and over, louder and louder."

"Shhh," Mora whispered in his ear, now holding him in her arms.

From just outside the door someone coughed. It was *Jarva* of Utina who had arrived to escort the *Holata Aco* of Utina to *Tacachale.*

For three nights and two days, without stopping, *Tacachale*, the celebration of a new fire, continued. To the side, pots of cooling cassina stood by to slake the thirst of the dancers, and to give them strength.

On the afternoon of the second day, the chiefs and elders of every village of Utina paraded before Coya's cabana, presenting gifts of tribute while he looked down on them from his high place.

On the second night, the Story of Utina was told, as the *jarva* directed the performance of the actors who represented the ancestors, telling of their great deeds of courage and sacrifice.

The air was cool, but the exertions of the dancers were so great that the dry earth was soaked with their sweat, and became mud that clung to their feet. Where they had danced around the central hearth, the ground was sunken, the way an animal trail grooves the floor of the forest.

The prayers of the *Jarva* of Utina, those of lesser *jarvas,* and the herbal magic of the *isucus* were lifted up into the darkness of the last night, as they had been from the beginning of the world. There was only one change from tradition, and it was on Coya's direct order. The boasting of warrior valor, the curses on their enemies, and the exhortations to dismember their bodies and scatter their blood was left out of the ceremony.

Here and there, those who were tired, but would not surrender their bench seats, slept in their places, only to be swatted awake by the palmetto whips of the village *jarva*, wandering about keeping discipline.

As the end drew near, *Jarva* signaled to Coya that he step down to stand at the fire. The chanter sang his song, each line higher and louder. "Save *Holata,* Bless *Holata*, Save the people, Bless the people, Prosper Holata, Prosper the people. . ."

For an old man, *Jarva* was lithe and quick and strong as he whirled about the fire. The crescendo of his dancing fed the excitement of the people who chanted with the leader, "Coya Ayacouta, live forever, People of Utina, live forever, Coya Ayacouta . . ."

Jarva released the packet of herbs and green magic into the flame. The explosion of color, sound and light echoed across the playing field, though the village, and beyond. The fire leapt high into the air with a great wind, as high as the trees it illuminated at the edge of the forest.

Those closest to the flame fell from their benches onto the ground. Coya rocked back on his heels, but recovered his balance and stood straight, facing the flame, his arms uplifted in acceptance of, and submission to, his destiny.

Then it was dark, the fire extinguished. Blinded by the sudden light, neither Coya nor the others noticed the second flame, no brighter than an ember jumping from a camp fire. Only Crying Bird, standing beyond the hearth, having shielded his eyes from the *Tacachale* fire, was able to see. He stepped in front of the man with the musket as it roared.

Osprey was blinded by the explosion of his musket, and lay on his back in the mud. He reached to touch his burned face. His right hand, all but severed from his arm, flopped about uselessly.

Crying Bird knelt beside him.

"Send me to be with my father," Osprey whispered.

Crying Bird removed the knife from his waistband and granted Osprey's last wish.

Chapter 21

Winter, 1607

Honoroso and Chilili returned to Ayacouta ten days after *Tacachale*. They brought with them workers for the new council house, and upsetting news for Coya.

"Some people of the river villages do not understand your choice of *inija*," Honoroso said. The three leaders sipped cassina and smoked tobacco in Coya's house early in the morning. Coya said nothing, but waited to hear more. Honoroso glanced at Chilili.

"I have heard the same thing in my own village," Chilili said. "Many ask me to explain it to them, and perhaps I need to hear it from you, so I can answer them correctly."

Coya fixed his father-in-law with a steady gaze. "If I am *Holata Aco*, it is my privilege to choose who I will as my second in command," he said. "You two should go home and say to these troublemakers that Coya Ayacouta Utina chooses who he will to govern them. Remind them that my word is law."

Honoroso laid down his pipe. He crossed his arms and lowered his chin to his chest. The greenstone gorget at his neck reflected the glowing embers of the fire. Presently he looked up. "I am here because I am your only living uncle, and because you may one day be remembered as the greatest of all

Utinan Chiefs. May I speak to you freely, as an uncle to his eldest nephew?"

Coya knew this moment would come when he chose Honoroso and Chilili as his vassal chiefs. Crying Bird had taught him well the lessons of respect. "No," he said. "You will speak to me with the respect owed by a vassal chief to his *Holata Aco*, not as a man might lecture a young pup, as if he knows nothing."

Seeing the look of hurt and surprise in Honoroso's eyes, he went on. "As always, your advice is valuable to me, and I welcome it."

Honoroso sucked on his pipe, and, realizing it had gone out, he relit it before answering Coya.

"These are not the people who followed Osprey and wished him to be the leader, and perhaps blame you for his death, who ask these questions. And they are not troublemakers, as you say. I will not name them unless you order me to, and even then I would prefer to be beaten rather than betray their trust in me.

"It is the elders who are most disturbed, and the shamans and other responsible people. These are the men who spoke for you in the councils and against Osprey, because he was not Utina's nephew, but only his son. They honor tradition and are disturbed by ideas that are new or foreign. More than anyone else, it is White Deer Clan, your own people, who need to understand."

Coya reached out and took the pipe from Honoroso. He drew deeply of the strong tobacco and blew a plume of smoke into the space between them. When it had cleared, he spoke. "They wish to know how a foreigner could serve as *Inija* to a *Holata* of Utina, am I right?"

Honoroso and Chilili nodded solemnly.

"And how, in my absence, a mere Acueran could look after their religious exercises and intervene with the spirits on their behalf in times of trouble. Is that what they say?"

"That is what worries them," Chilili said. Coya pondered the question, looking into the cooling embers of last night's fire.

"Explain it to them this way," he said. "Tell them their spiritual needs are met by me as their chief. When I am away, the *Jarva* of Utina speaks to the spirits on my behalf. Perhaps we should use another title other than *inija,* for Crying Bird, as it seems to confuse them. Perhaps they should look upon Crying Bird as governor. That was what he called himself on the Wekiva. That is what we will call him in Utina."

"That is a good answer with regard to his duties," Chilili said, "but some people will still object to an Acueran having authority over them."

"I have heard the same complaint from some of the chiefs of the river," Honoroso said. "They say it would be embarrassing and unnatural for an Utinan to submit to an Acueran."

Coya stood up and went to the doorway to look out. The skilled workers were erecting the main support poles for the council house roof, sinking the first of eight yellow pine trunks, each measuring exactly nine meters long, into the hole dug for it. Coya wanted to be with them, supervising, rather than sitting indoors all day solving problems.

He turned to face Honoroso and Chilili. "I promised that the man who brought Osprey to justice would be my *inija*. All of you heard me say that in the days before *Tacachale*. You should point out that it was Crying Bird whom the spirits chose as the instrument with which to take Osprey's miserable life. In a way, it was not my decision at all. The ancestors chose Crying Bird to be *Inija* of Utina."

The soldier sent by Governor Ibarra delivered the rolled parchment to the village of Ayacouta soon after Coya was made *Holata Aco*. Coya took it from him and read the Spanish greeting. Those who witnessed it were surprised when he then interpreted what was written into their own tongue.

It was a congratulatory greeting, and an invitation to Coya and his principal men to come to San Augustín to meet the governor, to render obedience and to discuss relations between Utina and the Spanish authorities. Such a journey had already been discussed at council among the leaders of Utina, but it was Coya's judgment that it was too soon, and that he should first consolidate his power and finish the new council house before traveling beyond the province.

"Please convey to the governor my apologies. Perhaps in the spring there will be opportunity for me to visit him," Coya said. It had begun to rain, delaying the soldier's journey, and Coya invited him into his house to talk. Coya would have written his own answer for the governor, but the soldier carried neither parchment nor ink.

"I was in San Augustín as a child, but too young to remember very much about it. I spent my youth at Misión San Juan del Puerto and studied under Father Pareja who taught me to speak in your tongue." Coya was enjoying the opportunity to speak Spanish for the first time in five years. "Do you know of Pareja?" he asked.

"I do not know any of the Franciscans personally," the soldier said. "I sometimes attend Mass at the church in San Augustín. Not very often, I am afraid. But the name Pareja is familiar to me. I believe he is the new custos of missions at the Franciscan monastery."

Coya's eyes opened wide in surprise. "That is very interesting, and gives me one more reason to accept the governor's kind invitation soon."

The soldier rose to leave, promising to deliver Coya's answer to the governor. "It is too bad you cannot come to San Augustín now. It promises to be an interesting time."

"Why is that?" Coya asked.

"We have many visitors coming now, chiefs from all over La Florida. But then you see Indians here all the time so that might not be interesting to you," the soldier said, laughing. "But we do have our little entertainments. For instance, there will be a trial of an Indian accused of killing a Spaniard, a hideous little man who was the governor's archivist. Some people have said it was a fair fight, but they can't just turn loose any old Acueran who kills a Spaniard, now, can they?"

"My influence extends well beyond Utina," Crying Bird said in a voice just loud enough to be understood by the other two men inside the house and none of the men outside who were busily preparing for a sudden journey.

"I can do what I promise. There will be no fewer than fifty warriors, the finest fighters, armed and trained for just this sort of encounter. With surprise working for us, we need only information on where my brother is being kept. In the dark of night, it will be a simple matter to overpower the guards."

Coya was already dressed in his finest clothing for the journey to San Augustín. He wore a new deerskin match coat, a gift from a river chief who had spoken for Osprey, but who now sought Coya's favor. He glanced at Big Bow who sat with his back against the wall on the other side of the room. "What does my *paracousi* say to such a plan?"

Big Bow stirred and rose to his feet to address Coya. "The Spaniards are not fools. They would be alert to a group of strangers lurking about the town. Still, if there were some diversion to draw the soldiers away . . ."

"That worked well once before," Crying Bird said. "Perhaps a fire. The Spanish are afraid of fire. We could burn the church."

"Not the church," Coya said. "And not the convento, if they have one." The sharpness in his voice startled both Big Bow and Crying Bird.

"We do not know what has happened in San Augustín, or where Marehootie is being held. This is no reason to go to war. I am *Holata Aco* of Utina, and have been invited by the governor to come see him. The governor will listen to me. When I tell him Marehootie is harmless, and my own grandfather, he will –"

Coya saw the look of disgust on Crying Bird's face. "You cannot say how many soldiers are about," Coya said, "or how they are armed. It would be foolish to walk into the mouth of the cannon and try to carry away a crippled old man. And Big Bow is right. A force of armed men would attract attention. Soldiers are not stupid about such things."

Crying Bird rose to his feet. "This is Marehootie's life we are talking about. Do you imagine they will just give him up because you ask it? All I ask is that we be prepared to do what we must to save his life."

Coya turned his gaze directly toward Crying Bird. "You will have only twenty men, no more, and you will remain to the west of the river crossing at Tocoi, avoiding contact with the people there. Big Bow will leave some of his guard there to keep you company.

"Big Bow and I will take only six men with us to San Augustín. If the governor will not give him up, at least we will discover where Marehootie is being held. We will send word to you of our plans. It may be impossible to get him out. We don't even know that he is still alive."

He nodded to Big Bow. "In the event we need to take some action to save Marehootie, my *paracousi* will lead the rescue. If it is to happen."

"I should be the one leading the fight," Crying Bird said. "He is my brother. I have led men in battle before either of you was born. This cannot be left to children. This is a task –"

"There will be no fight, no war," Coya shouted. The look of anger on Coya's face stopped Crying Bird cold. He sighed and shook his head sadly, then turned and walked out the door.

The delegation from Utina was housed at Soloy, a short walk from the government offices in the town. The governor's clerk had said they should return the next day, after siesta, when the governor would greet the visiting Indians and present them with gifts, each according to his rank. That would be followed by a banquet on the parade ground, paid for by Governor Ibarra, in which everyone would be invited to partake.

When Big Bow discovered that Coya had left the council house after dark, without a guard, he was upset and gathered some men to go looking for him.

"If he wanted your company, he would have told you to come with him," Chilili said. "Besides, the people here tell me the soldiers patrol the town after dark, and they get nervous when they see groups of Indians. You and your men will stay here until Coya returns."

Coya, the man, looked where Juan de Coya, the boy, would have looked to find Father Pareja after dark.

San Francisco, the new monastery of San Augustín, though much larger than the convento at San Juan del Puerto, was similar in that each had a shaded porch where the priest could meditate in the cool evening air. And there he was, sitting alone, his pipe aglow in the darkness of the church yard.

"Do you need an altar boy to assist you at Mass on Sunday?" Coya called from the shadows across the narrow courtyard between the south wall of the church and the monastery.

The priest looked up and peered into the darkness. "Good altar boys are hard to find," he said, "and once you train them, sometimes they run away."

The priest arose from his chair as Coya stepped onto the porch, and they embraced. "Have I changed so little in five years that you would recognize me so quickly?" Coya asked, tears dampening his cheeks.

"I prayed that you would not change, but change is nothing more than God's unfolding will, so we all must accept it," the priest said. He removed a kerchief from the pocket of his robe and wiped Coya's tears, and then his own.

"But you recognized me, even while I hid myself in the shadows."

Pareja laughed. "I had the advantage on you. I knew you would come, if not today, then tomorrow, or if not tomorrow, it would be soon. I sat here these last few evenings waiting for you. God rewards patience."

"Is it God who told you of my coming?"

"Not God. Only Marehootie, I'm afraid. He bragged to me of your growth, and predicted that someday soon you would become a great chief. When the governor announced there was to be a new *Holata* among the Utinans, Marehootie said they must have selected you. I did not believe him, of course. You know how he likes to make up stories.

"Then word came from the wilderness that the new *Holata* is called Coya Ayacouta Utina. Then I knew it was you, and I knew you would come. So you can see, I was waiting here for you."

The priest invited Coya to sit beside him, and he spoke a prayer of thanksgiving. When he was done, Coya held Pareja's hand as they talked.

"Tell me of Marehootie. A messenger from the governor says he will be tried for murder. When I heard that, I came immediately."

Pareja waved his free hand in the air. "That is settled. Marehootie has admitted he killed Suarez, and the witnesses all say he was trying to protect another man, that Suarez was the aggressor and it was a fair fight."

"So it was Suarez!" Coya said, rocking back on his chair. "I did not know that. I thought he died at San Juan."

Coya gazed into the darkness of the church yard. Above them the full moon came from behind a moving cloud and looked down on them, and then hid its face behind another. "It does seem like God's own justice," he said.

"I prefer to think of it as the Devil's due." A smile creased the priest's face. He crossed himself.

"What have they done with my grandfather?" Coya asked.

The priest's eyebrows arched upward in surprise. "So he is your grandfather now?"

"I have always thought of him that way. And his brother also, he is my other grandfather. They are the only family I have ever known."

A shadow of disappointment flitted across Pareja's face, but was immediately replaced by a broad smile.

"Marehootie is fine. When he was first taken, I'm afraid I threatened the governor with ostracism if a hair on his head was harmed. He was cleared of the criminal charges, but the feelings in town were such that it was decided that he should remain in custody."

Coya put his hands on the arms of the chair, as if to rise. “Where is the Spanish justice in that, imprisoning an innocent man?”

Father Pareja did not answer immediately, but gazed upward at the moon gliding from under a cloud. “Man’s justice is imperfect, but it is a solution that satisfies even Marehootie. When you see him tomorrow you will understand.”

Coya knew that the priest would have nothing more to say on the subject of Marehootie and his captivity. “And what of the man he saved?” he asked.

“Tried to save. I’m afraid he died from Suarez’ knife. Marehootie is very emotional and will not speak of him, but people say the two of them came here together.”

A sob escaped the throat of Coya. “I know the man. He was an old, deaf Indian from Cofahiqui. His name was Nihoto.”

They sat together a long time. The oil lamps around the village were all extinguished. A solitary soldier who had too much wine to drink lay snoring under a tree.

“There is something more I want to say to you. I have prayed about it every day for five years,” Coya said as the priest prepared to go to his bed.

Pareja stopped him. “I still carry wounds to my heart, and I know you must also. You felt that I had betrayed you by abandoning Marehootie to the evil of Suarez. To me, it was you who had abandoned me. Now, as it turns out, it appears to have been preordained.

Coya looked deeply into the friar’s eyes. “Can we just call it God’s unfolding will, and forgive each other?”

Father Pareja wrapped his arms around Coya and held him close. He did not bother with the kerchief to wipe away their tears.

Chapter 22

The palisade wooden fort overlooking the bay of San Augustín was massive, larger than the biggest council house Coya had ever seen. At each of its irregular corners, turrets jutted up and out, twice the height of a man, each armed with cannons and manned by guards with muskets and powerful crossbows.

Walls of interlocked cypress trunks ringed the outside. A double door of vertical pine slabs, hinged on each side, prevented entry. Today one of the doors stood open, and black slaves and Indian workers moved freely in and out carrying timbers and tools under the bored eyes of Spanish soldiers lounging in the shade.

Coya followed in the steps of the priest who nimbly moved among the workmen and their stacked materials, across a dusty yard, beneath the overhanging balcony of a second floor barracks and through a low doorway.

The darkness inside made it difficult for Coya to see, and Pareja waited for him and took him by the hand. "Until you know your way around, perhaps I should lead you. I come here almost every day. I am comfortable here, but I remember how frightening it was the first time." At intervals of thirty feet, oil lamps sputtered, putting out more greasy smoke than light.

They passed a grated door. From inside, cool air escaped. "That is the root cellar. The cooks use it for storage of dried corn and tubers and such."

"And here is the soldiers' armory," Pareja said as they approached another door, "where their hand weapons, armament and chain mail are stored. There is no gun powder stored here. Perhaps they learned from their mistake at San Juan." Pareja laughed over his shoulder as Coya stumbled behind.

They passed a large room where the door was grated and bolted shut. A young private armed with a musket lounged outside and acknowledged Father Pareja with a smile. The smell of stale body odor and filth wafted through the door, and groans and moving chains could be heard from deep in the room, but no light could be seen.

"This is the cell in which they confine the most unruly of the prisoners such as slaves who have run away, and Indians who are caught stealing. Soldiers who are imprisoned are not kept here," Pareja said. "They are lodged on the other side, near the water, so they can bathe in the river once a month."

Coya felt light headed, weak, and in need of fresh air.

They turned a corner and came to a hallway that led down a slope to storage rooms that lined the outside wall of the fort. The second room had a window on the south wall, above ground level. Morning sunlight flooded the room. The door stood wide open.

An old, emaciated Indian lay on a plank bed covered by a woolen blanket, a Spanish Bible on his chest, his hair white and scattered. He was sleeping and his breathing was raspy and labored. The sparse room also contained a single chair and a chamber pot. Against the wall stood a crude wooden table with a bowl of colorful daisies and magnolia blossoms.

"He does not walk now," Pareja whispered. "There is no opportunity for exercise here, as you can see, and he seems content to lie there too much. I have told him he should get up and move about, or he may never walk again. Perhaps you can speak to him."

Marehootie opened one eye and looked around. "You are talking about me behind my back again, Padre?" he said.

Coya moved to Marehootie's bedside and knelt, wrapping his arms around the old Acueran and lifting him so that he was sitting.

"I have never been hugged by a *Holata Aco*," Marehootie said. He held Coya in his bony arms and kissed him on the cheek.

"I have come to fetch you, Nariba." Coya said.

Marehootie and Father Pareja exchanged a look. The priest turned and stepped out of the door. Coya could hear him speaking to the guard.

"Who are you to say I need fetching? I am content here. As you can see, my feet will no longer allow me to walk about, even with a crutch. I have sunlight every day. People come to see me, and I have my work that keeps me busy. Why would I want to leave?"

"What people would come to see a dried up old skeleton?" Coya said, feeling the old man's bony shoulders.

Pareja slipped back into the room and stood in the corner, his arms crossed over his chest.

"I have many visitors. My sister Amita comes each day with food and fresh water and flowers from her garden, as you used to do at San Juan. Sometimes her daughter comes to talk to me. That old priest over there, he comes too on the days he is not too busy. I let him pray over me, and we talk about life and death and God and spirits."

"I need you with me, to help me rule." Coya said. "I will take you to Utina and make you *isucu*. You have so much to teach us about cures and magical medicines."

"Didn't the priest tell you? I'm needed as a teacher here. I teach Indian children to be interpreters in his school at the monastery."

Pareja stepped forward. "On good days he is carried on a donkey wagon to the school. He teaches the students to read and write, and the differences in the Timucuan dialects. Together, we train them to interpret for the new priests before they go to their missions."

Coya looked into Marehootie's face. "Crying Bird needs you too. He is my *inija*, but we call him governor. Most of the Utinans are so in awe of his powers that he can find no one to argue with him."

"Tell me about my brother," the old man said. "Does he still cough during the night? What does he do to occupy his time?"

"Most of the time he takes care of Yano."

"That toothless buzzard?" Marehootie said.

Coya could not suppress a laugh. "Yes, I'm afraid so. When you left Second Wekiva, Yano moved into Crying Bird's house. Now, at Ayacouta, they live together. Crying Bird gives him little jobs to do to keep him busy, but Yano soon forgets and wanders off looking for his people."

Marehootie lay back down and rested his head on a pillow.

"To tell the truth, I do not see him that often since I became *Holata*. His health seems good when he is around me. He never complains or asks the *isucu* for cures."

Marehootie pondered what he had heard, now unsmiling. "Is it, perhaps, that he travels about that you do not see him?"

"You know your brother well. He is away from Ayacouta much of the time. He wants to visit every village in Utina, which is understandable. He was the enemy of the Utinans for many years, and if he is to be governor, it is well that he make peace with his old enemies."

"Is that what he is doing, making peace?" Marehootie said.

Coya looked into Marehootie's eyes. "A strange question," he said.

The old man made no reply, but turned his head and gazed out the window.

Father Pareja spoke. "I must return to my duties. I'm sure you can find your way out." He paused at the door. "I have arranged for the cart to take you to the ceremony," he said, looking at Marehootie.

The old Indian made no reply, but continued to look out at the patch of blue sky and the occasional sea bird that flew past the fort.

Coya waited, respecting the old man's mood.

Finally, Marehootie turned and fixed his eyes on Coya. "I would not disrespect my brother. I would have died for him at any time, without one thought or regret. But I love you also, and for that reason I must give you one word of advice."

There was again stillness in the room. Not even the sound of workmen or calling seagulls intruded. From deep in the nearby jail cell a prisoner suddenly cried out, but then fell silent.

"My brother and I have lived our lives fighting against the Spanish. I have told you the stories, and they were all true," he said, "as far as they went."

Coya reached out his hand and placed his fingers on Marehootie's lips. "You don't have to say anything more to me. I know that in your life you may have killed soldiers, and that you did it for your people, and that in many ways you were justified. I also know that God forgives you, that you have confessed your sins, and that you have changed and that your heart is now right."

Marehootie took Coya's hand and held it tightly in his own.

"My brother has not changed," he said. "He has used his strength and his powers and his magic, and the pearls, and everyone and everything to rid our land of the Spanish by killing them and driving them away. His heart is not changed, and he seeks no forgiveness."

Coya wanted to reply, but now it was the old man's turn to place his fingers on Coya's lips.

"Beware my brother's power over the people. He carries in his heart a fire of hatred for the Spanish. It has been there since he was a child, and will never be extinguished as long as he is alive. He cannot help it. That is why he is called *Atichicolo-Iri*, the Spirit Warrior."

Coya straightened out the old man's hand in his own and inspected the long, thin fingers and the knuckles swollen from a lifetime of use. "Your brother is head-strong, and he does have a fire about him. That makes him a valuable *inija*. The people fear him and respect his powers, so they carry out my orders."

Marehootie pulled his hand from Coya's grasp and folded it with the other on his chest, closing his eyes against the glare from the window. "Tell me, Coya, when Crying Bird is away from your village, whose orders does he carry to the people?"

Coya caught up with Father Pareja as he entered the monastery. "I worry that he has nothing to occupy him. Even if he is so crippled that he cannot walk about, there should be something he can do to stay busy. Perhaps you could interest him in some diversion. He has artistic talents."

"I asked him if he wanted to become a carver," Pareja answered, "but I was forbidden by the sergeant major from bringing knives into the fort."

"For that old man? What harm could he possibly do?" Coya asked.

Father Pareja turned to face the young chief. "You and I know he would not hurt a flea, even if he had the ability, but the Spanish only consider that he killed Suarez with a knife. To them, he cannot be trusted."

"The Spanish are blind fools!" Coya said. "Sorry, Father," he added.

Father Pareja smiled broadly and patted Coya on the shoulder. "Let me give it some thought. Perhaps I can interest our friend in some endeavor that does not require lethal tools."

Later, as the priest and chief sat together over a light meal of parched maize and baked fish in the convento, Coya spoke. "When he is gone, send word to me and I will come and take him with me. He should be buried at Wekiva."

Father Pareja wiped his mouth with his napkin. "We have talked about that, he and I. It is Marehootie's wish that he be laid to rest in the floor of the church at San Juan del Puerto."

Coya looked into his cup of cassina, idly swirling it about. "Would a gift from the Utinan people assure that he will be buried near the altar?"

"That can be arranged," Pareja answered, smiling.

The afternoon sun shone brightly on the whitewashed steps of the Governor's House. Chiefs and principal men from four tribes listened politely as interpreters translated for them what was said. Governor Ibarra spoke eloquently of the King in Spain and of God in Heaven, both of whom loved the Indians and worked tirelessly on their behalf that they might have their souls saved for the next life, and prosper and be happy in this life. When he had nothing more to say, the governor introduced Father Pareja.

The priest told them of the missions established up and down the coast of the ocean, and those stretching southward on the river San Juan. He had with him another priest, Martín Prieto, who was charged with the responsibility of bringing the word of God to pagan Indians whose souls were yet to be saved.

"Some of you, and many of the chiefs of other tribes, have petitioned His Excellency, Governor Ibarra, that he send priests to your lands, that you and your children might be taught the word of God," Pareja said.

"You can see from here," he said gesturing toward the new monastery where the golden rays of the setting sun lighted its portico, "the new home of Franciscan priests in La Florida. We have waited and struggled and prayed for many years that we have a suitable friary in which to train new priests for the missions. It is through the leadership and good heart of His Excellency that it is finally completed." Father Pareja nodded toward the governor and clapped his hands together rhythmically. The honor guard of soldiers and musicians joined in the polite applause while the Indians looked uncertainly at each other.

When the interpreters made Pareja's meaning clear, the Indian women joined in with their chattering, bird-like calls, and their men voiced deep-throated harrumphs of approval, stomping their feet on the ground.

"And there is yet an even more wonderful blessing. Four new priests have come to the province, and are now receiving instruction in your language, that they may understand you better when they move to their duties at new missions to be established among you in the months and years to come."

Father Pareja went on to acknowledge Father Prieto who, he said, would soon organize an expedition to the province of Potano to establish the first mission beyond the River of the Sun.

Later, Coya and three other chiefs stood with their principal men before Ibarra and pledged loyalty and rendered obedience to the governor and his King. A chief from Guale was to be baptized on the Sabbath, and Governor Ibarra would stand with him as his godfather.

Father Pareja introduced Coya to the governor and said he was already a Christian, baptized years ago at Misión San Juan del Puerto.

Gifts were exchanged. The governor gave each chief a metal hoe for digging in the earth, beads, and colorful Spanish cloth and thread for sewing. Gifts from the Indians to the governor included arrobas of maize, deer skins and smoked manatee.

A clerk recorded the names of every Indian attending, with his title, the name of his village and the gifts they received.

Food was brought, and the Indians, the soldiers, and the governor sat together under the trees eating corn venison stew and baked fish. Governor Ibarra sat on the chair and ate at a small table provided for him. The Indians sat on the ground.

As the sun set, the donkey cart carrying the old Indian, Marehootie, made its way back to the fort.

Beyond the River
of
the Sun

Chapter 23

San Francisco de Potano
Summer, 1608

Father Martín Prieto arose from his cot and put on his woolen robe and sandals. He stepped from the crude hut and into the sunlight of a Potano summer morning.

"Not a good day for a walk," he muttered. The moist heat bathed his face and made it difficult to breathe. But walk he must. It was Tuesday, and he was expected to hold midday services in the *visita* of Santa Ana, two leagues to the west. On Thursday he would take the trail to the north, to the *visita* of San Miguel to teach the word of God to the rag-tag band of twenty heathen who farmed there. The other five days of the week he would labor here, in the village of Potano, arguing with the chief, cajoling him to supply enough skilled laborers to make progress in the construction of the mission church that was scheduled for dedication as San Francisco de Potano in less than thirty days.

Father Pareja, the Custos of Missions, had taught Prieto about the history of the chiefdom of Potano before he'd dispatched the priest and his young companion to the province west of the River San Juan. For as long as anyone could remember, so the story went, the Potanans had fought sporadically with their neighbors, the Utinans. Not warfare in the European sense, Pareja said, in which the object was to conquer territory and to inflict maximum casualties, but a more genteel conflict in which people might be killed, but the aggressor would be satisfied to have embarrassed the enemy and perhaps stolen a few women and children to be held as slaves. Later, through marriage or adoption, the slave would be accepted by a clan and incorporated into their new village.

The Utinans had succeeded in allying themselves with the French, and then the Spanish, in their warfare against Potano for the past forty years. Illness and disease decimated the Potanans further until they abandoned their villages along the river and hid in the swamps and less desirable lands to the west.

When old Chief Potano finally died, his nephew, who also called himself Potano, became leader of a dysfunctional, disparate, and dispirited people. To his credit, the young chief's first official act was to travel to San Augustín where he successfully sued for peace.

The terms dictated by the governor were simple and non-negotiable: the Spanish would cease further military operations in Potano, and the Potanans would be allowed to reoccupy the villages they had abandoned along the River San Juan. In turn, Potano pledged obedience to the Spanish government, agreed to supply maize to satisfy the hunger of the people in San Augustín, and to open the province to the Franciscans so the people might be taught Christianity.

Father Prieto and his associate, Father Alonso Serrano, were the first Franciscans dispatched to the province, and San Francisco de Potano was to be the first mission church, with *visitas* in Santa Ana and San Miguel. Beyond those three villages, Chief Potano would not discuss additional missions. Prieto believed Potano was such a weak leader that he lacked the authority over his subjects to expand the missions to the seventeen other Potanan villages scattered about the countryside.

Now, with Serrano having lost his nerve and returned to the comfort of the monastery in San Augustín, the burdensome sense of loneliness and isolation belonged only to Father Prieto. And to God.

In the pocket of his robe, a breviary bounced against his thigh with each long stride, as Father Prieto followed the meandering path that would take him, eventually, to Santa Ana. With his free hand, he used a kerchief to wipe away the sweat that already ran down his forehead and stung his eyes.

The path wound through a thin forest of hickory trees and stands of pine. Here the land was flat, and he could make good time despite the heat of the sun that beat down on him. Soon, the going became more difficult. The trail crossed a deep ravine, and as he descended, he grasped thorny bushes and briars to help him keep his footing.

Prieto stepped nimbly across the stream at the bottom of the ravine, and struggled to climb the steep hill on the other side. He paused to catch his breath.

It was then that he spied the strand of brown threads clinging to a bush of dense thorns. The threads were of the same cloth he wore, from a Franciscan robe. Serrano had come this way as he fled in terror from Santa Ana a week earlier.

Prieto had been supervising the Indians at San Francisco in the construction of the church when the natives stopped their work at midday, turning their heads about, listening.

Serrano burst from the forest, shrieking in fear. When Prieto first caught sight of him, he feared the younger man had been attacked by a panther or some other wild beast. His face and hands were stained with blood, and his robe hung in tatters. Serrano ran directly to the hut the two priests shared. When Prieto reached the house, he found the young priest lying on the dirt floor, his knees drawn up to his chest, whimpering and praying to God for mercy.

Later, with his wits restored, Serrano told Father Prieto what had occurred at Santa Ana. Things had gone well at first, he said. Each of the priests had been there several times before, and the Indians, if not eager for his message, were at least curious about what he had to tell them of the Spanish God.

Serrano had preached against the graven images of animal spirits the Indians displayed at the door of their council house, and elsewhere scattered throughout the village. "I said they were sinful graven images, and evil distractions from the word of God," he said, sobbing. "I tore them down and would have burned them, but their leaders turned on me and showed their anger by taunting me with their spears, cutting through my robe and pricking my skin."

Father Prieto bathed the cuts, those from the spear points and those from the briars and brambles Father Serrano had encountered as he fled his tormentors. He employed what little medical training he had received from Father Pareja, along with suggestions of the Potanan medicine man. Poultices of tree fungus and spider webs were applied, fixed in place with wrappings of palmetto fiber where the wound was to an arm or leg.

"These wounds were not meant to kill you," Father Prieto said. "They are superficial, and if we can prevent infection, you should be as good as new in a few days."

Indeed, within three days the cuts were scabbing over, and Father Prieto was quite proud of his work. Serrano was not so sanguine. He felt his own forehead and sensed a heat there, which he interpreted as the fever of some tropical infection. To Prieto, Serrano's skin was no warmer than his own.

A single thorn had penetrated the priest's leg, just above his ankle, and yet he insisted on the second day that it was the fang mark of a poisonous serpent, and that he should die if he were not straightaway removed to San Augustín, where he could receive proper medical attention.

"Alonso, snakes do not ordinarily attack with but one fang," Prieto said to reassure his young friend.

When Serrano openly questioned Prieto's medical competence and complained of the poisons flowing through his body, Prieto knew it was an argument he could not win.

"Perhaps you should return to San Augustín tomorrow," Prieto said. "When you are recovered sufficiently, you can rejoin me."

Within the hour, Serrano had packed his scant belongings, along with more than enough maize cakes and water for the journey, and prepared to leave the village of Potano for San Augustín, a three-day journey to the east. "I will return as soon as Father Pareja says I'm fit," Serrano said, as he paused at the head of the trail and looked back.

To Father Prieto, Serrano moved very well for a man dying of the bite of a rattlesnake. He certainly had regained a healthy appetite.

The Indian woman stood in the shade of a hickory tree. It was midday, and although the sky was now covered by low clouds, the heat had in no way abated. She was in a secluded spot, where Prieto was accustomed to pause for his final prayers before entering Santa Ana.

"You must go back," she said, stepping into the trail as Father Prieto approached. He recognized her from an earlier visit to Santa Ana. Though a mature woman, she was the granddaughter of the ancient village chief.

"I come in God's name to speak his Word," he said.

The woman was crying, and her hands shook as she tried to cover her face. Father Prieto stepped to her and put his hands on her shoulders to comfort her. "Why do you come to me thus, child?"

The woman shrugged off his embrace and turned her back on him. "My grandfather said you would not return after the disgraceful way the other holy man behaved in the village, but I knew you would be here, and I have come to warn you, to tell you to go away and not come back."

"I will speak to your grandfather. I have not met him. The first time I came to your village, I went to his house and asked him to come out so that I could greet him, but he did not answer me."

The woman turned and looked over her shoulder at Father Prieto. "My grandfather is very old. He is not rude. Because he lacks strength and sleeps much of the time, he asks me to talk to traders and other visitors for him."

"Perhaps I could see him for just a moment, to apologize to him for the other priest's bad manners. He is a good priest, but he is young and sometimes doesn't know how to speak respectfully. He will not return here. I will be your priest from now on."

Now the woman turned to face him. "You need to understand more about my grandfather. Perhaps when I tell it, you will do what I say and leave this village." She gestured that Father Prieto sit on a log. When he was comfortable, she sat on the ground before him.

The woman talked of a time when her grandfather was a child, and himself the nephew of a great Potanan chief. She spoke of the first Spaniard, de Soto, of how he and his men raided the land and stole the grain stored for winter. The chief resisted the Spanish, and threatened them to get them to leave Potano, and readied his men for battle.

"My grandfather was there when the Spaniards cut off the head of his uncle, and the other men of the clan of White Deer. Only my grandfather was saved and only because of his age."

"That has been seventy or more years," Prieto said.

"And for seventy years my grandfather has remembered. He is reminded of it every day of his life. The elders still speak of it. Even those who were not yet born have heard the story so often, they tell the tale as if it were a memory. Because my grandfather was White Deer, but too young for even the Spanish to kill, they cut off his ear with a sword to mark him as a member of the chief's family.

"When they return, if they are not welcomed and fed and given women and slaves, they will cut off his other ear. That is what de Soto promised my grandfather," she said.

Prieto dropped his eyes to the ground. "Surely your grandfather knows de Soto is dead these many years. Perhaps, in time, he will see that we are not all barbarians. We Franciscans come in the name of God to do good works."

"There was also a man who wore a robe who stood beside the devil de Soto," she said. "There is no forgiveness in my grandfather's heart. Perhaps when he and some of the older people are gone, you can return."

The rumble of thunder sounded in the west. A strangely-colored orange sky covered the horizon, and a cooling breeze scattered the leaves where they sat.

"We will get rain," Prieto said, looking around. "Surely your grandfather would not turn me away in the face of a storm." He stood up and brushed away the oak leaves that clung to his robe. Father Prieto stepped back onto the trail that led to the village. He paused and looked back. The woman had not moved to follow, but wept with her hands covering her face.

Father Prieto was seized roughly as soon as he entered the village. His hands were tied behind him and he was dragged by three men to the chief's house and thrown to the ground. Curious onlookers came from their huts, attracted by the commotion.

The chief sat on a low bench of cypress covered by a seat of deer hide. One man stood with a foot pressed to the priest's neck, grinding his face into the dirt. A second man reached into the pocket of his robe and removed his breviary and handed it to the old man.

Father Prieto spit dirt and tried to speak, but could not. The foot came down harder, now on his face, and sand blinded one eye.

"This is the holy man's medicine," the chief said, holding up the book and waving it about. "The devil de Soto had such a book."

With one good eye Prieto could see that the men were heavily armed with darts and spears and clubs. Their faces were painted in grotesque patterns. He thought of the five priests of Guale who, eleven years before, had been martyred for the Word of God. Was his death to come so soon, when his service to God had barely begun? Father Prieto prayed for his own salvation, and for forgiveness of these who would be his murderers. He relaxed his body and released his cares, commending his spirit to his Father in Heaven.

"Let me help this priest spread the word of his God. After all, that is why he has come, to save our souls," the chief said. With that, he ripped a page from the breviary, and then another. The pages were lifted from his fingers by the wind, and floated about before settling to the ground. Mocking laughter filled the village as the people enjoyed the spectacle.

The first page came to rest only inches in front of the priest's face, awaiting the next breeze to send it aloft. A dollop of rain splattered on the page, and then another.

The flash of white light was so sudden and blinding that Father Prieto thought it was the heralding of the return of Christ. The crack of thunder was so loud and piercing that his ears rang and ached.

The man whose foot had pinned Prieto's head in the dirt ran away, and the priest rolled onto his back, blinking his damaged eye and looking up. A tall pine tree, not ten meters away was split asunder, and smoke and flames danced from what was left of its trunk.

A sudden wind descended on the village, roaring and swirling about, knocking grown men to the ground. The air was full of choking dust and leaves, and branches of trees. In moments half the houses were blown away or flattened. A spear that had been held by one of Prieto's captors impaled itself in the trunk of a tree.

Then the rains came. Father Prieto closed his eyes as the waters of Heaven washed away the sins of the world. He opened them again. The chief sat where he was before, looking at the breviary. His own house lay on the ground behind him. Not a single pole remained standing.

As quickly as it had come, the storm was gone. After gathering their wits, people began to move about, digging through the wreckage looking for members of their families.

The chief was helped to his feet by his granddaughter, and gestured that the people return to hear what he had to say. They crowded around him in stunned silence.

"This shaman has great and powerful medicine," he said in a voice so soft and rounded by age it could barely be heard. He held the breviary in his hand, as well as the two ripped pages that withstood the storm and did not blow away. "We will hear what he has to tell us."

By sunset the chief's house had been rebuilt, as well as many of the others. Several people had broken bones and cuts and bruises from flying debris, and difficulty in hearing, but no one in the village would die.

Father Prieto's left eye was swollen shut and two teeth were loosened where his face had been stepped on. The chief's granddaughter brought a light meal for them to share, and a poultice for the priest's eye. He sat with the chief in his house and talked into the night.

"Perhaps you will read to me from your book some day," the chief said, handing Father Prieto his breviary.

When it was dark the chief lay on his back and closed his eyes. Father Prieto spoke to him of the Holy Father's love for all His creatures, and of the gift of divine forgiveness. Soon the old man began to snore. The sound became louder until the granddaughter slipped into the house and gently turned him to his side.

Chapter 24

The birthday of the patron, St. Francis of Assisi, was arriving quickly, but not quickly enough to suit the priest. San Francisco de Potano was Father Prieto's first church, and he was determined to make it the finest west of the mother church, Nombre de Dios, at San Augustín.

Delays tested the young friar's patience. With the coming of fall and cooler weather, fishing and hunting became more important to the Indians, who lacked the discipline to work until a project was completed. There seemed to be no end to their excuses.

The bones that were discovered while digging the northeast corner post had the effect of shutting down the work. There was no doubt in Prieto's mind that the Indians' fear was genuine, that they were greatly disturbed by the discovery. The man whose spade had exposed the bones was ordered out of the village by the chief, and he sat by himself in a grove of trees at a distance, weeping day and night and rubbing his hands in the dirt until they were raw and bleeding. No one would go near him, and no one would approach the church where the bones glinted in the sunlight.

Chief Potano summoned a shaman, called a *jarva,* from a distant village to conduct a curing ceremony to save the man who touched the bones, and to tell the village elders what must be done with the remains.

If Father Prieto had made any progress at all in turning the villagers from their pagan ways, and he thought he had, it was not in the area of burial practices. Despite his urgings that the bones be dug up and removed until the shaman arrived, no one would move a hand to help. To complicate matters, no one would talk to the priest about Potanan burial practices and beliefs, as they were clan secrets and not the subject of polite conversation.

Unwilling to be seen as acquiescing in the pagan rituals that were sure to occur with the *jarva's* visit, Father Prieto chose that time to travel to San Augustín to acquire iron nails for construction, and a brass mission bell. As it turned out, the bell was already available. It was the bell that was recovered from the mission at Tupiqui, in Guale, eleven years earlier when five priests were killed. With the assistance of Custos of Missions Father Pareja, Prieto was able to convince the governor to part with six pounds of iron nails.

When he returned to Potano, Father Prieto learned that the shaman had failed to save the man who had uncovered the bones. The priest went to where the man had last been seen. The fallen leaves where he had lain were the color of dried blood.

"What has happened to the man who lay here?" he demanded of Chief Potano.

"*Jarva* came too late. His magic was too weak to break the spell," Potano said.

"Look here," Prieto said, gesturing to the stained ground more than two meters across. "The man bled to death. He could not lose this much blood unless he was cut in some way."

The chief stood at a distance and would not come closer. "*Jarva* came too late," he repeated, but would say no more.

The bones found at the corner post hole had been removed by the shaman and the Indians were once again free to continue with construction of the church. They would not, however, dig any more holes. Further digging fell to Father Prieto.

Father Prieto stepped from his hut as the sun lit the facade of the church. It was, indeed, the finest of any of the mission churches, except Nombre de Dios in San Augustín, he thought. Measuring twenty-seven meters by eleven meters, with a pine plank altar floor and a sanctuary of hard clay, Prieto calculated it had a capacity of three-hundred and fifty worshipers. And it was the very first mission church to the west of the River San Juan, the river the Indians still called River of the Sun.

Three days before the dedication, Father Prieto received a letter from the Custos of Missions, Father Pareja, with the disappointing news that his duties in San Augustín prevented him from attending the event. Even Father Serrano, who had by now recovered from his earlier injuries, would be unavailable. Nevertheless, Father Pareja sent his blessings as well as a promise of painted clay effigies of St. Francis and the Blessed Mother to be delivered before the ceremony.

Father Prieto asked Chief Potano to send runners throughout the province inviting the two regional chiefs and each of the twenty village chiefs to attend a special Mass of dedication and feast, and to bring their families with them.

The day before the ceremony, a work detail of Indians from San Augustín arrived. They had crossed the river at Tocoi two days earlier and were worn out by the exertions of their westward journey. They carried with them the effigies Father Pareja had promised, and a baptismal font with holy water. While the bearers were fed and given the opportunity to bathe and rest, Father Prieto arranged the Holy Mother and the statue of St. Francis on a table near the altar, facing each other. He placed the baptismal font in the nave, at the entrance to the sanctuary. He would explain its use to the congregation later, perhaps at Sunday Mass.

When the time arrived, only the chiefs and principal men of local villages were present. The old Chief of Santa Ana and the Chief of San Miguel appeared with their retinues. Father Prieto waited an hour for late arrivals. Eventually he despaired and rang the brass bell to begin the service. Less than fifty people were present, huddled near the altar in the cavernous church.

"Where two or more are gathered in my name, there will I be, also," was the scripture Father Prieto selected at the last moment to begin the service of dedication.

As he read the catechism, none of the Indians could voice the proper responses, and only two or three seemed to know when it was time to kneel or stand. With up and down arm gestures he soon restored some semblance of liturgical order. The priest tried not to smile when one of the worshipers, unaccustomed to kneeling, toppled over.

Father Prieto was nearing the end of the service, when he was interrupted by voices from outside and shuffling feet at the church door. The faces of strangers peered around the corner into the sanctuary. The first man looked at the baptismal font, dipped his fingers, and touched the holy water to his forehead.

Four Potanan warriors, the chief's guard, leapt to their feet and surrounded their leader, displaying their knives. The man at the door spoke to his companions, and as they filed in they held their hands high. None of them was armed.

"Welcome to Misión San Francisco de Potano, my friends, the Lord be with you," Father Prieto said in the Timucua tongue as the arrivals entered the sanctuary. There were seven, led by a tall chief who could not have been more than twenty years old, Prieto reckoned. By their headdresses, Prieto knew they were not Potanans.

"And the Lord abide with you," the young chief responded in perfect Castilian.

The three Potanan chiefs met with the visitors in the council house when the Mass was concluded. Father Prieto was not invited, so he busied himself instructing the cooks on the preparation of the feast that was to be served. But he soon realized that his help was not needed, so he returned to the church to clean and store the ceremonial regalia in the sacristy.

As he turned to leave the church he was startled by the young chief who had approached silently and stood behind him.

"Father Prieto, I am Coya Ayacouta Utina. We have met before, but you may not remember me."

Father Prieto looked up into the young man's face. "I did not recognize you, and for that I apologize. I do know who you are. I remember you from San Augustín, and I have heard your praises sung by no less a judge of character than my superior, Father Francisco Pareja."

Coya smiled. "And it is also from Father Pareja that I have heard of you, and of your mission."

The two men clasped hands. "You may wonder why an Utinan dares to walk into a Potanan village uninvited and unarmed. You and I have much to say to each other. You will come with me now to the council house. My new friend, Chief Potano, has invited us to eat with him and talk."

Coya turned and walked from the church. Father Prieto followed.

Chief Potano afforded Coya the use of a fine cabana, directly adjoining his own and only half a meter lower. Father Prieto divided his attentions between the two chiefs.

"These benches are quite high," Prieto said to Coya. His legs dangled inches above the level below.

"There is good reason for this construction," Coya said. "You see, a flea can jump no more than a meter high, so the cabana is slightly higher. If you will lift your legs and sit cross-legged you will be comfortable, and I can promise you will not be bitten."

The priest crossed his legs in imitation of Coya. He shifted and tested his posture for a moment, then smiled at the young chief.

After they had eaten a meal of venison, tubers and maize cakes, Prieto reminded Coya of his earlier statement. "You were going to tell me why you are here."

"Curiosity, I guess you could call it," Coya said, sipping the hot cassina drink and peering over the rim of Chief Potano's ceremonial lightning whelk drinking vessel. "You see, I wanted to meet the famous Martín Prieto, the Shaman of

Santa Ana who has the magical power to call forth the God of Thunder to flatten a village and save his own life."

Prieto saw the mirth in Coya's eyes. "If it was a miracle, it was God's, not my own," he said.

"Then is it to God that I should address my complaint? The storm He caused that day crossed the river into Utina and damaged one of my innocent villages."

Father Prieto's mouth was open, but he could think of no response.

"In the future, I hope you will ask God to be more careful," Coya said, smiling.

"God's will be done," Father Prieto said, returning the smile. "If that is what brought you here today, it is proof that we must not question His wisdom."

When the food vessels had been removed, and before the planned entertainments began, Coya spoke once again to the priest. "I had hoped that Father Pareja would be here for the dedication of your Church."

"So it was Pareja, and not Prieto, that brought you to Potano."

Coya moved closer to the priest, and spoke quietly in his ear. "Father Pareja has told me of your calling, to bring the Word of God to the western Timucua and beyond. I am sure he has told you that I have been baptized into the faith. Perhaps I am the only Christian chief west of the River of the Sun. What you may not know is that I also have callings from God. The first is to serve my people, the Utina, and to lay down my life for them if necessary."

Prieto turned toward Coya, expectantly.

"My second calling, if you can call it my own, is to do what I can to help you fulfill your calling to spread the Word of God."

Chief Potano gestured to Coya to come close so they could speak privately. "This is a significant day for the priest, with the dedication of the first mission church this side of the river," he said. "But for us, the Potanans and the Utinans, it will be a day that will be remembered by our children's children as a day of peace, when enemies became brothers once again."

"There are still some who say in Utinan councils that the strength of a people is measured by the ability to make war," Coya answered. "Perhaps some Potanan war lords would agree. It is up to us, as leaders, to show our people that it is through peace and solidarity that true strength is achieved. Together we can become a powerful force to be reckoned with, a people that the Spanish cannot step on, but who must be respected."

"Well spoken," Potano said. "And if we succeed, the story tellers of Potano will honor Coya Ayacouta Utina for his courage in making the first gesture by sending his *inija* as an emissary of peace."

Coya did not reply, but considered what Potano had said.

"He is a brave man, your *inija.* When he came to this village he came unarmed, as you did, and had only a toothless old seer with him."

"He travels so much that it is hard for me to keep up with his movements," Coya answered. "How long ago was it he came to Potano?"

"Not long ago. It was before the last full moon. He had already been to five other Potanan villages when he arrived here."

A group of dancers filed through the council house door and mingled with the musicians who had already arrived for the entertainment.

"Give my regards to Crying Bird, and tell him he is welcome to visit Potano at any time," Chief Potano said.

The sound of drummers and flutists filled the council house. Skilled dancers whirled about, their copper bells and shell bracelets keeping time with the music. Chanters and singers joined in, their sounds as sweet as any choir Father Prieto had ever heard.

Before long, spectators left their cabanas and benches for the celebration on the floor, joining the dance that snaked around the central fire. Chief Potano stood and pointed his walking stick directly at Coya, and the uproar was deafening. Coya stood, spread his arms wide and leapt into the mass, where he joined the dancers in celebration.

Only Potano and the priest remained in their places in the cabanas above the dance floor.

"What hath God wrought?" Prieto asked himself as the excitement, energy and powerful spirit of the people filled the house.

As the night went on, the movements of the dancers became more frenetic and sensual, embarrassing the priest and making him ill at ease. In time, however, his foot began to tap with the rhythm.

"What hath God truly wrought?" he asked himself again.

Chapter 25

November, 1608
East of Yustaga

The priest sat quietly by the camp fire. With the coming of daylight, the previous night's inferno was reduced to glowing coals that would later be stoked to life when needed for warmth and cooking. Coya sat nearby, his back against a sapling sweet gum tree, watching him.

"So deep in thought, so early in the day?" Coya asked.

If the Franciscan heard him, he showed no sign of it and did not answer. It was not rudeness, Coya thought, but something else. Perhaps it was depression that had dogged the priest these last weeks. Prieto's natural exuberance, so inspiring to Coya in their early days together, had dissolved with the knowledge that not a single Potanan chief, other than Potano himself, would allow a church to be built in his village.

They had been here for three days, awaiting Big Bow's return from the Yustagan village of Potohiriba, where he had gone to ask the chief's permission for them to cross the river into his province. Perhaps it was the inactivity of waiting that darkened the priest's mood.

A gray squirrel descended from its nest in the high branches of an oak and perched on a low limb, barking its challenge to their presence and thrashing its tail. The priest looked up, a slight smile creasing the corners of his mouth.

"You slept late this morning," he said. "Your babies must be starved by now."

The squirrel hopped to the ground at the base of the tree and sat there on its haunches, studying them. In time it began to move about, searching among the fallen leaves and twigs for scraps of the men's meal from the night before. Buried acorns were not nearly as tasty as parched corn and bits of bread.

Father Prieto looked about, as if surprised to find Coya sitting so close. "Did you say something?" he asked.

"I just said that you appear to be deep in thought. Apparently I was right, since you did not hear me."

Father Prieto slowly extended his hand toward the squirrel. In his palm he held bits of maize and crumbs. The dark eyes of the squirrel fixed on the offering.

"Squirrels will not eat from your hand," Coya said.

"Patience, my friend," Prieto said softly so as not to startle the squirrel. "That is something we missionaries are good at."

Suddenly, Prieto laughed out loud and turned to face Coya. "Did you hear what I said? About priestly patience? What a wonderful sermon that was." The squirrel jumped to the tree and disappeared to the other side of the trunk.

Father Prieto was quiet for awhile before he spoke again. "I'm sorry, Coya, for the way I have been these last few weeks. As you know, I was disappointed at what we found in Potano. I expected that with the help of the paramount chief it would be a simple matter to win over his subordinate chiefs. There is need there for at least three additional mission churches to serve the people, particularly to the north and west of San Francisco de Potano."

"And you expected those people to eat from your hand just because Potano was your friend?" Coya asked.

"I see now that it takes patience, now that the mother squirrel has reminded me of it. I promise from now on to be patient, and to wait for God's own time. After all, this is His work, and I am only an instrument. One of His instruments."

"If you ask me why none of seventeen village chiefs would follow the example of Chief Potano, I say it is because he is a poor leader," Coya said. "For thirty years the Spanish and Utinans made war against him. His people suffered greatly. Now Potano suddenly sues for peace and allows a Spanish church in the main village. You can see how his vassal chiefs would lose respect for him."

"And I, a Spaniard, walk into their villages, escorted by you, an Utinan." The priest sighed, and looked at the tree where the squirrel now sat on a low branch.

"Exactly," Coya said.

"Patience, patience. Our reception in Yustaga will be better," Father Prieto said softly. "And perhaps before we leave here, Mother Squirrel will eat from Prieto's hand."

The squirrel alighted from the tree once again, but would not come close to the priest's outstretched palm. When his arm tired, Father Prieto scattered the food on the ground. The squirrel grabbed a piece of bread and scampered up into the seclusion of its leafy home.

Prieto stood up and brushed away the leaves that clung to his robe. "Chilili has asked me to go fishing with him. Will you go with us?"

"I will remain in camp. I want to be here when Big Bow returns with the answer of the Yustagan Chief."

Later, as Coya waited in the camp, a hawk spied the squirrel nest and, with barely a sound, made off with a newborn. The sorrowful wailing cries of the mother echoed through the forest. Father Prieto and Chilili still had not returned from the river when the mother vacated the nest and took her one surviving baby with her. Coya watched as she moved from tree to tree into the distance, searching for a new home where they would be safe from hawks.

"Not a good omen," Coya said to himself. "And not a story to be told to a priest."

Their reception at Potohiriba had not been a propitious one, Father Prieto believed. On the night before their arrival, Big Bow explained the terms that had been agreed upon in his negotiations with the *Inija* of Yustaga.

"You have to remember the history of these people," Big Bow said to the priest. "The first Spaniard, de Soto, murdered more than one hundred innocent people here. The Yustagans have never forgotten. It is only because you travel with the Paramount Chief of Utina that you will be allowed to enter. If you came alone, you would be butchered, priest or not."

Coya's guard, except for Big Bow, was required to remain outside the village of Potohiriba. Coya was provided a comfortable place in the council house, with servants to see to his every need, befitting his position as *Holata Aco*. Father Prieto received no such honor. He was housed in a small, flea-infested hut near the edge of the village, with only two Yustagan guards to protect him from harm.

In the morning, Coya and the priest met with Chief Potohiriba at his home, perched on a large mound near the council house. Father Prieto judged Chief Potohiriba, the Paramount Chief of Yustaga, to be a dour man. His face was painted black. Other than that, and a single hawk feather in his hair, he adorned himself in no way. He was polite, but taciturn, saying little and showing nothing in his face to betray his inner thoughts.

Only once, when Coya said that the Spanish had iron tools to trade, did Father Prieto think he saw Potohiriba's eyebrows rise slightly, but in the next moment, the chief's face was once again a mask.

In the late afternoon, Father Prieto spoke to the chief about God in Heaven who loved the Yustagans and had sent Prieto and the other Franciscans to serve them and save their souls. As the priest spoke, Chief Potohiriba seemed distracted by a conversation he carried on simultaneously with his *inija* who sat beside him.

When Father Prieto had said all he had to say, and ventured to repeat himself on an earlier point, Potohiriba waved his arm, dismissively. "No more holy men. We have all we need."

The parley was at an end. The *inija* escorted Coya and Father Prieto out of the chief's house and down the hill to the council house where they were fed a nourishing meal of maize and venison and entertained by dancers and musicians.

Before daybreak, Coya came to fetch the priest from his hut, and with an escort of twenty black-faced and heavily armed Yustagans they moved beyond the village, further toward the west.

"This river is the western boundary of the Timucua nation," Coya said, as they rested beside a small river two leagues from Potohiriba. "What you see over there is Apalachee. This is as far as we will go. You can now tell Father Pareja that you have been to the end of the world." In the distance, the land became rolling hills, topped with what appeared to be thin stands of small pine trees.

The Yustagan *Inija* offered them a hollowed gourd of sunflower seeds, and walked away downstream, keeping a careful watch for movement on the western bank of the river.

Coya still wore the black and red face striping with which he had adorned himself for meetings with Chief Potohiriba. He had his formal deerskin match coat to fend off the morning chill. Winter came sooner here on the edge of Apalachee than it did in the heart of Utina.

"I would like you to consider going further with me," Father Prieto said. "The governor asked me to visit the Apalachee if it were possible. Several years ago an Apalachee delegation appeared in San Augustín. They came by boat, having taken passage on a supply ship that served an outpost among the Pensacola who live beyond the Apalachee. Having come this far, it would be a shame to not visit them."

"I don't believe that would be possible or that Chief Potohiriba would allow it," Coya said. "These people are at war, and what you see here is a buffer, a no-man's land observed by both the Yustagans and the Apalachee on the other side of the river. Chief Potohiriba says that it keeps the peace very well, but that during his lifetime there have been many wars fought here. Sometimes over issues as simple as who should fish the river. Sometimes because the Apalachee are jealous of their maize fields, and accuse the Yustagans of thievery."

"Are there so few fish that men will kill each other for them?" Father Prieto asked.

"In fact, there are very few fish in this river." Coya answered. "They have all been seined out over time. There are many other good fishing spots in both Yustaga and Apalachee, and perhaps they all realized that. Now there is no more warfare, other than occasional skirmishes to collect hostages. If an Apalachee tries to cross the river and is seen, they will try to kill him. If he escapes, Potohiriba simply orders that a hostage be butchered, and his carcass floated across to the other side as a warning not to intrude on Yustagan territory."

"And if it is a Yustagan who crosses over?"

"A Yustagan corpse would wash ashore here. It's a way to keep the peace. They are quite proud of it."

"Does that not seem barbaric?" Prieto stood and began to move about. "Utterly, savagely, mindlessly barbaric? What about trade? Do they have any commerce between them?"

"Only the commerce of dead bodies, I'm afraid."

The priest paused to brush away the sunflower hulls that clung this robe. "These people are in great need of the Word of God, as well as a dose of common sense," he said.

Father Prieto strolled downstream, his hands clasped behind his back. He turned and took several long strides back to where Coya still sat. "Can you arrange for me to speak to Chief Potohiriba once again?"

"I don't know if he will see us again, Martín. When he and I spoke last night, he said that it was time for you and me to go home. I asked a personal favor of him, that he allow us to come here. I'm afraid he is done talking about religion. He told me that he might welcome talks concerning trade some day, but he will never allow a mission here. He promises to kill any soldier who crosses into Yustaga."

"Trade? He wants to talk of trade? Tell him that is precisely why I have come, to talk of trade." Prieto picked up his walking stick. Coya rose and followed behind as the priest moved eastward on the trail that led back to the village of Potohiriba.

"Our chief does not tolerate long speeches," the *inija* said before ushering Coya and Prieto into the chief's spacious home. "And he is not inclined to talk about matters he has already decided. You have his answers already. He will not allow your teachings among the Yustagans. Nor will he tolerate soldiers entering Yustaga. You have said you wish to speak of trade, and he has agreed to hear you on that subject alone."

Inside his house, Chief Potohiriba and three of his principal men, including his *inija*, listened politely to what the priest had to say.

Later in the day, after the chief and his council had discussed the priest's proposal, Coya and Father Prieto were once again summoned to the house.

"You wish to cross the river to meet with the Apalachee, and you ask that we release valuable hostages to lure them into talks of trade. Out of respect for my Utinan brother we have agreed, although none of us thinks anything good will come of this venture," Potohiriba said.

"*Inija* will accompany you as my representative. He speaks the Apalachee tongue, and neither of you do. We will send twenty of our warriors along with your guard. We will be badly outnumbered, but if they move to harm my *inija*, at least they will pay a price. We will see if the Apalachee have anything constructive to say about trade."

Potohiriba leaned forward and fixed his dark eyes on those of the priest. "We have three Apalachee slaves. Two will be released to return home with news of your pending visit. The other hostage will stay with us. She is the daughter-in-law of an important Apalachee chief. You should tell them as soon as you get there that if any harm befalls my *inija*, I will butcher their daughter and leave her where the buzzards will find her on the river bank."

Chapter 26

The Apalachee know we are coming. If they plan an ambush, they will wait until we are in the canoes," the *inija* of Yustaga said as he peered through a thin river fog from a stand of scrub oak. The joint force of Yustagan and Utinan warriors remained in the forest, awaiting orders to board the canoes that had been placed on the river bank before daylight.

A young Potohiriban boy left the trees and ventured onto the river bank, singing in a loud voice and waving his arms to attract attention.

"Who is this?" Father Prieto asked.

"Just an ambitious boy who wants to become a warrior," the *inija* said. "Watch him. He can be very entertaining."

The boy shouted taunts across the river as he strutted about, questioning the manhood of the Apalachee and making obscene references to their women.

Father Prieto's understanding of the Yustagan dialect was quite good. "Oh my," he said when the boy's meaning became clear. "He certainly is brave to say such things."

"He is as quick as he is brave," the *inija* said, "and his eyesight is excellent. If he attracts attention, he will see the arrows before they cross the river."

The young boy turned his back on the river and bent over, exposing his buttocks. Laughter erupted from the warriors waiting in the woods. The boy stood up and adjusted his loincloth, accepting the approval of the older men.

"Since this was your idea, Coya, your people will cross the river first. If they are not attacked, they can signal to us that it is safe, and the rest of us will join them."

"I agree with that plan, but I will be crossing with my men," Coya said. "You timid Yustagans may come after we have made it safely across."

Big Bow complained that it was his job to protect his chief, and that Coya should remain behind to cross with the Yustagans and the priest, but Coya insisted and the Utinans moved to board the canoes.

Coya took his place in the second canoe. Big Bow was in front, standing to catch any arrows that might be aimed at his chief. The priest sat behind Coya, slumped down to make an inconspicuous target.

In less than an hour, they reached the first of the rolling hills that were visible from Yustaga. What appeared from there to be young pine trees proved to be mature stalks of maize, laid out in orderly, straight lines that extended to the horizon. Interspersed with the maize, green, leafy vines of beans and squash covered the ground. *Inija* said that the Apalachee had abundant harvests twice a year. The narrow path they followed cut directly through the maize. Today, no one tended the fields.

"I have never seen so much maize in my life," Coya said, running his fingers through the fertile, red soil.

"Nor I." Father Prieto was short of breath from the exertion of walking hills that were steeper than any he had climbed since his childhood in Andalusia.

The Yustagan *Inija* spoke in low tones. "They know we are here. They have runners marking our progress. We need to keep up the pace."

As they moved forward, Father Prieto looked ahead. To the left and right, Yustagan and Utinan warriors shielded them from attack. In time, the path grew wider through the fields. The *inija* stopped suddenly and Prieto, who followed behind, stumbled on his heels. *Inija* held up his hand, signaling the others to stand still. He cupped his hand behind one ear, and the others did likewise.

Father Prieto heard a low murmur, such as the sound distant surf makes as it strikes the shore.

Farther on, they paused again to listen. Now what they could hear was much clearer. To Prieto it was the hubbub of many voices, as if he was again in the Madrid of his youth, and people gathered for a bullfight on a Sunday afternoon.

"We are nearing the village of Ivitachuco," the *inija* said.

As they moved on, a man appeared to the right of the trail, another to the left. Then there were others standing shoulder to shoulder, lining the way, unarmed Apalachee warriors, their skin dyed red and their shiny black hair piled high and festooned with colored feathers.

"That is ochre," Coya said to Father Prieto. "They color their skin with ochre."

The disciplined training of the warriors held, and they passed steadily within an arms length of the Apalachee men without incident.

"There must be hundreds of them," Father Prieto said. "There may be thousands."

The village center of Ivitachuco was dominated by an immense, round council house, so broad it blotted out the horizon, so high it would have dwarfed the largest house in Timucua. The plaza teemed with colorfully dressed, excited people. They were orderly, though some jostled each other to catch sight of the visitors. Some sang and chanted, raising both arms in salute. The sheer volume of their voices was deafening. The *inija* turned and spoke to his companions, but his words were drowned out, so he waived his arm, gesturing that Coya and Father Prieto follow him. And they did so, directly through the low doorway into the council house at Ivitachuco.

The warriors, Yustagan, Utinan and Apalachee, remained outside.

The council house was grander than any European cathedral Father Prieto had ever seen or imagined. Supported by fifty or more pillars of stout pine trunks, the coned ceiling soared upward fifteen meters to the smoke-stained center hole four meters across. In the very center of the house, the fire pit flamed, radiating gentle warmth, the smoke rising directly upward to escape through the hole. The priest peered upward at the huge umbrella of a roof, turning to take it all in, and then continued to turn as the dizzying immensity of it overwhelmed his sense of balance, leaving him light-headed.

Seventy or more of the leading chiefs of Apalachee occupied elevated cabanas around the entire circumference of the wall. Below them, *inijas* and *paracousi* and shamans had cabanas built at floor level, and they stood on their toes to see over the heads of principal men and advisors who populated the full inner circle of benches.

A tall man in a regal robe, his headpiece of dyed seabird feathers, slowly descended from the highest cabana until he stood on a wooden platform directly in front of Coya, Father Prieto and the Yustagan *Inija.*

He had the powerful voice of an orator and, as the others fell silent, his words reverberated throughout the immense hall. He was the *Inija* of Apalachee, and to Prieto he seemed a spirit-filled man with the dignity and magnetism of a born leader. *Inija* of Yustaga stood between Coya and Father Prieto, smoothly translating into Timucua all that his Apalachee counterpart said.

There followed the introduction of Chief Ivitachuco, the Paramount Peace Chief of Apalachee, who rose in his cabana to a thunderous greeting that rattled the very timbers of the house. Ivitachuco's brother, Anhaica, was next to be introduced as the Paramount War Chief of Apalachee. His reception was equally loud, and accompanied by a war dance performed by *paracousi* throughout the building.

The Yustagan *Inija* took advantage of the commotion to cover his words to Father Prieto and Coya. “Anhaica is a blood-thirsty animal,” he said.

The *Inija* of Apalachee continued with the introductions of seven regional chiefs, and then more than fifty village chiefs, calling each by name.

When all of the Apalachee dignitaries had been recognized, the *inija* called for something to drink, and it was brought to him by a servant whose hair hung down past his shoulders, and who wore only an elaborately painted breechcloth.

“This day we, the lords of Apalachee, welcome to our land outsiders who come to honor our chiefs and do homage to our people,” the *inija* said. “One comes in friendship and supplication, bearing gifts to appease the righteous anger of the Apalachee for a lifetime of crimes –”

A murmur, low at first, spread through the hall. Angry shouts and insults were heard, and fists were raised in anger. The Apalachee speaker made no effort to quell the outbreak. Finally, Chief Anhaica stood in his cabana and raised his arms, palms down. Immediately, quiet was restored.

“Three days past,” the *inija* continued, “the leader of the Yustagan people, embarrassed by his former criminal ways and seeking our forgiveness and mercy, released to us two of our warriors they have held as slaves.”

Again the Apalachee voiced their anger, but this time for only a moment.

“We are promised that the daughter of a village chief soon will be returned to her clan in a demonstration of the good will of the leaders of Yustaga.”

Again, a low murmur spread through the hall. The speaker approached and handed the steaming cup of cassina to the *Inija* of Yustaga who bowed to him and took a large swallow before bellowing loudly his approval, drawing polite laughter from some of the Apalachee men.

The Apalachee *Inija* continued. “A mighty chief has journeyed many days to bring us the greetings and friendship of his people. He is the Paramount Chief of a people known as the Utina. We know of their reputation as fierce warriors, feared by those who offend them, and respected and trusted by those who call them friend. He is called Coya Ayacouta Utina, and he comes to pay homage to Apalachee, and with offers of trade."

Coya accepted the cup and took a big drink, shouting his approval as the Yustagan had done. A cheer of welcome, a good deal friendlier than had greeted the *Inija* of Yustaga, arose from the cabanas around the house.

When the sound was quelled, the speaker continued.

"Seven summers past, the principal men of Apalachee journeyed to the Spanish town to the east. To avoid having to kill Yustagans, we went by boat. We exchanged gifts there, and spoke of peace between the Spanish and the Apalachee, and of trade. We were honored by their governor with his hospitality, and he fed us while we were there, but with foods of poor quality. It was the best they had to offer, that which the governor fed his own family. We invited the governor to visit with us and offered him safe conduct, to see how we lived, how well we feed ourselves. The Spanish governor is a busy man. Perhaps he feared to travel any way other than with his soldiers, which, of course, we could not allow to happen.

"But he has now sent to us his shaman, a holy man of great learning and wisdom. He is called Father Prieto, and he comes to talk of trade between our peoples, and to bless this land and our leaders with his prayers."

Father Prieto accepted the cup from the speaker. He blessed it and drank from it. "Good! Good!" he shouted, drawing laughter of approval.

Gathered outside the door, thirty or more bearers of wooden planks of food, meat, and fish, baskets of roasted ears of maize and cakes, and bowls of fruits and berries awaited a signal to enter. An Apalachee *jarva* danced about, blowing herb smoke into the air, chanting his incantations of blessing of the food.

The pleasant smells wafted into the council house and spread through the room. Soon more people were watching the doorway than listening to the *inija*, who announced that there would be more speeches after the feast.

While the bearers circulated throughout the house, distributing the foodstuff, the Apalachee *Inija* escorted Coya, Father Prieto and the Yustagan to the large, elevated cabana where Chiefs Ivitachuco and Anhaica and their principal advisors awaited.

Coya and Father Prieto sat across from the two Paramount Chiefs of Apalachee, separated only by garlands of flowers and bowls and baskets of hot food. The royal cabana was walled on the sides and large enough for thirty or more men. Attendants hung thick mats of soft, woven fabric, providing privacy and a quiet place for the leaders to talk, undisturbed by the noise of the feasting multitude.

Interpreters who spoke the Timucua tongue sat to either side. The Yustagan *Inij*a was seated at a distance, eating and conversing with men of his same rank.

The paramounts were impressive men, dressed regally. Chief Ivitachuco was friendly and outgoing, and he asked about the travels of Coya and Father Prieto, the places they had visited, and the people they had encountered. Anhaica seemed to be more interested in the subject of trade, and asked how the Spanish valued an arroba of maize, and whether grain could be bartered for iron tools.

When the conversation flagged, Coya spoke to Father Prieto in Spanish. "What do they call this meat, Martín?" He reached for a second piece of a glazed, roasted morsel. "I have never tasted anything like it. It is neither deer, nor turkey nor bear."

Before Father Prieto could answer, Chief Ivitachuco interrupted. "The meat is called pork. The only good thing the devil de Soto left us was his pigs. They thrive in the swamps to the south, and they also destroy our crops, so we have learned to enjoy their taste."

"And de Soto also left behind knowledge of our language, I see," Father Prieto said.

Ivitachuco chuckled and reached his arm across to shake the shoulder of the priest. "Sí, Padre," he said in Castilian.

When the pork was all gone, and the private talks concluded, the attendants were summoned to remove the privacy mats. Many of the men had left the council house to attend to their families, but by the time Chief Ivitachuco was ready to speak, they had all returned and waited expectantly.

Ivitachuco spoke eloquently of the blessings of peace, and promised to match his words with actions if the Yustagans would do the same. He said that his brother, Anhaica, had held the power to destroy Yustaga for many years, but had not done so in hopes that peace might some day prevail. He said that a formal treaty would be submitted to the council upon the return of the last hostage held by the Yustagans.

He spoke of the blessings of trade the Apalachee had enjoyed for many generations with kindred peoples to the north, the west, and the Pahoi and Calusa to the south.

"Now, perhaps, we can establish relations with our new friends, the Utinans, and with our old enemies, the Yustagans, if they have anything worthwhile to offer us in trade," he said. The Yustagan *Inija* sat stone-faced and said nothing.

"My brother Anhaica will journey to the Spanish town with the new moon, to pledge our loyalty to them, and to receive gifts and establish trade relations. They are hungry, and we have the maize to fill Spanish bellies. They have iron tools with which we can till the fields."

Anhaica rose to his feet. "They also have powerful weapons we need for hunting and for protecting ourselves from enemies," he said.

Chief Ivitachuco turned to look at Father Prieto. "And my brother will remind the governor that seven years ago we asked for priests to come to Apalachee. We are still waiting."

Their journey to Apalachee concluded, Coya and Father Prieto planned their return to Potohiriba, and then to Potano and finally to Ayacouta.

When the Chief of Potohiriba learned of the intention of the Apalachee Chief to travel to San Augustín to pledge loyalty, to establish trade relations, and invite the priests to come, he was greatly disturbed. He told Father Prieto that his only recourse was to travel to San Augustín and do the same, but to arrive before the Apalachee who planned to make the trip after the full moon. He said that in six days, the delegation of Yustagans would be ready to travel.

The Chief of Potano, learning of the Yustagan and Apalachee intentions, spoke to other Potanan chiefs and convinced them that unless they established good relations with the Spanish, they would soon be isolated and surrounded by potential enemies.

Chief Potano asked the priest to accompany him to San Augustín where he would request more priests for Potano. "If we move quickly, we will arrive first," he said. "You should explain to the governor that we are the nearest to the river, and perhaps he should provide us with the iron tools we will need to grow food crops. The Spanish and Potanans should be the best of trade partners."

During the ten day journey from Apalachee, Father Prieto had used the time in the evenings to begin his reports to the custos of missions and to the governor. As his successes were compounded, the reports needed to be rewritten. By the time Potano softened his position, Father Prieto had used the last of his parchment. The final reports would have to await his return to San Augustín.

On the night before their arrival in Ayacouta, Coya selected a camp site in a copse of pine trees at the top of a hill that afforded a beautiful view of the sunset. After eating a meal of soup made with what remained of the Apalachee pork, the two of them watched the colorful light show to the west as the sun went to its sleeping place.

"We have traveled far, Coya. You have shown me sights I could not have imagined, and people who are beyond imagination, also."

"It is as wondrous to me as it is to you," Coya said. "I had never been to Apalachee, and not even Yustaga."

"That surprises me, that you haven't been to these places before," Father Prieto said. "The *Inija* of Yustaga mentioned to me that your own *inija* had been there recently. Did you send him ahead of us so that we would be expected?"

Coya paused before answering. "It is time for us to get our rest, Martín. If we are to reach Ayacouta tomorrow, we will need to get an early start."

As darkness fell, Father Prieto lay down on his mat. He was asleep soon after. Coya sat with his back to a tree for a long time, thinking about Crying Bird, and wondering what business he might have in Potano and Yustaga.

"God has richly blessed our time together," Prieto said as he and Coya embraced on the morning the priest left Ayacouta for Tocoi crossing and San Augustín.

"Perhaps we have been too successful, Martín" Coya said. "There are not enough Franciscans this side of Spain to fill the churches that will be needed in four large provinces."

"We are the sowers, Coya. You and I merely plant the seeds. God will provide other men for the harvest."

Prieto picked up his bundle and nodded to the three guides Coya had provided that he was ready to be taken home. Potano and his delegation already awaited him at the Tocoi river crossing.

When he reached the edge of the clearing, the priest turned back. "Be thinking of a name for your mission. I will ask that the governor authorize the very next church to be built right here in Ayacouta."

"It already has a name," Coya answered, standing with his arm around his wife, Mora. "It will be called Misión San Martín de Ayacouta."

Chapter 27

"Bring Crying Bird to me," Coya said after Honoroso had finished his report on happenings around Utina during his absence.

Honoroso looked surprised. "Crying Bird is not here. He has been gone for a long time. I thought he was traveling around Utina, visiting the other villages, but no one has reported seeing him. We thought he might have gone to meet you in Potano, or perhaps to Yustaga."

"Crying Bird would have no business in any other province without my direct orders," Coya said.

Honoroso shrugged. "The last time he was here, he had with him the old man, Yano, and two skinny young boys from another village. Yano has come back, but no one else. I saw him in the council house today. Do you want me to fetch him?"

"Is he having a good day, today? Is his mind right?" Coya asked.

Honoroso smiled. "I have not spoken to him."

Coya rose to his feet. "I will go talk to him."

The old man was seated cross-legged in front of the glowing council fire, his back to the door. As he bent over his work, his shoulder blades and ribs protruded under his aged, leathery skin. To his left was a basket of irregular shaped pieces of stone, and on the other side, a blanket where he displayed finished arrow heads and spear points.

Age had taken from Yano the acute hearing of a younger man, as it sometimes robbed him of his memory. He seemed unaware that Coya had come in and was watching him from the doorway. Yano grunted aloud as the chert in his hand broke under the pressure of his antler tool.

"Excellent work," Coya said. The old man still didn't seem to hear him. Coya knelt beside him and picked up one of the thin arrow points. "Too large for hunting birds."

Startled, Yano dropped the antler tool and chert to the ground. He covered his face with his hands. "You approached so quietly, you frightened me," he said, pulling away from the touch of Coya's hand that rested on his shoulder.

"We have artisans who knap chert for our warriors," Coya said, giving the old man time to recover from his fright. "Many of our hunters prefer to do their own points, matching the size to the quarry. These spear points are large enough to kill a bear."

"I am a poor hand at it. I am just an old man who keeps his hands busy so they do not shake from age."

Coya turned to face Yano, smiling. "Not at all. These spear points are as good as any I have seen." He picked one up and ran his thumb along the edge. "See how thin, straight and balanced it is? With a proper shaft, a man with an atlatl could make a kill at many meters. Perhaps at a greater distance than a musket ball could travel. Crying Bird will be pleased."

Yano smiled broadly, exposing his naked gums. "I hope so. It is his chert. He traded a deerskin for it, and told me I should make twenty spear and one hundred arrow points. He showed me these samples." He picked up one of the spear and one arrow point. "He said to make the rest just like these."

Yano retrieved the antler tool and chert, and went back to his work. Coya watched as the old man bore down on the rock, flaking off slivers on each side of the point, sharpening it.

"Where is my *inija* now?" Coya asked. "I have business to discuss with him."

Yano's hand tightened on the antler and broke the arrow point in two, ruining it. "I do not know. Perhaps you should ask someone else."

"But you have been traveling with him," Coya said. "That is why I am asking you, Yano."

Yano reached into the basket for another piece of chert. Tears flooded his eyes and he dropped his chin to his chest, unable to go on. His voice was so low and choked with emotion that Coya could barely understand him. "If I answer you, will you tell Crying Bird I betrayed him?"

Coya patted the old man on the shoulder. "You will betray no one."

The two young priests appeared suddenly one day with no prior warning to Coya that they were coming. They had walked day and night from Misión San Francisco de Potano where they had slept last, and asked for a place to rest for a day before they continued their journey to their destination in Apalachee. Their Indian escort had taken them only as far as the river crossing at Tocoi, then set them on the trail to Potano.

The priests awoke from their slumber in the council house and ate a hearty meal. When they were done eating, Coya provided them with an escort that would take them as far as Potohiriba. Before they set out to the west, one of the young men recalled that they carried two letters for Coya, and they gave them to him.

When they were gone, Coya sat under a tree and inspected the envelopes. Both bore the seal of the custos of missions at San Augustín. One was in the familiar hand of Francisco Pareja. The other, thicker letter was written in the less precise scrawl of Father Martín Prieto. He opened this letter first.

"My good friend and fellow servant of God," it began.

Father Prieto told of his return to San Augustín. His reports had been enthusiastically received by both the governor and the custos. Father Pareja had relieved him of his work in Potano, and had replaced him with a younger man at San Francisco. Because of the successes in Potano, Yustaga and

Apalachee, the custos wished him to devote all of his energies to further mission expansion among the Surruque to the south of San Augustín, and the Acuerans who lived on the River San Juan.

"Unfortunately, they perceive that I have a talent in attracting new peoples," he said.

Father Prieto related the exciting circumstance of three major chiefs arriving almost simultaneously at San Augustín to render obedience to the governor. The Apalachee were feted royally, he said, with bolts of dyed fabric and iron tools. The Yustagans received copper sheets for making ornaments and two pounds of iron nails which served to confuse them, since they knew nothing of wood planking.

Even so, they were treated better than Potano's people who received only hand mirrors and a box of beads to ornament their clothing. When Potano complained, the governor relented and gave him a quantity of thread and a bright red Spanish shirt.

"Unfortunately," Father Prieto said, "the governor, for all his appreciation, has ignored my suggestion that a mission be established in Ayacouta. I might suggest you come to San Augustín to help me plead the case, but it may be that his motivations are such that he will be deaf to our entreaties. Three new priests have been trained and certified by Father Pareja for service on the frontier. The governor has designated them to go to Guale, to rebuild the missions where five of our brethren were martyred. Even the protests of Father Pareja are ignored. It is said around San Augustín that amber is found in Guale, and that it brings a good price in Spain. I sometimes despair of what we are doing here."

At the bottom of the third page the letter ended, "Your loving brother in Christ, Martín."

The letter from Father Pareja was on a single page of parchment.

"To His Excellency, Coya Ayacouta Utina, known to God and to me as 'Juan De Coya.'

"Father Martín Prieto has spoken of what a blessing was bestowed on him when God delivered him into your protection in Potano and the other pagan precincts to the west. He gives credit to you for saving his life, and for the success of his mission in Potano, Utina, and Yustaga and even among the Apalachee. It has been a rich harvest thus far. Glory to God.

"Regretfully, I write also to advise you of the ill health of our beloved friend, Marehootie. God will determine the day of his passing and, as with us all, none will know the day until it is accomplished. What is becoming clear, however, is that Marehootie is failing in his will to live. He is bed-bound now for a month, and incapable even of attending the monastery to teach the students. He sleeps more than necessary, in my opinion.

"I fear that if I wait too long to summon you, death may come suddenly, too swiftly for you to arrive in time to be with him. If you have something to say to him, words of love and redemption, write them to me in a letter and I will read them to him. His eyesight has failed him, and he lacks even the light to do the shell carving that has occupied so much of his time since you were last here.

"If you come soon, perhaps you can say the words to him directly. I pray that you not tarry until it is too late.

"Your loving brother in Christ, Francisco Pareja."

Chapter 28

Coya sent a runner ahead to secure canoes to ferry the Utinans to the eastern shore. The boy returned to camp late at night with unfortunate news.

"What do you mean, there are no canoeists?" Coya demanded.

The boy had run much of the night, and was so winded he could barely make himself understood. "I called across and no one answered me," he said, bending at the waist and holding his knees.

"You must have become lost in the dark. I should send you back to awaken those lazy people, and make sure the canoes are ready when we get there at sun up."

"It is possible the boy is telling the truth," said Big Bow. "I have heard that evil spirits have come to Tocoi. A trader told me that sooner or later everyone who works there dies, that their bodies break out with sores. The *isucus* have no medicine to save them, and the *jarvas* no magic. The only ones that survive are those who leave Tocoi before they become ill."

"I was not lost," the boy said. "The trail leads directly to the landing, and I could see the canoes on the other side of the river, but no people at all. Not even a camp fire."

Coya dismissed the messenger with a wave of his arm, and turned to his *paracousi*. "It is too late tonight. We all need to get our rest. We will deal with the people of Tocoi in the morning."

Soon after the sun rose, Coya and his band of twenty guards looked across the river at the abandoned village of Tocoi. It was just as the boy had said. There was no one to carry them across.

The river was swollen from heavy rains. Two of the strongest swimmers entered the water. The current was swift, and they were swept along by it, finally reaching shore north of the village.

Coya watched the boys struggle to guide the canoes to where the party waited. He turned to Big Bow. "The best swimmers are not always competent paddlers."

Coya went directly to the fort and was not challenged as he entered through the open gate, crossed the yard, and found the door of the dark passageway that led to Marehootie's room. Big Bow went to the monastery to find Father Pareja and to tell him where he could find Coya.

Little had changed since his first visit. The window admitted adequate sunlight into the room. One whitewashed wall was covered by a mural depicting a village with a small chapel, and thin smoke rising from a campfire.

Coya's heart leapt in his throat when he saw Marehootie lying on his bed, little more than a shriveled skeleton. He was not dead. From time to time he gasped for breath, or spoke a word or two to spirits who attended him.

When Father Pareja arrived, Coya was kneeling beside the bed, holding the old man's hand and praying. The priest cleared his throat. When Coya finished his prayer, he crossed himself, stood and faced the priest. His eyes were red and on his cheeks were painted black tear drops, the sign of an Utinan death watch. The two men embraced.

"Sometimes he awakens and wants to talk," Pareja said. "When we speak he tells me where he has been in his dreams.

"He told me of a quiet village to the south, Nocoroco, where two rivers join to meet the sea. Sometimes the old man is a lyrical poet in the images he evokes with his words. He describes moonlight glistening on the waters, and tall island pine trees stretching their fingers to dust the stars. It is always night time when all is quiet, except for the gentle lapping of the waters against his canoe. He says it sooths his soul to be there."

"Fanciful dreams?" Coya asked.

"Perhaps," Father Pareja said. "But there is such a place. I was so moved by his description that I looked at old maps until I found it, not four leagues to the south, but off the main trails and apparently of no interest to the soldiers."

"Marehootie has been many places in his life," Coya said. "I have heard all the stories, but if he mentioned Nocoroco, I must have forgotten it."

"I asked him that, if he had been there. He answered, 'not yet,' as if he has plans to go there in this life or the next. He spends much of his time communing with ancestors and Indian spirits, but I suspect that may just be mental confusion. Or perhaps the Lord has sent angels to carry him across."

Coya and the priest sat on the stone floor. Late afternoon sunlight illuminated the wall painting. "Who painted the mural?" Coya asked. "Surely he was not physically able to reach so high."

"He had help," Father Pareja said with a chuckle. "Children from the village of Soloy did the painting. His sister, Amita brought them here. Marehootie described the scene to them and supervised the work. He has a gentle way with children, and they were not satisfied until he pronounced the work to be perfect."

Coya stood and walked to the wall, studying the mural closely. "There are no people in this village," he said.

"I asked Marehootie about that. His answer was that it is the future, and all are gone. He made me promise not to say that to the children."

The priest stood and walked to a small table near the head of the bed. "There is something else you should see. The children bring Marehootie shells from the sea, and he makes interesting carvings on them. Then he gives them to the children. I have borrowed metal augers and blades and scrapers from the workers for him to use."

"Borrowed?" Coya asked, inspecting the tools laid out on the table.

"Perhaps they forgot I borrowed them. I have so much on my mind, lately."

The old man did not awaken during the day. Before Father Pareja left to return to his duties, he invited Coya to dinner at the new dining hall at the monastery.

"I should eat at the council house with my men," Coya said. "Besides, I have forgotten what you taught me about banquet customs. I would embarrass you with my bad manners."

"Nonsense!" Pareja said. "Martín Prieto will be supervising the cooks, and he insists on showing to you the same hospitality you afforded him. Besides, you are such a famous person that the governor has agreed to pay the cost of the dinner. Even better, he will not be there and we can all enjoy an evening free of his boring pomposity. I will send someone to fetch you."

Coya had seen the monastery on his earlier visit to San Augustín, but the dining hall that adjoined the kitchen was new. At the very center of the rectangular room sat a wooden table surrounded by ten high-back chairs of Spanish design, the wood polished to a high luster, reflecting oil lanterns suspended from roof beams.

Indian and black servants busied themselves placing white linen on the table, and metal platters as well as shallow bowls fashioned of colorful fired clay.

Coya was the last to arrive, having taken pains with his grooming to look his best. Father Pareja was there, as well as Martín Prieto, who each welcomed Coya with warm embraces. All of the priests wore their traditional brown, woolen robes despite the heat. Broad shutters were propped open to provide ventilation. Later, an evening sea breeze cooled the room so that they were all comfortable.

Father Prieto introduced Coya to four other priests, two of whom were young and made little impression on him and whose names he could not recall later in the evening. Father Serrano, who had served with Martín Prieto in Potano, was there. Coya recalled him as the young priest who fled Potano in fear, leaving the danger to Prieto. The other, Father de Avila, had suffered terribly during the revolt in Guale, and now attended patients in the hospital. His hands trembled as he greeted Coya.

Another guest, Francisco Menéndez Marquez, wore the finery of a wealthy landowner: a white cotton blouse, a soft golden vest of a fabric Coya had never seen, and a floppy hat of the same material.

When it was time, Father Pareja blessed the food of which they were to partake, and they took their places at the table. Pareja remained standing, and welcomed them to the banquet sponsored by the governor. "Unfortunately, His Excellency is away on government business in Guale, but he communicated to me his greetings and his regrets."

Father Prieto, sitting across from Coya, smiled at him. "Amber," he mouthed, rolling his eyes. Others had seen him and laughter rippled down the table. Señor Menéndez pretended not to notice.

Father Pareja ignored Martín and went on with what he had prepared to say for the occasion.

"We are honored to have with us his Excellency, Francisco Menéndez Marquez, the Royal Treasurer, and a member of the family of the founder of the colony, the Adelantano, Pedro Menéndez de Aviles."

A round of polite clapping filled the room, and Coya joined in.

"Tonight we are dining for the first time on this fine banquet table, and sitting on chairs fashioned by the most skilled artisans in Spain. We Franciscans have vowed poverty for ourselves, but the funds for this purchase do not come from the government situado. They are a bequest, a trust from Señor Menéndez, for the benefit of the monastery, for the entertainment of guests who have been of particular service in our mission of spreading God's Word."

Another round of applause followed, and Menéndez acknowledged it with a smile and a nod. Servants appeared, and poured wine into the small cups at each place.

"It is altogether fitting that we toast our benefactor." Pareja said, raising his cup. "To His Excellency, Francisco Menéndez Marquez."

The others echoed the toast, and then sipped thoughtfully on the soft Spanish wine.

"We have yet another guest, tonight. To me he is still my altar boy, Juan de Coya, the child I raised in Christ from the age of five and baptized into the faith at Misión San Juan del Puerto years ago. Today he is called Coya Ayacouta Utina. He is the foremost Christian *Holata* in all of Timucua."

Father Pareja was momentarily overcome by emotion. "Excuse me," he said, as he removed a kerchief from his pocket. He wiped his eyes, blew his nose, and replaced the kerchief in his robe.

"We have all heard how the powerful spirit of this young man led Father Martín Prieto to the conquest of souls throughout Western Timucua, through the provinces of Potano, Utina, Yustaga and, yes, even to the rich, fertile hills and valleys of Apalachee."

"I offer a toast to my son, Coya Ayacouta Utina. May God bless him in the same measure he has blessed all of us. To Juan de Coya."

"To de Coya," the others echoed.

A feast was served of lobster, shrimp, and baked fish of the sea. A bowl of parched maize, and another of beans remained on the table and were passed back and forth. More wine was offered, and accepted. Only Coya, who had no taste for the drink, declined.

Midway through the meal, the sergeant major entered the room, and after making excuses for his tardiness and bad manners, took his seat next to Señor Menéndez.

Coya could not stop staring, as he looked at the two Spaniards. Menéndez was of slight build, immaculately dressed with his beard neatly trimmed. The soldier was too well fed and had outgrown his uniform which squeezed him inside. His beard grew wild and red whiskers covered his mouth.

"I see you admire my vest," Menéndez said, when he caught Coya looking. "Would you like to touch it? It is called velvet, and it is the fashion in Europe." Menéndez stood and walked around the table to where Coya sat.

Coya reached out tentatively and felt the smooth softness, and noticed how it caressed his fingers.

"Would you like to have one like it?" Menéndez asked softly. Every eye in the room was on Coya at that moment.

"Thank you, but we have a fabric very much like it," Coya said. "It comes from the inner bark of the willow tree, and is spun into a soft material by our women."

The Spaniard looked surprised. "I would be very interested in seeing that. Perhaps it has some trade value if it is as soft as velvet."

Near the end of the meal, Menéndez once again addressed Coya. "We all know of your stature among the Indians, of your love of peace and the personal risks you have taken to strengthen and protect your people. Even the governor speaks glowingly of your accomplishments.

"I am what is called in Spain, a rancher. My family raises cattle there by the thousands. Here I have only a handful of beasts on two small islands."

"Do you have pigs?" Coya asked.

Menéndez paused before answering. "No. I have no pigs."

"The Apalachee have pigs," Coya said. "They were left by de Soto. They are very tasty. Their meat is called pork."

Again, Menéndez paused before he went on. "Cattle are cleaner than pigs. None of them smell good, but the odor of pigs and hogs is quite unpleasant. And I think beef from cattle is as flavorful as pork."

When Coya did not reply, Menéndez went on. "I propose to, one day, bring my cattle to the mainland where the grass is better, where they will be well-fed and provided more range. Your influence with the others is so strong I would like to have your assistance in finding good pasture, and convincing the other chiefs to allow it."

"You recognize, then, that you need that permission?" Coya asked. "That you are not free to take what you want?"

"The land is yours. We use only that which is legally ours. The governor has said he has no interest or authority to make land grants west of the San Juan River."

Coya studied the half-eaten fish on his plate.

Menéndez went on. "We will need to hire men to work our herds, and will pay wages. Those could be your people, the Utinans. Perhaps we will also share the cattle with the Indians if they develop a taste for beef."

"My people move around to pick nuts and berries and yaupon and coontie," Coya said. "They have their hunting grounds and fields where they plant maize. Already the deer destroy the fields. In Apalachee, the pigs dig up the plantings before they can be harvested. Perhaps there is no room in Utina for Spanish animals."

Señor Menéndez glanced to the head of the table, where Father Pareja sat. The priest did not look up from his plate.

The Spanish rancher smiled broadly at Coya. "Cattle do not dig up nuts or berries. The same is probably true of yaupon and coontie. They do eat maize, if you don't keep them out. I'll grant you that. But we will protect the places where your people harvest the fruit and other natural foods. All I ask is that you keep an open mind."

Coya continued to reflect on what was said. "Come and speak to me when you are ready. Perhaps we can reach some understanding that will be profitable for you and for my people."

As the dinner broke up, and the priests returned to the monastery, the sergeant major approached Coya.

"The governor asked me to speak to you on an urgent matter. Perhaps tomorrow morning at my office in the presidio?"

"I will be there in the morning," Coya said.

Chapter 29

Coya sat in the low, cushioned chair before the sergeant major's broad mahogany desk. He had arrived at the presidio too early, before the door was unlocked. But even after the clerks and soldiers appeared, well after daybreak, he was required to remain outside.

When he was finally escorted in, the sergeant major was there, seated behind his desk. A scrivener sat at a small working table to the side, a quill, an inkwell, and a stack of parchment before him. A black slave stood by with a palmetto fan to move the air and swat at flies that came in through the window.

"It is an amazing story that is told of your accomplishments among the western tribes," the officer said after Coya had declined the cup of hot tea he had offered.

"I am a Christian, as you are," Coya responded. "I was taught by Father Pareja the duty to spread God's Word. It might be remarkable if I chose to leave my people in darkness, thus condemning them to Satan. I do only what I have been taught is right."

The sergeant major peered at Coya, and then went on. "It is just that our military councils believed that extending the missions to the west would cost us much in terms of blood and treasure. You have simplified that greatly, and the governor has asked me to express his appreciation for what you have accomplished.

"We have always had good relations with the Utinans, from the time we first arrived here in 1565. Olate Ouai Utina, the Paramount in those days, was always a trusted ally. When you ascended to his place we hoped to continue good relations with the Utinans."

The sergeant major smiled broadly. It was not a smile that struck Coya as a warm one.

"What surprised us was your skill in winning over the others. The Yustagans, for example, killed fifty of de Soto's men in 1539."

"And de Soto killed ten times that many Yustagans," Coya said.

The sergeant major waved his arm, dismissively. "We had superior weapons."

Coya stood. "I accept the kind words from the governor. You may tell him that I, too, look forward to a close relationship between the Utinans and the Spanish. Is there something else you wanted to talk about, other than old battles?"

"I'm sorry," he said. "Perhaps I'm not handling this well. Please sit down. What we have to discuss may be as important to you as it is to the governor."

Coya sat down slowly, but with his back straight, on the front edge of the chair. The soldier had before him on the desk a stack of papers. He placed a looking glass on his nose, and bent over the documents, studying them closely.

"You are here to visit an Indian named Marehootie, a man to whom we provide a place to stay in the fort. Is that right?"

"I'm sure the soldiers report to you that I go to see him in his cell," Coya said. "He is a grandfather to me. Father Pareja uses his talents as a linguist to train the priests. I have come because he is dying."

"But you are not family. He is Acueran, I believe. Does he not have family? Perhaps a brother?"

From the corner of his eye, Coya could see the scrivener busily writing on the parchment. "You will have to ask Marehootie about his kin," he said.

"And as we both know, he is beyond answering questions." The sergeant major removed his eye glass and peered at Coya across the desk. Apparently he only needed it for reading.

"Then you have tried to speak to Marehootie."

The sergeant major did not answer, but using the eye glass he bent over another document, his finger moving across the page. "Do you know an Indian who is called – let's see – Crying Bird? Some people call him *Atichicolo-Iri*, which I believe means Spirit Warrior."

"Why do you ask?"

The officer looked up sharply. It was a moment before he replied. "We are looking for this Indian. He has for years made mischief," he said. The Spaniard began thumping his pointed finger on the desk. "No. That is an understatement. It is much more than mischief. It is a calculated, violent resistance against the authority of the Spanish government. We have traced his activities to Guale in 1597 when five priests were murdered. One reliable report dates as far back as Menéndez de Aviles' first incursion up the San Juan thirty years earlier."

"He must be a very old Indian by now," Coya said, unable to suppress a faint smile.

"Or perhaps this title *Atichicolo-Iri* has been passed down to a younger man," the sergeant major said. "You may have heard of the problem at San Juan, just last year. We arrested the Chief of Santa Maria for refusing to surrender criminals to us, and we were taking him to San Augustín for trial. The *Cassica* of San Juan tried to rescue him, and our soldiers were ambushed by her warriors. I lost two men that day. She confessed her involvement, and we hanged her. Others of her people said she was under the influence of an Acueran they called Crying Bird."

"Perhaps there are more Indians named Crying Bird," Coya said. "Maybe it is just a coincidence."

"Recently we had to arrest another *cassica,* at Vera Cruz." The sergeant major began to inspect yet another document. "She refused to hand over *cimarrones* who fled their mission and refused to return. She said that Crying Bird claimed we had no authority in the matter."

"Is it now a crime to leave a mission?" Coya asked.

The sergeant major ignored the question. "We have reason to suspect this Crying Bird is your *inija*," he said, fixing Coya with a stern look.

"As you have said, Crying Bird is Acueran. We are Utinans. What proof do you have that this man is connected with my people?"

"Oh, I have proof." The officer walked to a trunk in the corner of the room and retrieved a piece of heavy wood wrapped in a blanket. He discarded the blanket and laid the object carefully on the polished desk. It was the weathered stock of a Spanish musket, now pierced by sharp spikes, its barrel removed.

"This was recovered at San Juan. It was used by the Indians as a war club to beat my men," the sergeant major said. "This weapon was a gift from the governor to an Utinan named Osprey, for services to the Crown. Here, near the trigger guard, you can see the carving of a bird. It is Osprey's mark."

Coya hefted the weapon is his hand. It was remarkable how it had been adapted for a new use. He lay it down carelessly, leaving a thin scar on the desk.

"We have heard a story that when Osprey tried to use it to murder you, the barrel exploded, and that you made it a gift to a man named Crying Bird."

Coya stood up. "Thank you for your time. I will look into these matters." He turned and began walking toward the door.

"But, will you answer me?"

Coya stopped in the doorway and turned back. "When we crossed the river at Tocoi three days ago, there were no people to help us."

The sergeant major wrapped the weapon in its blanket and placed it in the trunk.

"We have had trouble keeping reliable people there. They keep dying on us. The governor has agreed with a group of Indians upriver to move their village to Tocoi. Perhaps they will already be manning the canoes when you go back home."

As he walked to the door, down the outside steps and into the streets of San Augustín, Coya tried to imagine what people lived upriver who would be willing to uproot their village to serve the needs of the Spanish.

The next day, Marehootie's eyes opened for a time, but he did not recognize Coya or the priest, nor speak to them. Coya held the old man's head above the pillow, and fed him tiny sips of fish soup from a bowl held by Father Pareja. Marehootie lapsed again into a deep sleep, his breathing rasping and irregular.

During the night, the old man began to speak softly. Coya awoke at the sound. He had made his bed on the floor. He moved close, so he could make out what the old man had to say, but could not understand the words. They were spoken in the language of the spirits.

On the fifth day, Coya met with Father Pareja at the monastery. He could delay his departure no longer. When they had agreed on what was to happen, Coya led his men from San Augustín toward Ayacouta. When they arrived at Tocoi, the village had come to life with men willing to transport them across the river. They were old men and boys, but sufficiently skilled for the job.

Chapter 30

When Coya returned from San Augustín, Crying Bird was again away from Ayacouta, and no one could say where he had gone. He had returned in Coya's absence, but stayed only one night. When he left he took the old man, Yano, with him.

In disgust, Coya assigned the duties of *inija* to his father-in-law, Chilili. Crying Bird was gone so much of the time that people had begun to complain that he was never there to resolve their disputes.

With Chilili's help, Coya addressed problems that had arisen in Utina in his absence. For two days, he sat in his cabana in the council house, sipping cassina and listening to the complaints of the people.

A young man had fallen asleep on guard duty, and Big Bow demanded he be put to death. "A guard who sleeps is worse than no guard at all," he said. "People who believe they are guarded will sleep soundly. Then everyone is caught unawares by an intruder. He should forfeit his own life as an example to others."

The boy's mother, a respected matron of Earth Clan, said that her son was ill, and unable to keep his eyes open, even during the day. While Big Bow argued for his death the boy fell asleep, his chin resting on his chest.

"No one could sleep when people around him are talking about taking his life. The boy is ill," Coya said. "It will be sufficient punishment that he be tied to a post and whipped, and stripped of his privileges as a warrior. From now on he will work with the men who clear the fields and dig the ditches."

The mother said it was a fair decision, and that Coya was a wise and compassionate *Holata*.

Others came before him. Village chiefs argued with each other about fishing rights, disputed fields and the theft by one of the other's maize. One man was accused of seducing another's wife. Coya ordered him whipped and banished from the society of Utinans. When he went on to say that the woman, also, should be punished, some of the women who were allowed into the council house to listen murmured among themselves.

Many of the arguments should have been resolved by the chief of the village in which the dispute arose, and Coya refused to hear them.

On the afternoon of the second day, a runner came to Ayacouta with a rolled parchment. He refused to hand it to Chilili, saying the priest meant it for Coya's eyes only. It was a short letter from Father Pareja. It said that Marehootie had gone to be with God.

Before he and his men set out for San Juan del Puerto, Coya dispatched runners throughout Utina to find Crying Bird, to tell him of his brother's death and where and when he would be laid to rest. They were also instructed to say that on the order of Coya Ayacouta Utina, Crying Bird was immune from arrest for any crime he had ever committed, going to and from the funeral.

From Ayacouta, San Juan del Puerto lay directly to the east, beyond rough, uninhabitable country laced with ravines and shallow creeks. "There is only the old, abandoned village of Molono on that trail," Big Bow said to Coya as they planned their journey. "The traders all say the best way to San Juan is to take Eagle Nest Creek all the way to the River of the Sun, and then use the fast current north."

They portaged their canoes along good trails for a day, and then navigated the winding creek for a full day and the following night. Once they reached the river, it took less than two days before they arrived at Misión San Juan del Puerto, a day earlier than anyone believed possible.

Father Pareja was already at San Juan, and as Coya walked into the church, he and the resident friar were studying the old burial records to determine where Marehootie could be safely laid to rest without disturbing the bones of those already there. Nearly one hundred souls were buried beneath the clay floor of the sanctuary, almost all under Pareja's direction while he served at San Juan. The ink on the journal was faded, but Pareja's memory was clear.

"There is one burial place that is not presently occupied on the row closest to the altar," he said, pointing to the location. "It once contained the remains of Father Blas Rodriguez who was martyred at Guale in 1597. He was later dug up, on the orders of the governor, and re-interred at Nombre de Dios."

Coya bent over the diagram, looking at the spot where Pareja's finger pointed.

"My reading of the manual of mission interments tells me that these four plots are to accommodate members of the clergy, governmental officials or soldiers. Beside them, a row of chiefs who have accepted Christ and been baptized. Beyond that row, the common Indians are buried," Pareja said.

"The Rodriguez plot, if we may call it that, has been consecrated already. Since it is vacant, I can find no prohibition against using it for a man of Marehootie's spiritual stature. Besides, I am custos of missions, and it is perhaps within my discretion to make such judgments."

Coya looked up. "Who lies here, on the second row, next to where you propose to lay Marehootie?"

"That is where Tacatacura, the Paramount of Mocama, lies."

"Marehootie and I were with Tacatacura when he was murdered," Coya said.

"I had heard that before. Marehootie told it to me."

The other priest had stepped into the sacristy. Coya spoke quietly to Father Pareja. "You should know that I suspect Marehootie was also at Guale."

Father Pareja was slow to answer. "Marehootie and I talked of many things before he was baptized. Father de Avila survived the Guale massacre, and says it was Marehootie who saved his life at Tulafina."

"So he will lie in the place of a priest, next to his old friend, Tacatacura," said Coya.

"Only his body will be there, my son," Father Pareja said. "The spirit of Marehootie is already with God."

Marehootie was laid to rest with great honors. All of the chiefs of Mocama attended, or sent their representatives if they were ill and unable to travel. Freshwater chiefs from miles upstream came, as well as Guale chiefs, Potanans and Acuerans. Old friends met and greeted one another, avoiding eye contact with old enemies who were all around.

Marehootie was laid on his side, his knees drawn up and his hands together clasping a gorget, a religious cross, expertly carved from shiny white seashell. Beneath the shroud, at Coya's request, Marehootie had his tools, the carving blades and metal awls, to occupy his time when he reached his destination, whether it be Heaven or the Village of the Spirits.

After the service, Coya spoke to no one, but walked from the church to the convento where he had lived as a child. There were no longer any religious students at San Juan, and the room in which they had slept was now used for storage.

Coya did not emerge from the convento for seven days. Big Bow stood guard at the door and would allow no one to enter. Each morning Big Bow placed a cup of water inside the doorway.

The priest had delayed his return to San Augustín, and was there, sitting on the porch, when Coya came out. Coya's face was gaunt with grief and his hair was cut short.

"I have something for you," Father Pareja said after Coya had broken his fast with cassina and corn cakes. Pareja opened a small wooden box and withdrew a carved sea shell gorget and handed it to Coya. It fit in the palm of his hand. The outside edge was finely scalloped, and the center had been cut away in four sections, leaving a cross suspended in the middle.

Father Pareja took it from Coya. "Watch this," he said, holding the gorget toward the sun. The shadow of a perfect circle and cross fell upon the priest's robe. "He made this for you. Our friend was very artistic, and this was his best work. He told me to give it to you upon his death. When he and I spoke for the last time, he said he had experienced a vision, that of a child, and his last wish was that you give it to your son."

"I have no son. Mora and I have had two babies, both born dead."

Father Pareja crossed himself. "Keep it. Marehootie was quite sure you will have an heir some day.

When Coya ordered Big Bow to return home with the men, the way they had come, the *paracousi* refused to obey the order. "My duty is to be with you, to protect you. You can kill me now if you wish, or deal with me as you will at Ayacouta, but I will not leave your side."

Coya gave up the argument. "Very well. Send the men ahead. You and I will go home by way of the village of Molono. It was abandoned when Olate Ouai Utina decided it was too remote to be defended from attack. We have few enemies now. Perhaps we will want to use that village once again as a hunting camp or perhaps to use the old fields to plant maize."

Chapter 31

Yano was having a very good day. It was he who had suggested to Crying Bird that they come to this old, abandoned, remote Utinan village, where they could work in secrecy, without fear of being discovered. And that very day, Crying Bird had bestowed upon Yano one of the highest honors of his life by naming him *inija* and placing him in charge of the ceremonies that would precede the historic business that brought them here.

The council house at Molona fared better than the other village structures, many of which had fallen down from years of neglect, some having disappeared completely. Even so, it was in serious need of repair. Cracks in the daub between the pine timber walls admitted thin slivers of sunlight during the day and cold air during the winter months. The fire pit in the center of the house sat directly beneath the circular roof opening, but the smoke, disturbed by the unwanted draught, did not rise up to escape, but drifted about inside.

Torches burning pine tar stood between the low benches and the higher cabanas, adding to the polluted air, irritating the eyes and making it difficult to breathe for the sixty men and boys who sat around consuming the last of the maize cakes that had been provided. A clay pot of cassina simmered on the fire.

An elevated cabana, directly across from the low entrance, was adorned by Yano with bowers of woven palmetto leaves and garlands of holly and mistletoe. He had hung fierce cloaks and headpieces of wolves, panthers and bobcats from low posts, symbolic spirits standing guard. Otherwise, the chief's seat was unoccupied.

To either side, a half-circle of cabanas on slightly lower levels provided seating for elder chiefs of lesser stature, their clothing, faces and headpieces reflecting a diversity of cultures. The others, mostly old men and boys, occupied benches and pulled their cloaks about them to stay warm while they waited.

A small speaker's platform sat between the cabanas and benches, and a man was there, trying to be heard. Only a few bothered to listen. He was Mayaca, and most of the others were Timucua and did not understand his words, nor care what he had to say, so they ignored him.

Yano, bearing the face paint of a high chief of the Ocale, busied himself going from cabana to cabana seeking volunteers among the chiefs to be the next to speak after the Mayaca was finished.

A village chief of the Mocama strode to the speaking stand, his hair decorated with the feathers of sea birds. He was an impressive man in appearance, tall and muscular, but a poor speaker who stuttered and stammered as he tried to say what was on his mind.

He was followed by the chief of a remote village of Utina, a man so old that he stood supported by a walking stick crooked under his arm to provide balance, his voice so faint, it was drowned out by the conversations of others. When he finished, the Utinan hobbled back to the low cabana provided for him. No one else stepped forward to speak. In time, some became restless, talking loudly or standing to look around.

Finally, as the crowd became unruly, Yano stepped up to speak. His appearance, that of an emaciated, toothless old man dressed in comical imitation of a chief, did little to silence them.

Yano lifted his attention stick and shook it, the small shells inside sounding a thin rattle. Still, the younger men continued to talk and look around. An elder chief with his own attention stick joined Yano, as did others. Some began to shout out, "Show respect," and, "Quiet!" Soon, a semblance of order was restored in the house, and Yano looked around, cleared his throat and began to talk.

"Welcome, you of the nations of the Timucua, the Mayaca, the Surruque, the Guale and the..." Yano looked down at his hand, counting on his fingers.

"And the Guale," he continued. "I recognize chiefs of the coastal lands to the north." He raised his stick and pointed toward the cabanas where Guale were seated. "The island nations to the east." He gestured toward the delegations of Mocama, Satureiwan, and Tacatacuran who sat as a single group on his left side. "And our brothers the Mayaca, the Ais and the Surruque, fierce warriors of the south."

Yano cleared his throat once again, but gained strength now that he had the attention of the crowd.

"We who live to the west, representatives of Acuera, Utina, Potano, Yustaga and Ocale, we welcome you. What can you take from that, what I have pronounced? Have I erred? Do I miscount? Are the Guale with us?"

"Haw!" the Guale shouted together, raising their fists in salute.

"Are the Mayaca here and ready to defend their homeland?"

Again, shouts and clenched fists were raised from another part of the house.

"And the children of Utina, are you at long last girded for war?"

So it went, through the roll call of the nations. Yano shouted his challenge and he was answered back in kind. Only when he called upon the Acuera was he greeted by silence, and he quickly went on to the next nation of eager warriors.

When all present had voiced their support, Yano went on, now in a deeper, softer tone. He had the men's attention and it was no longer necessary to strain his aged voice.

"I will recite for you a tale that is familiar to all of us who share the Timucua tongue. Perhaps the Guale, also, and the Jororo, and the Mayaca, if they consult their keepers of legend, will also recognize it in their heritage. Perhaps the name that is used among my people is different from yours, or my tiny details vary or sound strange or unfamiliar, but the essence of the legend is a gift of spirit for us all, and it is true.

"I first heard it as a child at the feet of a great Ocale Chief who was my grandfather. He told me first of the strength of a great people who inhabited a vast land between two seas. He told me of their traditions. Wise leaders who were compassionate in their just rulings, and were the objects of the love and obedient devotion of lesser people who knew their station in life and did their work well for the benefit of all. Wives who honored their husbands, and men who sacrificed themselves for their families. Children who cared for their parents and uncles, and who listened and remembered for a lifetime what they were taught by the elders. They respected the land, and took from it only what they needed. They spoke through shamans to the spirits of ancestors whose names and deeds they remembered and respected.

"They were a peaceful people with good relations among themselves and willingness to trade fairly with their neighbors. Yet their kindly nature and softness of speech was sometimes a sign to others of weakness or lack of spirit.

"When this occurred, as it sometimes did, and the enemy did not apologize for the insult nor offer recompense for a life taken or a field burned, then the people would rise up in righteous anger, and their wrath would shake the earth.

"Courage in battle defined them. The death of comrades only strengthened their resolve, and the sting of arrows was to them but that of a mosquito. They fought as a mother bear fights to protect her cub, or a panther beset by hunting dogs. They shed their own blood, but more blood of the enemy.

"Have you heard this? Do you know what I'm leading to?" Yano raised his voice.

"Haw! Haw!" the Ocale, the Utinans, the Potanans and the rest of those who spoke the Timucua tongue shouted in unison, raising their fists high. Those in the cabanas stomped their feet on the boards, while the ones who sat on the benches beat their feet on the clay floor. Only the Guale, Mayaca and Jororo looked puzzled.

"For those who have not heard it, I will tell you," Yano continued, growing stronger. "There was a day, in the Land of the Spirits," he began.

Shouts went up, and sounds of excited rejoicing were heard, interrupting Yano as many understood what they were again about to hear.

"There was a day when Wind whispered a message into the ear of the Spirit of War. 'I have been asked a riddle by the people, and I do not know how to answer them. They know you have said they will never be defeated in battle, so long as they are many and strong and well-armed, and alert to ambush, and fierce and unrelenting, and willing to give their own lives to protect the others.'

"'That is what I promised them the day they were created,' War Spirit said.

"'But the question they pose to me is this,' Wind said. 'How shall we win if the enemy is as strong, as well-armed, as alert to ambush, as fierce and unrelenting, and as willing to die as we, and yet he outnumbers us in warriors?'

"War Spirit puffed out his chest. 'Wait here, Wind, until I return with the answer.' Whereupon, War Spirit ran into a bramble of briars and bushes from which a loud uproar of yipping and snarling could be heard. Presently, War Spirit returned. He carried a wooden box, with slats in the side. Inside, a gray fox cried for release.

"'It was an impertinent question, a trickster's riddle,' War Spirit said. 'I knew he would be waiting there, hiding, to catch me with his joke. I will pronounce the trickster's punishment, after I answer the trickster's riddle.'

"'How shall we defeat an enemy who is as strong, as well-armed, as alert to ambush, as fierce and unrelenting in battle, and as willing to die, and yet outnumbers us greatly? It is a trick on the people to ask the question, for all I require for my promise of victory is that they trust me, that they believe my words will deliver them. But they have asked it, and now I must withdraw my assurance of victory or punish them for questioning my word. Which shall it be, Wind?'

"Then Wind said, 'It seems to me that punishment is appropriate, but it should be the trickster who is condemned, and not the people who were tricked into asking an impertinent question.'

"War Spirit marveled at the wisdom of Wind. 'The trickster shall have his punishment,' War Spirit said. 'From this day the gray fox will never again live with men, nor eat at their campfire. He will be shunned, and ignored, and his riddles will be answered with an arrow. Now, the people shall have their answer. But warn them, Wind, to never again question me on what I have promised, or the promise will be withdrawn.

"'On the day the people will be overwhelmed by a more numerous enemy that is as strong, as well-armed, as alert to ambush, as fierce and unrelenting, and as willing to die as they, when the last of their hope is gone, they will yet achieve victory. In those days I will come among them, an immortal warrior, stronger, better-armed, more alert to ambush, more fierce and unrelenting than all the mortal enemies who have ever lived. I will lead them to easy victory. The enemy will look at my face and fall on their spears. I will be called . . .'"

At this point, Yano paused and looked at the faces of the others. Even the heads of the Guale and the Mayaca and the others who were not of the Timucua tradition, nodded up and down in recognition and approval and expectation of what he would say next.

"In the language of my people, the Spirit of War that day pronounced the name, *Atichicolo-Iri.* Some of you might say, simply, Spirit Warrior."

Bedlam broke out. Feet stomped, attention sticks were pounded to splinters on the benches. "*Atichicolo-Iri, Atichicolo-Iri,*" they all shouted in unison. Louder, they shouted. The very air in the council house was moved by the sound, rising directly upward to escape.

Crying Bird stepped through the doorway, his face painted red ochre and black. He wore a match coat of finest deer hide, painted with a hundred brilliant red and white lightning bolts. A copper breastplate with a jagged hole at its center was suspended over his heart. On his head an eagle perched, its mouth stretched open in a silent scream.

He took his place in the seat of honor.

The *Paracousi* of Surruque pronounced the war plan devised by Crying Bird a sound one. “To kill *itori* you must first find its weakness, a soft, vulnerable spot where we can inflict a bloody wound. We turn the beast on its back, and our spears easily pierce the soft underbelly into its heart.”

The Surruque was the third warrior to speak, and his analysis was the same as that of the others. “We must fight the battle on our ground, and not his. As my brother from Potano has observed, the vulnerable spot on the Spanish alligator is the river crossing at Tocoi. It is their only access to re-supply from their friends the Utinans. I would respectfully disagree with Yano’s thought that Coya Ayacouta Utina may come to his senses and join us. That is only wishful thinking and not the fabric of sound war policy. The Utinans have been the friends of the Spanish since they arrived. Potano knows that better than anyone.”

Yano rose to defend himself. “I only meant to say that Coya might not support the Spanish soldiers. His love is for the Franciscans. It is they who nurtured him as a child. When he was beaten by the soldiers at San Juan he left there to join the resistance with Crying Bird, *Atichicolo-Iri*.”

Yano looked up to Crying Bird who sat in the highest cabana and who had not spoken a word during the discussion. Still, Crying Bird remained silent.

“When we assure Coya that the priests will not be killed, but will be allowed to withdraw with the rest, my hope is he will remain neutral,” Yano said.

“May I be heard?” It was a minor war chief of Ocale, standing among his delegation. “It seems to me that the mission priests should be our hostages. They are not well-defended, and the soldiers will not attack us at the risk of a priest’s death. It is the missions where I believe the Spanish are most vulnerable.”

From the delegation of Mayaca, another voice was heard. “The priests are Spanish, also, and they should be the first to die.” Shouts of approval echoed in the house.

A sharp crack was heard. Crying Bird had shattered his attention stick on the floor of his cabana. His voice rose above the rest. "The priests will not be harmed. They will be allowed to return to San Augustín without interference."

The man from Ocale rose to answer, but sat down after a brief moment of thought.

An hour later, the *Paracousi* of Surruque stood to summarize the plan to which they had all finally agreed. On the night of winter solstice, Crying Bird would lead a force of one hundred warriors, including Acuerans he knew he could depend upon, to seize Tocoi crossing and kill any Spaniard they found, as well as the Indians who worked for them.

The Surruque and Mayaca would move north, possibly as far as the River the Spanish called Matanzas, blocking the use of any trails. There was a small fort there, and not more than three or four soldiers, who could easily be killed.

Meanwhile, a force of Guale and Mocama would seize Misiónes San Pedro and San Juan del Puerto. Any soldiers who escaped to the south would be ambushed by the Satureiwans, who would move into position the day before to block the trails.

"There are fewer than 200 soldiers in the territory," the *paracousi* said. "They will have no choice but to withdraw. When they are gone, we will burn San Augustín and erase any sign of their presence in our land."

As Crying Bird was being greeted at his cabana by the most notable chiefs, someone pushed his way past the guards at the door and into the council house. It was Big Bow, the *Paracousi* of Utina. Behind him, Coya Ayacouta Utina stepped into the torchlight.

Chapter 32

The wounds to Big Bow's head were deep, but healed slowly under Mora's care. The *Isucu* of Utina conjured a poultice of spider web and comfrey leaves and the foremost *jarva* cast his spells and invoked the healing spirits. Coya Ayacouta Utina prayed to the Christian God that his *paracousi* might live.

For three days, no work was done in the village. Big Bow's stature had grown on news that he had taken a blow from a war axe that was intended for his chief.

Only the headaches remained, and the loss of memory. Willow bark cure eased the head pain, but there was no sign that Big Bow could remember.

For the first time since their return, Big Bow and Coya met in the chief's house. A wet winter storm had blown through the village the day before, and during the night it had become colder, leaving tiny arrows of ice hanging from the trees. A fire blazed in the hearth. Mora took her husband's bear skin robe and wrapped it around Big Bow's shoulders, as he still suffered chills.

"Do you remember the council house at Molona and what happened there?" Coya asked, as Big Bow warmed his hands on a steaming gourd of cassina.

"I remember leaving the others on the river, and searching for a trail that would take us to the west. You said you wanted to find an old, abandoned village. I don't remember anything else, except that I was angry and thought you were foolish to leave your guard behind."

Coya sipped from his own gourd, looking at his brother-in-law huddled on the other side of the fire. "I see you have lost only your memory. Your impertinence seems to be as strong as ever."

Behind Big Bow, Mora sat on a bench, mending clothes. She fixed Coya with a hard look, frowning and shaking her head.

"I will tell you what happened, because I need your counsel on what I should do next," Coya said.

"The *Holata Aco* of Utina needs advice from a lowly, impertinent soldier?" Big Bow asked.

"Only on matters of military tactics. That is a subject where I value your opinion greatly," Coya said, "but you need to know what you have forgotten, if you are to give me sound advice.

"We found Molona, you and I. How could we not? We camped that night beside an old, overgrown trail. It was difficult country with woods so thick and brambly we could hardly see into the trail at all, even in the winter. You woke me, saying that you heard sounds ahead of us, as if people were shouting and celebrating. We stumbled along the trail in the darkness, and there was Molona. The sounds came from the council house. Do you remember any of this?"

"No. I wish I did remember. Sometimes my head hurts too much to think at all," Big Bow said.

"You forced your way between two men who guarded the door. One of them swung his axe at me and you turned to block the blow. You used your head, which was probably not a good idea."

Mora cleared her throat and gave her husband a stern look.

"You were on your knees, and you pulled out your knife and tried to stand. The guard swung the axe once again. It glanced off my shoulder and struck you on top of your head. You fell on your face and did not move again. I thought you were dead."

Mora moved to where Big Bow sat, bent over and kissed his cheek. "My brother has a hard head," she said.

"As does his sister, my wife," Coya replied.

Mora tossed her head and returned to her sewing.

"We had walked into a secret war council. Crying Bird was there, as well as Yano. I saw one Utinan village chief, and a few other Utinans. Some were probably Mayaca, although I cannot be sure, and many spoke Timucua tongues. There were about sixty or seventy of them, but they were a sorry lot. There were three men who I judged to be *paracousi,* but they were so old it is laughable to imagine them leading men in war. There were boys, also, some barely old enough to be away from their mother's teat.

"I was unharmed, other than rope burns where they tied my arms and legs. They thought you were dead, so they didn't bother to tie you. We were thrown into a hut near the council house, close enough that I could hear much of what was said.

"They had agreed to a war plan, but they did not repeat what they had in mind, or when or where it would start. They argued among themselves, some saying that because they were discovered, I must be killed. They already thought you were dead.

"Crying Bird argued with the *paracousi,* saying that I did not know their plans, and they had nothing to fear from me. He told them that I am a Christian, weak-willed, soft, and not a strong leader. I would be afraid even to try to warn the Spanish. His words cut me more deeply than the ropes that bound me. He even said that his own brother, Marehootie, had become a Christian, and was so poisoned by it that he chose to rot to death in a Spanish prison, rather than stand up and fight as he did when he was younger." Coya rubbed the scar on his left wrist.

"Crying Bird warned them that if the Chief of Utina were killed, our people would rise up and join the Spanish and hunt them down and butcher every one of them. That convinced one of the *paracousi,* but some of the others doubted the wisdom of Crying Bird's words.

"You awoke, and although you were confused you loosened the bindings on my arms. When I shed the ropes you went back to sleep. Just before morning, while the others slept,

I heard someone at the door of the hut. When he walked away, I tried the door and it was no longer fastened shut."

"How did we escape? Was I able to walk?" Big Bow asked.

"I carried you on my back until it was daylight, then I dragged you into a thicket of briars and poison ivy."

"That explains the rashes all over my body," Big Bow said, scratching under his arm.

"They came looking for us, of course. They had sharp knives to cut away the bushes. They would have discovered our hiding place, but they saw the poison ivy and decided to look somewhere else. On the second day, you had wits enough to walk. They continued to look for us, but we avoided the main trails until we were near Ayacouta.

"Now, let me ask my question. As *paracousi*, if you were Crying Bird's man, how would you plan to defeat the Spanish?" Coya reached out and offered Big Bow his tobacco pipe.

After he had smoked, Big Bow handed the pipe to Coya and covered his face with his hands. He was with his thoughts for a long time. Eventually, he looked up.

"There would be more than one way to do it, but if I were Crying Bird's war chief I would seize a frigate or any boat in the bay that has cannons. I would shoot the weapons at the fort to draw their attention. Then I would attack the fort with warriors from the south. Once we controlled the fort, we would use their land cannons to destroy San Augustín."

Coya thought on what Big Bow had said, and tried to picture it in his mind.

"I don't know if there is much danger to the Spanish from Crying Bird. I suppose the Spanish can deal with a few old men and runny-nosed boys."

Coya studied the embers of the fire, and then looked up. "Still, if the missions or the Spanish town are attacked, people will die. Possibly it will be the priests. I cannot allow that to happen."

Coya stood and walked to the door, looking out at the bleak winter morning. It was raining again.

"Perhaps I should go to the governor and say that my grandfather, the man who raised me and made me a chief, is now intent on killing them all."

Mora spoke for the first time. "If it is not already too late," she said.

"I hope you know that a *paracousi* is not smart enough to tell a chief what to do," Big Bow said.

When Coya returned to his pallet and sat down, his *paracousi* spoke once again.

"On the night of our escape," Big Bow said, "did I not cry out at all?"

Coya's forehead wrinkled as he thought back. "You made some noise, but I covered your mouth with my hands."

"You should have left me in the hut, or killed me when I became a danger to you."

Coya retrieved a burning stick from the fire and relit his pipe. When the first cloud of smoke disappeared, his eyes met those of Mora. She smiled, and turned back to her work.

"I thought of that. Then I thought, if I kill my worthless brother-in-law, who will be the uncle to the child my wife carries in her belly?"

Seven days after the celebration of winter solstice, Big Bow came looking for Coya.

"I took my men hunting in the fields and forests to the east. We did quite well. Early this morning we killed a fat deer, and a little later we felled two turkeys. But we found something else you will want to see."

Coya followed his *paracousi* to the camp fire at the edge of the village where the hunting party butchered and smoked the venison and turkey. Sitting by the fire, warming his hands, was Yano. He was naked, but for the match coat of turkey feathers someone had draped over his shoulders. Other than briar scratches on his arms and legs, he seemed to be uninjured. He was offered roasted deer meat, and he went at it hungrily.

Later, after Yano had rested, he was brought to Coya's house.

"I know that I must die for what I have done. I did not come here on purpose. My sense of direction is not good. I was searching for *Atichicolo-Iri* when your people found me, and I was hungry and cold, so I did not try to hide myself."

"Is your belly full, and are you warm enough now?" Mora asked.

"Yes, thank you." Yano looked back at Coya who lay before the fire, leaning on his elbow.

"Will you tell me what you know?" Coya asked.

Yano was quiet for a long time before he answered. "I suppose it can do no harm, now.

"After you escaped us at Molona, I went with Crying Bird to Acuera where he hoped to collect fifty warriors. We knew by then that one of the *paracousi,* the one from Potano, had quit the war and gone home with his seven people. Crying Bird said that they could easily be replaced with Acuerans who are better fighters, anyway.

"We could find no one worthwhile in Acuera. We went to three villages. There were a few sick people and many already dead. Crying Bird took me further upriver to Second Wekiva. It was a wasted trip. Houses all fallen down, grass and weeds everywhere. Then it came time to meet the others to attack Tocoi."

Coya looked to his right, where Big Bow sat, listening. Big Bow shrugged his shoulders.

"Crying Bird always said we needed one hundred men to capture the crossing and hold it if the Spanish attacked us, but he had decided we could do it with half that number. There were only fifteen of us, not fifty. There were a few Yustagans. I suppose the chief from one of your villages up to the north must have got lost on the way to Tocoi, along with the twenty men he promised. Perhaps he lost his nerve when you recognized him at Molona.

"Crying Bird said that we would do it with fifteen men, that the others to the north and south would do their duty and we could not fail them. During the night, two Satureiwans disappeared into the woods. Crying Bird said we would do it with what we had left.

"We stole a war canoe that night and prepared to attack in the morning. That way, nobody could slip away from us in the daylight. Before the sun came up, Crying Bird and I went to the edge of the river and hid in the cattails to count how many of the enemy there might be. The people came out of their houses, and they started a fire to cook some cassina. We could smell it, and it made me want to eat instead of kill people. We could hear them talking with each other, and laughing."

Yano paused.

"They were Acuerans," he finally said, and he began to cry.

"It was too much for Crying Bird. He was still grieving the death of Marehootie. He could not kill his own people. He ordered me to go back and tell the others to go home. He said that when I came back, he would take me to a secret place he knew where we would be safe. I returned quickly, but he must have tired of waiting for me. I went looking for him and got lost."

Vaquero

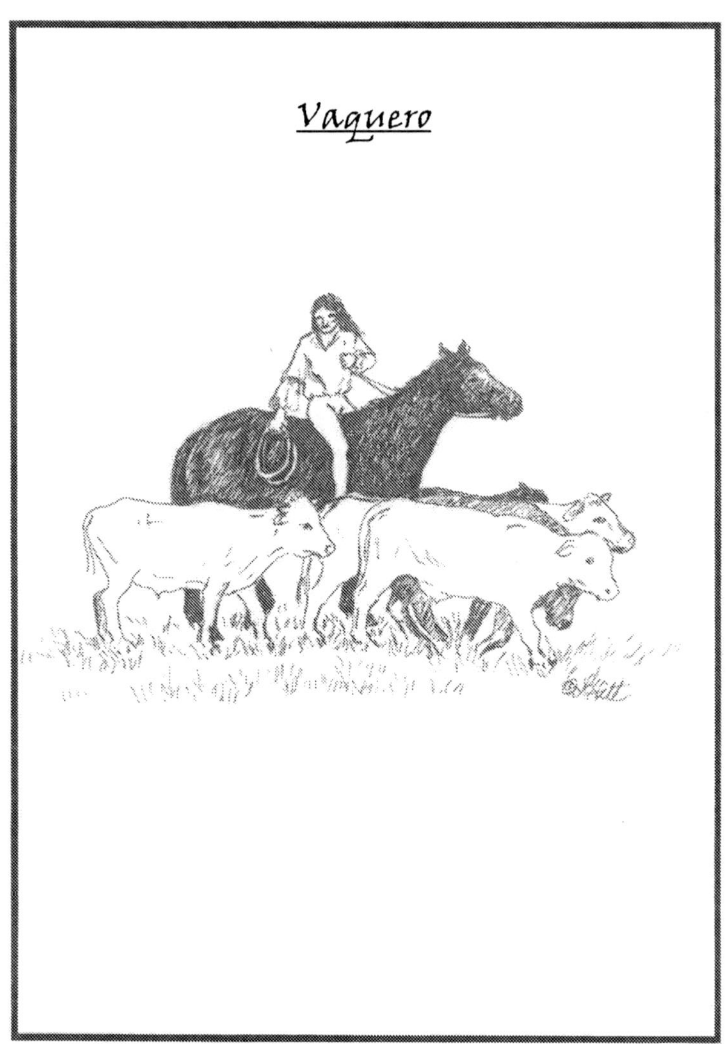

Chapter 33

La Chua Ranchero
Potano, 1635

The younger boy, the Indian, slowed his horse from a gallop to a fast trot and glanced behind him along the winding trail that marked the eastern boundary of the ranch. Juan Menéndez was nowhere in sight.

The last time the boys were together, they waded their horses across the creek. Once they reached high ground, the Spanish boy jumped into the saddle and spurred his horse, signaling that the race was on.

The sorrel, smaller by two hands than the roan, loved to run, and unencumbered by heavy tack, responded to the gentle urgings of its rider. By the time they reached the trail, Lucas had overcome the distance gained by surprise and passed his companion. Soon, horse and rider were well ahead, and then out of sight, as they followed the old trail to the southeast, paralleling the creek.

The trail came to a fork. To the left, it descended to rejoin the creek, and led to an abandoned village. Still, there was no sign of his companion. Lucas nudged the horse's flank with his right leg, and they climbed a gentle hillock, circling and avoiding the village, but providing an excellent view from the higher land which had once been a planting field. The maize was gone now, after years of inattention, but scraggly bean plants could till be seen baking in the sun and searching for corn stalks to climb.

Potanans had once lived here. Lucas' father, the Paramount Chief of Utina, knew the village and its history. It had never been a large village, just a dozen or so houses, with perhaps thirty or forty people. They were Earth Clan, for the most part, people who tended the fields. One or two families of Fish Clan also lived here, taking eels and turtles from the water. The Potanans were very strict in regard to the work of their clans, unlike the Utinans who would sometimes allow people to contribute based upon their talent and interests, rather than strictly on clan custom.

"A Potanan must do the work of his mother's family, even if he hates it," Coya had told his son at an early age.

"Of course, Potanans who are fearless warriors can escape family work if they are accepted into the *paracousi's* guard. Athletes who excel in the ball game would also be honored and exempted from menial clan chores, but that was the way it is with all Timucua societies," his father had said.

Lucas had always counted his blessings that he was not required to follow his birth clan. His mother was also Earth, just as the people who had worked this field. But she was the wife of the *Holata Aco*. Even her brother, Big Bow, escaped his destiny and served as *paracousi*, war chief of all Utina. Were Lucas not son of the chief, had he not born the title Beloved Son, he might be pulling weeds this summer, or chasing crows from the maize fields.

As it was, his father's influence allowed Lucas to escape menial work. Years earlier Coya had befriended Juan's father, Francisco Menéndez Marquez, a man of wealth who raised cattle in Spain. Coya gave permission that this land, where Utina and Potano provinces joined, be used for a ranch. Señor Menéndez, in turn, offered to employ Lucas to work with his son, Juan, to earn a wage and learn to run cattle.

After two years the boys were inseparable, except when Juan went with his father to San Augustín, or when Lucas was ordered to Ayacouta for religious instruction at the mission.

The work on the ranch was hard, and the sun hot during most of the year. But how else, Lucas thought, could he have the chance to ride a horse and learn the skills of a *vaquero*?

Evenings at the ranch were spent on studies. The friar at San Martín provided Lucas with tracts of Catholic teachings to be memorized and recited upon the boy's return to Ayacouta. Señor Menéndez ordered the boys to continue their studies, and provided old business records which could be turned over and used to practice their penmanship.

Juan taught Lucas to read and write in Spanish, and Lucas taught the young Spaniard the Timucua tongue. The Indian learned quickly, and in half a year could write clearly. Juan thought that writing Timucua was a waste of time, and Lucas had overheard him telling his father that the Indian language was useless to educated people. But Señor Menéndez had business dealings with the western tribes and saw value in his son's ability to write letters and agreements with Indians who had no understanding of Spanish, but who could read and write in their own language.

Riding a horse all day and chasing cows that stupidly lost themselves in the scrub was not easy, but to Lucas it was an enjoyable life, one that he shared with Juan who was as close to him as a brother.

As Lucas looked down into the abandoned village, he recalled his father's stories and his warnings to stay away. The village below the hill was cursed, his father said. Spanish soldiers had appeared there one day with orders that the people be moved to the mission village Santa Fé where they would receive the blessings of Catholic instruction from a priest. At the same time, they could work as bearers, carrying bundles between the missions at Santa Fé and San Francisco de Potano.

"You need Bear Clan people for this work," the village chief was reported to have said. "They have strong backs. We are the people who grow that which they carry about."

The chief was whipped for his insolence and humiliated before his people, and they were given no choice in the matter.

Many were unhappy with the move to Santa Fé, and half of them returned home. An illness befell the village, and they all died in less than a month. Of those who remained in Santa Fé, two drowned while ferrying heavy bundles across the river. Five others were ordered to travel to San Augustín, and never returned to their families.

Lucas let his horse graze in the thin grass as he sat on a tree stump thinking on these matters. From where he sat, he kept an eye on the fork in the trail. Time passed, and Juan still did not come.

Lucas remounted and rode back down the trail. The sound of a pistol shot echoed through the woods, and he urged the horse to a full run, ducking his head to avoid branches that overhung the trail, and leaning right and left to counter the sudden turns.

Another shot. This one was much closer. After one more jog in the trail, Lucas slung his right leg over the horse's withers, and landed on his feet, running. Juan Menéndez lay beside the trail, leaning on one elbow. The pistol in his right hand still smoked.

The roan lay on all fours on its belly, as if preparing to rise, but it did not move. Its neck and head were stretched out into the dirt, as if bowing to its master. Blood oozed from the bullet hole in its forehead and ran down its face. The horse's right rear leg protruded outward at a strange angle.

"Didn't you hear my shouts," Juan demanded, even before Lucas fell to his knees beside him.

"Don't move," Lucas said, cushioning one hand behind the older boy's head. Lucas took the pistol and laid it aside, and lifted Juan's arm so he would lie down on his back. "I must check for broken bones," he said.

The Spanish boy complained and cursed, but did not resist as Lucas began to examine him. Other than scrape marks on the side of his face, there was no sign of injury to the head or neck. Neither his arms nor legs showed any deformity other than scratch marks on both elbows that bled through the heavy woolen shirt.

"You killed the horse?" Lucas asked.

"His rear left leg is broken. Any fool can see that."

"Can you sit up?" Lucas moved behind him and reached under his arms to lift him. It was then Lucas saw the rattlesnake, slowly writhing in the dirt as if trying to determine why its head was all but severed from its body. A bullet had sliced through the white meat behind the head, exposing the tiny bones of the spine.

"Good shot," Lucas said.

"My father will kill us," Juan complained once he regained his feet and began to walk about, testing his legs. "He has warned us against racing the horses."

"How did it happen?" Lucas asked.

"Isn't it obvious? The horse stepped on the snake and reared up. I fell off. The horse's left leg gave way and it almost fell on me. Now, wouldn't that be a mess?"

Satisfied that his friend had no serious injuries, Lucas went to fetch the sorrel which by now had seen the snake moving in the path and showed signs of running away.

"I shouted for you, but you didn't come. The horse tried to get up but it was obvious the leg was broken. I shot him. I knew you would hear me and come back. I had my powder and shot in the pouch on the saddle bag and I crawled over there and reloaded the pistol. The snake was still alive, and I shot him too. Perhaps you will tell my father about my marksmanship and good judgment. Maybe that will save us both some of the lashes we will receive when we return to the ranch with only one horse."

Juan walked to where the snake lay and bent over to examine it. "Perhaps a meal of roasted rattlesnake will put my father in a better mood," Juan said.

Lucas' shouted warning came too late. Juan picked up the snake which reacted to the touch by jerking its head about and sinking it's fangs into the boy's forearm.

Lucas grabbed the snake and pulled its head directly back, loosing its teeth from Juan's flesh. A sticky stream of yellow poison oozed from the snake's mouth. Lucas severed the head from the body with his knife, and flung the head deep into the trees.

Juan was on the ground again, his face white as a cloud, his eyes wide and staring with disbelief at the twin bite marks, and the thin trickles of blood that ran down toward his elbow.

Lucas thought it was too soon for the venom to be working its evil, but Juan was already lying quietly. He was sweating now, and the pupils of his eyes were large. Lucas wiped away the snake blood from his knife and cut off his own shirt sleeve. He made a knot in the end and twisted the cloth repeatedly until it was wound into a rope. He tied it around Juan's upper arm.

By now Juan did not move, but groaned softly. Lucas held the arm firmly, and with the tip of his knife cut into the flesh across both fang marks. He sucked out the blood, spitting it into the dirt.

Later, he loosed the binding and sucked the blood and venom once again then tightened it securely. Lucas' uncle, Big Bow, had taught him to always carry a medicine pouch with him, and his father made the same point. Lucas found honey in it, and rubbed it into the wound, then wrapped it tightly with a bandage of tree moss. He mixed white willow leaf powder in water from the creek, and made Juan sip it from a cup.

In time, the Spaniard regained his senses and he was less frightened. He sat up, but said he was too dizzy and weak to stand or walk.

On a ranch of seventeen miles square, it was fortunate that they were so close to the ranch house. As the sun was setting, they arrived home. At Juan's insistence, Lucas had taken the tack from the dead horse and saddled the smaller animal. Still woozy, Juan sat slumped in the saddle while Lucas walked ahead, holding the reins. In his other hand he carried the dead snake.

Señor Menéndez was conducting business away from La Chua Ranch, but returned immediately when informed of the injury to his son. Two days later, he came looking for Lucas who was working with ranch hands, removing a cow that had become stuck in a bog.

"My son has explained to me how the snake bite happened. It was poor judgment on your part, challenging him to race the horses over rough ground. Sometimes you Indians are too wild for your own good, and others' safety. I will speak to your father. Coya is honorable. I will ask him to recompense me for half the value of the horse that was lost."

Lucas sat on his horse, his head down. Another worker came and removed from the horse's neck the harness and ropes used to rescue the cow. The cow stood unsteadily on its mud-caked legs.

"That is the way the horse was lost, was it not?" Menéndez asked.

Lucas opened his mouth to speak, but said nothing. He kept his eyes down and would not look at the Spaniard.

"I have decided to forbid you from riding my horses until this matter is concluded. I have only a few remaining, and they are expensive and difficult to replace," Menéndez said.

Lucas dismounted and handed him the reins.

"You can work on foot, the way the other men do," Menéndez said, as he turned to lead the horse away. Then he paused, and looked back at Lucas.

"I shall never forget that your courage and skill saved my son's life. For that, I can never repay you. You are like a son to me. Perhaps I will say that to your father, when I tell him about the horse."

Chapter 34

"A strange letter." Coya reached out, as if to hand the parchment to Chilili, but drew it back. His *inija* could not read.

"It was a Potanan messenger who delivered it," Chilili said.

Coya went to the doorway, knelt and threw back the door flap so he could study the document in the sunlight.

"Chief Potano may be very proud that he can write, but his penmanship is so shaky he should have a scrivener, as the Spanish do." The letter was written in the Timucua tongue, but on poor quality paper and with ink that had already begun to fade.

"He is asking that we meet together and talk about our problems. The new Chief of Potohiriba will be here, also. Potano suggests that Ayacouta would be a convenient place for such a meeting, since it is midway between Potano and Potohiriba."

"So he is inviting himself to come here?"

Coya sighed and massaged his forehead. Mora had said that his worries were making him an old man before his time. When he looked into the mirror that was a gift from the governor, Coya no longer recognized the face starring back, haggard, wrinkled and with gray hair showing at the temples. Strange, that he had not noticed it before Mora spoke.

"Potano has asked that we meet at a time when the priest is away from San Martín, and that our meeting be in secret."

Chilili stood and straightened his tunic. "In other words, the Spanish are not to know," the *inija* said. "Father Rogero will travel to San Augustín for six days to collect supplies for the new church. He plans to leave after Mass on Sunday."

Coya went to another part of the house and soon returned with a writing board, paper, turkey quill and ink.

"I will send letters to Potano and Potohiriba today, and we will meet with them in six days. That should give them enough time to arrive, and the priest will not be here to make them uncomfortable."

Chilili gathered his shell cup and pipe and prepared to go.

"Tell me about this Chief of Potohiriba. I have never met him. You attended his baptism and the dedication of the new church when Mora was ill and I could not leave her." Coya said, leaning over his writing.

"When I met him it was a time of celebration. He was a new *Holata* with a beautiful new church, and he was now a Christian. He appeared to be pleased with the honors that were given him."

Coya looked up. "But?"

Chilili paused before answering. "I saw something else. Perhaps it is because he paints his face black, in the old Yustagan custom. There is a certain wildness about the man. I saw it in his eyes."

"Let's hope the priest has tamed him with the Gospel," Coya said. "Potohiriba leads a nation of five thousand Yustagans. I would be more comfortable living next to a peace loving child of God, than a powerful warlord."

There was little in the way of ceremonial honors bestowed on the *Holatas* of Potohiriba and Potano upon their arrival in Ayacouta. Chilili, on Coya's orders, showed them the fine new church of Misión San Martín and the friar's convento.

"Our first church was little more than an open shed, with one wall behind the altar," the *inija* said as they stood in the sanctuary. "For fifteen years, whenever it rained everyone got wet, even the priest."

Chief Potano leaned back and looked up at the ceiling, the height of three men standing on each other's shoulders above the clay floor. "This is a little bit larger than the church at San Francisco de Potano," he said.

Chilili spread his arms apart. "Eight meters wide, twenty meters long, and the ceiling a little less than nine meters high," he said. "Father Rogero says it is almost as large as the church at Nombre de Dios. There is nothing nearly as large west of the River of the Sun."

"You must be very proud," the younger man, the Chief of Potohiriba said, moving toward the open doorway.

Coya Ayacouta Utina was waiting when the visitors were brought to the council house. He wore the deerskin match coat he reserved for entertainments and formal occasions. Potohiriba and Potano had changed from their traveling clothes, and were suitably dressed in turkey feather match coats. They had only their *inijas* with them. Their guard remained outside to be fed and entertained by the people of Ayacouta.

"I welcome my old friend, the *Holata Aco* of Potano," Coya said, once they took their places in the cabanas specially constructed for the occasion. Coya's seat was slightly higher than the others.

"I'm afraid that '*Aco*' no longer describes me," Potano said with a pleasant smile. "My people are greatly diminished in their number and in their villages. I thank you, however, for the honor of using the old title. Perhaps I was once worthy of it, but no longer."

"And my new friend, the great Chief of Potohiriba, welcome to Ayacouta and to Misión San Martín. I visited the land of Yustaga years ago and I remember the people of Potohiriba fondly. I only regret that I was unable to attend the dedication of San Pedro de Potohiriba, and the celebration of your baptism. May I address you by your Christian name, 'Don Diego?'"

It was a cloudy day, and dark inside the council house. Coya could see the whiteness of his eyes and the flash of his teeth as the man with the black face answered him.

"Only the priest calls me Diego. My people still call me Potohiriba. I prefer it that way," he said.

"Then, Potohiriba it shall be," Coya said.

Steaming cups of cassina were brought in, along with hickory nut cakes and honey. When they were done eating, they talked politely for awhile. After a time, when the visitors had told of the events of their journey to Ayacouta, they all fell silent. Coya would not be so impolite as to ask the reason they had come. Finally, Chief Potano cleared his throat.

"We have much in common, the three of us. Each has his own chiefdom to rule and people to keep safe. Even in the old days, before the time of the wars between Utina and Potano, my uncle told me of how hard it was to rule so many people over such a large province, dealing with the jealousies of our vassal chiefs and the other problems. Then, when the French and Spanish came, the wars between us only got worse. Instead of joining together, we continued to fight among ourselves. Those wars are finally at an end. Some of us just lost the will to fight any more, or perhaps we came to our senses. But still the problems plague us, even more so than before. We thought, Potohiriba and I, that it would be helpful if we met to talk among ourselves."

Potano glanced at Potohiriba who sat quietly with his arms folded, looking into the cold hearth in the middle of the room.

"I suppose that might be good to talk to each other about common problems," Coya said. "Sometimes I feel alone with my problems. Luckily for me, my *inija* shares many of my burdens." He glanced at Chilili, who had his eyes fixed on Chief Potohiriba.

Finally, Potohiriba spoke. "You were not surprised, Coya, when Potano said he was no longer *Holata Aco,* Chief Over Many, but only a simple *Holata*. He admits that his people are diminished, no longer even enough to start a decent war."

Potano lowered his eyes to the floor in front of him.

"Tell me, Coya, how is life among your river people?" the Yustagan said. "There was a time when there were thousands of them. I have heard from traders that some of your villages are now abandoned."

Coya did not offer to answer the question.

"And how many Surruque are there? Or Mayaca? When is the last time you have seen an Acueran trader?"

"What are you saying?" Coya asked, looking beyond the darkness of Potohiriba's face and into his eyes.

"We are all diminished. Not just Potano, but the rest of us, also. Only the Apalachee are still strong. They are as plentiful as fleas on a camp dog, and it is because they raise large crops and are favored by the Spanish."

"How can you say that? Have you counted them?" Coya asked.

Potohiriba smiled for the first time. "Yes. I have counted them. Not all of them, but we have been to Apalachee villages and know they are more plentiful than ever."

Coya smiled back. "You Yustagans have nothing better to do than count Apalachee?"

"You forget your history. The Apalachee have been our enemies for as long as we can remember. We would be at war today if it were not for the Spanish who forbid it. Tell me, Coya, how many Potanan men there are of fighting age? If you cannot say, you need to get yourself a better *paracousi*. I'm sure Potano, as diminished as he may be, could say how many Utinans live within a day's walk of his province."

Potano continued looking at the floor.

"What are you saying to me? What does all this mean?" Coya demanded.

"I'm simply saying what you must already know to be true. The Spanish work our men too hard, carrying maize to San Augustín and working as canoers at every river crossing. Now sometimes they force men to remain in the Spanish town, working on their fort. Young women do not have babies because their men are dead, or ill, or away from home.

"When I complain to the soldiers or to the governor, they do not listen to me. Even the priests are blind to what is happening. Now they are making more demands on us."

Potohiriba again glanced at Potano, who would not return his look.

"Tell him, Potano. Tell him what you came here to say. Do not look away," Potohiriba shouted, rapping his walking stick on the wooden floor of his cabana.

Potano looked at Potohiriba, and then turned to face Coya.

"The governor ordered me to abandon three villages in the north and to move the people to the trail. The priest said it would be good to have the people near a mission, so they could be taught the Word of God."

"Neither of us believes that is the reason for the order," Potohiriba said. "They want more men to work on the trail, to replace the ones who have died."

"The worst part," Potano continued, "is that the old people are ordered out of their homes, where they have lived their entire lives, and marched cross country to places they do not recognize. These are harmless people. Many still practice the old ways, but they do no harm to the Spanish or anyone else. In one village, many people live as they have lived from the beginning of time. They now plan a ceremony, a *Tacachale*, to ask the spirits if they should move as the Spanish demand, or whether it would be better that they die."

"I have not heard of a *Tacachale* in this land for many years," Coya said. "I was taught that ceremony by a man I considered my grandfather. Utina honored me with *Tacachale* when I was chosen *Holata Aco*. I am sure the priests would not allow it today." He thought for a moment. "But isn't that a little dramatic, this 'obey or die' notion?"

"Perhaps you should ask the people of Chiso, in Mocama province," Potohiriba said. "They ignored the Spanish order. Some were beaten or had their ears cut off. They were the lucky ones. Seven people died on the trail and their chief was hanged for resisting."

Coya sat quietly, stroking his chin. "I have heard that story, but my understanding was that the chieftess was hanged for failing to return *cimarrones* who had fled the mission."

Potohiriba and Potano looked at each other. Potohiriba smiled tightly and turned back to face Coya. "Respectfully, you are mistaken. The incident you mention occurred at San Juan.

But what is the difference? How is it that the Spanish have the right of life or death over us? How is it they can kill some for staying at their homes, and still others for moving from their homes?"

In the morning, after the visiting chiefs had left to go home, Big Bow came to see Coya.

"I spent time with our guests, the *Paracousi* of Potano and Potohiriba, as you had instructed. They were quite talkative. They said the chiefs came to honor you with the title, Paramount Chief of all Western Timucua, so you could speak with one strong voice to the Spanish regarding their grievances."

Mora brought cassina for her husband and her brother.

"Perhaps they forgot why they had come," Coya said. "Or maybe they changed their minds about me after they got here."

Chapter 35

The friar of San Martín prided himself and drew praise from his superiors in San Augustín for his successes in converting the Indians of Ayacouta and those who lived in villages clustered throughout the countryside of Utina. Of course, it was an advantage that Coya Ayacouta Utina had been a Christian all of his life and set an example of regular attendance at Mass. Even so, Coya resisted Father Rogero's suggestion that attendance be made mandatory and that slackers be whipped, as was done in some other missions closer to San Augustín.

Father Rogero's annual reports to the governor and the custos of missions listed the names of those undergoing religious training and those who had been baptized. The only comment he received from the custos, and Father Rogero considered it a rebuke, was that the past three reports listed the son of the chief as one being catechized, but never baptized.

"He is a boy, and strong-minded like his mother," Coya responded when the subject was first raised by the priest.

The next year Rogero was less inclined to accept excuses when Coya answered that Lucas spent most of his time at La Chua Ranchero, and as a boy had little time to devote to his studies.

"He is here perhaps half of the time," Rogero said. "And he is no longer a boy. Lucas finds time to be entertained by the young women, but little time for memorizing the catechism.

This has become a source of embarrassment for me in San Augustín."

When Coya told Lucas that he would not be allowed to visit the ranch again until he completed his studies and was baptized, the son devoted himself energetically, if not enthusiastically, to his studies. Within a month, Father Rogero came to the chief's house and said that Lucas had done all the memorizations required and answered all of the priest's questions correctly. He was ready for baptism.

"Shall I write to the governor to arrange the services in San Augustín? The governor might wish to serve as godfather, as he has done with some notable families."

"No," Coya said without hesitation. "Governor Ibarra treated me shabbily when I was last in San Augustín. He showed disrespect by sending me to the home of a soldier for my dinner. In the past, he has always entertained me at his house. Besides, he does not know the boy. For him to stand as godfather would be an insincere gesture, a sham. Señor Menéndez has said that when the time comes, it is his desire to be godfather. He loves Lucas and I trust him to fulfill his obligations more than I would Ibarra."

Rogero's brow furrowed. "You run the risk of offending the governor by disrespecting him in his own town."

"Then the baptism will take place right here, at our own mission," Coya said. "And you will have the honor of consecrating Lucas to the Lord's service."

"I will advise my superiors of your decision, Coya, and it will be an honor beyond measure for me to preside. Thank you," Father Rogero said.

"One more thing," Coya said as the priest prepared to return to the convento. "I know it is the custom to bestow a Spanish name when an Indian accepts Christ. His mother named him Lucas at his birth at the suggestion of Father Pareja who was custos at the time. It was a good decision to name him after the patron saint of healers. It fits him. Lucas has said that he also wishes to honor the man who has consented to be his protector, and unless there is some impropriety to it, my son will be baptized as Lucas Menéndez."

On the second Sunday of December, 1638, the son of the Paramount of Utina, Lucas Menéndez, was baptized by Father Diego Rogero at the front door of Misión San Martín de Ayacouta. Señor Francisco Menéndez Marquez, the Royal Treasurer of La Florida, stood by his side and pledged an oath of guardianship.

When the moment came for Father Rogero to place the silver cross around Lucas' neck, he produced, instead, a shell amulet of a cross, the size of a man's palm, a gorget tethered by a tightly woven fiber. Rogero held it aloft and asked God's blessing.

"A gift from the heart of an old man you never met in this life," he said, "but one who looks down upon you today with a grandfather's love."

Delegations from throughout western Timucua joined in the celebration, along with the leaders of Apalachee, Acuera, and Mocama. More than a thousand people attended. The council house could not contain the ones who came for the feast, and only the chiefs and their families and principal men were allowed in. The common people ate their fill of roast pork, maize and venison, along with sweet cakes in the church yard.

Señor Menéndez and the men from La Chua brought a cow which they butchered and roasted at the village barbacoa. Some people, whose taste ran to venison, bear and opossum, thought the beef had a strange and wild flavor.

Señor Menéndez also brought a gift to his godson, a small female dog he had acquired in San Augustín to herd his cows. "She is too timid," he said. "She nips and barks and runs in circles, but the cows ignore her. She will be a good village dog, and will kill rats and other vermin who invade the storage rooms."

A minor governmental official from San Augustín appeared as the meal was being eaten, apologized for his tardiness, and delivered a letter expressing the best wishes and blessings of the governor, as well as his regrets that his duties prevented him from attending.

Lucas held the dog in his lap while he ate, feeding it pieces of beef. He called the dog Efa.

Chapter 36

La Chua Ranchero

"Do you know the word '*Tacachale*?'" Juan Menéndez asked his companion. They were half a day's ride from the ranch house, camped on the side of a hill in a grove of ancient live oak.

Lucas looked up from the sassafras root he had carved into the shape of an alligator, and wiped his arm across his forehead to dislodge a mosquito that feasted there. "I know the word. Are you serious about learning the Timucua tongue, or is this a test to prove how smart you are?"

"Just a word I heard, and do not know its meaning."

The Indian tossed the alligator to the Spaniard who caught it deftly and leaned toward the light of the fire to inspect it.

"'*Taca*' means fire. '*Chale*' sometimes means to cleanse or purify. When said together, *Tacachale* speaks of an ancient ceremony. The fire is a path for the ancestors to speak to us through a *jarva,* a shaman. Some of the old people use the word when they talk about the good days. My father said that the last *Tacachale* in Ayacouta was the day he became chief."

The dog, Efa, trotted into camp clutching a dead mole, and laid it beside Lucas, who grasped it by the tail and threw it away. Efa sprung up and ran into the bushes to retrieve it.

"So it is a celebration, then?"

Lucas looked up through the low branches of the tree at the smoke that rose and bent to the east. There would be rain in the morning.

"My father has told me old stories, not the superstitions about the spirits the priest complain about, but things that happened in his life, and things he has been told by people he trusts. One story is about a *Tacachale* that was held when a great chief died, so maybe they do it in times of great sadness, also."

Juan rubbed the sassafras alligator with a rag soaked in bear grease, and it shined in the firelight. "Would people do *Tacachale* to find answers from the spirits, like when they are confused or worried about something they cannot control?"

Efa returned with the mole and gave it to Lucas, who ignored the offering.

"Do you mean like going to a *jarva* to learn the future? I suppose they could do that, but I expect asking the *jarva* would be less trouble than having a *Tacachale*, for people who still believe in those things."

Juan stood up and walked to where Lucas sat against the tree. He knelt down and handed him the carving. "Would you go with me to a *Tacachale*?" he asked.

"I do not think the padre would allow it. My father might banish me, he would be so embarrassed," Lucas said, looking at his friend. "You are serious about this, aren't you?"

"My father has been invited to a ceremony in a village four leagues north of La Chua, a place called Anohica. The village chief and his *inija* came to the ranch one day. Their dialect was strange, and Father had difficulty understanding them, but they wanted him to visit them for a ceremony, and they said the word '*Tacachale*.'"

"That sounds strange to me. I'm sure there are uncivilized people far out in the country who still observe the old ways," Lucas said, "but why would they invite a stranger and risk censure or punishment by the priest?"

Juan shrugged his shoulders. "Perhaps they have no priest, and the people do not know it is evil."

"Everyone knows the old ways are the works of the Devil," Lucas said.

"The old chief said that his people want to be good neighbors for the ranch, and to trade. He even said his people would work, and perhaps be paid with food. My father believes in making friends and fears that if he does not honor them they may start feeding themselves on stray cattle. It is much easier to kill a cow than a deer, and beef is much tastier."

"That is your opinion. I'll take roasted venison anytime, over stringy beef."

"They also said that my father would better understand them if he came to *Tacachale*, and that perhaps he would become their patron, or protector."

Efa lay down against Lucas' outstretched leg, and soon was fast asleep.

"When is this *Tacachale*?"

"It is in four days. My father has told me to go on his behalf, but I am afraid to walk alone into a village of Indians I do not know. I would not ask this of you, but you are my only friend."

Lucas looked up into the Spaniard's face, and then closed his eyes and leaned back against the tree. "If you promise not to tell my father or the priest, I will go with you."

Efa dreamed. Her legs jerked and she yipped softly as she chased a phantom rabbit.

"Why do you call her Efa?" Juan asked. "Doesn't 'Efa' mean dog in the tongue of the Mocama Indians?"

Lucas reached down and rubbed the dog's head. "She is the only dog I have ever had, and I'm not likely to ever have another. Do you want me to call her Rabbit?"

The trail leading northeast from La Chua was little more than a deer path, winding through thick woods and brush that appeared never to have been disturbed or cut. Rains had fallen, erasing any footprints left in the soft, sandy earth. Where the ground was of hard clay, only the hooves of deer left their mark.

"Not many traders come this way," Lucas quipped.

"Nor soldiers," Juan said, climbing to the top of a small knoll and looking around. Ahead the land gradually rose to the north, where a forest of pine reached toward the clouds. To the left, along a wide, shallow creek they had crossed earlier, a ridge as high as a man's head went on for a distance.

"Step down from there," Lucas said.

Puzzled, Juan took two steps down the slope and jumped to the ground.

Lucas took his walking stick and poked around in the side of the hill.

"Snake hole?" Juan asked.

Lucas continued to probe into the dirt until the pressure gave way and the stick moved freely in and out. He stepped back.

"We must go a different way," he said. "This place is very old. There may be spirits here. I think the hill you climbed may be the burial mound of someone's ancestor."

"Surely, you do not believe the old superstitions!" Juan exclaimed.

"Even the Holy Scripture frowns on defiling the places left to the dead," Lucas said, striking off in a different direction.

Anohica was small compared to the villages strung along the major Indian trails. It contained a cluster of twenty small houses hidden beneath a forest of tall trees. Juan and Lucas were welcomed by the village chief, his *inija* and his advisors. What struck Lucas first was that they all smiled warmly and greeted them with open kindness. As he looked them over, he could see that they were old people. There were no children, and only one or two women who might be of child-bearing age.

If the people of Anohica were disappointed that the ranch owner had sent his son in his stead, they did not show it. Their excitement and wonder at the appearance of two such strong young men made them giddy, and they chattered among themselves.

Lucas spoke for the Spaniard, explaining that Juan's knowledge of the Timucua tongue was not good. Before long, Lucas was comfortable with their accent and able to communicate well.

When Lucas and Juan had bathed and refreshed themselves from the trail, a feast was had in the center of the village. The chief and his *inija* spoke privately with the guests.

"A soldier came to Anohica," said the chief. "He called himself Pérez. He was the first soldier we have seen since the man called de Soto was here before my father was born. We are not ignorant. We know they are everywhere, nowadays, with their weapons and their profane curses. But he was the first one to come all the way up here. We prayed that they would never find us, but they did."

Lucas interpreted what the old man said into Spanish, so that Juan might understand every word.

"He came with orders for us. He said the King wants our land. Why the King would want to live in Anohica, I don't know. Our creek is almost dry and the planting fields are tired, but it is the only home we know. We are too old to move.

"He said there is a place to the south where the villages are all strung out in a row, where everyone is well fed and happy. I asked him why the King doesn't live there, and leave us alone. The soldier became angry and he beat me with a whip. It is embarrassing to be so disrespected in front of family. Unless we are gone before he returns, he said he will bring hounds to chase us. De Soto had hounds."

"Perhaps a move would be good for you, away from this tired place," Lucas said.

"We will die here," the chief said. "*Tacachale* may show us the wisdom of the ancestors, to tell us what to do."

The chief turned to face Juan. His eyes were glassy with tears. "Your father is a powerful man and he is good to Indians. He allows them to walk upon the ranch, to gather nuts and pick fruit as they have done forever. And he welcomes trade, as we would welcome his. Perhaps, after he gets to know the people of Anohica, he will tell the King to leave us alone."

It was a village with a very small council house, and apparently no shaman of its own. When it was dark and time to light the *Tacachale* fire, the man in charge was beautifully dressed in a deerskin cape with his chest stained with pulverized White Sea shell and black markings for his ribs. On his head, a wolf's head perched and raccoon tails dangled from his ears.

"I have seen that man before," Lucas whispered to Juan as the ceremony began. "He is a Potanan, and he sometimes travels with their chief when he visits my father. These people had to borrow a shaman."

Juan laughed, but by now the shaman had begun his chant, and the laughter was drowned out.

A troop of dancers, all of them old but spry, beat the ground with their feet as they circled the fire at the center of the council house, keeping perfect rhythm with the flute players and drummers. A chorus of men chanted while the shaman stood to the side. Lucas recognized it as a story of creation, of spirit beings from the distant past, of sacrifice, of shared pain, of birth and death.

On and on it went through the night. Lucas was transfixed, stirred deeply beneath the veneer of his religion, in places he never knew. Half way through, Juan rudely dozed, and his head nodded until Lucas elbowed him in the ribs, waking him up.

The *jarva* moved back and forth, constantly, then stopped directly in front of Lucas and Juan, where they sat nearest the fire, chanting to them and about them. He swung a club on the end of a rope above their heads. Juan squirmed and leaned away.

The shaman bent at the knees, facing them, and then with a clear gesture that they arise, he stood up. Lucas rose to his feet. The Spaniard merely smiled and waved his arm dismissively, looking away.

Lucas joined in the dance. Awkwardly, at first, he mimicked the shaman's movements. Encouraging calls of the people dissolved feelings of embarrassment, and he moved with the music.

When the shaman finished with Lucas, the young man flopped to the ground next to Juan, exhausted by the effort but exhilarated. The shaman next engaged an old woman, the matriarch of the village, who danced as if she were a girl. Then the chief stood up and danced, and then his *inija.*

Gradually the music changed. The joy and excitement were gone, the shouts and laughter but a memory. The mood was now somehow dark and hard to comprehend for Lucas. The shaman ceased his dancing, but strutted about facing the fire, his arm raised in summons to the spirits of the ancestors, while the drummers beat out a slow dirge.

"We should leave," Juan said, touching Lucas's arm.

The *jarva* began to speak in a staccato, high pitched tone, imploring the spirits, whom he called by their ancient names. He spoke the names of thirty or more, and as each name was spoken Lucas thought the fire responded, with sparks that popped out, licks of yellow flame that jumped above the rest, and colors that mutated and changed.

Again, Juan gestured that they depart, the whites of his eyes wide and reflecting the fire light. Before Lucas could reply, the *jarva* spun about three times, and as he did so his hand dug into a leather satchel at his waist. He scattered a handful of magical herb into the fire.

The flash of white light blinded Lucas. For an instant it was full daylight inside the house. A lick of blue flame jumped from the fire pit and flew to Lucas and circled his head three times. Juan lunged to the side, away from Lucas and the heat. The blue flame suddenly retreated into the hearth. In a moment, a great whooshing of air was felt and the camp fire flickered into nothingness and died.

Lucas was on his knees, his hands stretched out before him, digging where smoking embers had become ash.

Neither Lucas' head nor his hands showed any effect of the fire. Not even a hair was singed.

The shaman accepted payment for his services, but was embarrassed by his performance. "I was unable to call forth your ancestors," he admitted to the chief. "Two angry old spirits were here, arguing so fiercely the others were afraid to appear. I begged them to leave us, saying to them that they were lost and did not belong in Anohica, but they would not listen to me. They were fighting over the boy, the Utinan."

Humbled, the shaman walked out of Anohica before the sun arose.

As they followed the trail southward, Juan had many questions for which Lucas had no answers. Finally Lucas told Juan to shut up, insisting that he had nothing more to say.

"Answer me one more question," Juan demanded. "Why did you reach into the flames?"

Lucas stopped in the trail and reached into the pouch he carried around his waist. He pulled out the shell cross gorget. The twine had been burned through.

Chapter 37

The message from Coya arrived at La Chua hacienda three days after Lucas and Juan returned from Anohica. It was delivered by a runner and written in the chief's own hand.

"Return home to Ayacouta immediately, but do not speak to anyone on the way. Use secondary trails, and avoid being seen." It was signed by his father.

Lucas left Efa in Juan's care, as he intended to travel faster than the dog's short legs would carry it.

"My father must be ill, or perhaps it is my mother," Lucas said to Juan, explaining why he must leave so suddenly.

He rode a horse to the southern boundary of the ranch and left it tied to a tree where Juan would later retrieve it.

Now on foot, he moved swiftly in the moonlit night. One trail was unfamiliar, and he made a wrong turn, arriving at a place he did not intend to be. He had wasted precious time, but retraced his movements and found the correct path. Early in the morning the trail was blocked by a bear out for a stroll with her cub. Lucas followed a deer path that led away and circled back to the trail beyond the bear.

As he neared Ayacouta, a young boy spotted him and leapt from a tree and ran ahead to announce his coming.

Lucas found Big Bow waiting for him at the edge of the village, but his uncle would answer none of his questions. The *paracousi* brought him directly to the house of Coya, leaving him in the main room where he sat alone, waiting.

Coya ducked through the doorway, followed by Father Rogero. Neither man smiled. Lucas recognized the look on his father's face, the one he wore when he thought he had been lied to or betrayed.

"There is a story being told that you attended a pagan ceremony in a village north of the hacienda," Coya said. "Many of us are disturbed by the rumor. I thought it must be a lie spread by my enemies, but before I accuse them I want to hear what you have to say."

Lucas had seen his father this angry only once before, when the man he entrusted with the storehouse stole food and traded it to the soldiers. Perhaps the presence of the priest would make Coya cautious with his words, but Lucas could see the swollen blood vessels of his father's forehead and neck.

"It is true," Lucas said. "I went to Anohica, and there was an old ceremony. I beg your forgiveness, and that of God. I will speak of it at confession and accept the priest's penance, and your just punishment."

"Do you know what you have done? The story of the *Holata Aco's* son attending the Devil's worship has spread throughout Utina and beyond. The Potanan *Jarva* has bragged to the people that his powers are greater than the priest's, and even those who live at the missions now question what they have been taught."

"The people of Anohica did not believe it was the Devil," Lucas said. "No one claimed that. They saw only the spirits of ancestors."

Father Rogero spoke for the first time. "Those people are pagans without the knowledge of God. They would be blind to Satan's power. You, on the other hand, have been baptized, and consumed the blood and body of Christ."

Coya glared at the priest. "Thank you, Padre. I will deal with my son. You may hear his confession later."

When Father Rogero was gone, Coya sat on a bench cushioned by a gray fox pelt, looking at his son. "Rogero and the other priests, all the way back to Father Pareja, have condemned such wicked practices. Twenty years ago, every village had a shaman or a wizard who blinded the people from the truth with their lies and tricks. In these enlightened times they have all been exposed and ridiculed. There are no new *jarva* at all. Only a handful remain among the non-Christians.

"Now you, my son, have worshiped among them, and it delights the old people, those who have only lately come to know the one true God. They say to the priests that through *Tacachale* they can produce proof of the old spirits, and they ask the priests to show them God."

Lucas looked up into his father's eyes. Now he saw more sadness than anger. "Father, I have sinned. I deserve to be punished and I will suffer it gladly. I will do whatever I can to repair the damage I have thoughtlessly brought upon your reputation and the church.

"You have spoken to me of your childhood," Lucas continued. "You told me of a *Tacachale,* and your participation in it at Second Wekiva. You said that even here, when you were made chief, a *Tacachale* was celebrated –"

Coya interrupted. "You are a smart son, and you have a good memory. You ask why you should be punished for sins that I, myself, have committed more times than once. The answer, Lucas, is that the times have changed. What I did, in those days, was harmless. I had been baptized, but did not know the evil of *Tacachale*. Today, almost everyone knows. Maybe not those old people in Anohica, but the rest of us do. Devil worship affects the weak-minded, those whose faith is not strong. It endangers their very souls."

Coya fell silent. From outside, the sound of an eagle's call could be heard.

"Will you walk with me to the river?" Lucas asked.

Big Bow was outside the house and he fell in behind Coya and Lucas as they descended the small hillock into the village.

"I'm going nowhere," Coya said, waving off his *paracousi.* When they reached the path that led to the river Big Bow still followed at a respectful distance.

The morning fog had disappeared and the winter sun warmed the breeze from the west, brightening Coya's mood. "We should come back late in the day. The sunsets can be quite beautiful this time of year."

Father and son sat on a bench on a bluff three times the height of a man above the languid waters. To the right, the river flowed around a bend, past the embarcadero. To their left, the river widened, gathering strength for its two day journey to the water the Spanish call the Gulf of Mexico.

"You spend too much time with cattle and too little time at Mass. Father Rogero wants me to make a law that slackers should be punished," Coya said. "What do you think about that?"

Lucas shook his head, laughing. "I'm just a vaquero. Herding people into church would be harder than moving cows about. That is a chief's duty."

Sea gulls from the gulf floated on the air, diving for minnows in the shallows. Coya stood and walked near the edge, looking to the north where seven men bearing bundles of maize from the farming village of Guacara hailed the canoers on the other side.

"Could you do it?" said Coya. "If the decision were yours, could you order your people about even if they did not understand it was for their own good? Or could you tell those bearers who expect to return to their beds tonight, that they must continue all the way to San Augustín because there is no one in Potano to carry the corn?"

Lucas looked down, embarrassed by his father's questions.

"For many years, I consulted my advisors, and usually they helped me decide to do what the people wanted to do, anyway. The people said I was a wise leader, and my clansmen felt I respected them, and they honored me for it."

"I never think about such things," Lucas said. "I don't know how to answer."

Coya turned to face his son. "Now, when the priest needs workers and there are none available, or when the governor says for me to send men to work at the presidio, but they are all sick, what am I to do? If I ask my *inija,* he sometimes tells me not to do it. Sometimes I miss having a *jarva* to tell me the future, even if he is just a sorcerer."

A tandem canoe was launched to cross the river to the waiting bearers.

"So much has changed. Ceremonies and feasts and games that were entertainments for the people are now condemned. Where once I led the people, now I drive them like the cattle of Señor Menéndez. I hope not to their slaughter."

Coya returned to the bench and sat down heavily. He closed his eyes and faced the warm rays of the sun.

"Father, when I was a child you told stories about your grandfather, a man you called Marehootie, and of his brother."

"He was not my grandfather. I just called him that. He and his brother were Acuerans, and they raised me after I left the mission. There is, perhaps, a lot I have not told you. Things you do not need to know."

Lucas leaned forward, holding his face in his hands.

Coya opened his eyes and looked at Lucas. "Why do you ask about Marehootie?"

"Do not be angry, Father. Something happened at Anohica that I do not understand."

Coya sighed deeply. "Is it that the *jarva* said there were two spirits who fought over you? That they tussled so that the Anohica ancestors were afraid to appear?"

"Then you know about it," Lucas said.

"I know a wizard's trick when I hear one. The people wanted to hear from their ancestors, and I'm sure the *jarva* could call none of them by name. So he invents two lost souls to interfere. Then he throws the powder into the fire to dazzle everyone and goes home with his payment."

"You have told me of Marehootie's death and his burial at San Juan. Does his brother still live?"

"His name was Crying Bird. He fancied himself *Atichicolo-Iri*, a legendary spirit warrior. In the end he was a criminal, and maybe a crazy one. He was very old. Crying Bird disappeared into the Wekiva swamp before you were born. He was seen once or twice. I sent a search party, but he could not be found. He would be very old by now. I am sure he is dead."

"Did Marehootie and Crying Bird fight over you, and what sort of chief you should become?"

"Yes, yes," Coya said, smiling. "Those two were as close as any brothers. They would each die for the other. But they argued like blue jays. Why do you ask? Have you been fooled by the shaman's trick?"

Lucas reached into his pouch and withdrew the shell cross gorget and strand of charred woven fiber. He handed them to his father.

"Crying Bird resents Marehootie's gift of a cross. He burned it from my neck and cast it into the fire," he said.

Chapter 38

Tocoi crossing, 1646

Tocoi was as Coya had described it to Lucas: a busy river port with people headed in all directions. East to west, a trail stretched from San Augustín to Apalachee. Those people going north were bound by dugout for Piccolata or as far as San Juan del Puerto, while those southbound were likely going to Acuera or Mayaca.

Big Bow went with Lucas as far as Tocoi, and left him on the trail to San Augustín before turning back toward Ayacouta.

A farmer with a canoe load of grain and a trader dealing in deer skins haggled with a Spaniard who drove an ox. Eventually they struck a deal, and the wagon was loaded to the rails with baskets of maize and animal skins.

When the farmer and the trader climbed onto the wagon, the Spaniard shouted, “Do you want to kill my beast?”

The men pretended they did not understand what he meant until he took his whip and lashed them, then they got down to walk behind.

There were many people on the trail to San Augustín. Lucas heeded Big Bow’s warning about bandits, and walked with a group of Potanan and Yustagan traders who carried heavy bundles of clay pots and chert for sale in the town.

Late in the day they arrived at a camp with a central fire pit and lean-tos scattered about. Old women who were good cooks offered a filling meal and a place to sleep in exchange for bits of cloth or beads. Later, women who could have been their daughters offered other services in exchange for Spanish coin, copper bells or even cowry shells.

After he ate his meal, Lucas separated himself from the others and made his bed at a distance. Coya had said that the lean-tos were full of fleas. During the night the traders laughed and told stories and cavorted with the young women. Perhaps traders do not need to sleep, Lucas thought.

When he awoke the sun was not yet up, but it was light enough to read. Lucas pulled from his packet the two letters his father had written for him. They were written on parchment in Coya's careful hand, rolled and tied with string. The first was addressed to Governor Luis de Horruytiner, introducing Lucas as the Beloved Son of Coya, and heir to the Utinan Nation. The letter asked that his son be treated as a prince and that he be gifted as befitted one of his station. The second letter was addressed to a priest.

An old woman arose and saw him sitting alone and brought him a gourd of cassina tea, still warm from the night before. As she approached, Lucas replaced the letters where he carried them. The woman's eyes were red, as if she were on the edge of tears.

"How is it that you are here, and not with your family?" Lucas asked. He immediately regretted his question when the woman's face dissolved into tears. When she had wiped her eyes, she answered him.

"I am a widow. My husband died last year working for the Spaniards in San Augustín. When I saw you sitting here, with your back turned, you reminded me of my son. He wanted to follow in his father's footsteps, but I forbid him to go to the Spanish town, so he worked at Tocoi."

The traders were now on the trail, but Lucas stayed with the old woman. She was not yet done with her story.

"He died also, three days ago. Tocoi is full of evil spirits. Perhaps it is as bad as San Augustín."

When their talk was done, Lucas gave the woman one of the Spanish coins he had been given by his father, and hurried along the trail. He overtook the others before the sun had climbed above the trees. He encountered no bandits.

———

The night before Lucas' departure, Coya had told his son that the time had come for him to go away from the life he knew, the one in which he was comfortable, to discover his own nature. His father had made such a journey at the insistence of Marehootie, and it was on that wandering exploration that Coya had met Mora, Lucas' mother.

"Though I do not suggest you come back married, with a child in the woman's belly," Coya had cautioned.

Coya wanted Lucas to visit San Augustín to establish himself with the governor, and to see how the Spanish lived and how happy the mission Indians were. Perhaps Lucas could visit the monastery and meet Father Pareja, if he was still alive.

They had talked before, Lucas and his father, about such a journey. Perhaps Coya chose this time to get his son away from Ayacouta until the incident at Anohica faded from the people's memories. No, he decided. His father was not deceitful. Lucas would stay away from home and travel for half a year or more until he knew what he would do with his life. He could not be a vaquero forever.

He hoped he would not be so changed that his dog, Efa, would not recognize him when he returned.

———

The soldier standing guard at the office of the governor stopped Lucas at the door and asked his name and the purpose of his visit. He spoke in the Timucua tongue, but so poorly that Lucas smiled and answered in Spanish.

"I am Lucas, son of Coya Ayacouta Utina, *Holata Aco* of the Nation of Utina. I bring greetings from my father to his Excellency, the Governor of La Florida."

"You may enter," the man said, but made no move to open the door. Lucas looked at the latch, similar to the one at the mission. He pressed down on it, then pulled on the handle to swing the heavy wooden door outward.

Inside, a clerk sat at a desk making entries in a ledger. He glanced up at Lucas standing in the doorway and gestured for him to sit in a chair beside the door.

"My name is Lucas Menéndez. I am the son of Coya Ayacouta Utina, *Holata Aco* of the Utinan people. I come with greetings for His Excellency from my father."

"Sit down," the clerk said. "I will be with you soon." Lucas shut the door behind him and continued to stand. Sunlight entered through the unshuttered window beside the desk, illuminating the dust motes that floated about. Presently the man closed the ledger and set it aside. When he looked up, he seemed surprised that Lucas was still there.

"You said your name was…?"

"My Christian name is Lucas Menéndez."

"Of course," the man said. "Do you have a letter of introduction?"

Lucas removed the letter from the sleeve of his tunic and handed it to the clerk. "It is for the governor."

The clerk unbound the parchment and spread it on the table before him. "Come back later," he said, after he had read the letter from Coya. When Lucas made no move to leave, the man waved him toward the door. "Scoot, scoot," he said.

Late in the afternoon, after Lucas had wandered about in the outdoor market, talking to the vendors and inspecting their crudely made pots, he returned to the office. Again, he was asked to wait.

"The governor is too busy to see you," the clerk said when he finally got around to speaking with Lucas. "But he has asked me to give you these." He laid two strings of beads upon the edge of the desk, one of a green glass and the other of copper, and a piece of brightly colored yellow cloth.

Lucas inspected the gifts. Two of the glass beads were discolored. The cloth was imperfectly woven, with pulled threads. "Thank you," Lucas said, as he had been instructed by his father.

"You will be entertained for dinner at the house of a soldier who is fluent in your language. I assume you will be comfortable sleeping in the council house? Good. Please let us know if there is anything else you require while you are here. His Excellency conveys his warm, affectionate greetings to his good friend, your father, Don Carlos."

"Coya," Lucas said. "My father is Coya Ayacouta Utina. He is *Holata Aco* of the Utinan Nation."

The clerk looked up. "Of course, Coya," he said. "Please remain outside. The soldier will be along to fetch you."

Eventually, a soldier appeared at the front door of he governor's office and introduced himself as Lucas' host for the evening. The man had the smell of strong drink on his breath, an unpleasant odor Lucas had sometimes smelled on Spaniards who visited the hacienda at La Chua.

"You are Utinan. I can tell by your manner of dress," he said as they walked through the town to the soldier's house. "His Excellency is engaged in important governmental matters tonight. Otherwise, he would ask you to his home. He has designated me to entertain you at my house."

The soldier bragged that his wife was the daughter of a Mocama village chief, but he did not introduce her to Lucas nor mention her name. She served the meal of pork and maize without speaking to either her husband or Lucas. Once, when she poured tea into Lucas' cup, their eyes met, but she quickly looked away.

"You overcooked the pig meat," the soldier said. When she came to take it from him, he slapped her hand away. He was drinking a dark red wine.

The soldier had little to say to Lucas, other than questioning him about criminal Indians who might be hiding in Utina. "These *cimarrones* should be hunted down like mad dogs," he said.

When the meal was done, the soldier said it was time for him to sleep. Lucas thanked him for the food and said it was cooked well. He left the governor's gifts on the floor beside his chair and set out for the council house.

"Do you want work?" the black man asked Lucas the next day as he walked about the town looking at the mixture of poor shacks and fine houses that lined the streets.

"I do not know how to work," Lucas said.

"You will learn to work when you become hungry enough."

"I can ride a horse, and herd cattle, if you call that work," Lucas answered.

The black man bent over, laughing. "I do not have a horse. Perhaps you can ride this shovel," he said, displaying a metal spade with a wooden handle.

Lucas hefted it in his hands. "If you will teach me how it works, maybe I will be a good shoveler," he said.

Lucas spent the rest of the day digging a trench that the black man, Samuel, called a latrine. Samuel sat in the shade, hollering encouragement to Lucas, reminding him to cut a straight line that led behind three small houses used by soldiers and their families, down a slight hill toward a cluster of Indian houses.

Samuel thanked Lucas for his work at the end of the day. They walked together to the commissary office where the black man was paid for his day's work with seven cowry shells.

"Two for you, two for me and three for the master," Samuel said, placing two shells in Lucas' outstretched palm.

Samuel invited Lucas to stay with him and his wife and child in a small hut, but it was so crowded inside that Lucas thanked them and returned to the council house.

A market was held on Saturday, and Lucas wandered about, seeing what there was to trade. He traded cowry shells for a small mirror. The face that looked back at him was older than he remembered.

A vendor of pottery had a blanket spread in the shade. In one of the bowls he displayed a necklace of copper beads and another of green glass beads. Beside them was a yellow cloth with imperfections in the weaving.

"If you have three cowries, you may have both necklaces," the trader called out as Lucas walked away.

Lucas attended the singing on Saturday and the Mass on Sunday at Misión Nombre de Diós. The music was beautiful, better than any he had heard, and the priest reciting the Mass had a pleasant voice. Lucas thought of home, and of his father and mother, and his friend, Juan Menéndez, and wondered whether they missed him as much as he missed them.

As he left the church, Lucas paused to speak to the priest. He held a letter in his hand.

"Are you Father Pareja?"

"No," the friar said. "Father Pareja is no longer here. He is gone to Mexico. Why do you ask?"

"My father was a religious student at San Juan," Lucas said.

The priest seemed already to have lost interest. He was looking over Lucas' shoulder, smiling and gesturing at the people leaving the church. Lucas put the letter in his pocket and walked away.

Samuel said that Lucas could find work at the fort being rebuilt near the water. As the sun came up the next morning, Lucas followed a group of Mocama workers from the council house through the front gate into the fortress. In the dusty yard, men with saws and other tools moved aimlessly about among stacks of lumber, piles of cedar and pine logs and barrels of iron nails.

Many of the workers were Guale and spoke a tongue Lucas could not understand. Others were Mocama, some were Apalachee, and some were from Yustaga and Potano. Soldiers sat in the shade drinking water, telling the men what they wanted done.

The sun was hot in the sandy yard where walls and door frames were constructed. Lucas picked up a hammer and began to drive iron nails into the wood. He liked the sound of metal striking metal, and the ease with which the nails pierced the wood.

Lucas watched the other workers carefully, and mimicked what they did. When the others looked for places to hide from the sun at midday, Lucas picked up unattended tools and learned their use. Within a week, the soldiers had made him the boss of the others. No one seemed to mind, even the ones who had been there before him. In time, he mastered the use of the saw, the adz and the lathe.

With the coming of winter and cool weather, Lucas worked even harder. With each passing day he became stronger and more confident in his talent as a builder.

One morning in February, the Apalachee whispered excitedly among themselves as they worked. Lucas had been around them long enough that he could understand some of what they said. They spoke of reports of an uprising among their kinsmen at the village of Bacuqua.

The soldiers, also, seemed to be stirred by the reports. For two days no work at all took place at the fort, as the soldiers of the presidio gathered at the drill field, marching about and practicing with their muskets. The next morning half the soldiers of San Augustín marched to the west, bound for Apalachee province.

Those who remained soon gathered the Indians to continue work on construction of the fort. They had fewer Indians to supervise. The men from Apalachee had fled over night into the woods and did not return.

Lucas made no friends among the Indians because he would not talk about who he was, or where he came from. Sometimes he met Samuel in the village, and they walked around, talking about Samuel's family and what it was like to be a slave. Samuel was a happy man, content with his work and satisfied. He had a generous and kind master, he said. One Saturday Samuel was not there when Lucas looked for him. The next week he was back, standing under a tree near the market. He looked tired, and his smile was gone.

"My son is ten years old," said Samuel. "Master said he is now a man, and he sold him to a planter who took him to Cuba."

When Samuel had gone back home, Lucas sat near the marketplace with his back to a tree. It was summer again, and perhaps it was time for him to leave San Augustín.

Lucas heard a woman speaking to a man nearby. Her voice sounded familiar. When he turned to look, he recognized her as the old woman he had met on the trail from Tocoi, the widow who had lost her son.

"When I saw you sitting here, I thought you were my son," she said to the stranger. "He died three days ago at Tocoi."

As Lucas watched, the man and woman continued to talk. Eventually, the man handed her a Spanish coin and she thanked him and walked away.

The next morning Lucas walked out of San Augustín. Coya had talked to him about a village called Nocoroco, where two rivers come together, twenty leagues to the south.

"I have never been there," Coya had said. "I do not know anyone there, but I have heard of it and somehow it is a place I have always wanted to see. You can go there, and tell me about it when you come home."

Chapter 39

Sergeant Bartolome Pérez arrived at San Martín de Ayacouta unexpectedly, and instead of paying a courtesy call to the chief or his *inija* to announce the reason for his visit, went directly to the convento where he spoke at length with Father Rogero.

Coya was in the council house with Chilili, hearing a dispute between two chiefs regarding fishing and turtling rights to a stream midway between their villages. Twenty old people, who had nothing better to do, sat on low benches listening as Chilili skillfully questioned the chiefs to establish the exact location of the creek and the history of its use. Coya sat in his cabana, looking solemn and listening carefully to what was said. From time to time he motioned to his *inija*, and Chilili would climb up to him and Coya would whisper a question he wished to have answered.

Big Bow ducked through the low doorway, and gestured to Chilili who paused in his questioning and went to speak to the *paracousi*. Together, they climbed to Coya's box.

"There is a soldier in the village, the sergeant called Pérez," Big Bow whispered. "I did not know he was coming, and received no warning from any of the other villages that there was a Spaniard about."

"Where is he? What is his business?" Coya asked.

"He is with the priest. He said he will be here presently, when he is done with the friar. He also said that he will speak to you privately. I don't know if that means that Chilili and I should not be present, but he did not want anyone else to hear what he had to say to you. He made that very clear."

Big Bow wore a tunic of green Spanish cloth, the uniform of a member of the Indian Militia which had been organized two years earlier on the orders of the governor. Coya had agreed with the governor for the need of a militia, but the wearing of the uniform made him vaguely uncomfortable. On his sleeve, Big Bow wore a marking denoting him as a leader.

"Tell him I will be with him when my work here is done," Coya said. "And perhaps you should educate him on the protocols he must follow when entering an Utinan village."

Chilili reached out and touched Big Bow's arm. "Tell him also that Coya decides who will listen when Coya speaks."

Big Bow looked unhappy, but left the council house to carry out his orders.

When Big Bow was gone, Chilili continued with the dispute that was being heard. When that was done and the decision announced, Coya said that he would hear the next argument.

It was late in the day by the time all the questions had been answered, and the Spaniard was admitted to see the *Holata Aco* of Utina. Coya had put on his formal coat, and on his order everyone was excluded other than his *inija* and *paracousi*.

"I bring you greetings of His Excellency, Luis de Horruytiner, the Governor and Captain General of La Florida," Pérez said.

He was a small man, a head shorter than Big Bow. His full beard and close-set black eyes gave him an angry look.

"I am here under his authority, and I must protest the way I have been delayed." Even from his place above, Coya could see spittle fly from the soldier's lips.

Chilili took a step closer to the soldier. "There are protocols to be followed, agreed to by the governor, before a soldier can enter a village. You must –"

"I carry his orders," Pérez said.

"When you have apologized –" Chilili paused when he saw Coya's gesture, and he sat down.

"What are these requests that the governor has for my consideration?" Coya asked.

Pérez did not answer immediately. His chest heaved under his tunic and his face was red and perspiring. In time his breathing slowed, and he was ready to go on.

"I will leave this order with you. It bears the governor's seal which is still intact, but I am authorized to tell you its contents and to explain to you the reasons behind it. His Excellency believes this is so important that he dispatched me all the way from San Augustín to deliver it to you, personally.

"Over the past several months the governor's commissary had noted a diminishment in the flow of corn and other products along the Royal Road. The same is true with trade goods and mission supplies flowing westward. Bearers to carry the burdens have become scarcer than they were in earlier times. There are still many strong men willing to do their part in Yustaga and Apalachee, but there has been a severe loss of manpower in Potano and Utina. Personally, I believe that the Potanans have become lazy and unwilling to work. But it is the governor's judgment that they are doing what they can," Pérez said.

"This brings us to Utina and in particular the villages of Santa Fé and San Martín. Last month you gave less than 1,200 man-days to the effort. That is equal to only forty men working for the thirty days. Do you know how that compares to a year ago at this time?" Pérez took a paper from his pocket, looked at it and held it aloft. "Last year at this time you sent sixty men each day."

Coya looked at Chilili and Big Bow who had puzzled looks on their faces. Then he turned to Pérez. "What does that mean in terms of arrobas of grain?"

Sergeant Pérez looked at the paper in his hand. "I am a soldier, not a clerk."

Chilili spoke up. "Perhaps the governor should send his clerk to Ayacouta."

Coya looked at his *inija* and frowned. "We have had illness and death here, too," Coya said. "Perhaps not as much as in Potano, but these are significant losses. We have barely enough men for planting and harvesting, and many of the bearers have been crippled by the loads they carry. Some, those we send all the way to San Augustín, do not return at all, and we hear stories that they are ordered to dig ditches or work on the fort."

Pérez shook his head. "I have spoken to your friar, whose responsibility it is to organize the workmen, and he paints a very different picture of the failings in Utina. He acknowledges there have been some deaths. His fellow priests are the ones who bury the dead, so they should know the truth of it. And that truth is that many of your people have absented themselves from the mission and fled into the woods to avoid work. The same is true in Potano to a lesser extent. In Utina it is an epidemic. Two villages are completely abandoned, and even here in San Martín more than thirty people have disappeared in the last month. These people –"

"Ayacouta," Chilili interrupted. "This village is Ayacouta. San Martín is what you Spanish call the mission."

Pérez ignored Chilili and looked directly at Coya. "These people are slackers, *cimarrones,* and criminals. Both here and in Santa Fé. And we know exactly where they have fled."

"That would be news to me," Coya said.

Pérez reached into his satchel and withdrew a map. He handed it to Chilili who studied it for a moment and then took it to Coya.

"I have marked the map with an X, at a place the Indians call Laguna Oconee, just to the east of a large swamp. Traders tell us that what has been for years an abandoned village is now fully populated by people who speak the Potanan and Utinan tongues. It is three days travel northwest of Mission San Juan, and the same distance northeast of San Martín."

"Ayacouta," Chilili corrected.

Pérez gathered himself to his full height and extended the sealed order to the *inija.* "You have been ordered by the governor to send a force of fifty Indian Militiamen, under my command, to enforce the return of these *cimarrones* to their villages. Their leaders will be punished upon their return. I will leave here for Potano. I will return in four days. On the fifth day the expedition to Laguna Oconee will begin. Your war leader, Big Bow, will accompany me to identify the leaders."

Coya huddled with Big Bow and Chilili while the sergeant waited. Finally, the three separated and Chilili addressed the soldier. "You may send word to the governor that Coya Ayacouta Utina will consider his request."

Coya, Chilili, and Big Bow met together in the chief's house until late in the night, smoking and sipping cassina. The smoke from the fire pit did not rise rapidly to escape to the outside, but lingered in the air.

"I will not go with him unless you order me to go," Big Bow said. "But perhaps you will want me to go with him. It is a long journey, with several dangerous rivers to cross."

Coya smiled. Here, with his closest advisors, he could relax and show his feelings. Carrying the stern countenance of a leader had never come easy.

"And you would teach him to swim with rocks in his pockets?"

"It had occurred to me," Big Bow said.

"You will go with him, and if there are Utinans at that place, you should bring them home. But they are not to be punished by the sergeant. I will listen to what they have to say, and if they are to be punished it will be Coya who decides."

Coya stood up and walked outside with the others. There was no moon, and the stars spread out above their heads.

"There is something you should know," Chilili said. "Earlier today, while we were in the council house and Pérez was kept outside, he became angry."

"It is my duty to tell it," Big Bow said. "That little camp dog, the one Lucas calls Efa. You know how it runs around some people, nipping at their feet? Especially Spaniards. That dog hates Spaniards."

Coya drew in a deep breath.

"Pérez ran it through with his sword," Big Bow said.

Chapter 40

"You appear to be lost."

Lucas was startled by the voice. For two days he had followed the ancient, abandoned trails to the south and had seen no one at all.

The late afternoon sun was still bright, but the shadows had deepened and it took a moment for his eyes to adjust. Then he saw a shriveled old man sitting under a palmetto tree to the left of the trail.

"I have a good sense of direction, but I have never walked this path before," Lucas answered.

"Then you are lost. If you have never been where you are going, you cannot get there from here without my help. For a cowry shell I will set you straight and you can be on your way."

Beside the old man's right knee, there was a small woven basket stained with the juice of palmetto berries. Only two berries remained. To the other side, seeds were scattered where the man had spit them on the ground.

"If you share your berries with me, you shall have a shell. If you can direct me where I'm going, you will have another."

The old man looked into the basket, as if trying to decide. "Half the berries I have left and accurate directions? You drive a hard bargain."

Lucas sat beside him. He reached into his pouch and withdrew a poultice and began to treat the bloody scratches that had accumulated below his knees from the low vines that grew along the trails.

"You are an *isucu*? A medicine man?" the old man said.

"My father taught me never to let scratches go untreated. He learned it from an Acueran *isucu.* I know enough to collect the proper herbs, when I can find them, but I'm a long way from home here and don't recognize most of the bushes."

"You came from the north. I thought you might be a mission Indian fleeing from the Spanish. If you are, the soldiers might give me ten shells if I take you back."

Lucas laughed out loud. "They would not give much for me. I am Utinan. My father sent me to San Augustín to study the Spanish and see how they live. I was there for almost a year and I have seen enough of the Spaniards to last a lifetime. Now I'm on my way home."

"Then you are more lost than I thought. I may have to charge three cowries," the old man said. He put a berry in his mouth and handed the last one to Lucas.

"Before I go back across the River of the Sun I plan to visit Nocoroco."

The old man bit down hard on the berry and winced in pain. "There is nothing to see at Nocoroco, and they do not like strangers."

"But that is where I am bound," Lucas said. He reached again into his medicine pouch and withdrew a twig with five angular leaves attached. He removed the leaves and twisted them into a wad and handed it to the old man.

"In Utina, we call this toothache tree. Bite down and see what happens."

The old man stuck the leaves between two jaw teeth where one was missing, and bit down, closing his eyes. In a moment he looked up. "That feels much better. I wish we had your toothache tree at Nocoroco."

"Now, perhaps you will take only two of my shells," Lucas said.

"No more berries and not much sunlight left," the man said, struggling to get to his feet. Lucas grasped him under the arm and lifted him.

"I don't think you are a spy, and I will take you to Nocoroco with me. You can stay for four days, but then you must leave and promise never to tell others how to get there. It will cost you four cowries for food and a place to sleep. Plus, of course, the two you already owe me."

Nocoroco sat on a point of land where two meandering, reedy rivers came together. They formed a bay, and to the east Lucas could see the inlet which led to the ocean.

The sun was still up, but a communal fire was already lit in the center of the village, and the people sat around eating a meal of fish.

The old guide introduced Lucas to the others as a great *isucu* of Utina, and then left him there. Lucas ate his meal quietly and listened to the talk around him. They were different peoples, from different lands. They all spoke the Timucua tongue, but there were five or more dialects spoken around the fire, one or two of which Lucas could not identify.

None of them, other than the old man, had been born in these parts, and most of them avoided answering Lucas's questions about where they came from. Eventually, feeling his questions were somehow rude, Lucas stopped asking, but listened instead as the people talked among themselves.

There was a family of Potanans that had fled their village to escape an illness that ravaged their province. Three Mocama men and their families had left their mission village because of the hard work they were require to do, carrying arrobas of maize from Tocoi to San Augustín. A black slave who had run away from his master was also there.

A woman came with a pot of what looked like the crayfish Lucas had seen in the creeks of Utina. Lucas took one to be polite, and watched the others peel away the shells and head before eating what was left.

Lucas took a small bite. It had been cooked with onions and garlic and other spices, basted in fish fat. He had never tasted anything so good, and looked around for the woman to ask for another.

"We call it shrimp," someone said. It was a Potanan boy who had been watching him eat. "My mother cooked them. Would you like more?"

Lucas nodded and the boy jumped up and scampered away. Soon he returned with a palmetto leaf wrapped around three shrimp, and he sat beside Lucas and watched as he ate them.

"If your mother were not already married, I would take her home with me to Utina," Lucas said.

The boy laughed. "You would not keep her, even if my father would consent. It is the shrimp you would be after, and you would find that they do not travel well. These were caught last night, and already they are beginning to spoil. If you smoke them, they lose their flavor and taste just like crayfish."

Lucas wrinkled his nose in disgust at the thought of crayfish.

"I can take you fishing for them if you want more. Tonight there is a full moon, and this is the best night of the year for shrimp. The men are going shrimping, but they say I am too small, and they won't let me go with them."

The boy took Lucas by the hand and they descended a steep, chalky trail to the river where the boy kept a small canoe and cane poles with fiber nets on the end.

"You watch for their eyes as they swim by under the dugout, and you just scoop them up. Don't worry. It is very easy. I will teach you. It will cost you only one cowry shell, and you can keep all the shrimp we catch."

When the boy's mother gave her consent, they followed the other canoes up the river to the north. The fire in Nocoroco was extinguished, and even as the moon rose higher in the sky over the river, the village disappeared into the trees.

The boy tied the canoe to reeds at the side of the river. The men had all done the same. They were waiting for the time the shrimp would run, the boy said. In the dark water around the canoe, the moonlight flickered with sparkles of blue and green.

"Are those the shrimp?" Lucas asked.

The boy looked. "No. The shrimp's eyes look red or sometimes white. There will be two of them coming toward the boat, and you just scoop them up. I think that's just the moonlight you see shining in the water."

Finally, a torch was lit and passed from canoe to canoe down the line where it was used to light smaller torches in each dugout. Soon the men in the lead canoe paddled to the middle of the river and drifted slowly with the current, shining their light in the water. Behind them, the other canoes followed in an orderly, silent procession. Lucas and the boy paddled the last canoe. When the lead canoe reached the point where it met the other river, directly across from the village, it went back upstream in the shallows, then maneuvered back into the middle to begin again.

On the third drift, a man hollered, and soon nets were being dipped into and out of the water. For the most part, the men remained quiet as they worked. Even without a torch of their own, Lucas and the boy had no trouble spotting the shrimp as they moved down the river. Their eyes were fire red in the moonlight, and they swam only a few feet below the surface.

As suddenly as they had begun, the shrimp disappeared. The basket the boy's mother had given them was half full, and covered by a cloth to prevent the shrimp from jumping out.

"There will be another run, just before daylight," the boy said as they tied up in the rushes on the other side of the river. The boy lay down and soon was asleep.

Even with the full moon, a blanket of stars stretched above them. Wispy white clouds floated past on a south wind, and the soft sound of owls, passing manatees, and other night creatures could be heard. To Lucas, it was the most beautiful time and place he could recall in his life.

He thought of home. He wanted his father to see this place, and hoped he could describe it to him as he had promised. Most of all, he missed his mother and father, Big Bow, Efa his dog, and Juan Menéndez.

He moved the blade of the paddle back and forth, barely touching the water, watching the million blue and green points of light glow against the darkness. This was not moonlight reflected in the water, he decided. When the moon went behind a cloud the glow from the water seemed even brighter than before.

Lucas moved the paddle slowly and watched the water. The river around the canoe was now a blue-green cloud, alive, moving, and with form. A face appeared in the water, that of an old man with lively eyes and long white hair. The mouth of the apparition moved soundlessly, speaking to Lucas in a silent, forgotten tongue.

Lucas braced himself and leaned out over the water. The cross gorget, suspended from his neck, dangled on its string. The water spirit smiled. It rose up higher under the surface. Lucas could make out the form of its shoulders, and a face wrinkled with age. On its chest it wore a gorget of a cross carved from seashell. It was the same as the one Lucas wore. Lucas fell back, grasping his own gorget in his hand. The eyes of the spirit closed and it sank deeper into the river, faded, and was gone. The last image to disappear was the gorget, glowing in the moonlight.

Chapter 41

The astonishing news of the revolt among the Apalachee came suddenly and without warning. Coya had finished his morning meeting with his advisors and was sitting in his house when he heard the pounding of horse hooves outside.

Mora lay on her bed as she had for seven days. The priest had gone to the convento, having delivered his morning prayer for the recovery of the chief's wife, and Coya sat beside her bed watching her and wiping the sweat from her brow.

"Is that a horse I hear?" Mora said, blinking away the sleep she seemed to need so badly. Her eyes had a strange yellow caste to them. Her hair was wet and stuck to her head.

Coya patted her arm. "The only horse in these parts is the one ridden by Dog Killer. If he has business here it will be with Big Bow. Get your rest. I will stay here with you."

Mora's eyes fluttered and closed.

Coya could hear the excited voice of the horseman outside and the deeper sound of Big Bow's questions.

The *paracousi* entered quietly and touched Coya's shoulder, gesturing for him to go outside. "Sergeant Pérez is here with bad news," he whispered. "He wants to speak to you immediately."

"What could a killer of dogs have to say that would take me from the side of my sick wife?"

Big Bow hesitated. "You will want to hear what he has to say. The news he carries is very grave."

Coya massaged his forehead, stirring the worrisome thoughts that resided there. "Take him to the council house. Find Honoroso and Chilili. I will join you there soon."

The news was, indeed, grave. The Apalachee had risen up against the Spanish, Pérez said. The Deputy Governor, Claudio Luis de Florencia, had been lured away from his hacienda at San Luis to Bacuqua for a festival to be celebrated at the village mission. When he arrived, the Apalachee suddenly attacked him and his family.

Governor Florencia was tortured, along with his wife, his older daughter and her husband. The younger daughter cried out to God, and preached to the Indians, and she was mutilated along with the others. Three priests also were murdered that day.

"How is it you lived to tell the story?" Coya asked.

"I was assigned to stay at the hacienda that day to protect against thieves. A Christian Indian brought me the news of what happened, and said the murderers were led by Chief Anhaica, and that his men were coming to San Luis to kill me."

"And now you ride for San Augustín to tell the governor?"

"And to alert you and the other Christian chiefs. Chief Potohiriba is already gathering his men. You should do the same. I will be in Santa Fé by nightfall and in Potano tomorrow. I should reach the presidio by Thursday night. I am sure the governor will send sufficient soldiers. By Tuesday we will all congregate in Potohiriba. I will have more orders for you then."

Coya looked at Big Bow who stood beside the sergeant, a stern look on his face. Big Bow wore the tunic of the Indian Militia.

"Suppose the governor has different ideas? Suppose he leaves you in San Augustín to guard against thieves and sends the sergeant major to fight the Apalachee?"

Pérez flinched as if he had been slapped. His dark eyes smoldered. "I will abide the orders of my governor. If you wish me to tell him that you refused my request to prepare for battle, I shall tell him that."

"You have no authority to issue orders in Utina," Coya said. "But since you now ask my help instead of ordering it, I will gather my men and be in Potohiriba with the others."

When Pérez was gone on the trail to Santa Fé, Coya met with his advisors and considered what should be done.

"We have a plan for what the Indian Militia should do in the event of an attack," Big Bow said. "We always thought it would come from the Chiscas or some other pagan tribe, never from the Apalachee. If you order it, I will send runners throughout Utina telling the village chiefs to send their fighting men to Potohiriba. The chiefs already know how many warriors will be required of them. They will also arrange for bearers to carry the maize and cassina the men will need for a long battle."

Coya considered what his *paracousi* had said. "We have enough time that everyone can congregate here in Ayacouta. The bearers can proceed directly to Potohiriba. Chief Potohiriba has enough men to repel the Apalachee if they are so foolish as to cross the river."

Thirty-one Spanish soldiers armed with muskets and arquebusiers joined five hundred Timucua warriors at the Yustagan village of Potohiriba. Only a handful of Potanans appeared. Two hundred Utinans were there, led by Coya and Big Bow. The rest were Yustagans under the direct command of Chief Potohiriba. The soldiers were led by the sergeant major. Sergeant Pérez was there, carrying a musket.

The battle lasted only one day. The Apalachee thought they were seizing an advantage when they moved in great numbers to the east side of the Aucilla River to fight in Yustagan territory. The sergeant major delayed his attack for two days because of the heavy rains that fell. When the assault was launched, led by the heavily armed Spanish, the Apalachee found themselves with their backs to a swollen river.

By morning, a few Apalachee who had not been killed in battle or drowned in the river made their way back to their homeland. Over the next three days, Christian Apalachee came to Potohiriba. The rebels had suffered great losses and believed their leaders had blundered badly.

On the third day, the *inija* of the Paramount Apalachee Chief appeared with his personal bodyguard, carrying a white flag. The sergeant major directed that he be brought to the council house. Chief Potohiriba sat in the highest cabana. Below him, and to either side, Coya and Potano were seated. The sergeant major and his interpreter arrived after the *inija* was brought in, and sat at a wooden desk near the Apalachee.

"The Apalachee Paramount, Ivitachuco, sends his warm greetings to his brothers," the *inija* said. He was nervous, and although a great orator, his voice shook.

"He prays to God in Heaven each day for peace with the Spanish, and with the people of Potohiriba and with Utina, and sends a bottle of his own tears to show the ache and suffering he feels in his heart." The *inija* produced a stoppered glass vial of a clear fluid to demonstrate the sincerity of his chief.

The *inija's* guard took the vial and stepped toward the sergeant major, holding the bottle as an offering. The sergeant major sat with his arms folded and made no effort to accept the gift. Slowly, he rose to his feet and stepped around the desk until he stood eye to eye with the *inija.*

"Do you think tears will suffice to absolve the Apalachee of these black sins?" the sergeant major asked. "Does your understanding of penance require only frightened tears to pardon the murder of innocents whose only sin was to give their lives that your miserable souls might be saved?

"Shall I summon the priest that he may hear your confession and that of your chief? Would you agree that ten Hail Marys would be appropriate? Or that fifty or one hundred would suffice? Or do you say that for this butchery, this blasphemy, God should require continuous Hail Marys every moment of every day of every year of every century until His Son at last returns to establish His Kingdom here on Earth?"

The sergeant major returned to the desk and slammed his fist down so hard that the crack of the wood echoed through the council house. Even the bravest warriors jumped at the sound.

The soldier stepped away from the broken desk and walked to where the *inija* stood, his loincloth stained by his own urine.

The sergeant major lowered his voice, as if he were carrying on a normal conversation. “In four more days, my army of two thousand Spanish regulars will join me here in Potohiriba. Unless every bloody-handed Apalachee is delivered to me in chains by that day, I shall order the destruction of every village, every house, every council house, every field of maize, every canoe, and every store house in the province of Apalachee, which will from that day cease to exist.

“There will be no more need for the Apalachee Province, and our men of God can retire to work for more worthy people, for every Apalachee man between the ages of twelve and one hundred and twelve will be dead and every woman and every child removed to San Augustín as rewards to the brave Spanish soldiers.”

The sergeant major turned and walked from the council house, followed by his aides. The Apalachee *inija* stood in embarrassment and shame, his head down, as the Timucuan chiefs ignored his presence and walked single-file out into the sunlight of a winter day.

Three days later, Chief Ivitachuco came to Potohiriba without his *inija* who was too ill to travel. He carried a white flag and was accompanied by only four lightly-armed personal guards and a fifth man in chains. Coya recognized the man. He had met him years before at the grand Apalachee council house. The black hair was now streaked with white, the eyes lacked the fire of youth and the shoulders were rounded and hunched. But there was no doubt.

“This is the mighty Anhaico, the War Chief of Apalachee,” Coya said to the sergeant major.

Chief Ivitachuco said that within fourteen days he would deliver Anhaico's personal guard of one hundred forty warriors, the men who had murdered the Spanish. Some had fled to the south, he said, but they would be found soon enough.

"That will be a good start," the sergeant major said.

The following evening, a nephew of Chief Potohiriba had a dispute with his wife and she sent him away, placing his belongings outside their house. It had happened before, and the young man, whose Christian name was Carlos, knew what was expected of him. Perhaps his wife would change her heart in the morning, as she had done before. Instead of going to the home of his mother, he walked into the council house, looking for a warm place to sleep. Carlos lay near the fire, surrounded by soldiers, traders and visitors of sufficient rank to be there.

Sergeant Bartolome Pérez returned to the fire after being summoned to speak to the sergeant major concerning what was planned for the morning. When Pérez saw Carlos lying there, where he wished to sleep, he kicked him in the side.

"Get out, you dog," Pérez shouted. He grabbed Carlos by his hair and dragged him out the door into the cold night. As Carlos sat in the dirt, he could hear the laughter of the soldiers inside.

Chief Potohiriba summoned Coya and the leader of the Potanans to his house late that night, after the Spanish were asleep in the council house. The soldiers were comfortable with Yustagan guards on watch. Coya had with him only his *paracousi,* Big Bow.

"The Spanish are saying this was a great victory," said Potohiriba. "They believe that the Apalachee have lost their heart for the fight, and I suppose that is right. Anhaica counted only his own losses, and not ours. Fifty-one of my people died. Almost as many Utinans were lost, and I will never forget their sacrifice, Coya. You have proven to be a great leader, and perhaps some day I can repay you for what you have done here."

In the last five days, Coya and Potohiriba had become friends, and felt comfortable calling each other by their first names.

Chief Potohiriba turned to Potano. "You also have done what you could. You say you have only thirty fighters in your province, and that seven of them are now dead. I grieve with you for that loss."

The Yustagan Chief lit a tobacco pipe and handed it to Coya.

"I can understand why the Apalachee rebelled. They have their reasons, their grievances against the Spaniards, as we all do." Potohiriba was again looking directly at Coya. "The Spanish forced the people of Asile to clear the fields and build a hacienda there to feed the Spanish at San Luis. It was brutal work, and many of the people of Asile died. It is said that it was the priests who ordered the work done.

"Every season, more land is taken from the Apalachee and more of their men are turned into bearers, pack animals for the road to San Augustín. And like your people," Potohiriba said, nodding first toward Coya, then Potano, "many never return home. They die on the trail, or are drowned in the rivers, or simply disappear with the people who are forced to work in San Augustín."

"Are you saying we were on the wrong side of this fight?" Coya asked.

A smile crossed Chief Potohiriba's lips, but his eyes were hard. "I have no pity for the Apalachee. I only regret that we did not kill them all."

Coya wanted to get back to his bed, but he knew that sooner or later the chief would make his point, so he kept silent and listened.

"There comes a time when grievances should be addressed. We have all suffered under the Spanish. They take our land from us. Soldiers mistreat our women and take them away to their homes. Even the priests now order sick people to get out of bed and carry maize to San Augustín. We are no longer respected. We petition the governor to be treated more fairly, but we get only promises in return. And we are dying. As surely as Potano was once a great nation, and now has only a handful of men left, it is happening to Utina and Yustaga."

"We have talked of these matters before," Potano said. "It never does any good. It is a waste of time."

Potohiriba looked at the old chief sharply, and then turned his gaze back to Coya. "There are twenty-seven Spaniards, and their sergeant major, sleeping in the council house at this moment. The sergeant major bragged to me that half of all the Spanish fighting men are here, and that what remains are in San Augustín."

Coya laughed. "I understood him to tell the Apalachee that he has two thousand men in reserve."

"But you and I know the truth, don't we?" Potohiriba said. "The time has come for us to be men. We may never again have such an opportunity, but unless we act together we and our people are doomed.

"If you will support me, I am prepared to act now, at this moment. My men are standing by with buckets of pine pitch." Potohiriba nodded to his war chief who stood by the door. "We will burn our council house. When the soldiers try to escape, we will kill them like rabbits fleeing a burning field."

Chapter 42

Lucas stayed at Nocoroco four days. Each morning the old man who was his guide showed him the sights and answered his questions, and at the end of the day collected from Lucas another cowry shell for his services.

Where the rivers came together, the village jutted out into the bay like a fat log. On either side, the banks were as high as a man's head, sloping steeply to the water below. Steps had been carved out to provide a footing for the men to get to their canoes and so the people could swim or fish.

There was not much sand in the village. The ground was covered with shells of river clams, oysters, fragile snail shells and others Lucas had never seen. Squat bushes covered the steep banks as far down as the water mark of high tide.

Where rains had grooved furrows in the ground and on the sloping banks, Lucas picked up pieces of old pottery with strange designs, hand scrapers and broken tools fashioned of chert. He found arrow heads and spear points. Lucas asked the old man about what he found. "Our ancestors are here with us, under our feet," his guide said.

"How is it the water rises and falls from day to night?" Lucas asked on the second day when he noticed an unmanned canoe had floated away from the shore.

"It is the way the spirits clean the rivers," the guide said, and launched into an old story of a struggle between the spirit of water and the spirit of earth for the affections of Moon

Woman, and how Earth stands up to gain her attention when she awakens and looks around, and how Water is jealous, and climbs out of his bed so that he might be noticed.

"And they are still at it. Constantly, up and down, for as long as our people have been here to watch. They never fail, and they never give up, so deep is their love of the fickle Moon Woman who can never make up her mind."

Lucas was amused, but too polite to laugh at the old man's story. "But you said the spirit uses the rising and falling to clean the river."

The old man chuckled. "You have the curiosity of an *isucu*, and to satisfy it I will tell you a truth very few people recognize, and it is this: Any struggle, no matter how hopeless or frustrating it may be, is worth the effort put into it, whether you succeed or fail. Moon Woman worships Sun God, as we all know, but she keeps Water and Earth hopeful so they will continue to struggle. Up and down the water moves, up and down the land climbs, flushing the dirty water of the river until it moves out to sea, making room for clean water to come in its place.

"Our women clean their cooking pots in the water leaving grease floating on the surface. Fish and turtle are butchered and the leavings are thrown in. We urinate in the water at night, for we know that by morning the dirty water will be gone and we and our children may bathe and swim where the water is again clean."

As it was getting dark on the last day, Lucas asked the old man to go with him to the canoe landing on the east side, and he helped him down the steps to the narrow beach. "Do you see a light in the water?" Lucas asked.

The ripples washing up on the narrow shore glowed green and blue.

"That is Water, using his torches to keep an eye on Earth, so that he does not rise up suddenly to flirt with Moon Woman. We spoke of this before. Have you already forgotten?"

"Are you sure that is all? Is there something else here to see?"

The old man became quiet, staring into the water. "When I was a young man," he answered, "we had a *jarva,* a wise shaman, who lived here. He would go out in a canoe late at night and summon the ancestors to show themselves in the water and to talk to him.

"A priest came and lived among us for awhile. He heard what the *jarva* was doing and ordered him to stop. We have no more *jarvas* here. Neither do we have a priest, anymore. It has been so long since anyone asked about the ancestors in the water, I had almost forgotten."

True to his bargain, the old man took Lucas to a trail that led to the River of the Sun. "I have one last place to visit before I return home," Lucas said as he paid the old man for his services and picked up his bundle. "My father speaks of a place called Wekiva that lies two days south of a large lake."

"I see you will need a river guide, also," the old man said. "By midday you will come to a dim trail that leads to the left, just beyond a bog on the right side. Follow it to the River of the Sun. There is a village where river traders live. If you are lucky you will find one going upstream toward Mayaca."

The trader enjoyed having someone to talk to, and did not charge Lucas for the canoe ride. Southbound, carrying only Spanish trade beads, cloth, and a few iron tools, there was plenty of room in the canoe for Lucas and his bundle. "If I were going to the north, my canoe would be filled with deer skins and alligator meat," he said. He was now the only trader who traveled the river as far as Mayaca, and had no competitors. There was no reason to hurry.

He also knew of the Wekiva, and in his early years had traded at a small village called Second Wekiva. "I will show you where the first camp was, and then I will leave you on the trail to Second Wekiva. There are probably no people living there, either, certainly not enough to make it worth my time to go there for trade" he said.

The mouth of the Wekiva River was easy to find. The willow trees that once overhung the entrance had been chopped down by the soldiers, the trader said, and the bottom was dredged and widened to accommodate a Spanish gun boat.

"This is where the fish camp stood," the trader said. They pulled the canoe on shore and walked around. Nothing remained to be seen of the camp.

"Not even the soldiers come here now," the trader said. "After twenty years of searching for a man called Crying Bird, and looking foolish, they decided he must be dead."

"They are probably right. He would be ninety years old by now," Lucas said.

The trader turned and looked at Lucas. "You seem to know a lot about Wekiva, for an Utinan."

"Is the name 'Marehootie' familiar to you?" Lucas asked.

The trader's eyes were now wide with surprise. "My grandfather spoke of him often."

"Marehootie and Crying Bird raised my father here on the Wekiva," Lucas said.

"Then you are the son of Coya," the trader said, "the *Holata Aco* of Utina. It is a great honor to have you in my canoe."

There was more to see at Second Wekiva. The village had long since been burned to the ground, most likely by the Spanish, but from the descriptions told him by his father, Lucas found it was easy to locate where Crying Bird had made his house at the top of a chalk-white hill. Charred posts still marked its outline.

Next to it, on either side, two smaller houses could be imagined. Lucas could not remember if the house shared by Coya and Marehootie was to the right, or whether that was the one in which the toothless *inija,* Yano slept. The *inija* would be to the right, he decided.

With his knife Lucas dug through the thin topsoil and grasses that covered the hill. Just below the surface he found the clay that would have been the floor of his father's house. He put some of it in a pouch to take home to Coya.

Lucas could imagine his father sleeping on the hill top, which would have afforded some protection from mosquitoes. But there was a strong breeze blowing, so he decided to make his bed beside the water.

The sun was near the horizon and shot its last arrows through the cypress trees to where Lucas lay on the river bank. Barred owls called to each other that it would soon be time to hunt. A flight of more than a hundred white ibis filled the air, flying down river at treetop height, bound for their rookery.

Another bird, speckled brown in color and larger than the ibis, settled onto a nearby tree branch, then fluttered to the ground and began to walk around searching in the grass and leaves for a last meal before nightfall.

Have I been so quiet, thought Lucas, *or are you so blind that you cannot see me?* It was a limpkin, the skittish bird Acuerans and other swamp peoples called crying bird. Lucas hardly breathed; afraid he would frighten it away.

The bird was thin and looked old and bedraggled, and was missing some of its tail feathers. Slowly it moved about, closer to where Lucas lay propped against a tree. The bird, though now aware of Lucas, did not fly away, but looked at him with curious interest, soft sounds coming from its long throat.

The last rays of sunlight glinted on the shell gorget Lucas wore on his chest. The bird was now attracted by the shiny ornament, and moved closer, turning its head about to see it with each eye. Still, Lucas remained quiet and did not move.

Without warning, the bird moved toward him, its long neck extended, pecking at the cross gorget.

Lucas pushed the bird away and grasped the gorget in his other hand. The twine broke, and he put it in the pouch at his waist. The bird appeared confused, fluttered about and then returned to the tree branch from which it had come and rested, its breast heaving mightily.

"Have I hurt you?" said Lucas. Still it did not flee.

Now the sun was gone below the trees and darkness came.

The sound of a fish jumping in the river distracted Lucas, and when he looked back the bird was gone. He listened for its call, but it never came.

Perhaps this is a story I should keep to myself, thought Lucas. It might upset my father to hear it.

Chapter 43

Lucas imagined his return home with no warning, after more than a year's absence. As he moved along the brambled, overgrown secondary trails, he was warmed by the thought of the tears of joy that would run down his mother's face, and the broad smile that would crack the austere, chiefly countenance of his father.

To make his return a surprise, he kept to the back trails, avoiding villages and other travelers who might send word ahead and alert Coya of his coming. The roundabout way delayed him, as did the bulky bundle of gifts he carried on his back: the bolt of bright yellow Spanish cloth for his mother, the blue military tunic with metal buttons for his father, and even the dried pig's ears the people of San Augustín gave their dogs to chew, for Efa.

As he neared Ayacouta, he heard the sounds of a multitude of people in the village. Perhaps they were aware of his coming, he thought, and had gathered to welcome him home. But as he drew closer, it was not the sound of the excited chatterings of women greeting a welcomed guest that came to his ears. It was, instead, a high-pitched sorrowful sound of wailing, of mourning.

Lucas doubled his pace and left the trail, running through a rough thicket, between the small huts and gardens and into the center of the village. Death had come to Ayacouta. The day of joyous homecoming was not to be.

The village was crowded and the church yard of San Martín was packed with people awaiting entrance. Some saw Lucas and swarmed about to speak to him. He pushed them aside and moved past the guard at the front door and into the church.

Father Rogero was there, with another priest, supervising workmen digging a hole in the floor.

"Thank God you are here," Father Rogero exclaimed when he saw Lucas enter the sanctuary. "Your father sent runners everywhere, looking for you. They all returned, saying you could not be found. We had given up hope, but God has delivered you to us."

"My father?" The anguish showed itself on Lucas' face.

Rogero put his arms around Lucas' shoulders. "I'm sorry, my son. It is Mora. Your mother has gone to be with God."

The wife of the *Holata Aco* of Utina was interred beneath the floor of the church, on the right side of the sanctuary, near the altar. Her head was laid toward the northeast and she was covered over with clay. The red ocher brought in tribute by her family from the village of Chilili was not mixed with the burial soil. Father Rogero had forbidden its use, saying the custom reflected non-Christian beliefs. Hers was the first Christian burial of a member of the royal family of Utina, and the priest was determined that it be done properly.

Coya and Lucas stood together at the front. The chief's scalp was red with blood, where he had cut off all his hair in his grief. Lucas, also, had shorn his top knot, as was expected of a son who had lost his mother.

When the long burial Mass was over, and the family had shoveled the earth over Mora's remains, Coya went directly to his house to begin his private mourning. Lucas stood in the nave with the priest, Chilili, the aged father of Mora, and her brother, Big Bow, accepting the condolences of all who came to do her honor.

"It was a fine service," Father Rogero informed his superior in San Augustín in his written account of the funeral, "without elements of the pagan rituals so often insisted upon by Timucua leaders when we bury their dead. It was also well attended. The chief's heir, Lucas Menéndez, spoke to more than five hundred mourners, each in turn.

"The sergeant major attended, along with Sergeant Bartolome Pérez who has responsibilities with the Indians west of the river. The Honorable Francisco Menéndez, Royal Treasurer, ably represented His Excellency the Governor, Benito Ruiz de Salazar. He had with him his son, Juan Menéndez, who is the proprietor of La Chua hacienda and cattle ranch.

"All seventeen village chiefs of Utina were here, and they were well-behaved. We even had the pleasure of entertaining the Paramount Chief of Yustaga, Don Diego, who traveled from Potohiriba for the occasion, although he left immediately after the service.

"It was, in all, a good day for reconciliation between the Spaniards and the Indians. There are so many conflicts and misunderstandings these days, and so little opportunity for the parties to meet and talk. Perhaps we should take better advantage of these occasions in the future. The Indians observe the death of prominent people not only as sorrowful occasions, but also as social gatherings with great feasting. Perhaps we could learn from them in that regard."

Ten days into the period of grieving, Coya still allowed no one to be admitted into his house other than his son and the women who carried food and water to him, and who removed the previous day's food that had gone untouched.

"I am very worried about my father," Lucas confided in Big Bow as they sat on the bluff above the river watching the sunset. "I suppose I should get used to it. He is deeply wounded by her death. He has no interest in resuming his duties now. It may be a long time before he gets back to his work."

"I would guess it will take half a year or more before he comes outside," Big Bow said.

"That long? I know it is the traditional way for Utinans to mourn. I only wish he would show a spark of spirit, along with his grief. I showed him the gifts I brought him from San Augustín, but he was not interested in them. I also confided in him of two spiritual encounters I had on my travels, hoping he would interpret them for me. He brushed me off like a mosquitoes and would not answer me. Perhaps he will in time."

Big Bow stood and walked to the bluff, then turned to face Lucas. The rays of the sun outlined his broad shoulders and powerful physique. "Lucas, it is more than just your mother's death that burdens your father. He has been sad for a long time, since even before she fell ill."

From the council house, the sounds of women singing floated on the evening air. They would sing every night for half a year, just at sundown, in memory of the loss.

"I first noticed that he was quieter than usual and withdrawn soon after you left Ayacouta," Big Bow said. "The Governor was angered that so many people were fleeing the missions and hiding in the woods, and he ordered your father to go after the people who had gathered at a place called Laguna Oconee, a remote village three or four days to the north.

"I went, on your father's orders. We found fifty people there, living quietly and peaceably in a river valley. Most were Utinans, although a few were from Potano. They were doing no one any harm, just farming maize and beans and gourds. The soil was very good, and there were plenty of fish and turtles and deer. They were mostly old people or others who were crippled from carrying the Spanish bundles. They did not want to come home with me, but I had my orders so we gathered them up."

Big Bow turned his back and wiped his face with a cloth. "It shames me to say that I allowed a soldier to burn their fields. Winter was coming and they would have nothing to eat. So they came back to Ayacouta with us. They were so old and crippled it took us six days to get home. We were gentle with them and took our time."

Big Bow blew his nose on the rag, but still would not look at Lucas.

"Four of them died on the trail, and another three died soon after we returned. Your father took it all on his shoulders. He said he was to blame for not standing up to the governor. There were hard feelings against his decision throughout Utina, but no one condemned him quite as much as he blamed himself. I tried to take responsibility, but Coya said it was his order that I had followed."

A large female osprey flew down river, chirping her call to the nest. Presently her mate, smaller and more compact, followed after her.

"You have heard, of course, of the rebellion in Apalachee?" Big Bow said.

"Everyone knows about that," Lucas answered. "I was in San Augustín, and the people talked about nothing else."

Big Bow returned to the bench and sat down. His eyes were as red as the water reflecting the last shafts of sunlight.

"There is more. No one is supposed to know this other than the people who were there. We were all sworn to secrecy, but I suspect it is becoming common knowledge. It is so hard to keep secrets nowadays. If anyone needs to know this, it is you.

"After the Apalachee gave up, Chief Potohiriba told your father that the time had come to strike the Spanish, once and for all. We could have easily killed half of all the Spanish soldiers in one night, there in Potohiriba."

Lucas sighed and leaned over, shaking his head.

"Coya said he would not allow it to happen, that he would turn his men on the Yustagans if one Spaniard was harmed. Potohiriba argued with him. He promised to protect the priests, to leave all the missions standing. It was the governor and his soldiers who were the enemies of the Indians, after all.

"Your father backed him down. He accused Potohiriba of being a poor Christian and a sinful pagan. Coya was prepared to go to war with Yustaga even to protect the soldiers. It may have been a bad decision. Chief Potohiriba and even Chief

Potano lost all respect for your father. Coya was once considered *Holata Aco*, Paramount over all chiefs. Even many Utinans now talk behind your father's back, calling him half-breed."

"How quickly traitorous people can turn against their leader," Lucas said.

Big Bow dropped his head and covered his face with his hands. Then he looked up. "These are the same people who were most excited by the religious experience you had at Anohica. Not just the pagans, but many mission Indians feel the same way. They have started to observe *Tacachale* in some villages, and there are now two or three shamans who claim they can call forth the spirits.

"Many people believe you are the proper heir of your father. They have decided that your clan is no longer important. They say you have spiritual power, and that you would be a strong *Holata.*"

"But I am a Christian. Don't they realize that?"

"They know it well. Most of them are Christians, also, but in some ways they still cling to old beliefs. And the priests think you would be a good choice, as well as Señor Francisco Menéndez who has powerful influence over the governor."

"But it is not up to the governor or Menéndez or the priests," Lucas said. "It is not even a decision for the people. My father is *Holata* for life. If I am to succeed him, it will be upon his death, not while he lives, and I will fight at his side to put down any rebellion against his authority."

Big Bow was smiling. He put his hand on Lucas' shoulder. "It will not be quite that dramatic, my friend. The decision was your father's. It was his plan even before your mother died. He was waiting only for your return."

Lucas bolted from his seat and whirled to face Big Bow. "Why would he do such a thing? My father is not one who walks away from a fight or worries about what ignorant people think of him."

Big Bow crossed his arms over his chest and stared at his feet for a moment. Then he looked up into Lucas' eyes. "There are things I know that I am sworn to keep secret, even from you. I can say this much. Your father has taken a chief's oath of obedience to the governor. Coya's word is everything to him. There is something he is forbidden to do as *Holata* that he feels compelled to do as a man and a Christian. He's stubborn, just like you. No one can change his mind. Like it or not, Lucas Menéndez, you are destined to be the next *Holata Aco* of Utina."

By now the sun had almost disappeared from view, but still illuminated fleecy pink and orange clouds that were reflected perfectly in the dark water of the river.

"How did my dog die?" Lucas asked, breaking the silence. "No one will say what happened to Efa."

Big Bow sat for a long time before answering.

"That was my fault. I was responsible for watching a soldier while he was in the village. He became angry when I would not allow him to see your father. He killed your dog with his sword."

Lucas' eyes squinted almost shut, filtering out the last rays of the sun. "What is his name?"

"You met him at the service for your mother. His name is Bartolome Pérez."

Chapter 44

The sudden death of Francisco Menéndez Marquez drew as many Indians as Spaniards to the cathedral in San Augustín, although the church was so crowded that, of the Indians, only chiefs were allowed inside while their advisors and family members remained in the street. Don Diego came from Yustaga and stood to the right side, closer to the altar than the small contingent of Apalachee chiefs. Chief Potano and two of his village chiefs were lost amid a delegation of Mocama Indians from the coast.

The newly appointed Chief Lucas Menéndez and a delegation of seven Utinan chiefs stood where they were directed to stand, half way to the altar, but against the wall. Lucas could see the backs of the heads of the large Menéndez family, the children and their spouses, the widow and her nurse and the cousins, stretched across the front.

"Father loved you so. As his godson, he would want you to have a place of honor if there was room," Juan Menéndez had said to Lucas before the procession into the church. Juan was dressed in a fine European suit of clothes. His beard was neatly trimmed, and except that he was a head shorter, and thinner, he looked very much like his father.

"I thought you would be more comfortable standing with your people, than with my family."

Two days after the burial, Lucas went to see the governor to render obedience, as was the custom for a new chief. The ceremony took place on the steps of the governor's house and was followed by a banquet that was held inside because of a squally rain that blew in from the sea and lashed the town.

Lucas sat next to Governor Salazar, and the sergeant major was on his other side. Before the food was served, gifts of animal skins and iron tools were exchanged. When they began to eat, Lucas watched how the others picked up their food.

"What became of your father?" the soldier asked midway through the meal of roast venison. "I met him many times here in San Augustín, and he was a valuable ally when we had the difficulty with the Apalachee two years ago. We were sorry to hear he stepped aside as chief."

Lucas lay down the metal spoon he had been using and, with his fingers, picked up a piece of meat and put it in his mouth. "My father also speaks highly of you," he answered after he'd swallowed. "I will tell him you asked about him."

"Then he is still living at Ayacouta?"

Governor Salazar had stopped eating, and was leaning to the side, listening.

"My father has many friends in many places. He travels about, visiting with them," Lucas said.

"I thought he would be here for the funeral," said the governor. "I know he was a good friend of Menéndez."

"I do not know why he is not here. There was so little time. We left Ayacouta immediately when we got the sad news. Perhaps my runners could not find him."

"Or it might be that he is so far away from Utina there was not enough time for him to make the journey," the sergeant major said.

Lucas did not answer further, but took another piece of meat in his mouth and chewed leisurely.

Sergeant Bartolome Pérez rode into Ayacouta from the southeast, the direction of San Augustín, and tethered his horse to a post. He had been there before, but it was still a novelty to the children to see such a large animal, and they flocked around, keeping a safe distance from the rear hooves of the sweating mount.

Big Bow came to get Lucas. “Sergeant Pérez is here and wants to see you,” he said. Lucas set aside the letter he was writing to Juan Menéndez.

“I heard him ride in. His horse was panting hard enough to wake the dead.”

“That is the only way he knows to ride: full out.”

“He has no respect for the beast. No more than he had for my dog,” Lucas said. “Take him to the council house. I will not have that man in my home. Also, find my advisors and have them there.”

When Lucas had entered and had taken his place in his cabana, he nodded that he was ready to proceed. Pérez stood below him at the speaker’s place. He held in his hand a role of parchment. Even at a distance, Lucas recognized the blue wax seal of the governor.

“I bring the greetings of His Excellency, Benito Ruiz de Salazar Vallecilla, the Governor and Captain General of La Florida,” the sergeant said, “as well as those of my immediate superior, Diego de Rebolledo, the provincial sergeant major. They are anxious for reports of your good health and well being, and of any help you require to make your sworn service to the Crown easier to accomplish.”

Lucas glanced at Chilili and Honoroso who sat to either side of him, then turned his gaze back to the soldier. “You may convey the cordiality of my greeting to them. We are well here in Ayacouta, at least most of us. There are some people dying in other villages, but not as many as last winter.

“If you are sincere in asking how you may help us, I would suggest two things. First, that the governor should reduce the maize levy. It is more than one thousand arrobas above what we were required to produce last year, and my chiefs report that there will be nothing left for our people to eat if you take it all.”

Pérez looked about, uncomfortably. "I will tell my superiors what you have said."

The soldier looked at the document he carried, and prepared to break the seal.

"Secondly," Lucas said, "we find the labor demands for burden bearers and river-crossing people are beyond our ability to provide. The men who should be harvesting your maize are carrying it, and those who should be serving in the Indian Militia are, instead, manning the canoes here and at the other river to the east."

Grunts of approval moved through the house, as the advisors showed there agreement with what Lucas said. By now, Pérez had removed the official ribbon and prepared to unrolled the parchment.

"Before you read that document you brought, I want you to commit to carry my words to your masters. I did not know you were coming, or I would have been better prepared. I shall write a letter to the governor, and require that you take it with you."

Pérez' face was red, and his hands shook as he unrolled the parchment. "I will tell them what you have said today, and I will carry with me whatever you want to send them. But it is my duty today to present you with this order, signed by His Excellency and witnessed by the sergeant major. It is quite lengthy, and since you can read and write in Spanish, I will leave it for you to review."

Big Bow moved toward the sergeant to take the order from him, but he stopped when Lucas raised his hand.

"I prefer to have you read it aloud, so that all of us may consider the wishes of the governor," Lucas said.

The sergeant unrolled the parchment and held it up as if the lighting was not good. He began to read, slowly and haltingly. He was a poor reader, and he struggled with the words and with his own anger and embarrassment.

Despite his poor reading and speaking skills, the intent of the document was clear. Informants had told the governor that *cimarrones* from Utina had once again fled the missions and villages and had returned to a place known as Laguna Oconee, where they were forbidden to go.

Because the governor had once before made such an order, and his authority had been so flaunted, any Indians who had returned to Laguna Oconee for the second time would be delivered to San Augustín for duties to be assigned by the soldiers. Those who were found there for the first time should be returned to Utina and whipped by the chief in the presence of all Utinans as a sign that violation of the lawful orders of the governor would not be tolerated.

When he was done reading, the sergeant handed the order to Big Bow who carried it to Lucas.

"You shall have my letter and my answer for this order. Both will be in writing, so there will be no misunderstanding," Lucas said.

One hour before sundown, Lucas sent word that he was ready. The council house was now nearly full. Word had spread and the people were excited by the way Lucas had earlier spoken to the soldier.

Big Bow presented the sergeant with a manuscript of three pages, written in Lucas' own hand.

"I would like you to read my response, so that if there is any question of my meaning it can be answered now," Lucas said. "It will not be necessary for you to read it aloud, unless you want to." Lucas and the others watched the sergeant's lips move as he read the document.

"I cannot speak for the Governor," the sergeant said when he had finished reading. "I do not believe he will be satisfied with the response, but at least your meaning is clear." The sergeant smiled. "And your tone is respectful."

"As for a response to the order you brought me," Lucas said, "I have written my answer across the face of it, so that there would be no misunderstanding."

Pérez accepted the original order from Big Bow and unrolled it. "Refused" had been written across the page, in bold letters, and it was signed by Lucas Menéndez, *Holata Aco* of the Utinan Nation. The writing was the color of blood.

Chapter 45

Office of the Governor
April 19, 1656

Diego de Rebolledo, former Sergeant Major of the presidio and now the twenty-second appointed Governor and Captain General of San Augustín and its provinces, found the current sergeant major, Adrian de Canizares, waiting for him as he entered his office.

Rebolledo let his dusty travel cape slip from his shoulders and fall to the floor, where it was quickly retrieved by his aide. "Good afternoon," the governor said as he took his seat behind the expansive oak desk.

"Sir, I trust you had a profitable and pleasant visit with the Ais," Canizares said. He stood before the desk, his hands folded behind his back.

"Sit down. Sit down," Rebolledo said, leaning forward and examining the neatly stacked documents prepared for his signature. "As the traders told us, the Indians collect great quantities of amber. We came home with almost two arrobas of it, all of the finest quality."

"Have you calculated its value?" the sergeant major asked.

"Twenty, perhaps twenty-five pesos an ounce is the going price in Havana." Governor Rebolledo began to write figures on a tablet. Eventually, he looked up and smiled. "Fifteen thousand pesos," he said, stretching out the words. "And all it cost me was the metal from a surplus cannon."

Canizares whistled, shaking his head from side to side.

"They have no idea of its value," Rebolledo said. "The Ais believed they got the best of the bargain. Next time we may carry beads and trinkets. There may be no gold or silver here, or precious stones as we found in Peru, but there is money to be made by an investor with a sharp eye."

"That would describe you well, sir," Canizares said.

Rebolledo turned to the second page and then thumbed through the copies that lay beneath. Humming to himself, he slowly read the top page of parchment.

"What do you think will be the reaction of the Indians to my order that they come defend us against the English here in San Augustín?"

The younger man stroked his beard and considered his answer. "Sir, you have been here much longer, and I would defer to your judgment on that question," he said.

The governor smiled and leaned forward over the desk. "They will come. I am certain of that. They have no love for the English, and are dependent on us in many ways."

"As we are dependent on them," Canizares said.

"A mutual dependence. That is the formula for dealing with these people. We save their souls and protect them from their enemies. In turn, all we require is that they bring us a share of their produce. It is not too much to ask that their militias come to the defense of the presidio."

The governor busied himself signing the orders, spreading them out so that the ink would dry. "Has there been further word concerning the English?"

"We had only one ship in port in your absence, and it was bound for Seville," Canizares said. "The last communiqué from the Crown warned all the governors of the Indies about the English attack on Hispañola and the seizure of the Island of Jamaica."

"You have three copies here?"

"Four, including the last one that is addressed to the Apalachee."

Rebolledo stood and walked to the window, looking down on the dusty street. "Potano will comply without hesitation, but he has so few able men. If he provides thirty militiamen I will be satisfied. Chief Don Diego of Potohiriba has a powerful army, and I will accept no fewer than three hundred Yustagans."

The governor turned back toward the sergeant major. "The Utinan, Lucas Menéndez, he is the questionable one. Have you met him?"

"I have not been beyond Potano, sir," Canizares answered.

"Let me tell you about Lucas. He is unpredictable and sometimes irrational in his actions. Among the western Timucua chiefs, he is considered their paramount. The others fear him, and look to him for leadership."

Canizares turned in his chair to face the governor. "Do you think he will resist a lawful order?"

"He has done so in the past. It was seven years ago, during the first year of Salazar's term as governor, and I was sergeant major. It was a simple order to go to the north and retrieve some of his people who were too lazy to work and had abandoned their posts. Lucas' own father, Coya, had obeyed such an order a few years earlier."

Rebolledo moved back to his desk, sat down and rummaged in a drawer. He withdrew a document and handed it to the sergeant major.

"Look at this. It is Salazar's order. You can see the Indian's response."

"These brown markings. Is that blood?"

"The word 'refused' and his signature. When blood dries on parchment, it turns brown."

"What did Salazar do in retribution?" Canizares asked.

Rebolledo laughed. "I told him to hang the Indian, but the coward backed down, saying that we had too many problems just then to go chasing Utinans. In truth, it is doubtful we could have found twenty soldiers for the operation. So Salazar did nothing. Lucas got away with his insolence and became a hero to the others.

"Now he is just a complainer. No order goes without challenge on his part. But when the time comes, we ignore his complaints and he ultimately obeys. For the past seven years, he has behaved himself. I expect him to object to this new order, but when the time comes, he will be here with his vassal chiefs and principal men."

Governor Rebolledo inspected the documents once again. "This second page?" he asked.

"It contains the logistical requirements, those you and I discussed," Canizares said. "Sergeant Augustín Villareal and an interpreter, Esteban Solana, are standing by to deliver them. The first to Potano, the second to Lucas Menéndez and the third for Chief Don Diego. The last one is for the Apalachee."

The sergeant major watched as the governor sealed the orders. Then he stood, saluted smartly, and was excused to do his duty.

Potohiriba
Yustaga Province

A runner arrived in Potohiriba during the night, carrying a document and an urgent message from the Chief of Potano. Chief Potohiriba was standing outside his house when Lucas arrived at midday. They immediately went inside. Potohiriba did not read the Spanish language, and asked Lucas to interpret the writings for him.

When they understood the meaning of the governor's order, Chief Potohiriba sent a man to the convento to fetch the priest, and soon the two chiefs were joined by the friar, Alonso de Escudero.

The priest read the document that was handed to him. When he was done, he read it a second time before returning it to Chief Potohiriba. "How did you come into possession of this document, Don Diego?"

"Potano received it and sent it to me with word that the Spaniards were on the trail to Ayacouta, and then they would be coming here. While the Spaniards slept in his village, Chief Potano sent runners to warn Lucas, and me," Potohiriba said.

"Until we three chiefs agree what to do, it is best we stay out of sight," Lucas said.

"I have heard rumors of English ships in the islands," the priest said. "Perhaps the governor is desperate. He has never before called upon the chiefs and their principal men to prepare for battle."

Don Diego looked at Lucas, and then back to the priest. "We do not oppose the order to go to San Augustín. We pledged to the common defense long ago. We may be nobility and lords of the land, but we are men, first. For me, and the chiefs of Yustaga, we are not afraid of a fight."

"Nor are we," Lucas said. "We will meet with the governor's men in seven days at Ivitachuco, as he orders. And we will fight to defend the presidio in San Augustín if we must. But what is said on that second page, that our chiefs must carry their own weapons and provisions, is an insult. For us to be saddled with three arrobas of grain, to become pack animals in front of our people, is unacceptable."

Through the afternoon they talked. Word came of soldiers approaching on the trail, and the chiefs moved to the convento where the priest prepared them a place to work.

When the soldiers came they were told by the Yustagan *Inija* that Chief Potohiriba was away and would not return that day. Because there was no chief to greet them, the soldiers were told to find another place to sleep, in another village.

Into the night, by candlelight, the two chiefs wrote letters to the governor agreeing to go to San Augustín to defend the presidio, if bearers would be allowed to carry their burdens. The priest wrote the letter for Chief Potohiriba, since he could neither read nor write. When he was done, Fray Escudero wrote a letter of his own, explaining to the governor that manual labor was unknown to royalty of the Timucua, that the suggestion of it was insulting and demeaning.

"Just as you, Sire, would not be required as governor to perform menial labor, so it is with these men of high position," Father Escudero wrote. "Their authority is grounded in the respect with which they are viewed by the commoners. It would be a mistake to disrespect them in this manner."

Before sun-up, the three letters were dispatched by runners to San Augustín. "The governor will amend his order. I'm sure of it," Fray Escudero predicted.

Seven days later, Lucas and Chief Potohiriba met again in the Apalachee town of Ivitachuco. They had with them their militiamen and vassal chiefs, a force of two hundred armed men.

Again, knowledge of the governor's response traveled faster than the courier who carried it. Potano arrived in Apalachee. He had twelve fighters with him, the entire Potanan militia. He also carried a letter from the governor responding to the pleas of Father Escudero, Chief Lucas, and Chief Potohiriba.

The governor's letter scolded them, and said that his first order was to be obeyed without exception, reservation or delay. The three chiefs of western Timucua, to whom all other chiefs were vassals, resolved what they would do.

Lucas penned a letter to Juan Menéndez, and sent it to him at San Pedro, where he lived with his family. The letter was written in Timucua, in case it fell into unfriendly hands.

"We have problems with the governor, we Timucua," Lucas wrote. "Until the issue is resolved, I urge that you not return to the hacienda at La Chua. It might be wise for you to remove your household to San Augustín. I address you in all friendship, brotherhood, and love."

Soon after daybreak, the governor's messenger, Augustín Villareal addressed the five hundred Timucua and Apalachee chiefs and principal men at the council house at Ivitachuco. He read aloud the order signed by Governor Rebolledo, including the provisions relating to the transport of supplies.

When he was done, none of the men objected or voiced any opposition despite the order's harsh and uncompromising tone. Within the hour, the contingent of Timucua set out for Potohiriba, under the command of the interpreter, Esteban Solana. They would arrive in San Augustín in six or seven days. To alleviate congestion at river crossings, Villareal ordered that the Apalachee would leave with him the next day.

"They are afraid the Timucua and Apalachee will steal from each other if we travel together," Lucas whispered to Don Diego.

"I have no doubt that it would happen," the Yustagan chief said.

Sergeant Bartolome Pérez set out on horseback for the farm at Asile with two Apalachee, to collect additional grain for the journey. He would rendezvous with the others at Santa Fé.

At five o'clock in the afternoon, Fray Joseph Bamba of the mission at Asile violated his vows of poverty by riding a horse into Ivitachuco. "Murder! They are both dead," he shouted, as he dismounted and ran into the council house where Sergeant Villareal was talking with two Spanish soldiers.

Chapter 46

Sergeant Bartolome Pérez was attacked and killed at Asile, where he had gone for corn. It was the nephew of Don Diego, a Yustagan, who had done the murder, Father Bamba reported.

On his way to Ivitachuco to deliver the news to the Spanish authorities, Father Bamba encountered a man on the trail.

"I do not know it to be true. I pray it is not, but the man said Esteban Solano also died, that he was murdered by the Timucua Militia when they reached Potohiriba." Agustín Villareal met with the Deputy Governor for Western La Florida, who made his home at Misión San Luis.

"Suppose it is a general revolt, and one in which the Apalachee will soon engage with the Timucua?" Villareal asked.

"Then we are all dead," the Deputy Governor said. "The only man I trust here is Chief Ivitachuco. He swears to me that his personal guard is not a part of this uprising, but he cannot speak for some of the other chiefs."

Villareal ordered that all Apalachee militiamen disburse to their homes and villages. It was remarkable to him how quickly they were gone. Chief Ivitachuco's guard was retained and positioned to repel any possible attack from the east side of the Aucilla River. The friars of Apalachee were gathered together in the council house, along with the Spanish civilians and government workers.

Before daybreak, a courier left San Luis on horseback, heading south toward Pahoi. His orders were to avoid Yustaga and Utina territory, but to make haste to San Augustín carrying urgent messages for the governor.

Forty leagues to the east, an early morning fog blanketed the valley below the hilltop hacienda, providing concealment for the twenty Utinan and Yustagan warriors who awaited the order to attack. It was not yet sun-up, and no lamps were visible in the house or barn.

Almost without sound, Big Bow lay down next to Lucas behind a fallen tree.

"For a big man, you move with the stealth of a deer," Lucas whispered.

The *paracousi* did not answer immediately, but panted deeply trying to catch his breath. "There are seven horses in the stable. I did not see anyone awake. They have no one on guard."

Lucas cursed under his breath. "Did you say there were seven? There should be no more than five."

"There were seven. One was a large sorrel, perhaps fifteen hands high."

Lucas cursed once again, and rolled onto his back, staring into the shroud of gray fog. "The sorrel belongs to Juan Menéndez. No one else is allowed to ride it. If the horse is here, Juan Menéndez is here as well. The seventh horse would belong to the soldier who guards Juan on his travels."

Lucas lay there, thinking. "It will be light, soon," Big Bow reminded him.

"This is what we will do," Lucas said. "Take two men with you who are not afraid of the horses. Remove them quietly and tie them together in the woods behind the barn. Leave the men there to guard the horses. When that is done, come back to me. I will then go into the hacienda alone. When you see me sitting on this log, you may signal your men."

Big Bow said he understood, and prepared to carry out his orders.

"Remember, if there is a priest, or a woman or a child, they are not to be harmed," Lucas said. "Tell that to all the men. If they harm an innocent person, they will answer to me." As silently as he had arrived, Big Bow disappeared into the fog.

Lucas Menéndez looked down at Juan Menéndez lying on his bed, breathing slowly and steadily. The Spaniard wore a long woolen undergarment to fend off the chill night air.

Lucas removed his knife from its scabbard and held it in his right hand, behind his thigh. With his other hand, he reached out and covered the mouth of the sleeping man, grasping him tightly under the chin to prevent him from crying out.

Juan was immediately awake, his eyes wide with fright and confusion, struggling against the pressure of Lucas' grip. Lucas hovered over him, their faces only inches apart.

"Be quiet, Juan. Be quiet," Lucas whispered. In a moment the Spaniard stopped resisting, and laid quietly, but was still visibly frightened.

"If you promise not to cry out, and to go with me quietly, I will take my hand away. If you cry out, I have this," Lucas said, showing the knife. Juan looked at the blade, and then cut his eyes back to those of Lucas. He nodded his agreement. Moments later, the two were outside, running down the sloping hill away from the hacienda.

"Sit here, Juan," Lucas ordered, gesturing that the Spaniard should face away from the house. Lucas sat beside him, still clutching the knife. Juan was barefoot, and he shivered in fear and against the cold.

"I wrote to you, begging you to stay away from La Chua. Why are you here?"

Juan's teeth chattered as he tried to answer. "I could not read it, but carried it with me so someone could read it to me here. You wrote it in Timucua. If it had been in Spanish, perhaps . . ."

"If it were in Spanish, anyone who saw it would suspect the reason it was sent," Lucas said. "I could trust you, but no one else."

Behind them they heard the sound of splintering wood as the militiamen crashed through the front door. Juan jerked his head around to see.

"Do not look," Lucas commanded, and the Spaniard once again looked straight ahead. The horizon showed the approach of first light.

"Who is in the house?" Lucas asked.

"Only my escort and two Indians. And two vaqueros who work the cows."

Lucas sighed deeply, and his shoulders slumped. "I will tell you why we are here, and why this is happening," he said. "When you have heard it all, you may judge it as you will."

Lucas told his friend of the order from the governor and of the willingness of the chiefs of Timucua and Apalachee to obey, and to give their lives if need be in defense of San Augustín.

"But we could never accept his command that the lords of the land act as their own beasts of burden, like oxen laboring under their loads, while the ones who are suited to that work remain at home, planting the fields to produce more corn for the governor's belly.

"The Friar of Potohiriba wrote to Rebolledo, explaining to him how the chiefs would be diminished in the eyes of our people and no longer worthy of respect if we did this. It is a difference, I suppose, between our worlds, yours and mine."

Behind them, the screams of the dying and injured could be heard from the hacienda. Juan started to turn, but then looked straight ahead. He covered his ears until there was no sound.

"I suppose there is more to it," Lucas said. "We are so diminished by illness and death. There are few Potanans left on the face of the earth. Utina also suffers, and we have only half the number we had even seven years ago when I became *Holata.*

"The governor requires of me fifty burden carriers this year. Last year it was only thirty-six men he asked for. The governor says we are lazy people and stupid."

Lucas hung his head, looking at the ground between his feet. The knife slipped from his hand. "I will never forget your father. I was not his son, only his godson, but I loved him as much as I love you, my brother. In a way, he was godfather to all of us Indians. Never did he try to keep our people away from their hunting grounds, even if they trespassed here." He looked out over the vista of La Chua.

"He allowed us to harvest nuts, berries and coontie. He never asked for a share for himself, but some of the people would leave him gifts on the porch before going home. No one ever said he cheated them in any way.

"Most of all, I remember him for the way he always took our side when the governor made unreasonable demands on us. Since your father died, they never listen to us anymore."

The hacienda was afire, and the smoke rose up and followed the wind toward the southwest.

"What is to become of me?" Juan asked.

Lucas breathed deeply, and let the air out slowly. "We saved the horses. You should go back to San Augustín where you will be safe. There is no place for a Spaniard this side of the River of the Sun. I will provide two men to guard you as far as Tocoi crossing. They will also have horses, so you can move quickly."

"Will we ever meet again?" Juan asked.

"In God's own time. Perhaps in six years you may come back when our hearts are not so full of anger. The priests are free to remain here, but I will understand it if they choose to leave. I have ordered that they be respected and not harmed."

The two men stood and embraced for what Lucas knew might be the last time in this life.

Juan was crying. "I will address this issue with the governor, and stop him from making war," Juan said. "He is a stupid, insensitive man. If he refuses to rescind his order, I will sail to Spain to have the King remove him from office."

Lucas held him at arms length, searching his face. "You have that sort of power, to tell a governor what to do, and to complain even to the King of Spain?"

Juan straightened his back. "I am Menéndez. My great-grandfather was Pedro Menéndez de Aviles, the Adelantano. La Florida all began with him. My father named seven governors, and advised the King on whom to appoint next. The Menéndez family has powerful friends. Rebolledo is a puppet. He will not challenge me."

Before the smoke cleared, Juan Menéndez and his guards rode to the southeast on a less-traveled trail leading to the River of the Sun. In four days he would visit the governor.

Dénouement

Chapter 47

S.C.C.M.

To His Most Sanctified, Caesarian, Catholic Majesty,
The Emperor Don Felipe IV, Our Lord King

May the serene and beneficent light of Our Lord Jesus Christ shine everlastingly on Your Majesty, Don Felipe, divinely appointed Emperor, and by the Grace of God, ruler of Castile, of Leon, of Aragon, of the two Sicilies, of Jerusalem, of Navarre, of Granada, of Toledo, of Valencia, of Galicia, of Mallorca, of Seville, of Sardinia, of Cordoba, of the Caribbees, of Algeciras, of Gibraltar, of the Canary Isles, of the islands and lands of the Ocean Sea, of the Indies, of Mexico, of Peru, and of La Florida.

Most High and Mighty Majesty, Our Sovereign Liege. From the town of San Augustín La Florida, this twelfth day of the month of September, of the Year of Our Lord one thousand six hundred fifty seven, a greeting.

Your Majesty commands of the Bishop of Santiago de Cuba, His Eminence, Gabriel Diaz Vara Calderon, that he arrange for the provision of detailed and verifiable accounts of the recent unhappy and tragic events that occurred in His Majesty's province of La Florida regarding an uprising of the

Indians of Western Timucua and Apalachee against the constituted authority of your appointed governor at San Augustín.

His Eminence, having no personal knowledge of those events, other than reports from myself and fellow Franciscan friars of La Florida, has charged me with the heavy responsibility of investigating the facts and answering Your Majesty's request. At the outset, let me say that I did not choose this duty for myself. There are others I might name, some of those who have counter-signed this document, who are more skillful in the art of crafting reports, and as knowledgeable as I of the events in question. I protested to the bishop that since I, myself, have been scurrilously attacked and vilified by at least one report that has been circulated, I would be considered a biased and unreliable witness for Your Majesty.

Bishop Calderon's response was that I do the best I can, that I circulate this report among my fellow Franciscans who witnessed these events, and that I note any error of fact or objection to tone that any of them might have to this, the final report. (It will be noted that each of the undersigned Friars have reviewed it and some have made suggestions that I have followed, and others have related facts and occurrences outside my personal knowledge. These have been included, and the source of facts not known by me has been noted and attributed to its source.) By their signatures, each signatory friar has agreed that these are the true accounts, and the judgments expressed are unvarnished and supportable.

We set forth here that which we all believe to be true. Our purpose is not to duplicate that which is already at your disposal, including copies of documents collected by the Council of the Indies, the judicial notes of the trials that were held in Apalachee, the Residencia testimony, and independent and unsolicited reports, including that of Fray José de Urritia, about which I will have more to say later. However, nothing herein should be interpreted as verification of the authenticity or veracity of any such document.

The testimony and documents of Governor Rebolledo, we urge, should be viewed with care, insofar as they conflict with other, independent sources of information to the contrary.

It is our understanding that this testimony may be used for Your Majesty's personal information and edification, for referral to the Council of the Indies in their investigations of the events themselves, and of the official conduct of the former Governor of La Florida, Diego de Rebolledo, or for any other purpose that suits Your Majesty.

By Your leave, where shall I begin?

The beginning is always a safe place to start, but so much of the history of this colony is so well known by Your Majesty that you, yourself, could report upon it from your indelible memory and the detailed studies you have conducted, perhaps better than I. For that reason, I shall begin in the days and months that led up to the events that occurred between April 19, 1656 and November 15 of that same year. Where I digress, it will be noted.

State of the Indian Nations, circa 1650 A.D.

By use of the term Indian Nations, I refer to the Western Timucua, consisting of chiefdoms of Potano, Utina and Yustaga, and others, lying west of the River San Juan, and to the chiefdom of Apalachee that lies west of the Aucilla River and to the shores of the river noted on the maps as Ochlochonee.

Beginning at the time of the westward expansion of missions (1608 to 1656 a. d.), the western Timucua have been greatly reduced in numbers, due primarily to the contagions that swept their lands. For three periods, beginning in 1614, in 1632 and 1642, small pox and other scourges decimated the provinces of Potano and Utina.

To demonstrate the impact, perhaps it will suffice to compare the Franciscan records of pagan conversions. In 1625, the number of catechized Western Timucua stood at more than 60,000. Twenty five years later, there were only 26,000 Christians counted by the friars, despite the increased number of priests and missions. The plain fact is that a higher percent of all the Indians were Christian in 1650, though their total number was less than half of those counted twenty-five years earlier. There were far fewer Indians still living at the time of the later census.

There were few deaths because of conflict between the tribes or with the soldiers. Mortality was high, however, among the Indians conscripted to carry produce to San Augustín and supplies to the missions. It pains us to say that in the early days of the Royal Road that stretched from the capital to Apalachee, we Franciscans recruited Indians for the work.

The work was hard and the heat intolerable. Bearers carried as many as three arrobas of grain on their backs, on a trail that extended more than one hundred leagues. Of one group, two hundred men left Potohiriba and San Martín for San Augustín, carrying five hundred and forty arrobas of maize (slightly less than six tons). Of those who did not die on the trail, some were conscripted for work on the fort. Only ten of the original two hundred men ever returned to their families.

Men, women, and children were required to work in the fields, planting and harvesting two maize crops each year, mostly without the benefit of efficient tools.

Some friars went without supplies for the missions, rather than burdening the Indians with more work.

The governor's appetite for Indian corn was insatiable. Of course the people have to eat, and the soil around San Augustín is sandy and unsuitable for crops, but the corn levy was beyond the Indians ability to provide.

Governor Rebolledo, in particular, was unreasonable in his demands of the Indians, although it was an issue of contention between the friars and many of Rebolledo's predecessors. In 1652, the governor required the Utina Chief to supply sixty bearers, compared to thirty-eight the prior year. This, despite a summer epidemic that took more than one hundred men, women and children. It was so hard on the Indians that they left the villages and missions and fled into the woods to escape the diseases and hard labor that diminished their numbers and spirits.

As true as they were to their Christian faith, they soon associated the missions with unhappiness and death itself. As villages along the trail were emptied of their inhabitants, the governor ordered them to return and sent soldiers and Indian militiamen to fetch them back. When Potano was so depleted of men, Utinans were ordered to go there to live and work. In 1650, there were so few Utinans left, Yustagan boatmen were enlisted to ferry people across the rivers of Utina. Only Apalachee remained strong in terms of manpower.

Governor Rebolledo's Order of April 16, 1656
Leading directly to Insurrection

Your Majesty alerted your several governors of the Indies, Cuba, Jamaica, Puerto Rico, and La Florida of the threatened invasion by the English in the spring of the year. To his credit, Governor Rebolledo acted promptly in issuing an order calling upon the most valorous western Indians to come to San Augustín to defend the presidio. Much to his discredit, in the implementation of his order, Governor Rebolledo gravely offended his loyal subjects in such a way that rebellion became almost a certainty.

I promised Your Majesty that when I digressed in this narrative, it would be noted. This is such a time.

Leaders among the Indians, the caciques, holatas, etc., are exempted from labor in their societies. Historically, the Timucua chiefs have been members of the White Deer Clan, although presently there are some of other families who rise to leadership roles.

Just as governors, bishops, and (by your leave) Kings do not ordinarily labor in the fields, so it is among the Indians. A chief's fields are tended by his subjects, as tribute. In early days he was carried about on a litter, so that he would not be required to stand or walk if it did not suit him. Only the meanest of his servants carried his bundles. A chief's exemption from physical labor is a manifestation of the love and respect of his vassals. By analogy, it is the glue that binds the society together. The chief's word is law and to be obeyed. He carries the heavy burden of leading the people, and in turn he is afforded great respect by his vassals who provide the physical labor.

These were the societal rules that led common Indians to rise from their sick beds, to bury their dead, and to obey their chief's orders that they carry the bundles to San Augustín in behalf of the Spaniards. And these were the principles that were trodden under the boots of Governor Rebolledo when he directed that the most valorous men come to the defense of the presidio, and that they carry their own bundles of provisions, sufficient to sustain them for one month. It was a grievous error, but one that was yet correctable.

I can say it no more cogently than does the wording suggested by my friend and mentor, Fray Gomez de Engraba:

"The governor, like a man of little experience, made such an issue of this that he forced them to revolt, as they stated that they were not slaves, that they had become Christians to obey the Holy Gospel and the law of God and that which the priests had taught them."

And it was on this point of contention that your worshipful servant, Fray Juan Escudero, became an unwitting actor in this tragic drama.

To Acquaint Your Majesty with the Leaders

Before I begin again with the narrative, I beg leave of your Majesty for yet another digression. At the risk of disclosing a disorderly mind, I feel it is important that you be made aware of the personalities, the strengths and weaknesses, and the life stories of two Indians. By our leave:

Don Diego, the Yustagan chief, was my close friend. It was I who brought him to Christ and baptized him. Even after his baptism, he was addressed as Potohiriba by his people. Diego was a pious, faithful Christian and a strong and respected leader of his people. He was not, however, as some reports have held, the paramount chief. That honor belongs to Lucas Menéndez, the Chief of San Martín de Ayacouta, an Utinan.

Lucas Menéndez was the son of the former Utinan Chief, Coya Ayacouta Utina. He was the godson of your Majesty's good friend and faithful servant, the Royal Treasurer, Francisco Menéndez Marquez, may God rest his soul. You are, of course, familiar with the family and its history, and I will not repeat that here.

Coya, in turn, was an interesting person. He was a religious student at San Juan del Puerto in his early years, and was spirited away by two Acueran brothers. The elder of the two was called Marehootie, who was later befriended by Fray Francisco Pareja, and assisted Father Pareja in his language studies. Perhaps Marehootie may be mentioned in some of Father Pareja's writings.

The other brother was called Crying Bird. He was a criminal in the eyes of the Spanish military, and he was rumored to be the legendary Indian Spirit Warrior, *Atichicolo-Iri*. If true, he was the man who opposed Pedro Menéndez de Aviles on his journey on the River San Juan in 1565, and who fomented the revolt in Guale in 1597, and numerous attacks on Spanish interests until about 1620, when he disappeared. Whether the legend is true or not, most Indians I have met believe it. The Indian was so clever in escaping the military patrols for so many years, even the soldiers sometimes spoke of him as a spirit.

As the son of Coya, Lucas Menéndez was to the Spanish eye a friendly leader of the Utina, and a good Christian. There was one recorded incident of his having refused an order of the governor, but he served valorously in the Apalachee revolt of 1647 and was honored by the governor for his service.

Lucas Menéndez was, by the remaining pagan Indians and many of the Christians, believed to be the reincarnation of both the Christian Marehootie and the *cimarrone*, Crying Bird. He was a powerful chief of great intellect and courage, and the paramount leader of all Western Timucua. Lucas Menéndez was willing to go to San Augustín to defend the presidio, but it was he who rejected the governor's order that chiefs become pack animals. He chose to die rather than submit.

I have recorded the date. It was April 26, 1656. I was called to the chief's house at Potohiriba. Don Diego was there with Lucas Menéndez and his leading militiaman. Don Diego had an order in his hand. It was Rebolledo's order of April 19, the copy addressed to Chief Potano.

I will not recite the order. Your Majesty undoubtedly has the original. Don Diego and Lucas were fully in accord that they take their vassal chiefs and principal men to defend the presidio. Despite the veneer of Christianity, these men do not shrink from war and their excitement shown in their faces. Their objection was, of course, to the provision that they bear their own burdens.

To me it was a clear error of judgment on the part of the governor or the sergeant major who advises him, that the chiefs become pack animals. To disrespect the leaders, at any time, would be detrimental to their rule. In wartime, it might be fatal to the Spanish cause.

It was my judgment that the governor should recognize the affront he had inflicted on the leaders, and relent, allowing workers to carry their leader's burdens. I so advised Lucas and Don Diego. For that purpose, I wrote a letter to Governor Rebolledo asking that the change be made. I sent it, along with individual letters written by the two chiefs, pledging their support.

It was my letter that has led one person to accuse me of encouraging the Indians to revolt. I will have more to say about that, presently.

The letters were received by the governor five days later. His response was unequivocal and immediate. His first order was to be obeyed, he said, with no amendment or exemption.

I was not in Ivitachuco the day Governor Rebolledo's men published his orders. Don Diego was there, as was Lucas Menéndez and their militias. By now the story is well understood. The interpreter Solana took the Timucua men to Potohiriba and the Apalachee militia was to follow the next day, to keep the Indians from stealing from each other and to prevent confusion at river crossings. Solana was murdered when he reached Potohiriba.

It was then and there that Lucas Menéndez declared the rebellion, ordering that all Spaniards west of the San Juan be killed, with the exception of the friars who were to be protected and their churches and possessions unharmed.

Sergeant Bartolome Pérez was likewise killed that day at the Asile farm, where he had gone to collect maize for the expedition to San Augustín. This was more an act of revenge than warfare. The murderer was the nephew of Don Diego, and a member of my church. He was a proud man who had been insulted and kicked by Pérez on an earlier occasion, and chose that day to extract his revenge.

There were several other deaths, perhaps four more, over the next several days. None were witnessed by friars, and Your Majesty is undoubtedly better informed than we.

Machava Fortress

The governor was informed of events but took no immediate steps to retaliate or restore the peace. Those in rebellion established a fort near the village of Machava. It was palisade, with wooden walls, having been built by Indians who had worked on the fort in San Augustín.

Perhaps two hundred Indians were there, primarily Yustagans and Utinans, but with a few Potanans and others I did not recognize. In the beginning they were a belligerent mob, looking for the opportunity to kill Spaniards. As time went by with no sign of soldiers, some tired of it and wanted to go home.

I was there from time to time, and this is another accusation against me by the ill-informed Fray Urritia. What was I to do? These were Christian men in need of the sacraments afforded by the church. I went at night, and carried the blood and body of Christ with me and gave them Communion. I admit to the charge that I heard their confessions, the content of which I will share with no man.

I and my fellow friars take umbrage at the report of Fray Urritia, a man who the records will reflect was in Cuba at the time in question, and came to La Florida for the first time after the events of 1656. His report is considered a work of tawdry fiction based on unreliable hearsay. I do not hide the pain of the personal wound it has inflicted on my heart, and if Your Majesty will allow it, I reject it here as a point of personal privilege.

Lucas Menéndez was there, and was their leader. He told them all that there would be no need for war, that his brother, Juan Menéndez, would set the governor straight, and tell him to apologize to the chiefs and provide bearers for their journey to San Augustín where they would be welcomed as heroes.

In time, some of the men went home. Lucas wanted the Apalachee to come to the aid of the Timucua. He had witnessed how Governor Rebolledo, when he was sergeant major, stopped the Apalachee revolt in 1647 by telling them a lie about the strength of the Spanish army.

Lucas sent a false message to Ivitachuco saying that the Apalachee Chief in San Augustín had been imprisoned by the Spanish. The Apalachee were not fooled. They sent someone to verify the story which was proven false.

Another time, Lucas sent word to the northern Utinan villages, who were not involved in the uprising, that the fort at Machava was under attack and their assistance was needed. That also was exposed as a lie.

I will never forget what Lucas Menéndez said to me. "We are poor liars, we Utina. The Spanish are much better at it than we."

Lucas still believed that Juan Menéndez would prevail over the governor. Lucas' worst day was September 4, 1656. That was the day Sergeant Major Adrien de Canizares arrived with his army at the Machava fortress, demanding that the leaders come out and surrender to him. Standing behind Canizares, in the uniform of a Spanish Lieutenant, was his second-in-command, Juan Menéndez.

I visited the fort that night and I spoke with Lucas. The light was gone from his eyes. He walked out of the fort that night and disappeared into the woods. His *paracousi*, Big Bow was with him.

Your Majesty knows the rest of what happened. Two days later, on a flag of safe conduct, the remaining chiefs walked out of the fort to parley with the Spanish soldiers in the council house. They were quickly arrested and disarmed. Don Diego was there, with his men, as was Chief Potano.

Within days, the other chiefs were gathered up. Lucas did not resist. They were all taken to Ivitachuco in Apalachee where they were held in the council house and imprisoned until their trials. Big Bow was not found. Rumor has it he went to Laguna Oconee where other Utinans were known to have fled.

Governor Rebolledo came from San Augustín and conducted the trials.

The nephew of Don Diego said, of his killing of Sergeant Pérez, that he knew when he did it he would have to pay for what he did. He said that he was a Christian, but not a man until the insult of the sergeant was avenged. Just before he was garroted, he smiled and said he was content.

Ten chiefs of the Western Timucua, including Don Diego, the old man Potano, and Lucas Menéndez were executed and their bodies put on display at Potohiriba.

Lucas Menéndez' last words were mild. "If we are to perish," he said, "it is better that we do so standing up."

The same might have been said of the peoples of Mocama, Acuera, and Potano, who scarcely survive today, but are few in number and scattered around the countryside. The same might yet be said of the remaining Utina, the Yustaga and the Apalachee.

Indeed, with all respect, unless men of character and intelligence are sent here by Your Majesty to lead us, in the light of the English threat, the same might someday be said of San Augustín, La Florida, and Your Majesty's grand designs on this continent.

Sire, may our Lord God and Jesus Christ His son watch over and preserve Your Most Excellent Majesty for many years in His holy service.

Of your S.C.C.M., the loyal and prayerful chaplain

(ecce signum) Fray Juan Escudero

San Pedro de Potohiriba

Witnessed, and verified: This twelfth day of the month of September,

in the year of Our Lord, one thousand, six hundred fifty seven

Fray Lorenzo Solis, San Francisco de Potano

Fray Juan Gomez de Engraba, San Augustín de Urica

Fray Joseph Bamba, San Miguel de Asile

Fray Diego Rogero, San Martín de Ayacouta

Epilogue

The downward spiral of Timucua society, a pattern that was evident from earliest contact with the Spaniards, was only accelerated by the Timucua Revolt of 1656. Governor Rebolledo's execution of ten chiefs and pincipal men of Potano, Utina, and Yustaga provinces left the Western Timucua leaderless and their people dispirited and scattered into the woods.

Attempts were made by the Spaniards to establish and promote new leaders, and to consolidate villages along *El Camino Real*, the Royal Road, which was the lifeline to Apalachee corn for the beleaguered colony of San Augustín. Chief Lazaro Chamile was ordered to relocate his people to Ayacouta, to man the river crossings on what are now the Suwannee and Santa Fé Rivers. It is unclear whether the order was followed, but Ayacouta was last mentioned as a way station on the road in 1660.

Potano Province was seldom referred to thereafter. Utina, which was the largest of the western provinces, was severely depopulated, many of their people having fled to country outside Spanish influence, such as Laguna Oconee in present day Georgia. Yustaga survived, but was greatly diminished. Apalachee, which did not participate in the revolt, remained the center of Spanish attention, owing to its rich resources of laborers and grain.

Accusations placing blame for the revolt were heated. The Franciscans accused Governor Rebolledo of insensitivity, of having fomented the revolt by showing disrespect for the mores of Indian society. Rebolledo countered that the problems were related to the friars' mistreatment of the Indians, although there was little in the record to support that assertion.

Father José de Urritia, who cast blame on Father Escudero for having written a letter to the governor in support of the Timucua chiefs on the issue of carrying their own burdens, and for having ministered the sacraments to them at the fort at Machava, was treated harshly. In referring to Urritia, the Provincial Franciscan leader remarked that it made them blush that the Order held such a man.

The Council of the Indies investigated the circumstances leading to the revolt and was influenced by the testimony of the priests. Governor Rebolledo was formally condemned by the Council, and in 1657 it issued an order for his immediate arrest and detention in Cuba until he could be delivered to Spain for trial.

Governor Rebolledo died before the order could be executed.

Acknowledgments

To admit to standing on the shoulders of others is trite, and a cliché. Nevertheless, it is true, and an admission I make readily. The historians, archaeologists and anthropologists who have written about the Timucua and other prehistoric Indians of the southeast have my undying respect and admiration for their work. I have spent time in archives at the St. Augustine Historical Society and the Timucua Cultural Preserve, following in their footsteps.

The works of Jerald T. Milanich, John Worth, and Michael V. Gannon fill my library shelves. Although not always in agreement on finite detail, each has contributed to my understanding and appreciation of the Timucua.

In particular, I want to acknowledge the time and patience of John H. Hann and Bonnie McEwan who sat with me at the marvelous re-creation of Mission San Luis at Tallahassee and answered questions. I learned that day that in the early years, there were no plate glass windows in the missions, since no archaeological dig had found glass shards. That knowledge saved me from making an error. Thank you, Dr. McEwan.

And a special word of appreciation goes to Dr. Joe Knetsch, Historian for the Florida Department of State for introducing me to Mission San Luis, and to Dr. McEwan and Dr. Hann.

Charles Tingley of the St. Augustine Historical Society labored with me over archival microfilm records of four-hundred-year-old letters.Thank you, Charles.

David White Wolf, world-class 'knapper' of arrow points and the repository of infinite knowledge of natural foods, Indian cures, and weaponry has been with me from the start, sharing his expertise and advice.

One afternoon, I walked into The Pearl Shop in the St. Augustine old town, leading to a conversation with Terry Auten, who knows as much as any man alive about freshwater pearls, and how they might deteriorate.

A collective huzzah to Dr. Nick Wynne, Debra Wynne, and the Florida Historical Society for anointing my first Timucua novel, *Wekiva Winter*, with the Patrick D. Smith literary award as Best Fiction for 2006. See what a little encouragement does?

My good friend and mentor Bill Belleville, author of *River of Lakes: A Journey on Florida's St. Johns River*, and *Sprawl: How Progress Ate My Cracker Landscape*, was among the first to see what I'm struggling to do in bringing the Timucua back to life.

Jim Robison, history columnist for the Orlando Sentinel, was there about the same time as Bill Belleville, and lent his support and encouragement.

Tom Wallace, my editor, whose sharp eye for typos is exceeded only by his talent for turning a non-sequitor into a well-turned phrase, has helped me bring *Beyond the River of the Sun* to fruition.

Ron Carson keeps my computer working and my web page, www.fredricmhitt.com, up and running with information on forthcoming book signings and talks.

And to Linda Silsby Hitt, my loving wife, confidant, resident artist and, when necessary, my critic, my undying love and appreciation. Linda painted the cover art, authored the map of Timucua territory, and penned the illustrations.

Lastly, a nod of appreciation to my muse, Marehootie, who watches over me as I write.

There are others, and I hope no one is slighted by not having been mentioned here. You, and I, know your contributions. Thank you.

Fredric M. Hitt

2007

Printed in the United States
108324LV00001B/1/A

9 781602 640764